SWORD BRETHREN

SWORD BRETHREN

JON BYRNE

The Book Guild Ltd

First published in Great Britain in 2024 by
The Book Guild Ltd
Unit E2 Airfield Business Park,
Harrison Road, Market Harborough,
Leicestershire. LE16 7UL
Tel: 0116 2792299
www.bookguild.co.uk
Email: info@bookguild.co.uk
X: @bookguild

Typeset in 12pt Adobe Jenson Pro

ISBN 978 1835740 798

British Library Cataloguing in Publication Data.
A catalogue record for this book is available from the British Library.

Dedicated to the two girls in my life: To Anja, whose support and belief in this book kept me going through the dark moments of self-doubt, and to my daughter Sara who helped me with the maps.

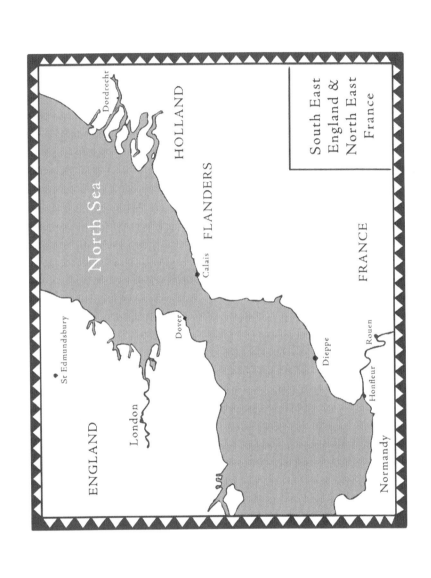

South East
England &
North East
France

North Sea

HOLLAND

Dordrecht

FLANDERS

Calais

FRANCE

Dover

Dieppe

Rouen

Honfleur

St Edmundsbury

London

ENGLAND

Normandy

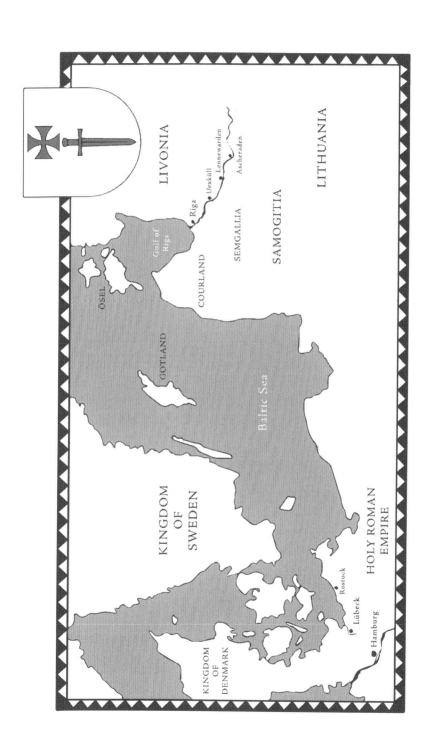

LIVONIA

LITHUANIA

Riga
Uexküll
Lennewarden
Ascheraden

SEMGALLIA

SAMOGITIA

COURLAND

Gulf of Riga

ÖSEL

GOTLAND

Baltic Sea

KINGDOM
OF
SWEDEN

HOLY ROMAN
EMPIRE

Rostock
Lübeck
Hamburg

KINGDOM
OF
DENMARK

Prologue

YURIEV MONASTERY, NOVGOROD
REPUBLIC, APRIL–MAY 1242

We were already in disarray when the arrow slammed into my shoulder, punching through my mail-coat and nearly felling me from my horse. Our charge across the ice had been peppered with missiles fired with deadly accuracy, and the freezing air was raucous with the screams of dying men and thrashing animals. I could still see the eyes of the mounted archer who had loosed the arrow widen in triumph. His face I would never forget. Was he a Mongol? For some reason it mattered to me. I had never fought these fierce people from the steppe but their reputation and ferocity were well-known. I was not even aware they had been part of the Novgorodian army. Whether this had affected the outcome of the battle, only God in all his wisdom knew. We had been so confident. Overconfident. Our defeat had been absolute.

I woke in a room with whitewashed walls. An old, bearded man, his craggy face not unkind, loomed over me, his fingers gentle as he probed my wound and changed my dressing. Nevertheless, despite his care, searing flames coursed through me with every touch of his parchment-dry fingers. When the burning finally subsided, I blinked my eyes open. Through tears, I saw a small picture on the opposite wall of a man with a halo around his head spearing a serpent. It must have been Saint George killing the dragon. The halo made him look more like an angel. The bearded man mumbled to himself in a soft voice as he worked, however, the language was unfamiliar. It sounded Slavic, probably Russian. That could only mean I was a prisoner.

With any movement, shafts of fire shot through my body, an agony so great I thought I would pass out again. By Christ Almighty and all His Holy Saints, I just wanted it to stop. But, of course, it didn't. It was unrelenting. Perhaps when I was younger, I would have borne it better. Who knows? At my venerable age, death should come as a welcome relief and I almost felt ready to succumb to it – to give up my fight and drift into the hallowed afterlife. Almost, but not quite. I was not yet ready to die. There was still too much to be done. There was still my vengeance to be had. A vengeance that stretched back to my youth.

The room was cool, but at times I felt like a sizzling pig roasting on a spit. The old man put strips of damp cloth on my face, but it hardly helped. Only blessed unconsciousness relieved me of it. My body fought a desperate battle to survive.

It is strange that, despite everything, the gift of life is most precious when it is about to be taken away.

But survive I did. In the weeks following the battle, the fever gradually released its grip and I could feel my strength slowly returning. I was still as feeble as a child, but my bearded nurse nodded his head and smiled encouragement as he spooned a watery cabbage soup through my cracked lips. Perhaps I would live after all.

Now, at least, I could sit up in bed, but any other movement still sent stabbing bolts of pain through my chest. I was too weak to get up, and one time the effort broke the healing scabs on my wound, causing me to sink back into the pit of sweat my cot had become. It was clear to me now that the bearded man was a monk, a monk of the heretical Greek church, and I was in the infirmary of a monastery. Nevertheless, my skin crawled and itched with lice, my hair was filthy and unkempt, and there was nothing I could do about it. Outside, the bells of a church clanged the times for prayer. Never in my life had I felt so helpless, unable to piss or shit without help from the bearded monk and one of his helpers, a pale-faced youth of no more than seventeen or eighteen winters.

I still did not know how long I had lain there, but one morning I received a visitor. Or, more accurately, two visitors. I had been dozing when the door banged open without warning and the bearded monk led in two men. The first was tall, at least my height, and I am taller than most, but younger – young enough to be my son. He had the athletic build of a warrior, and his angled face was framed by a shortly trimmed beard and sandy-brown, shoulder-length hair, plastered across his head with sweat as if he had just taken off a hat or helmet. He wore a red cloak edged with fur worn over his left shoulder, fastened with a gold clasp fashioned in the shape of the three-barred Greek cross on the right shoulder, and a blue brocade surcoat over a long-sleeved white shirt. On his feet were high, leather riding boots of obvious quality, although they were spattered with mud. When he looked me in the eyes, I felt the power behind his gaze despite his youth. There was a harshness there, a cynical coldness strange in someone so young. He said something to the other man, who was older, of slight build, with long auburn hair tied back from the nape of his neck. This man was no warrior. He looked more like a scholar, and his chestnut-coloured, homespun tunic, although of good quality cotton, clearly denoted his lower rank. It was this man who spoke to me in Latin.

'Prince Alexander Yaroslavich Nevsky of Novgorod the Great, welcomes you to Yuriev Monastery and hopes you are recovering from your wounds.'

His words slapped me in the face. Alexander Yaroslavich had commanded the Russian army in the battle on the ice where we had been defeated, as well as being victorious against the Swedish army two years earlier on the Neva River. My surprise must have been obvious because the young prince, Alexander, smiled at my reaction, speaking again quickly before waiting for his words to be translated.

'You are one of six German knights captured in the battle,' the interpreter continued, 'but you were the most badly wounded. Prince Alexander says that under Brother Dimitri's care and with God's grace, you have made a vast improvement. But it is doubtful that at your age you shall ever be able to take up arms against his people again.'

'How long have I lain here?' I said in Latin. As a warrior monk of the Livonian Order, my Latin was respectable, though not as good as my Low German, or Norman French – the language of my birth.

'The battle by Lake Chudskoe was over a month ago. You were carried here in a wain.'

A month already. I struggled to rise but the bearded monk who had tended me all this time, whom Prince Alexander had named as Brother Dimitri, came forward to restrain me. I collapsed back in a wave of dizziness. While I lay there panting, my weakness open to all, the three men spoke quickly to each other.

'What are you saying?'

They looked at me and Alexander motioned for the interpreter to translate again.

'Brother Dimitri had to remove the arrow that was still lodged in your left shoulder when you were brought here. He says some links of mail also had to be extracted from the wound before the arrow could be pushed through and pulled out with forceps. You were close to death and had lost much blood. Luckily, no organs or bones had been damaged...'

'Then how could I have been in this bed for over a month? I have seen many arrow wounds in my time... I should have recovered by now.'

The interpreter glanced towards Dimitri before answering. 'As recommended by renowned physicians, Dimitri inserted a strip of bacon to help drain the pus and then dressed the wound with compresses. But nonetheless, the wound went bad. You have been fighting this poison for the last weeks.'

'And what happens now?'

The two of them turned to Alexander who said something in his language.

'Prince Alexander has not yet decided. You will be treated until you have recovered fully, then probably be ransomed back to your Order. But there is one thing...'

'What is that?'

'Brother Dimitri thinks you are not German, despite wearing the insignia of a Teutonic knight. When you were delirious, you spoke in another language, a language unknown to him despite his learned status. Prince Alexander is interested to know from where you originally hail?'

I closed my eyes for a moment. I must have been babbling in Norman French. It had been so very long since I had seen my homeland. 'I am a Norman, from a country far to the west of here. A country called England.'

The interpreter flinched as if he'd just smelt a latrine. After a moment's hesitation, he translated my words and fixed me with eyes suddenly hostile. Was it my imagination or had something cold entered the room?

He translated Alexander's reply. 'Prince Alexander knows of your land,' he said. 'He is most interested to know why you would travel so far to make war on his people.'

I looked the interpreter directly in the eye. There was no mistaking his enmity – enmity that had not been there before. 'And what do you think?' I said, addressing my question to the scholarly interpreter.

'I think it is normal for the bastard Norman English to take lands that do not belong to them.'

He had spoken in French, although his accent was strange. 'And what is an Irishman doing working as a translator for the Prince of Novgorod?'

He looked uncomfortable at my question and I saw Prince Alexander watching our exchange with amusement. Dimitri was oblivious to the hostility in the room, nodding his head and smiling. Alexander said something in his language to the Irishman.

'Prince Alexander desires to know your name?'

'My name is Richard,' I said. 'Richard Fitz Simon. And what is your name, Irishman?'

The interpreter looked to Alexander, wanting to avoid the question. But despite the Russian prince's lack of knowledge of our language, he seemed to know what we were talking about. The man was intelligent, but then again, he had defeated our army. Our proud Christian army. Alexander said something and the Irishman turned back to me. 'My name is Fergus,' he said reluctantly.

Alexander said something more while I waited patiently for a translation.

'My lord is intrigued by your story,' Fergus said. 'He comes often to Yuriev to pay respects to his brother Theodor and the other Novgorodian princes who are buried here. He shall come and see you again. You have aroused his curiosity and he is interested in your story. It seems we are all destined to meet again.'

And with that they left, leaving me to my thoughts and pain.

Three days later, they allowed me up for the first time. I was supported by Grigori, the pale-faced youth who had assisted me before, and, of course, Brother Dimitri. Our progress was slow, passing through a dark passage lit by an oil lamp ensconced in the wall that reeked of fish oil, exiting through a door into sunlight. I blinked in discomfort, unused to the brightness after the gloom of the infirmary. We hobbled past a small herb garden built alongside a squat wooden building that formed one of the walls of the monastery. The monastery itself was enormous, with an expanse of grass stretching to a colossal, barn-like church topped by three silver domes. As big as any cathedral I had ever seen, it looked more like a fortress, with tall narrow windows and white flaking paint that fluttered in the breeze. It must have stood over a hundred feet high. Of course, I had seen Greek churches in Dorpat in Estonia and Pskov but this was, without doubt, the largest.

A sharp pain stabbed at my shoulder and we stopped at a low wall where I could sit for a while. It was a balmy day and the sun on my face felt good. A kitten, one of the many cats that wandered freely around, came and rubbed itself against my leg, purring happily. I studied the huge building. Despite it being a heretical church, I would have liked to have gone inside, but Dimitri made it clear by a shake of his head that this was not possible. As if this was not clear enough, Grigori spoke in faltering Latin. 'No allowed… monks pray now… now you must indoors.' He picked me up again, supporting my good shoulder, and we returned the way we had come, back into the wooden building and the gloominess of the infirmary.

Prince Alexander visited again the next day. I was sitting up in bed, daydreaming of the past, when the door opened and the tall nobleman and his Irish interpreter entered. This time, both men pulled up stools and sat on either side of my bed. Fergus was carrying a letter, its seal of a horseman with a raised sword in his right hand still unbroken. There was no sign of Brother Dimitri.

'Prince Alexander is pleased to see you are recovering,' Fergus said in a neutral voice.

'As am I,' I replied. 'Last time you were here you told me some of my brethren knights had also been captured. It would please me to see my old comrades again.'

Fergus translated my words and Alexander shook his head.

'This will not be possible,' the Irishman translated. 'They have already been ransomed back to your Order. You are the only German…' he coughed to cover his mistake, knowing I was as much German as he was, 'still confined here.'

'And now that I am in recovery,' I said, unsurprised at the news, 'when will I be released?'

'You are far from a recovery,' Fergus translated. 'Prince Alexander believes releasing you too early could jeopardise all the good work done by Brother Dimitri. You are unfit to travel and, in the meantime, must remain a guest of Novgorod the Great.

He also believes you are of a higher rank than the other captured knights and therefore worthy of a more… fitting payment.'

Without knowing the identities of the others captured, I had no idea of the truth of this. However, it was credible; I was one of the highest-ranked knights in the Livonian Order.

'And of course,' Fergus said, smiling maliciously, 'you are no longer a young man.'

That was true enough; I was fifty-three at my last count, an old man. And at that moment, I felt every year.

An idea came to me, although in truth I had been considering it for a while – I'd had nothing else to do. If I was to be confined to my bed or as a prisoner I might as well use the time. 'As I am to be kept here longer,' I said to Fergus in French, 'then I would like to have the chance to write to my son… an account of my life perhaps, so he understands his background and heritage.'

I waited patiently as Fergus relayed this. To my surprise, Alexander clapped his hands together and beamed at me, speaking quickly to the Irishman who then slowly translated his answer.

'Prince Alexander finds your idea of merit,' Fergus said. 'But only on the condition that whatever is written can be translated into Russian.' His face crumpled as he understood the implication of what he had said. He would be tasked with the duty himself. 'It is normal among the Rus' for written records to be made. Even as we sit here, in this very monastery, scribes are writing up a chronicle of the history of Novgorod.'

I regarded Alexander, who was grinning in enthusiasm. All the power and harshness of his face had disappeared and he looked young, very young. This only made me feel older and more irritable. But at least I would have the chance to write my memoirs for my son, to let him know his responsibilities and inform him of his birthright, in order for him to seek the vengeance I might not be able to achieve.

'Prince Alexander is interested to learn how a warrior monk can have a son,' Fergus went on. 'Did you not swear a vow of chastity before joining your Order?'

I sighed and turned away. Of course I had, but life was never easy. The Devil finds ways to lead even the most pious from the path of purity. And being pious had never been one of my strengths. 'I have no wish to talk of such matters now. If the Lord Prince wants to know, then he will have to read what is transcribed.'

The Irishman translated my words and for a moment I thought I had angered his master. It is no easy thing to defy a prince – even if he was the enemy. But the shadow that flashed over Alexander's face was replaced with a smile. He spoke quickly to Fergus, who appeared to question what had been said, dropping his head and nodding. I waited, interested for the translation.

'The Lord Prince Alexander says you are still too weak to undertake this chore alone. He desires that I,' Fergus's voice had fallen so low I thought he would gag over the words, 'come here daily from the city to act as your scribe and write your words. I am then to translate them later into Russian for the Lord Prince.'

I looked at him and laughed, enjoying his predicament. I have never liked the Irish. It seemed this dour, unenthusiastic helper and I were going to spend much more time in each other's company. I did not realise then how fruitful that task would ultimately prove.

But where to begin? My early recollections were so distant they felt like they belonged to someone else. I glanced at the letter, cradled on Fergus's lap, and a memory came back to me, of another letter, so many years ago. A letter that had changed my life. That would be as good a place to begin as any.

We started the chronicle the next day.

PART ONE

ENGLAND, 1203

CHAPTER ONE

My name is Richard Fitz Simon and this is my story. It is the truth, as God is my witness, although if I am honest, I think the Almighty gave up on me many years ago.

It is not a story I should have to tell. As the first and only son of the Lord of Cranham, my future was preordained. I would inherit my father's castle and estates, continuing to rule much as he had, until I too grew old and feeble and passed it on to my own son. That was the way of things. Or at least the way it should have been. However, life for me turned out differently.

I was born in the year of our Lord 1189, the same year Henry II died and his eldest son Richard was crowned king, before he took the cross. When I was a child, I was naively proud of sharing my name with the Lionheart. Now, this memory is just a child's foolishness. Richard was probably one of the worst kings ever to rule over the Kingdom of England, mainly because as an adult he was hardly there. When not on crusade to Outremer or imprisoned by the Duke of Austria, he spent more time in Normandy or France than he ever spent at home. England proved to be little more than a golden goose for him.

In my opinion, King Richard was a vain bastard interested only in his own glory. But when I was a child, I thought differently. I was proud of my kingly name. But then the young have always been fools.

The Lionheart may have been dead a long time now, but sharing his name was not the only thing we had in common. I too spent most of my life abroad, on a near-permanent crusade in lands most people have never heard of, far from the hot suns of Outremer and the Holy Land. I fought in the forgotten wars to help bring the light of Christ to the pagans of the eastern Baltic. It was a life of duty and hardship. And it was a thankless task.

My story begins at the point when I was just fourteen, early summer in the fifth year of the reign of King John. I remember peering over the battlements on the keep of our castle at Cranham with my father, Lord Roger. He was never a talkative man, and as a child I found him more than a little intimidating. It was sunny, with clouds skimming across the sky and the sheep-shearing season underway. My father had summoned me to the roof, and I stood waiting for him to speak. Despite living in the same castle, he was rarely at home, and when he was, he had always been unapproachable; a distant and stern figure I would normally only see at mealtimes. In his hand he carried a letter, its seal broken, which he must have just opened. The frown on his face suggested displeasure at what he had read. I had seen the messenger sitting in the hall on my way up and was curious about the news it contained.

For the first few moments we stood in silence, gazing out over the castle, feeling the breeze brush our hair.

'Take a look, Richard. Everything you see is our land. Our barony is small compared to most, but it is fertile land, good land. And remember we are the feudal tenants-in-chief. Do you know what that means?'

'The land belongs to the king…?'

'All land in England belongs to the king!' my father growled. 'What makes a feudal tenant-in-chief different?'

I could not remember and shook my head.

He frowned. 'It means I have no liege lord. Our family own the land directly from the king and we answer only to him. The biggest landowner in this area is Lord Bigod, Earl of Norfolk.' He pointed off towards the south-east. 'He owns most of Suffolk and Norfolk and has several castles much bigger than this one. But he is not my liege lord.'

Little did I realise then that he planned for me to squire for Lord Bigod – but I am getting ahead of myself.

My father changed the subject. 'When she was alive, your mother used to enjoy coming up here. She said she felt like a goddess looking down on the world…'

My memories of my mother were vague. She had died giving birth to my little sister Alice. I think my father never forgave my sister for that unfortunate fact. He had never really spoken about my mother before, though I knew he missed her. I wanted to know more. 'Did you marry mother for love?'

'Of course not,' my father said, irritated again. 'No one marries for love. But I grew to love her. If your mother still lived, things would be very different.'

I said nothing, scared of ruining the moment.

'Alice would have turned out differently, I am sure. I blame myself for her being so wild. If only she could be more like Isabella.'

Isabella was my older sister by four years. She had recently been given in marriage and now lived with her new husband miles away. I did not miss her; we had never been close. Alice, on the other hand, felt more like a little brother. I had spent most of my earlier years playing with her. She hated all things girlish and loved to climb trees and play knights in the castle yard, outwrestling most of the younger boys of the household and often coming home with scuffed knees or a torn dress, much to the chagrin of her nursemaid or my father.

What could I say? Alice was by far my favourite. She was a wildcat.

'It is why I never remarried,' my father continued. 'I did not want to sully your mother's memory. There will never be anyone quite like Mathilde, God rest her soul... not for me anyway.' My father turned and fixed me with his hard stare. 'Sir Hugh says you are progressing well with your weapons training. He also says you are growing into an accomplished rider. All of this is good, Richard, but do not neglect your studies with Father Bertram. A lord needs to know more than just how to fight. Learn everything you can from whomever is teaching you. Knowledge is power. Always remember. Knowledge is power.'

My father's acknowledgement of my successful training with Sir Hugh de Burcy filled my heart with pride. Praise from my father was praise indeed, however qualified. Sir Hugh was my father's chief knight, a grizzled old warrior and veteran of the same crusade to Outremer led by King Richard. My father had told me that was why he had kept me at our castle in Cranham rather than sending me to another noble family for fostering at the age of seven, which was the custom. He wanted Sir Hugh to tutor me as a page. There was little about swordplay or riding he didn't know. In addition, as a page, I began to learn the things I would need to know to be a squire and ultimately a knight.

And of course, it was true I enjoyed everything Sir Hugh taught. I may not have been the best swordsman in the kingdom, but I was very fast and better than most my age.

Hugh would spend hours in the practice yard teaching me and the other two boys he tutored the rudiments of combat. Scarcely a day would pass that I would not go to bed with a new bruise or cut somewhere on my body.

I looked at my father, but he was staring out across the river and the fields beyond and did not seem to notice. He was not a tall man, in fact at fourteen I was only half a head shorter myself, and despite being over forty, his grey hair was only slightly receding.

I turned to look over the castle. It was a modest affair, consisting of the small stone keep on which we stood, surrounded by a palisade built of wood in the Norman fashion. Another palisade split the outer bailey with the much smaller inner one, where my family lived. It was nothing compared to some castles in the realm, but it was ours and it was home.

My father waved the letter towards me. 'We shall be receiving visitors in just over two months. Your Aunt Cecilia and your cousin Walter. They will be here by Michaelmas.'

Aunt Cecilia was the wife of my uncle, Gilbert, who was fighting for the king in France. I had never met Gilbert, my father's younger brother, but I looked forward to hearing about his exploits in the war.

'I assume you are aware of the situation in Normandy from discussions at dinner. Your uncle has lost his holdings to King Philip of France. Cecilia and Walter are not just coming to visit. They shall be coming here to live. They have nowhere else to go.'

At the time, I did not understand the implications of this. Family coming to live with us was surely a good thing.

'Your Aunt Cecilia...' My father paused.

I had never seen my father when he was not in total control.

'She is not the easiest of women.'

'Yes, Father.'

'Listen carefully,' my father growled. 'This is important. You do not understand what this means. I do not want you to give her any cause for judgement. You are my only son and a direct reflection on me and the entire family. I am expecting you to help welcome them – especially your cousin Walter. I have yet to speak with Alice, but that can wait. I am trusting you to help control your little sister. All she cares about is her damned horse. God knows how difficult Alice can be at the best of times, but she seems to listen to you. I shall be holding you responsible for her behaviour.'

This was not good news. Alice didn't listen to me any more than she listened to anybody else. And although we were still close, my studies and training had created a distance between us.

'I am thinking of sending her away, anyway,' my father said. 'She needs to learn how to behave like the lady she shall one day become. Either that or send her to a nunnery.'

If it was not my father speaking, I would have burst out laughing. I could no more imagine Alice in a convent than a Saracen in a church.

There was a pause as my father gazed out across our land, before turning to me again. 'Always remember, Richard, one day when I am just bare bones crumbling in the earth, all of this shall belong to you.'

I knew that already, of course, but the words still felt like honeyed mead. A feeling of contentment surged in me. These were happy times. Little did I know that my problems were just about to begin.

It was a month before Michaelmas in 1203, Saint Giles's Day I believe, although I am not sure anymore. I was confined to the cramped room next to the chapel that served as the classroom, learning Latin with my two fellow students, John de Vere and Robert Percy, both sons of knights that served my father and decent enough companions. I have never been good with my letters and listening to the chaplain droning on had almost sent me to sleep. We all jumped when the door was flung open and Sir Hugh appeared. 'Excuse me for interrupting, Father Bertram, but Lord Roger summons his son at once.'

My heart immediately started thumping. What could be so important he would disturb my lessons? I followed him out of the tiny room into the bustle of the castle yard.

'Your father is waiting by the stables,' Sir Hugh said, leading me in that direction. The outer bailey was reasonably large, with a blacksmith's workshop, stables, chapel, storerooms and the new hall my father was building. A sandstone gatehouse that housed my father's men-at-arms led to the village.

By the entrance to the stables, I saw my father waiting with another man. A messenger dressed in a yellow tabard with a red cross – the livery of Lord Bigod. My pulse surged.

My father turned to us as we approached and he gave a rare smile. 'This is Richard, my son. Please repeat to him what you just told me.'

The man bowed his head. 'I have been instructed by Lord Bigod, Earl of Norfolk, to accept your father's request for you to enter into the service of my liege as a squire. You are to arrive at Framlingham in November, on the day after Martinmas.'

Words caught in my throat. This was everything I'd always wanted. I beamed at him like a simpleton.

'You are to attend with your own horse and weapons. Sir Hugh de Burcy has spoken well of you and my lord looks forward to accepting your service.'

'Thank you,' I managed to say. 'It is a great honour.'

'Are you sure you will not break bread with us?' my father said, addressing the messenger. 'You have ridden far. I can arrange for your horse to be fed and groomed.'

'Please excuse me, but I must regretfully decline. I have further messages to deliver and the sun is already high in the sky.' The groom held the horse as the messenger swung himself up into the saddle.

My father thanked him, and I watched as the gate to the village creaked open and the messenger walked his horse through, disappearing from view. This was one of the proudest moments of my life, especially as Sir Hugh had spoken so highly of me. I would be sent to Framlingham, one of the greatest castles in all of East Anglia.

'It is a great honour to be accepted by a noble of such high rank, Richard,' my father said. 'I expect great things of you. Act your best at all times.'

'Thank you, Father. I will not disappoint you.'

He nodded in satisfaction, turning to return to the keep. 'Now I have work to do. We shall talk again later.'

My father left me with my mind reeling, excited about the prospect of becoming a squire, and dreaming of being a knight.

The next few weeks saw frantic activity around the castle and the surrounding fields. It was the busiest time of the year and the peasants worked tirelessly, harvesting crops from their fields as well as the demesne land that belonged to my father. Extra labourers were hired to get the crops in and help transport them to the barns and most of the village were involved. The days were long and tiring, but after a wet early summer, the last few months had been unusually hot with no rain. While the weather had not completely ruined the harvest, it was still bad compared to the years I could remember as a child. And the last three harvests had been even worse. So, the work progressed, with everyone working towards the feast that would take place at Michaelmas, although it promised to be a frugal affair. My father was particularly busy, receiving rents due, hiring new servants and collecting debts, working closely with his steward, Wilhelm, on the household accounts as people continually came and went.

I was in the Northmead, the meadow directly next to the palisade that ran down to the river, practising mounted swordplay with John and Robert under the watchful eye of Sir Hugh. The Northmead was left untilled because it was often prone to flooding, but the previous two months of dry weather ensured the ground was hard and the grass yellow. I was mounted on my young courser, Cobalt, a gift from my father when I had become a page. He had given both my sisters horses as well, but I was particularly proud of mine, a spirited grey mare. Robert was reeling from a clout round the head I had just given him with my wooden practice sword, when a servant from the castle appeared, speaking briefly with Sir Hugh.

'Richard!' Hugh waved me towards him. I cantered over to where he waited. 'That was a good strike, but remember to keep your shield up, otherwise you leave yourself vulnerable. Your father has sent a message. You are to prepare yourself and go to the hall to welcome your aunt and cousin who have just arrived. You are relieved of training for the rest of the day.'

Excitement welled up in my chest. It was early afternoon with the sun directly overhead, which meant I had most of the day free, a rare opportunity. My father had told me Walter was already fifteen, a year older than me. It would be good to have another friend of my own age to train with. I rode Cobalt back across the Northmead, past the wattle houses of the village and through the outer gatehouse, stabling her quickly and instructing the groom to rub her down and feed her. I passed through the second gate and into the inner bailey. The main keep was not large, squarely built of tan-coloured stone and three stories high, acting as the last line of defence as well as being the family home, although since becoming a page seven years before, I now lived in a low building next to the brewery and the falconry mews. I returned to the room I shared with Robert, stopping to stroke Gaston, an old, half-blind spaniel that liked to sleep at the end of my bed. I hung my sword on its hook above my narrow pallet, shaking off my mail *hauberk* and padded gambeson underneath. The room was cramped, with a sloping roof, wooden walls and a small shutter, which we always kept closed because it opened out to where the shaft from the privy in the keep dropped its waste. I changed into my finest black tunic and rushed out to respond to the summons.

Alice was on the steps that led up to the entrance to the keep. I called to her and she smiled, waiting for me on the top step. We entered through the stout wooden door, pushing through the curtain that hung to keep out the worst of the draughts and into the gloomy smokiness of the hall.

The chamber had a high table on a raised dais at one end where the family normally sat for mealtimes and two lower tables. Fresh rushes covered the floor. Four men and one woman were finishing a meal of soup and bread at the nearest table and I assumed these were the retainers and servants who had accompanied my aunt. My eye passed quickly over them to the high table where my father sat with his steward, Wilhelm, a woman in her late thirties and a youth I presumed was Walter.

My father stood and waved us over to where they were seated. 'Let me introduce my son Richard, and my youngest daughter Alice. This is your Aunt Cecilia and your Cousin Walter.'

I bowed my head towards my aunt. She wore a chemise underneath a long aqua-blue gown with tight sleeves widening to the wrist in a trumpet shape. On her head was a wimple and veil of the same colour. She gave me a long stare, as if trying to see into my heart. She gave a pinched smile and inclined her head. Fine lines spread from her eyes and whilst not attractive, she possessed an aristocratic air that made her appear almost regal. I disliked her immediately.

Walter looked to be roughly the same size as me. In contrast to my dark hair, his was sandy brown and cut shorter, and he wore an emerald doublet with bright silver buttons. He looked at me briefly, turning to stare at the embroidered wall hanging of a hunting scene that hung along the main wall next to the fireplace. My first impression was that he didn't want to be here.

'Richard,' my father said, 'why not show Walter the castle? I am sure he would like to see his new home while I discuss matters with Lady Cecilia.'

Walter came to his feet reluctantly, and I saw he was only slightly taller than me. I led him outside and Alice followed.

'Will you be joining us for training?' I asked Walter. We descended the steps. 'Our instructor is very good. He took the cross with King Richard in Outremer.'

Walter shrugged. 'It is beneath me to train with children. I am used to fighting with the squires and adults.' His accent sounded strange to my ears and I bristled at his words, but he didn't seem to notice. 'My father is a great soldier. He always made sure I got the very best of training. Unfortunately, things have changed.'

I stifled a comment and looked round at Alice and rolled my eyes. She laughed.

Walter stopped to glare at my sister. 'What do you find so amusing?'

To her credit, Alice just shook her head. 'It was nothing. Come and see our horses. Perhaps we can all go for a ride and show you our father's land.'

We led Walter through the inner gate and into the outer bailey. He looked around, hardly hiding his disdain.

'In Normandy,' he said, 'the castles are built of stone. This place would not hold for long if it was besieged.'

'England is peaceful at the moment,' I said. 'All the fighting is in France.' I looked away to see Robert Percy striding across the yard. 'I need to speak with my friend for a moment,' I said, glad to get away from our new guest. I said to Alice, 'Take Walter to the stables and I will catch you up.'

Walter and Alice walked in the direction of the stables and I called Robert over. My friend had a bruise on his forehead where I had struck him with the practice sword earlier.

'You landed me a good one in training,' Robert said with a wry smile. He pointed with his head towards the back of Walter and Alice who were entering the stables. 'How is your cousin? You don't seem very happy? I thought you were looking forward to him coming.'

'I was, but he seems to be an arrogant shit. He thinks he's too good for us. Anyway, forget him'. Why are you not training? Did Sir Hugh realise that without me your sword practice would be pointless?'

Robert laughed. 'He released us. I am going fishing in the river. Want to come?'

I shook my head. 'I have to look after my cousin. I will see you later.'

Robert continued back to the room we shared in the inner bailey and I walked towards the stables. I was about to open the door when I heard shouting coming from within. It was Alice.

I flung the door open and dashed inside, stopping in shock. Walter was whipping Alice's rouncey Angel with a leather strap. He was like a man possessed, flaying at the horse with all his strength. Alice was distraught. Tears streamed down her face as she begged him to stop, but he hardly seemed to hear. She stepped between him and the horse and he turned his attention on her, whipping the strap across her face.

Anger exploded inside me and I rushed forward, shoving him away from my sister. He stumbled forward and turned, his eyes wild with fury, pulling his arm back to lash me. I smashed my fist into his face, hearing his nose crack and feeling blood splatter across my hand. He howled in pain, dropped the strap and clutched his face. Giving him no chance to recover, I hammered my knee into his stomach and grabbed his hair as he doubled over and continuing to punch him in the face with my free hand. He fell to the ground and I rained more blows down on him. After what he had done to Alice, I could have beaten him senseless, but two powerful hands grabbed me from behind and flung me into a bundle of hay in one of the empty stalls.

'Stop this lunacy immediately!' It was Sir Hugh, black with rage. 'This is no way for a lord's son to behave.'

Walter was groaning on his hands and knees, his face a bloody mess. Alice was sobbing, a red welt vivid on her cheek.

'Your father will be furious when he hears about this,' Sir Hugh snarled at me, looking at Walter who was whimpering. 'And hitting girls might be acceptable behaviour in Normandy, but it most certainly is not here!'

Walter came to his feet, clutching his nose, his eyes wild with hostility.

'You had better go and get your nose seen to,' Sir Hugh said. 'It looks like it's been broken.'

Walter almost ran for the door. Hugh let him go, looking at me as his anger finally cooled. 'I thought I taught you about the importance of keeping a level head and not losing your temper.'

'He struck Alice. What was I supposed to do?'

'You did not have to beat the boy half to death. Wait until you have calmed down and go to the hall and see your father. Go before you are summoned – it might go better for you.' He turned and left, shaking his head.

I looked at Alice. She had stopped crying and was comforting Angel. 'I hate him,' she said. 'I wish you had killed him. I'll get him back for this, just you see.'

'No, you shall not,' I said. 'I've punished him enough and do not want Father to have an excuse to send you away. He is thinking about it, you know.'

Alice shrugged. 'If that pig is going to live with us then maybe it will be better.'

'Do not say that,' I said. We hugged and I wiped the tears from her face. My knuckles were bruised and I cleaned the blood and snot from them with a cloth. 'We had better go to Father and face whatever punishment he has for us. He must have heard from Walter by now.'

Outside, we received looks from the household servants. I groaned at the thought of the whole castle learning about what had happened. We walked into the inner bailey, my feet moving ever more reluctantly towards the punishment I knew would follow. But I had no regrets about what I'd done. Walter was a bastard and he deserved everything that had happened.

Inside the hall, my father sat anchored in his chair at the high table, idly stroking one of his hunting dogs. Walter was being tended at one of the lower trestles by my aunt and a servant. Everyone looked up as we entered.

'Is this the way you treat guests in England?' Aunt Cecilia's eyes narrowed as she glared at me. Walter at least had the dignity to look ashamed. My father's gaze bored into me before he turned to Alice. 'Walter says your horse attacked him in the stables, and when he tried to discipline her you attacked him.'

My sister raised her chin in defiance. 'That is a lie.'

'And that you, Richard, came up behind him and punched him in the face.'

I shook my head. Surely my father could not believe this nonsense.

'This is a serious matter,' my father said. 'I would not tolerate it when servants fight, let alone my own family. Lady Cecilia and Walter are guests in our house. I want to know the truth of the matter. Alice, tell me what happened in the stables?'

'I was showing Walter the horses,' Alice said, without hesitation. 'He started laughing at Angel and hit her around the head...' I could see she was fighting to hold back tears. 'Angel tried to bite him... but she did not... she didn't touch him. Then Walter said he knew how to punish bad horses and he... he whipped her with a strap. I tried to stop him and he began to hit me with the strap—'

'She lies!' Walter shouted.

My father came to his feet. 'Quiet! You have said your piece; now it is Alice's turn.'

Cecilia stood up. 'Are you going to believe this little girl over my son?'

'Please sit down, Cecilia. You are my brother's wife and a guest in my hall, but I am the lord here. My Alice can be wilful, but I have never known her to be deceitful. Richard, give us your account.'

I took a deep breath and explained what I'd seen when I entered the stables. 'And I saw Walter strike Alice so I lost my temper and hit him... I was pulled off by Sir Hugh.'

'So, you freely admit striking Walter,' my father said.

'Yes... but only because he struck Alice.'

'It looks like you almost killed him.' He thought for a moment, before turning to a young servant that hovered by the edge of the high table. 'Go and fetch Sir Hugh. I shall hear all witnesses of this sordid affair before making any decision.'

The servant disappeared. I looked at Walter who scowled at me, taking satisfaction in his swollen face, although the bleeding had now stopped. Sir Hugh arrived a few moments later. His gruff voice resounded around the hall as he recounted what he'd seen. When he had finished, I looked at my father. Although his face remained impassive, I knew his punishment would be harsh.

'I am very displeased with all three of you,' he began. 'For this episode to have taken place on the day of our guests' arrival only makes it worse. You are all to blame for what happened in the stables. Tomorrow is a holy day, the Feast of Michaelmas, but after mass, instead of celebrating, all three of you shall spend the time keeping a vigil in the chapel under the watchful eye of Father Bertram, where you can reflect and seek guidance from God.' He looked at Walter and then me. 'You are both on the cusp of manhood. I do not wish to interfere with your training to become knights. Your vigil shall be followed by twenty strokes of the birch the following morning, to be carried out by Sir Hugh.'

I knew better than to say anything, but Walter groaned. Lady Cecilia flushed in fury. Nevertheless, she kept her mouth shut.

'Alice. It is clear to me that unfortunately at Cranham you have failed to learn the virtues and finesse required to be a lady. Soon you will be of marriageable age, but your behaviour to date makes that an unlikely prospect. I have decided to send you away as soon as I can find a noble house willing to take you.'

My heart dropped and I stole a glance at my sister. She looked as though she would cry, but I sensed the news did not entirely displease her. It was a normal thing to be sent to another noble's household. I could hardly wait myself to go to Framlingham. Maybe it was for the better, but I would miss her terribly. All because of that bastard Walter. It was clear we would never be friends.

CHAPTER TWO

So, the next day we missed the feast and had to keep a vigil in the chapel, supposedly in prayer, although I spent most of the time thinking of ways to get back at Walter. The following morning we were punished. Being whipped with the birch was painful, but it was not the first time, and I sensed Sir Hugh's heart was not really in the strokes he delivered. I refused to cry out or scream and took the punishment without complaint. I would not let Sir Hugh see my weakness. Afterwards, I did my best to cast the ordeal from my mind, but I could not help feel some resentment towards my father who had ordered it, even if he had felt there was no other choice.

Two days later, Wilhelm, my father's diminutive and taciturn German steward, told me at dinner that my father had left at dawn for Norwich on business expected to take over a week. We had not spoken to each other since I had received my punishment and he had not bade me goodbye. At noon on the same day, Lady Cecilia had moved into my mother's old chambers on the top floor of the keep where my father had previously slept, split by a wooden partition from his own solar which he now used. She avoided the rest of the household at mealtimes, preferring to eat alone or with Walter in the privacy of her chamber above the hall. Walter and I had barely spoken since our fight, but every time I saw his swollen face, I felt a satisfaction.

Unfortunately, although expected, Walter started training with us under Sir Hugh. The veteran knight was careful to avoid pairing us together at first, but with only four of us, this proved impossible to maintain. It was a cold windy day with heavy clouds racing across the sky and the threat of rain ever constant, when he matched us with each other to practise sword training on foot in the fenced-off enclosure next to the outer gatehouse. Walter looked at me maliciously, as though he had waited a long time for the moment, and I knew from seeing him batter my friend Robert the previous day that he was a competent swordsman. Sweat trickled down my spine despite the weather, and I vowed to myself I would fight my best and deal out as much punishment as I received. Before we started, Sir Hugh spoke with us both out of earshot of the others.

'Remember, you are both noblemen of the same family. This is only a training session. If either of you take it too far, then I shall report it to Lord Roger when he returns. You have been warned.'

When he walked away, Walter glared at me through narrowed eyes. 'This time you shall not take me by surprise, little cousin. I am going to enjoy humbling you.'

'Do your best.'

Of course, from the first blow the fight was for real. We both wore gambesons, a quilted jacket normally worn under a *hauberk*, and had shields, but despite our wooden swords, there was the very real danger one of us could get hurt. I didn't care – I wanted to hurt him as much as possible. Walter attacked in a flurry of slicing strokes that forced me onto the defensive, desperately parrying or using my shield to block his assault. He was older than me and strong, and he was better than both Robert or John. I swung my sword at him in a blow that would have taken his head off had it struck, but he took it on the top of his shield, grunting with the effort as I attacked again, forcing him back towards the others who were watching our contest. We were roughly matched and, when he caught me with a stinging blow on my forearm, I replied with a cut that hit his upper leg above the knee underneath his gambeson. After a short time, sweat flowed down my back and face. I stole a glance at Sir Hugh, seeing him glower, as Walter slashed at my head, catching me on the side of my helmet with a blow that made my head spin.

'Stop!' Sir Hugh bellowed, striding forward. 'What did I say before? It is over for today. Both of you are to go and see Father Bertram for extra Latin!'

We both groaned. Our hatred of studying was the only thing we had in common.

'And if I catch either of you fighting again, I shall be forced to bring it to the attention of Lord Roger. He shall not be so lenient with you both next time.'

Walter muttered something unintelligible and stormed off. My head still rang from the last blow and I could already feel a bruise coming on. I was glad my father was away. Hopefully, by the time he returned the episode would be forgotten.

Life at Cranham carried on over the next week or two and things settled down. Outside the castle, the peasants ploughed for the winter crop of wheat and rye to be planted in the field that had lain fallow all year. The hedges were opened to allow the cattle access to the harvested fields to graze on the stubble as the weather took a turn for the worse. Hardly a day passed without rain and winds buffeting the shutters, whipping around the castle yard like demonic ghosts seeking the souls of the living.

An uneasy truce developed between me and Walter. Mostly we shunned conversation, but when it was unavoidable – when we trained together, learned together, and ate many meals together – we were almost over-polite. Neither of us wanted to be disciplined again and we both knew another incident between us would lead to greater punishment. Walter kept to himself most of the time, completing his training and studies with us, but making no effort to make friends with either Robert or John. What little free time he did have, he spent playing knucklebones with the four retainers who had accompanied him. I was glad of his aloofness, able to enjoy the company of my peers without interference.

Mealtimes in the hall were usually solemn and unpleasant, and though I was no longer required to wait on the tables, I could never get away quick enough, even if it meant much of the afternoon confined to the classroom. As before, Lady Cecilia avoided most of the meals with the household, at least when my father was absent. On the rare times she did make an appearance at the high table, she would studiously ignore me, although on a couple of occasions I caught her glaring when she thought no one was watching. We never spoke.

My father's trip to Norwich was successful; he had arranged for the family of William d'Aubigny to take Alice as a lady-in-waiting. Alice told me he was particularly pleased as d'Aubigny was the 3rd Earl of Arundel and one of King John's favourites.

'He says I should be proud of the honour,' she confided to me in the stables. 'And I suppose I am. But I would rather stay here. I shall learn etiquette and act as a servant for his wife, Mabel of Chester. I bet she's a right witch.'

'Maybe not,' I said, more to try and cheer her up than actually believing it. 'We cannot stay children forever. Anyway, I will be squiring for Lord Bigod soon. It seems Father is sending us to some of the best families in the land.'

Alice pulled a face. 'He wants to marry me off and have me gone. He hates me for killing Mother.'

I hated this conversation whenever it came up. 'You did not kill Mother. And he does not hate you. He is hard on all of us.'

'He was not so hard on Isabella before she was married off…'

'But you know that's the role set for us. We have no choice.'

'At least you shall get to inherit Cranham. I will probably be married to some fat pig twice my age!'

There was nothing I could say to that. It was probably true.

Alice was due to leave the day after Saint Luke's Day. This was usually a happy time of the year and it rekindled my hatred of Walter, knowing he was partly to blame, but Alice was not entirely faultless and what I had said was true; we were both almost adults and could not avoid our fate.

The night before the feast day, we lit candles in the chapel for the sick and poor and kept a vigil. With my father and most of the other senior members of the household present, I had to dig my nails into my palms to stay awake as the prayers droned on. I am a bad Christian, and I found the countless days of fasting and prayer unbelievably tedious – strange, considering how my life would turn out.

On Saint Luke's Day, Father Bertram gave a rambling sermon in the chapel about the martyrdom of Saint Edmund, an East Anglian king killed by the Danes over two hundred years previously. He then went on to talk about the healing power of Saint Luke and his life as a physician, before becoming a disciple to the apostle Paul. We recited what felt like an endless stream of prayers. The following feast in the hall was a dour and miserable affair – at least for me, worried about what awaited my sister the next day. Alice did her best to put on a brave face, but I could see she was terrified and fighting not to cry and bring dishonour to the family. Lady Cecilia, sitting next to my father, made small talk with him, smiling and laughing at everything he said. It was as if she was playing a game and, of course, she said nothing to me. She was a viper. I hardly touched the main dish of goose and, in an effort to get through the feast and afternoon entertainments, I drank far more wine than normal. I hardly remembered the minstrels and jugglers my father had employed. Subsequently, I spent most of the evening vomiting into my chamber pot, much to the amusement of Robert with whom I shared a room.

Pouring rain greeted us at dawn the following morning and I did not envy poor Alice who had to make the journey to her new home in such atrocious weather. She was accompanied by a maidservant and two of my father's men-at-arms. The goodbyes were said swiftly as everyone wanted to get back inside, and I didn't manage to overhear the few words my father said to her.

I embraced her as the rain hid the tears I knew were flowing down her face. 'You will be fine,' I said. 'You are the lucky one. I wish it was my time to leave…'

'I will miss you, Richard.' Alice bit her lip. 'And I hope you beat up Walter again.'

I smiled and gave her a hug. I whispered in her ear, 'May God keep you safe.'

Her escort was already mounted and a groom helped her climb into the saddle of Angel before they all turned to the outer gatehouse. Walter was also there to witness her departure and I saw a smile of satisfaction on his smug, arrogant face. It took all my self-control not to punch him into the mud and finish off what had started when he'd first arrived. As if reading my thoughts, I caught a look from Sir Hugh who shook his head slowly.

The wooden gates opened and we watched them disappear into the rain. A great weight settled in my stomach like a rock. I had lost my little sister. My little wildcat.

The next morning, I was working in the stables mucking out the stalls when a rider arrived with news. He was a messenger from Gilbert Fitz Simon, my father's brother and Cecilia's husband. My uncle had been wounded fighting for King John in Normandy and wished to recuperate at Cranham with his wife and son. He would be arriving the following day. At the late-evening dinner in the hall, Cecilia was more animated than normal, and she even gave me a self-satisfied smile, saying with pride what a great soldier her husband was.

My uncle arrived after mass the following day. It was raining again, not the heavy downpour of the day Alice left, but a fine drizzle that permeated everything like a mantle of mist. We heard the creak of the main gate opening before we emerged from our morning prayers in the chapel. My uncle and his men rode through the outer gatehouse. There were twenty of them and they wore mail and carried shields, swords and spears, sitting hunched in their cloaks as if they had just come from battle, which I suppose they had, having recently arrived from Normandy. As the horses stamped and snorted in the muddy yard, several grooms, including my friends Robert and John, came running to take the reins and lead them to the stables. I stood watching next to my father and Sir Hugh. My father's face was an unreadable mask but that was normal for him: he rarely showed his emotions.

My uncle dismounted, handed the reins of his horse to a groom and approached my father. 'Roger,' he said, bowing his head.

'Welcome back, Gilbert,' my father said. 'You and your men can come to the hall where we can break our fast.'

'It has been a long time since I was last here,' my uncle said. 'It looks almost the same.' He looked at the half completed new hall in the outer bailey, turning his attention to Lady Cecilia and Walter whom he greeted warmly. 'What happened to your nose?' he said to Walter. 'You look like you had a fight.'

'I had… a little accident.' Walter turned and scowled at me.

My uncle followed his gaze and looked me directly in the eyes. 'You must be my nephew, Richard. I have not seen you since you were a small child.'

I bowed my head, not really knowing what to say.

'Come inside,' my father said. 'There shall be plenty of time to talk out of this damned rain.'

My father led the way and we skirted the puddles, through the second gatehouse into the inner bailey and the keep. A few moments later the hall was a bustle of activity, with the servants having to set up more trestle tables to seat the new arrivals. My uncle's men sat apart from the household and the garrison, taking up one complete side of the room. They looked tough and grim and they devoured the hunks of bread and cheese eagerly in relative silence as if they had not eaten for a long time. On the high table, my uncle sat to the right of my father, talking in low tones about the war in France. I studied him carefully in between bites of food. He was taller than my father and well-muscled, looking like the soldier he was. As I watched him more closely, I noticed he was disinterested in the conversation around him. His eyes were never still, darting around the hall, taking in everything that was happening. There was a slyness that was hard to define.

'The war is not going well, as you have probably heard,' he said to my father. 'The family holdings in Normandy have already been lost, along with the land I received from Cecilia's family when I married. She is very upset about the loss… as am I. It is a grim business.'

My father said little, even less than normal, and again I wondered about his relationship with his brother. 'How long do you intend to stay in England?' he finally asked.

'Until my wound has healed.' My uncle did not look especially hurt. 'If the weather improves, maybe we can go hunting. It has been a long time since I've enjoyed that particular pleasure.'

'I have little time for sport,' my father said. 'And the weather is hardly suitable.'

'Time should always be found for hunting. There is no better way to spend one's free time.'

'You said you were wounded,' my father said. 'Tell me, what happened?'

'It was at the beginning of the siege of Château Gaillard. We got into a skirmish in woodland near the castle and I took a sword-stroke on my arm. My mail saved me, but the arm was badly injured. It is still heavily bruised.'

'You were lucky,' my father said. 'I assume when you have recovered you will wish to rejoin the king in Normandy?'

Gilbert smiled. 'All in good time. I might be one of the king's most trusted captains, but he is not expecting me back immediately. Anyway, I suspect he will return to England soon enough himself. In the meantime, I am pleased to be able to catch up with my family again – and to revisit my childhood home.'

My father stared ahead as if he had not heard. I felt a tremor of unease. What would my uncle's arrival mean for life in Cranham?

The next day was colder, but at least the rain had stopped and the sky was clear and blue. Despite what he had said the previous morning, my father announced at breakfast he would indeed be going hawking with my uncle in the afternoon, and he would need me to squire for him. My father rarely hunted, with hawks or otherwise, and I went to my morning class with uplifted spirits. But when Walter told me, after a tedious lesson of Latin, he would be joining us too, my mood soured. I should not have been surprised, but I had hoped otherwise. Nevertheless, I intended to have fun anyway and enjoy the change in routine.

Dinner in the hall was busier than ever. In contrast to the day before, my uncle's soldiers were much louder, but they kept apart, away from the rest of the garrison. On the high table, I was dealt a further disappointment when Lady Cecilia declared she also wished to come hawking with us.

We gathered outside by the mews where Edmund, my father's falconer, waited. He was a short, compact man, who always reminded me of a barrel with arms and legs, but he was good-natured, and he presented my father, my uncle and Lady Cecilia with the hawks they would be using for the hunt. My father's peregrine falcon was especially impressive – a magnificent bird of blue and grey named Striker. The falcon was hooded to keep it quiet.

We collected the horses and hunting dogs at the stables. Ralf, the huntsman, oversaw the dogs, half-a-dozen or so spaniels. I knew every dog in the castle, often spending my free time playing with them, and they barked and jumped over me in excitement as the rest of the party climbed into their saddles. Walter sneered down at me but I didn't care. We rode out of the gate through the village, heading for the Northmead and the river. There were seven of us and we followed the river for several miles, the dogs barking and yapping around the horses' feet. The river had flooded in some places after the heavy rain and my father cast a critical look over the waterlogged fields. I rode behind him, keeping a respectful distance, avoiding eye contact with Walter riding on my right. Because of the flooding, we had to change our route several times. After a while we reached the area of wetland and stopped. My father spoke quietly with Edmund, while the dogs nosed around and the rest of us waited patiently.

'Here is a good place for wild ducks and other waterfowl,' my father said, unhooding Striker. He released the bird, letting it fly upwards. I watched it gain height until it was just a small speck in the sky. Everyone dismounted, except Lady Cecilia, and my father turned to me. 'Look after the horses.'

Walter openly gloated as he handed me the reins of his horse. Lady Cecilia had a sparrowhawk on her wrist and she turned to scan the ground for any sign of hares to hunt. The others walked towards the river, the dogs dashing ahead to rouse the ducks.

My uncle released his hawk, a lanner falcon. Walter waited behind; his job was to help collect any birds brought down by the hawks. I watched them walk further away, the ducks taking flight in a tumult of noise as the dogs chased around the reeds at the edge of the river. I shaded my eyes against the glare of the sun, looking in the sky for the two hawks that had been released. There was a flash of speed and I saw the peregrine dive and strike one of the ducks, knocking it out of the sky before the falcon circled back and landed a few feet away. There was a reason why he was named Striker. The falcon hopped over onto the wounded duck, which was dead a moment later. Edmund gave it part of a dead hare as a reward.

He swung the lure and the peregrine flew back to it. A moment later, my uncle's hawk made its first kill, Walter collecting the dead duck and bringing it back to the others. This carried on for much of the morning and I brought the horses up to where my father waited with Lady Cecilia. I shivered in the cold air, watching everyone else enjoy themselves.

My uncle, Gilbert, was further off, but he walked back to where we stood, climbing back onto his horse. 'I want to go on a little further,' he said to my father. 'I will take young Richard, so he too can enjoy the sport.'

Walter came up and scowled sulkily. Now it was my turn and I flashed him my smuggest smile, climbing onto Cobalt and following my uncle, leaving my aunt to chatter to my father. We rode across the meadowland and once we were away from the others, my uncle slowed down, letting me bring my horse alongside. The lanner falcon on his arm observed me with hooded eyes.

'It has been a while since I have been able to enjoy hawking,' he said. 'I used to hunt ducks here whenever I was home as a squire many years ago. But I prefer hunting deer – or even better, boar. I shall have to convince your father to go to the chase soon.'

I nodded, hoping he would succeed. I had not been on a proper hunt with my father for over a year.

'Is everything well here? A great deal has changed since my time. The garrison is smaller than before.'

'I don't think so. There are still three knights and a dozen men-at-arms. A couple are away escorting my sister Alice, but they should be back in a few days.'

I remember even now, though it pains me, how proud I felt that my uncle was talking to me like an adult. I did not trust him, but that was just an indistinct feeling. Nevertheless, he was talking to me in a way my father rarely did and I was babbling away like a child... like the foolish child I still was. But as I said before, the young have always been fools.

'And Sir Hugh de Burcy is still in command? That is a surprise... he must be very old now.'

'But he is still a formidable warrior. He is in charge of my training. I have learnt so much from him.'

'I'm sure you have. Walter speaks well of him.'

I found that hard to believe; I could not imagine Walter spoke well about anybody at Cranham.

'And he is loyal to your father?'

It was a strange question, but I did not realise it at the time. 'Oh yes. He is the most loyal of my father's vassals.'

My uncle considered this for a moment before changing the subject. 'But your father's steward, the German man, what is his name... Wilhelm? He is new, is he not?'

'Not really. He has been in my father's employ for at least five years.'

'Where did your father find him?'

'In London, I think. He was a merchant and my father helped him. That is all I know.'

'But it seems strange to have a German as a retainer – at least in such a senior position.'

'My father says he is very honest. And he is loyal as well.'

Gilbert stroked his beard. He released his falcon which climbed quickly to a position to be able to swoop down on any prey. The dogs splashed around in the water flushing more ducks into flight and a few moments later the first was brought down. For a while I collected the dead ducks, until the light began to fade and it was time to return to Cranham.

We rode back the way we had come. When we approached the village again, my father let his horse drop back, allowing my uncle and Lady Cecilia to lead. He drew his horse next to mine and leaned over. 'I saw your uncle talking with you. What was he saying?'

'He was asking some questions about life in Cranham...'

'And you told him what he wanted to know, I suppose? Learn when to talk and when to listen.' My father kicked his horse forward again, not even waiting for my answer.

I was confused, wondering what I had done to displease him. By the time we were riding past the wattle buildings of the village, my mood was dark.

That evening, supper in the hall was as busy as ever. I sat next to my father but he spoke instead with my uncle about the situation in Normandy. After the meal, they remained, drinking wine, although I observed my father hardly touched his. They both seemed to have forgotten I was there, so I remained, eager to hear more about the war in France.

'We heard Prince Arthur was moved from Falaise by the king and is now locked up in Rouen,' my father said.

My uncle hesitated for a moment, then leaned towards my father. I could only just hear him. 'He was, under the charge of William de Braose, but the king got rid of him.'

'Got rid of him?'

'Before Easter this year. The king was drunk and killed the boy himself, dumping his corpse in the Seine. I should know, I was with him at the time...'

My father sat in silence for a moment as I listened stunned. 'And you serve such a man?'

'As do you,' my uncle said. 'He is the rightful king of England and your liege as well as mine.'

'He is despicable. You have confirmed it with your own mouth, king or not. And there are many who believe Arthur should have been the rightful king after Richard. For Christ's sake, Richard even nominated him as successor until changing his mind on his deathbed. That a king of England could stoop so low.'

My uncle, Gilbert, shrugged. 'Kings do what they must.'

'Must? To murder his own nephew? The man has no honour.'

'I would be careful what you say, brother. He is known for being unforgiving to his enemies.'

'Don't be ridiculous, I am not his enemy. But there are many in this land who consider him so. He is hardly a good Christian and taking noblewomen as mistresses hardly endears him to his barons. And on top of it all, to lose our ancestral holdings to the French king… But we are on thin ice, of that you are right. Let us talk of other things.'

'Which reminds me,' my uncle said. 'I have some valuable documents I would like to deposit in a safe place. I assume you have somewhere secure – a place where you keep your own valuables?'

'Of course,' my father said. 'Give what you have to Wilhelm and he shall take care of it.'

My uncle pulled his beard, nodding in thought.

My father seemed to remember that I was still sitting with them. 'What are you still doing here? Go and finish your chores.'

So, that was that, I was dismissed, my mind reeling from what my uncle had said.

CHAPTER THREE

My father woke me before dawn the next morning with a hand on my shoulder. 'Get up, pack clothes for a few days, ready your mail and weapons and come to the chapel.'

A short time later, I pushed open the door of the chapel and entered, bleary-eyed and curious about where I would be going. Inside, it was gloomy, with only the few candles on the altar giving any illumination. My father was kneeling on the cold floor, his head lowered in prayer. I knelt next to him and after a moment he turned and spoke to me in a low voice. 'You are going to accompany Wilhelm on a trip to Little Tamfield, and then on to the abbey of Saint Edmundsbury. I would go myself, but I cannot leave the castle at the moment.'

His words chilled me. What was behind this?

'You will leave as soon as possible. I have given some important documents to Wilhelm, which he shall deposit for safekeeping with Abbot Samson in the monastery of Saint Edmunds. No one here knows that Saint Edmundsbury is your ultimate destination and it must remain that way. I shall say you are going to recover tithes at our manor near Thetford.'

'What documents are we carrying?'

My father sighed. 'The deeds and titles relating to lordship of Cranham. Your uncle Gilbert is not to be trusted. I want you to go so you know where they can be found if anything happens to me.'

'Anything happens to you?'

'It's just a precaution. But it shall be good for you to learn how to manage the family's estates and manors and no one can teach you better than Wilhelm. He is waiting for you in the stables. I would like to send a couple of men-at-arms with you, but I need them all here. In fact, I would like to hire more, but it is not so easy now with the war in France. Go now and may God protect you.'

When I reached the stables, Wilhelm was already leading his horse out. He nodded to me and waited while I prepared Cobalt. The steward wore a long grey cloak edged with fox fur at the collar, and he had a sword strapped round his waist, although I couldn't imagine him using it. As usual, he wore a red felt cap on his head to cover his balding pate. A few moments later, we were ready to leave. Outside was still dark but I could detect a faint lightening of the sky to the east. I shivered in my cloak as I climbed into the saddle. The gate opened and we rode out towards the village. When I looked back into the outer bailey my father had already disappeared.

By the time it was light enough to see my own breath, we were well clear of the castle and village. The road was barely more than a track, rutted and uneven, but at least in the cold it was no longer a quagmire. Thin tendrils of mist clung to the surrounding bushes and trees giving the landscape an eerie, ethereal feel. We rode alone in silence.

I had a thousand questions I wanted to ask Wilhelm. I drew my horse up alongside him. 'Tell me what you know about this, Wilhelm?' I said. 'Why does Father fear my uncle?'

'Your father does not fear him, Richard. He is just being careful and taking precautions. He is worried about why Gilbert has come back to Cranham... what his motivations are. He has more soldiers than your father's garrison.'

'But he is my uncle. He is family.'

'Do not be naïve. Your uncle has lost all his holdings in Normandy. He has no home anymore.'

I remembered my uncle's questions when we had gone hawking – and my pathetic pleasure at being treated like an adult. The reason for my father's reaction was clear to me now. 'But there are laws. My uncle cannot simply take what is not his.'

'Ja, in normal cases you are right, but these are difficult times. Laws are often flouted in times of war. Your father does not want to take chances, which is why we go now to Saint Edmunds monastery.'

Wilhelm spoke almost perfect Norman French and it was only occasionally I could hear it was not his native tongue. I considered his words, absently fingering the silver cross around my neck.

We passed through an area of open woodland, the last of the autumn leaves falling in the cold breeze, the bare trees stark and skeletal. Alerted by our movement, a squirrel dashed up the nearest tree, disappearing into the tangle of branches. Above us, flocks of migrating swallows soared across the cloud-scudded sky, swooping over the tops of the trees. Despite being weak, the sun managed to burn off the early-morning mist. Although we had not seen a single person since leaving Cranham, this changed when we reached the Thetford road. A line of packhorses carried wool, probably heading to Dunwich for export to Flanders. A group of pilgrims headed south and two oxen driven by a peasant family pulled a cart heaped with firewood for the coming winter.

After turning onto another minor track for a mile or so, we reached my father's manor of Little Tamfield in the afternoon, with the sun gradually slipping towards the tops of the surrounding trees. A gaggle of children ran alongside our horses as we trotted up the rutted path that led to the manor house. I flipped them a couple of cut pennies from my purse and they whooped with excitement, scrubbing around in the dirt. Wattle houses with sagging thatched roofs streaked green with lichen lined the road, looking as though they would collapse under the weight. Little Tamfield was far smaller than Cranham and not as prosperous. The manor house was at the end of the track ringed by a wooden palisade, opposite a stumpy stone church surrounded by a stand of poplars. Inside the gate, the actual house was the only two-storied structure in the village, the ground floor built of stone with a wooden upper floor and roof. A servant took our horses and led us into the main hall where we were met by my father's mesne lord, Sir Henry Danneville, a knight even older than Sir Hugh de Burcy but with none of his energy or physical intimidation. We spent the evening sitting in Sir Henry's draughty hall, sipping sour wine and listening to him and Wilhelm drone on about manorial finances. I tried to pay attention, but with the conversation about land management, livestock and crop productivity, they might as well have been talking in another language, and I soon lost interest. When it was finally time to bed down on a pallet set up at the edge of the hall, I thanked God with relief.

The next morning we left early for Saint Edmunds Abbey. Wilhelm, as usual, said little, but I wanted to know more about how he'd come into my father's service and he was surprisingly open. 'Your father helped me when things went wrong with my business in London,' he explained. 'Without his help I would probably be dead now.'

'But why were you in London anyway?'

'I was born in the Holy Roman Empire in a large trading city called Lübeck, although it is occupied by the Danes now. I was a wool and cloth merchant. I travelled often to England and when my business picked up, I bought a warehouse and property in London. Not long afterwards, I moved there permanently, selling the holdings I owned in my hometown. I met your father about ten years ago – Lord Roger had business with me. I bought raw wool from him, among others, to export to Lübeck. We had dealings with each other over a number of years.'

'How did you come to Cranham?'

'My business had a few problems… My ship sunk in a storm in the German Ocean… my warehouse in London burnt down. I lost everything. Your father needed a new steward and he offered me the job. We had always had a good relationship and he respected my business competence. I owe your father everything.'

The road wound through an area of woodland. A few hundred paces ahead I saw several figures closing on two horsemen. Next to me Wilhelm drew up his horse, '*Scheiße!*'

'Sorry?' I said.

'Looks like trouble. Richard, you have better eyes than mine. What do you see?'

I squinted and looked at the scene before us. There were six men on foot. One of the riders was pulled from his horse as the other drew his sword and began striking at the figures around him. 'Outlaws,' I said. 'We must help.'

I still remember my reaction clearly, all these years later. My reaction was the foolishness of a fourteen-year-old who thought he was immortal. I whipped Cobalt forward, drawing my sword and waving it above my head. Behind me, I could hear Wilhelm shouting but I ignored him, caught up in the excitement.

He had no choice but to follow. We galloped down the track towards the fight. One of the riders was on the ground unmoving, but the other was still fighting, slashing wildly left and right with his sword. As we got closer, one of the attackers turned and saw us thundering towards them and he shouted a warning. They ran, dispersing in all directions and fading back into the trees. I pulled Cobalt up. The man who had been fighting had a gash down his arm that was bleeding, but he paid no heed to his own wound, instead rushing to check on the condition of his companion. Unfortunately, the other man was dead.

Wilhelm arrived, his face disapproving. 'Richard. Are you mad? What were you thinking?'

'This man is wounded,' I said. 'Help bandage his arm.' To my surprise, Wilhelm dismounted and obeyed. I scanned the trees around us, fully aware they could attack again at any moment. 'We need to get moving before they realise there are only two of us.'

It was only later I reflected on how I had taken control of the situation. I was to be fifteen in a few months, but both older men obeyed without question. Then again, I was big for my age and of noble blood.

'I thank you,' the man said as Wilhelm wrapped a strip of cloth torn from the dead man's tunic to staunch the flow of blood. 'I am Thomas of Lynn. We were on our way to Normandy to fight for the king.' He looked at the dead corpse of his companion. 'Although poor Simon shall fight no more.'

'We will not leave him here for the wolves,' I said. 'We shall take his body with us to Saint Edmundsbury. But we have to leave now.'

Thomas and Wilhelm lifted the dead Simon and tied him quickly over the saddle of his horse. I could still hear movement in the tangled undergrowth and half expected an arrow shaft to strike us at any moment. Nevertheless, in the brief time we were waiting, nothing happened. We all mounted, cantering away until we had left the scene behind us. As the danger decreased, a ripple of exhilaration flooded through me. Although I had not fought anybody, our opportune arrival had seen off the outlaws and probably saved Thomas's life.

'You will be able to get your arm seen to in the infirmary at the abbey,' Wilhelm said. 'They will also be able to give your friend a proper burial.'

Thomas shook his head. 'The outlaws must be desperate to risk attacking two men-at-arms. I'd have thought the bastards would have waited for easier prey.'

'Winter and hunger are never far apart,' Wilhelm said. 'And hunger makes people desperate.'

We continued in silence for a few miles. I thought about what my father had said the previous morning and I brought my horse alongside Thomas. 'My Father, Lord Roger Fitz Simon of Cranham, has need of men-at-arms far closer than Normandy. Would you be interested?'

'Perhaps,' Thomas said, 'depending on the terms.'

'You can decide after they have seen to your arm at the abbey.'

Thomas looked competent as a fighter, and he was armed well enough, with a falchion, shield and crossbow slung over the side of the packhorse. As we got closer to the town, the road became more crowded with people. We passed a group of pilgrims travelling in our direction. They were barefoot and chanted songs praising God and Saint Edmund. I looked at the bleeding sores on some of their feet and I wondered if this was what God wanted? I could not see how God, Jesus or the Holy Ghost could benefit from this kind of devotion. We kicked our horses into a canter again, glad to leave the noisy pilgrims in our wake.

Ahead, I could see the tower of the abbey church, reaching up like a finger pointing to the heavens and dominating the surrounding countryside. To the right was a heath on which gallows were erected, two bodies hanging, the rightful fate that awaited outlaws.

We entered through the north gate as the bells from the town's churches rang out for Sext. The streets bustled with people and the deafening noise overpowered my senses. As well as the bells, there was the clang of a blacksmith hammering, people shouting, and dogs barking. The stench of shit and the stink of too many people living too close to each other assaulted my senses. Father Bertram had always preached about the danger of noxious smells and I believed him. After traversing a long street, we reached the abbey gate and passed into the relative serenity of the abbey itself. Here we had to leave our weapons. To our right, the abbey church was magnificent, bigger than anything I had ever seen. Scaffolding covered the entire western side and I could see the façade was being extended, although no one was working at present. Inside, we were met by two servants who took our horses. Monks in black habits came from all directions and headed towards the church but, after Wilhelm announced our purpose, one of the servants led us in a different direction, while the other escorted Thomas to the infirmary.

We were led across a wide muddy courtyard, edged by the last browned tufts of the original lawn and surrounded by other stone buildings. I was amazed how large it was. Looking around, I could see that in addition to the huge abbey church, there were a further two churches within the complex. It made Cranham seem insignificant in comparison. The servant conducted us to the abbot's lodgings, an imposing two-storied palace where he showed us our room. We were given a comfortable chamber on the ground floor with intricate leaves carved into the stone arch above the doorway, and he brought us water in a jug to wash off the dust and dirt of the road, telling us that we would be summoned to eat dinner with the abbot after he had prayed. Not long later, he returned and ushered us upstairs to the abbot's personal hall, where we were greeted by a short man of at least sixty with a worn face and the last remains of wispy white hair around his tonsure, and a taller man of middle age with heavy bags under his eyes.

The elderly man's voice was surprisingly strong and his eyes sparkled as he introduced himself as Samson, Abbot of Saint Edmundsbury, and the other man as Prior Adam. 'Shall we speak in Latin or would you prefer French?' Samson said.

'My Latin is passable,' I said, 'but French is easier, of course.'

'Then French it is. And to what do we have the pleasure of this visit? It has been a while since I last heard from Lord Roger. How is life at Cranham?'

'We have some documents we wish to deposit with you here, father abbot,' Wilhelm said. 'And of course, we would like to make a generous gift to your establishment.' Servants appeared carrying a large array of dishes they deposited on the table. As it was Friday, most of them were fish. Even at my father's table I had never seen such an abundance. There were platters of fried sole, dace, lampreys and roasted eel in a wine sauce, pike in galantine and smoked salmon, along with bowls of leeks, peas and beans served with brown bread. It seemed that the monks lived well here at Saint Edmundsbury and I realised how hungry I was.

'Why do you wish to deposit the documents here?' Abbot Samson asked. 'Surely Lord Roger has somewhere secure in his castle?'

Wilhelm pulled a sealed letter out from his tunic and passed it to the abbot. 'This is from Lord Roger Fitz Simon.'

Samson broke the seal and quickly read the letter. 'Lord
Roger requests that only three people should have access to
the documents,' he said. 'Himself, Wilhelm?' He looked at
Wilhelm and then me. 'And young Richard, here. Is there
something more I should know about?'

Wilhelm shook his head. 'Nein, Lord Roger believes that
these deeds and titles would be better kept here for safekeeping,
that is all. With the current war in Normandy everything is
uncertain... and Saint Edmundsbury is a house of God.'

Abbot Samson grunted, clearly not convinced. 'Well, for a
generous gift I am sure we can come to some arrangement. I
shall speak with the Treasurer this afternoon. As for the war
in Normandy, it is a burden that affects us all. Unfortunately,
our current king lacks the good sense of his brother.'

I ate and listened as Abbot Samson talked about the war
and the situation in the kingdom.

'I hear that you were attacked by outlaws on the road from
Thetford,' he said. 'It is a sad state of affairs to see how things
have deteriorated. But it is cause for concern. In the four years
or so since Richard died, things have got worse. King John was
here after his coronation,' he lowered his voice as if we might
be overheard, 'but he donated a mere thirteen shillings – as
King of England! Can you believe it? As you can imagine, I
was appalled.'

'Hopefully, he shall be more generous of spirit on his next
visit,' Prior Adam said between mouthfuls.

'We can but hope,' the abbot said. 'But his lack of piety is
known to everyone. He has robbed the church of its property
and openly mocked our rituals and rites – failing to observe
fasts or other ceremonies and making irreligious remarks. We
have heard that he has even questioned basic Christian tenets.'

I thought about what my uncle had said about the murder
of Arthur of Brittany, but of course, I said nothing.

'And he is on dangerous ground with the pope as well,' Prior Adam said. He took another mouthful of food. 'I must say, Brother Fidelis has excelled himself today. These lampreys really are quite delicious.'

We continued the meal, making small talk, although I chose to say little as Abbot Samson held court. I found his forceful personality daunting and I remembered my father's words about knowledge being power. Time to listen and learn. Afterwards, Abbot Samson and Prior Adam excused themselves, citing important work.

A servant was assigned to show us the main abbey church, and we entered under the scaffolding and through one of the three enormous bronze doors where massive columns and rounded arches towered above our heads. Colourful patterns adorned the walls and for a moment I just stood there, too stunned and overwhelmed for words. This was surely a house of God if ever there was one. There was a stream of pilgrims wanting to visit the shrine, and we shuffled in line with them and down the nave, passing the choir stalls. At the far end, behind the altar, we came to the shrine of Saint Edmund. It was impressive, looking itself like a small church, dwarfing us on its marble plinth. The top half was covered in gold plating with figurines adorning its side, and it shone in the candlelight, illuminating the pilgrims praying on their knees. On a table nearby, gifts were stacked in the hope that Saint Edmund would bestow his blessings upon them. Our servant guide explained that the shrine had been damaged in a fire previously, although I could see no evidence of it. I wondered if the saint's relics really were contained within, and despite my awe at the church building I found it hard to believe they really could cure people of their ailments and infirmities. Father Bertram had taught us that a saint's relics were highly sacred and could perform all kinds of miracles, but my natural scepticism found this dubious. Now, forty years on, as an old man, my natural scepticism has only hardened into outright cynicism. I think it is all a pile of shit.

Next to the shrine was a reliquary that our servant said contained a piece of John the Baptist's beard and the finger bone of Saint Peter. How a piece of John the Baptist's beard made it all the way from Outremer to England over a thousand years ago only Our Lord knew? It seemed so unlikely I could not help but doubt its authenticity. Afterwards, I felt guilty about my lack of faith so I spent half a penny and bought a pilgrim badge. Maybe then God would not condemn me for my lack of conviction.

We retired to our chamber early, my mind in turmoil over my doubts. Of course, I was a Christian, everyone in my world was, but it had never *interested* me. All I had ever wanted, from when I was a small child, was to be a knight. Father Bertram taught us the scriptures and I prayed, fasted, kept vigils, went to confession and served penance like everybody else. But this was because I had no choice. I could not wait for dreary Latin in the classroom to end and my training with Sir Hugh de Burcy to begin. I hated the endless church rituals and ceaseless praying. Did this mean I was condemned to hell? I didn't know the answer to that and I am too old to care about it anymore, even though my time in this world is nearly over. But I remember how it worried me at the time and gave me many sleepless nights.

Next morning we were woken by the bells ringing for Prime. Outside, rain drummed down and a biting wind lashed around the yard, buffeting the shutters that covered the windows. I dressed quickly and we hurried to the abbey church to say our prayers, laughing at the sight of some monks, who had hitched their habits up to reveal bare legs, running across the rain-soaked mud. Wilhelm and I joined them, shivering in the nave of the church as the monks sang a hymn, followed by psalms and a reading. My mind wandered to what would await us later in the day when we returned to Cranham, but our journey had been successful. Abbot Samson had agreed to safeguard the documents for a fee, or donation, of ten shillings, which I considered a staggering amount but was much what Wilhelm had expected. Afterwards, we went to the infirmary to see if Thomas had recovered enough to travel back with us to Cranham, if that was indeed his intention. He declared he was fit, able and willing to come and speak with my father about employment. 'It's many leagues closer than Normandy,' he said, showing us the bandage around his arm. 'And one master is as good as another.'

We left Simon's body in the care of the abbey and departed shortly afterwards. The weather had still not improved and after collecting our horses and picking up Thomas, we passed out of the same gate of the abbey that we had entered and back into the town. In contrast to the busy streets we had seen the day before, it was almost deserted. We took the town's eastern gate, clopping over the bridge and the swollen waters of the River Lark. I sat hunched in my cloak, letting the horse make its own way, shivering as the track wound through waterlogged fields. Water dripped down my neck from my cap and my limbs ached like a taut bowstring, ready to snap. Although the journey back to Cranham would only take half a day, it was too long as far as I was concerned. We travelled in silence.

Sometime later, we reached the track that led back to Cranham, retracing our steps from two days previously. The rain had not relented and visibility was poor. Ahead, through the mist, I could see a wagon slewed across our path. One of the wagon's wheels was broken and two men crouched down repairing it. The scene looked innocent enough and I nudged my horse to ride single file past them, my two companions following behind. When I drew level with the first man, he abruptly stood and grabbed Cobalt by the reins. Instinctively, I pulled her away, but I glimpsed a flash of steel. The horse's sudden movement saved my life as the dagger missed me but scored Cobalt's flank, causing her to rear up and my attacker to step back to avoid getting kicked. I drew my sword, hearing shouting behind me. 'Get the boy!' cried the man who had attacked me.

There were more figures around us and Cobalt jumped forward, knocking another man over as the first drew a sword and came for me. My horse circled round and I leant out from the saddle, as Sir Hugh had taught me, and hacked at the first attacker. It was like striking the quintain in arms practice. The man screamed as my blade cut his upper arm and he dropped his sword and fell to the ground. Behind me, Wilhelm and Thomas were engaged with more attackers and I pulled Cobalt round to come to their aid. Another man screamed a challenge from out of the rain and attacked from the right, swinging an axe. But he slipped in the mud and went tumbling past me. Cobalt jumped over him, the blood from her wound mingling with the rain, as I went to help my companions.

But Thomas had fought his way past the wagon, parrying several blows and slashing back at his attackers. Behind him, Wilhelm was also defending himself desperately. I drove Cobalt into the back of a man blocking off Thomas and Wilhelm, sending him sprawling into the mud. For a moment the way ahead was clear and I shouted for them to ride. I wheeled Cobalt round again, parrying another blow with my sword, sending shooting pains down my arm and almost causing me to drop my weapon. Wilhelm and Thomas thundered past me and I dug my heels in, leaning forward as Cobalt sprung ahead again, galloping after the others and leaving our attackers behind.

I glanced quickly over my shoulder, seeing the outlaws disappear into the rain behind us. We let the horses run, bent low in our saddles to avoid the branches of the surrounding trees. I could see the squat houses of the village looming out of the mist ahead. We slowed down and I bent over to look at the rain-washed streaks of blood down Cobalt's flank. The wound didn't look deep.

'They got the packhorses,' Wilhelm said. That was ill news, my mail *hauberk* was on one of them.

'But they did not get us,' I said. 'And I wounded one of them!'

'*Ja*. Nevertheless, it is concerning to see how dangerous the roads have become for innocent travellers. Two attacks by outlaws in as many days... and so close to Cranham.'

'When I tell my father, he will send men to track them down and bring them to justice.' I hoped above everything that I would be allowed to accompany them. Something about the incident nagged at me, but I could not think what it was and put it out of my mind. By now the rain had died down to a mere drizzle and we rode through the deserted village. Ahead, I could see the gatehouse of the castle and we picked up our speed again, trotting over the wooden bridge and through the open gateway.

It was then my life changed for ever.

CHAPTER FOUR

At first, I didn't notice anything different. We were greeted at the gate by Godfrey, my father's dim-witted man-at-arms, who bowed his head as we passed into the outer bailey. There were more people around than I would have expected, considering the weather, and I observed a group of my uncle's soldiers dressed in mail, milling around, talking near the gatehouse. Despite this, there was a subdued atmosphere, but I thought nothing of it, dismounting from Cobalt and instructing the groom to treat her wound while I went to find my father. I was so eager to speak with him that I left Wilhelm and Thomas at the stables in my haste. The steward could catch up with me when he was ready.

I strode through the second gateway into the inner bailey, passing another couple of my uncle's men. Ahead was the main keep where I expected my father to be. When I approached, the door at the top of the steps opened and my uncle emerged. He was deep in conversation with Ralf, my father's huntsman, and for a second, he did not see me. Then he glanced down in my direction and his eyes widened, stopping me in my stride. For a brief moment we stared at each other before he recovered his composure, leaving Ralf and descending the steps towards me. 'Richard, it is good you have returned. Come with me to the great hall, there is something I must tell you.'

I followed him up the stairs and into the hall, my heart pulsating. Inside, I scanned the top table for my father but there was no sign of him. Instead, I saw Cecilia, sitting talking to Gervase, my uncle's chief retainer and second-in-command. She looked up and I saw surprise on her face, quickly replaced by her familiar contempt. What had I done to earn such hatred? Several of my uncle's soldiers sat at one of the side tables and, apart from the odd household servant, I realised everyone present was a stranger to me. Where, by Christ, was my father?

My uncle called for ale and waved me over to a table where we sat down. I was aware of many eyes on me and it was a relief when Wilhelm appeared out of breath in the doorway.

'We were attacked on our way back,' I said to my uncle, 'only a mile or so from the village. Where is Father? We may still be able to apprehend the outlaws.'

'It is of your father I wish to speak,' my uncle said. 'Yesterday, we went hunting – for boar and deer this time, not waterfowl. There was an accident. I am afraid that your father was grievously wounded. He died of his injuries.'

His words slapped me in the face. I sat stunned. Wilhelm joined us and my uncle repeated the news, but I hardly heard him.

'How did it happen?' Wilhelm asked.

'We were hunting a hart by bow and stable in woodland. Lord Roger left his position and rode towards our prey as one of my retainers fired an arrow. Unfortunately, it struck Lord Roger in the back, piercing his lung. We brought him back here, but he died shortly afterwards…'

'Where is his body?' I said.

'In the chapel.'

I came to my feet, tears stinging my eyes, but I was damned if I would let anyone see me cry. Wilhelm said something to me but I didn't hear him as I stumbled to the door. I had to see for myself.

Outside, I saw Ralf by the mews. I headed towards him, determined to find out more. 'What happened?' I demanded. 'How could my father get killed?'

Ralf lowered his head. 'I did not see the accident, my lord.'

'How could you not see it? You were my father's huntsman – you should have been with him. You should have been protecting him!'

Ralf refused to look me in the eye. I walked off in disgust, passing through the gateway back into the outer bailey. I skirted some large puddles and pushed open the door to the chapel.

Inside, it was gloomy. The sweet scent of frankincense pervaded the air and the banks of flickering candles illuminated my father's body, wrapped in a white shroud and lying on a trestle table before the altar. In front of him, two figures knelt on the cold flagstone floor, praying. I lingered for a moment at the door as my eyes adjusted to the poor light; the figure nearest to me was the burly form of Sir Hugh.

I went to the altar. Despite knowing what my uncle had said was true, it was still a shock to see my father's immobile face staring up at me. He seemed composed and peaceful in a way he never had when he was alive, showing no sign of the wound that had killed him. In truth, he had always been a stern man, hard to please and lacking in warmth. I thought about the last time I had seen him alive, when he had roused me to leave only two days before. The thought of this strong man being dead was inconceivable. What would become of me? What would become of Cranham? I felt cast adrift.

Out of the corner of my eye, I noticed that the other person present was Father Bertram, mumbling prayers in a dull monotone. I knelt and said a few of my own but, after a few moments, my mind was blank of prayers. There were things I had to do. Something was not right about my uncle's story and Ralf had been terrified when I had spoken to him. I came to my feet and caught Sir Hugh's eye, motioning with my head that I wished to talk with him by the door of the chapel.

I pushed the door open and led him outside into the drizzle. 'Something is wrong.'

'I am sorry for your loss,' Sir Hugh said. 'Your father was a good man.'

'Yes, he was,' I said. By the outer gatehouse Thomas was talking to the group of my uncle's men-at-arms. 'On the way back, we were attacked by outlaws barely a mile from Cranham.'

'That is strange,' Sir Hugh said. 'I have never known outlaws to be so brazen in daytime.'

'Do you know any more about what happened to my father?'

Sir Hugh shook his head. 'Unfortunately, I was not with the hunting party. Your father wanted me to remain here to safeguard Cranham. Most of your uncle's retainers took part, except the four that left in the morning on a trip to Norwich. Your father took half a dozen of his own soldiers too, as well as Ralf—'

I remembered Ralf's reluctance to talk with me. 'I tried to speak to him but he wasn't very helpful. In fact, he acted very suspiciously. But what about these four men that left for Norwich?'

'Yes. Four of Gilbert's men left Cranham on an errand after breaking their fast. I do not know any more than that.'

The nagging feeling I'd had earlier returned. The men had shouted, 'Get the boy', when they had attacked us. There was nothing particularly strange about that, except they had shouted it in Norman French. Why would English outlaws speak Norman French – the language of nobility? Suddenly, everything became clear. The four men had been Gilbert's retainers. Why had it not occurred to me before? My uncle was responsible for the attack on the road. I had no doubt either that he was behind the death of my father.

'I think Father's death was no accident,' I said. 'And my uncle tried to kill us on our way back.'

Sir Hugh's mouth opened and I could see him struggling to grasp my words. 'Your father did express doubts about your uncle, but I thought he was...' He stuck his chin out. 'No matter, everything is clear now.'

'We do not have much time,' I said. 'Can you rouse the men-at-arms as quietly as possible – without my uncle realising what we're doing?'

Sir Hugh looked across at my uncle's men still talking to Thomas. 'We will need to secure the gatehouses and armoury. What do you intend to do?'

I looked towards the inner gatehouse to see Wilhelm scuttling towards us. Behind, I could see my uncle, Gilbert, accompanied by his second-in-command Gervase and Walter, hurrying to catch him up. My hand dropped to my sword as Wilhelm reached us.

'Your uncle wishes you ill,' he gasped.

'I know,' I said. 'The question is what can we do about it?'

My uncle walked across the outer bailey towards the group of his soldiers standing near the gate. He did not look at me nor show any haste. Apart from four or five of my father's men-at-arms on duty, patrolling the stockade and manning the gates, none of the garrison were armed or armoured. By now, my uncle had reached his men and was giving them instructions.

'We have to leave,' Wilhelm said. 'We have no chance of securing the castle. I shall ready our horses again.' He headed towards the stables leaving me standing with Sir Hugh.

I could see he was right. We had lost before we had even started. Three of my uncle's men were striding towards the main gate where Godfrey stood looking confused. My uncle was talking to Gervase and looking in our direction. Sir Hugh shouted to a couple of my father's guards on the wall to come down and join us, but we were still heavily outnumbered.

My uncle walked towards us flanked by Walter and Gervase and with three of his men-at-arms bringing up the rear.

Sir Hugh unsheathed his sword. 'I have seen better odds.'

My uncle stopped five paces before us. Next to him, Walter smirked at me but I ignored him. 'Now, why have you drawn your sword, Sir Hugh? Are you expecting a fight?'

'Perhaps,' Sir Hugh said. 'It certainly looks as if you are.'

'On the contrary. After the unfortunate death of Lord Roger, I am merely concerned for the well-being of my nephew.'

'Your nephew is the new lord of Cranham.'

'My nephew is too young to inherit, as are his sisters. He is the ward of the king now and I am a good friend of the king. You would do well to remember that, Sir Hugh.'

'Richard is the rightful heir,' Sir Hugh said. 'You would do well to remember the law.'

'Well, the king will be the judge of that. I do not imagine young Richard shall be in any position to pay the relief he will demand.'

I looked at the stables some fifty paces to my right and saw Wilhelm emerge with two grooms, one of them Robert, leading our horses back into the yard. The gate was still open, with Godfrey bravely refusing to back down from the men confronting him. Three more of my father's men had joined us from the wall, taking up position behind Sir Hugh, but there was no sign of the rest. Several of my uncle's soldiers had entered the gatehouse and probably taken them prisoner.

I glared at my uncle. 'Did you kill Father?'

'Has the grief addled your brain? He was killed in a hunting accident, as I told you.'

'Well, I do not believe you. I think you killed your own kin.' I could see my words had struck him.

But before he could react, Father Bertram rushed up, waving his crucifix as he stepped between the two groups. 'God is watching,' he implored. 'There must be no bloodshed between families. Let us all calm ourselves and parley.' Behind him, I could see more of my uncle's soldiers hurrying through the inner gate towards us, as well as another two on the stockade walkway opposite, armed with crossbows. They outnumbered us by more than two to one.

Using the distraction caused by Father Bertram, Sir Hugh grabbed my arm and pulled me back, leaning in to whisper in my ear, 'You have to leave with Wilhelm, but your uncle will try and stop you… We will hold them off until you get clear.'

'No. I am not going to run away and let my uncle win.'

'He will win if you stay. There shall be another time. You have no choice. After everything I've taught you. Remember, you have to pick your battles – battles you can win. And this is a futile fight.' He pushed me towards Wilhelm who had already mounted his own horse.

Bertram was still pleading for peace when my uncle suddenly had enough. He back-handed the priest across the face, knocking him to the ground and bloodying his nose. He drew his sword, shouting to his men at the gatehouse. 'Close the gate!'

Then my uncle attacked, slashing at the unarmoured Sir Hugh in a flurry of blows, any of which would have killed the grizzled old knight if they had landed. But Sir Hugh had been expecting the attack and he sprung back, parrying every stroke like a man twenty years younger. Gervase and Walter followed up the attack, being met by two of my father's men-at-arms standing behind Sir Hugh. Wilhelm called my name and I turned my gaze away, looking towards the gate where the three soldiers of my uncle were attacking Godfrey, forcing him back, away from the gate itself. Two more of my uncle's men were trying to close the gates.

Wilhelm called me again. 'Come, Richard. We have to leave!'

I was torn between helping Sir Hugh and obeying their instructions. When Wilhelm shouted a third time, I ran the short distance to Cobalt and swung myself up into the saddle, drawing my sword. It was nearly too late. One of the gates was already closed and the two soldiers had almost closed the other.

I looked back at Sir Hugh. He was defending against my uncle and Gervase, my uncle engaging him, allowing Gervase to flank and attack from the side. Sir Hugh, seeing the danger, feinted against my uncle, swinging his sword at Gervase and slicing him on his upper leg just below his mail *hauberk*. Gervase fell back with a howl, but my uncle recovered and darted in quickly, thrusting his sword into Sir Hugh's chest. I watched appalled as the old knight staggered backwards, blood pumping from his wound, falling to his knees and collapsing face down into a muddy puddle. My father's three remaining men-at-arms who were still fighting immediately yielded, dropping their weapons and raising their hands. We kicked our horses towards the gate.

All this time, Thomas had been watching the fight in complete bewilderment. But as the two soldiers had nearly closed the doors of the gate, he saw the danger we were in and jumped forward, drawing his falchion in one swift movement and stabbing one of the soldiers in the back.

'Stop the boy!' my uncle screamed. Wilhelm and I reached the gate.

The other soldier turned towards me, trying to block my escape, and I swung my sword, catching him in the face. The blow jarred my wrist but he fell screaming in a spray of blood, his face a mangled mess. More men were running towards us and a crossbow bolt whistled past my head. Wilhelm drove his horse through the gap, shouting again for me to follow. I glanced back to where Sir Hugh lay dying, whipping Cobalt towards Thomas standing in the gateway. 'Get on my horse!'

Thomas turned to climb up on the back when another crossbow bolt, fired by one of my uncle's soldiers on the wall, hit him in the back. He collapsed into the mud, twisting round onto his side, blood bubbling from his mouth. I could see immediately he was dead. More of my uncle's soldiers were almost upon me, so I spurred Cobalt onwards, springing through the gate and across the wooden bridge, galloping after Wilhelm and into the village. Behind, I could hear more shouting and ducked down in the saddle as another bolt skimmed past my ear, missing me by inches. We galloped on, clattering through the village and leaving it in our wake. We did not dare stop, knowing my uncle would send men to hunt us.

My mind was reeling from what had happened. Tears streamed down my face, mingling with the rain. What in God's name were we to do now? Where would we go? I had lost my father and I had lost my home.

I had lost everything.

We galloped until our horses were exhausted, slowing reluctantly to an easier pace. The rain had finally stopped, but the roads were still a quagmire and by now it was getting dark. We had spoken little, both absorbed in our own thoughts, wondering what the future held. But we needed somewhere to stay overnight, somewhere where my uncle wouldn't find us.

In a small area of woodland, we found what was an old forester's cottage, little more than a ruined hovel, with a gaping hole in the wattle walls at one end and a sagging, rotting thatched roof partially open to the sky. Nevertheless, one side was reasonably intact and we managed to find some wood dry enough to make a small fire, hidden from the road by the walls and surrounding trees. We led the horses through the decaying door-frame but they were reluctant, which suggested they detected the odour of some animal that had previously made the hovel its home, but it was empty now and, after some coaxing, we managed to calm them down and settle them inside. But we had nothing to eat and I was hungry – probably hungrier than I had ever been in my life. Wilhelm was shaking as we talked about what had happened.

I told him about why I thought my uncle's men had carried out the attack. 'What did you talk about with my uncle after I left the hall?'

'He wanted to know where the deeds and titles to Cranham were,' Wilhelm said. 'First of all, he was friendly... telling me I could carry on as steward and offering me gold. When I would not tell him where they had been hidden, he threatened me. That was when I came to warn you.'

'I think my uncle arranged for us to be ambushed and I think he killed my father.'

Wilhelm nodded.

'But there is the law. How can he steal Cranham like this?'

'I think that he hopes by killing you and your father he would be able to inherit your father's estates. With both of you dead the title would resort to your sisters together, but they are both young and he probably thought that his relationship with the king and ability to pay any relief would mean he would get preference. Knowing King John and his need for money, he is right. After all, Isabella's new husband is a knight of little means.'

'He said something like this to Sir Hugh before he attacked us.'

Wilhelm nodded. '*Ja*, I think he must have been surprised to have seen us when we returned from Saint Edmundsbury. He was probably waiting for his own men to return before taking over the castle peacefully. That would explain why they were all prepared and waiting for the order to move.'

I remembered the look of shock on both my uncle's and Cecilia's faces when they saw me and knew that Wilhelm was right. 'And now Sir Hugh is dead. Without him we would never have escaped... and Thomas. He died keeping the gate open for us.' All my new-found confidence of the previous days had evaporated. I felt like the boy of fourteen I was, fighting the urge to cry again. 'What do we do now?'

'We have to get away from Cranham. We should go to London. I know some people there that might be able to help us.'

'What is London like?'

'It is a city unlike any other – at least in England. But you must take care... it is a violent and dangerous place.'

'We should go to the king. My uncle said to Sir Hugh that with the death of my father I am a ward of the king. He must surely see the injustice of what has happened...'

'Under the terms of military tenure, you would become a ward of the king, which means that he will send you away to a royal castle to continue your training until you come of age at twenty-one and can swear fealty. He would also maintain the right to arrange your marriage. During this time Cranham would revert to him and he would reap all profits. However, considering it is a small barony the profits are relatively meagre – I should know. But King John is desperate for money to fund his war in France. He may well decide to give it to your uncle if he can pay the baronial relief, especially as your uncle is a known retainer and already occupies the main fief and castle. I am afraid that gold is sometimes everything, and the current king's decisions have been arbitrary to say the least. He has often flouted customary behaviour.'

'But I have to speak to him,' I said. 'We may have to go to Normandy.'

'Or we wait until he returns to England. It would be the safer option. Normandy is not somewhere I would choose to visit at present.'

There was little to say to that and we both lapsed into silence.

I sat there as the enormity of what happened sunk in. Father was dead, Sir Hugh de Burcy was dead, and I had lost Cranham. Despite my best efforts, tears streamed down my face, this time without being masked by the rain. And I let them. Wilhelm said nothing, but he moved closer and put his arm around me. I buried my face in the crook of his arm and I don't mind admitting now that I cried like a baby. Shortly afterwards, I drifted into a fitful sleep disturbed by nightmares of my uncle and the death of my father.

CHAPTER FIVE

Next morning, the weather was dry with a pale-blue sky littered with ragged clouds that heaped up on the horizon. As we saddled the horses outside of the hut, I spoke with Wilhelm. 'About last night...'

'What about last night?'

'It will not happen again.'

Wilhelm paused in fixing his saddle and looked at me. 'There is nothing to apologise for, Richard. Last night, I merely helped comfort a young man who has lost everything.'

'It will not happen again.' I turned to mount Cobalt.

We headed south, picking up the main road that led to London. Wilhelm had some money in his saddlebag, money my father had given him for our trip to Saint Edmundsbury, and I still had a few silver pennies in my purse. It was mid-morning when we passed through the town again. We decided to leave the deeds and titles unmolested with Abbot Samson. Our new life was too uncertain to risk losing them on the road to either outlaws or, worse still, my uncle and his retainers who may have been pursuing us. As long as my uncle was ignorant to their whereabouts, they would be safe. So we did not stop and I hardly gave the abbey church a glance as we continued onwards. We decided to pose as a merchant and servant returning to London so as not to draw any attention and we picked up the road leading west towards Newmarket, joining a merchant caravan of over twenty wagons carrying wool. I felt more secure with the armed guards and settled down into a morose silence, mulling over everything that had happened. We spent the second night at an inn in Cambridge, a medium-sized town of wood and thatch located on the River Cam and dominated by a stone castle. The river was busy with boats and people. Wilhelm told me that transporting goods by water was cheaper and the Cam flowed into the Great Ouse which straddled the fens and stretched all the way to Bishop's Lynn on the coast. Unfortunately, the inn was packed so we couldn't get a room, choosing instead to sleep in the hayloft above the stables rather than in the common room. This allowed us to keep a watch on our horses. However, it was not normal for well-dressed travellers on good horses to sleep in such humble surroundings and I noticed this attracted attention. I wondered if they believed our story about Wilhelm being a travelling merchant and me his servant. But at least I ate well, devouring my bean soup and bread like a fasting man on the last day of Lent, before retiring to our cold loft.

The next day, we continued our journey south. The road was busier now and it was even paved, the legacy of Roman road building, and we decided to leave the caravan as our progress would be faster alone. With so many people abroad, the risk of outlaws attacking us was remote. By late afternoon we had reached Ware, where the Old North Road crossed the River Lea, and a thriving market allowed us to buy some much-needed provisions. All the inns were full of pilgrims heading north to the shrine of the Virgin Mary at Walsingham, so we spent the night in a priory north of the road, although our accommodation was nowhere near as grand as Saint Edmundsbury. The following day was the Feast of Saint Simon and Jude. It meant fasting the evening before, and so we ate a meagre fish soup that was far too salty for my taste. The monks did not seem to notice and the priory was full nonetheless. We retired for an uncomfortable night sharing a pallet in a crowded dormitory.

When we awoke, we were obliged to attend mass in the chapel before being able to continue our journey. As it was a holiday, the fields were empty and the road was busy, nevertheless we made good time. When the bells began to ring out across the countryside for Nones, we emerged from a tract of woodland and caught our first sight of the city. It was dominated by two low hills and spread across the whole valley before us, with stone walls bigger than anything I had ever seen and the spires and towers of hundreds of churches within. One soared high into the sky towards the heavens, although the tower was unfinished. I thought this must be the cathedral dedicated to Saint Paul that Father Bertram had spoken of. Grey fields and meadowland, interlaced with tracks and small rivers, stretched from where we had stopped down to a gate in the city walls, flowing into an area of marshland next to which dozens of hovels and animal pens clustered together.

'Where are we going to stay?' I asked. I really did not want to stay another night in a house of God.

'I have an old friend… a wine merchant who lives by the river. We shall go there first. I do not think he will deny us – at least not for a day or two.'

Despite my loss, I felt a quiver of excitement at what lay ahead, Wilhelm's words of caution already forgotten. I had always wanted to see London and now I had my chance.

Hopefully, the greatest city in the kingdom would not disappoint.

We descended the hill, passing through a village and over a rancid ditch that surrounded the wall, reaching a gate capped by two grisly heads, their flesh long picked away by the birds and decayed black. One of them still had several wisps of blond-coloured hair fluttering with every gust of air. Wilhelm explained this was the Bishopsgate, and due to the number of people ahead of us it took a while to gain entry. Inside, we followed the main road that led towards the river. The streets were packed and there was a cacophony of noise with people shouting, vendors selling food, the rattling of carts over the uneven cobbles, the ringing of bells and barking of dogs. It was overwhelming and it made my impression of Saint Edmundsbury trivial in comparison. The street was wide, but with so many people progress was still slow. Around me were folk of all descriptions, some wearing velvet, fur, satin and damask in every conceivable colour. I saw a man as black as a raven and stared mesmerised, wondering if he was a Saracen, until an old crone clutched at my leg with gnarled hands the colour of wood, thrusting an alms bowl up at me. With no money to spare, I nudged my horse onwards, hearing her curse under her breath. I strained my neck to catch sight of the Saracen again, but he was already lost in the crowd.

The smell was intense, the stench of animal waste, offal and excrement hanging in the air like a noxious cloud, infused with the scent of perfume and the aroma of spices. From a crowded tavern on my left, I heard a flute accompanied by raucous laughter and singing. Despite it being a holiday, some people were working nonetheless. Servants darted through the throng, picking their way on their masters' errands between the heaps of animal dung and the open sewers that flowed on both sides of the road. Water carriers and porters manhandled their burdens and the sound of a hammer on steel rang from a side street. At the junction with a church, we turned right into another street called Cornhill, lined with shops and bakeries, and I could almost taste the freshly baked bread that wafted up from the earthier odours of the street. Nearby was a pillory with two men and a woman sitting punishment. Most of the normal townspeople ignored them, but a group of urchins were enjoying the spectacle, jeering and throwing dung. One of the men had blood over his face from where a stone had struck his head.

There were beggars everywhere shaking their bowls, and because we were riding horses we were constantly implored to hand over our coin. In some of the narrow alleys, rats scurried around the heaps of refuse along with packs of dogs and the odd pig covered in muck, nosing through the rubbish. Most of the buildings were made of wood, some of them even three-stories high, and in the narrower streets the upper floors hung over the people below, blotting out the fading light so it was like walking through a tunnel.

We came to an intersection of many streets with a thriving market taking up most of the space. Everywhere there were vendors shouting and customers haggling. Progress was slow and most people were reluctant to move out of our path. I thanked God we were mounted but nevertheless, we were continually pushed and shoved by the crowds around us. A large man with a shaved head and well-muscled arms shouted at us to buy one of the dozens of chickens that hung from hooks on his stall, their legs trussed. Despite the hollow rumbles in my belly, I knew we didn't have the money to spare, so I shook my head and he turned his attention elsewhere.

We crossed over a small stream clogged with filth that stank so bad my empty stomach lurched and I thought I would vomit. We turned left down a small street that led towards the river and away from the mass of people. Now it was quieter and we could ride together.

'It is a little chaotic,' Wilhelm said. 'But we are nearly there.'

We turned into a wider street and I caught glimpses of the river between some of the buildings. A pungent smell of fish hung in the air and I could hear the shouting and bustle of a fish market close by. The street was busier again, and a line of loaded wagons pulled by oxen clattered past in the opposite direction. Wilhelm led us down a small alley that opened into a courtyard directly by the river. I could smell the Thames before I saw it. It reeked of human waste and rotting meat. A few moments later, I got my first glimpse of the river and I paused, looking at the forest of masts from the dozens of ships. It was an impressive sight. From here, ships sailed all over the known world, from the Middle Sea to the far Baltic, loaded with all manner of exotic goods. Ships would sail to Outremer from here. How exciting it would be to see the Holy Land! Maybe fighting Saracens would help dispel my doubts in God.

Wilhelm waited patiently, but we had already reached our destination. On the other side of the courtyard was a set of wooden doors set in a high wall. This was where Wilhelm's old friend lived. The German dismounted and knocked on the gate. On the other side, a dog began barking, but Wilhelm was unperturbed. 'This quarter of the city is known as Vintry – many of the houses belong to wine merchants. My friend Edward is one of the most successful.'

The door was opened by a red-haired servant who fought to keep a large barking Alaunt bulldog at bay. Despite its ferocity, I went and stroked its head, murmuring reassuring words. It quietened immediately, much to the surprise of the servant that still clutched its leash as if it would rip my throat out. I have always had an affinity with animals, and dogs in particular. Now I am an old man, I think I actually prefer dogs to most people. In my opinion, they are easier to manage and more loyal.

The servant told us to wait while he conveyed our arrival to his master. Although we were unexpected, I reflected that Father would never have left guests standing outside the gates of Cranham and I swallowed my irritation. However, we were admitted a few moments later and led into a smaller, cobbled courtyard, surrounded by several outbuildings where a stable-hand took our horses. The main house was a large, two-storey structure with a stone undercroft and wood-framed first floor topped by a tiled roof. The servant led us up the outside steps through the iron-studded entrance door and into a large hall on the upper floor.

The hall was half full of people who had just finished a feast. A man sat before a roaring fire playing a harp and most people were listening to him strum the instrument with long, deft fingers. Our host introduced himself as Edward Payne and invited us both to sit at his end of the table, the members of his family making room for us. Edward seemed genuinely pleased to see Wilhelm. He was a portly, balding, middle-aged man with a face flushed with wine and a large wart on the side of his nose, dressed in a crimson velvet jacket with bright gold buttons. His wife was small and dark-haired, but she personally served us the meal of goose and it was clear that she also held Wilhelm in high regard. With them sat their three children, a girl roughly a year younger than me who avoided eye contact and two younger boys who chattered away like sparrows.

Wilhelm talked to Edward in soft tones that made it hard for me to overhear, so I gave up and listened to the music. I was in no mood for conversation anyway. Time passed and most of the people in the hall left, disappearing into the cold evening outside. With the music over, the rest of Edward's family retired, leaving the three of us. Now at last I could hear what Wilhelm and Edward were discussing.

'Of course,' Edward said, drinking another long draught of wine. 'As an alderman now, my obligations have greatly increased since you were last here.'

He was speaking in English, a language with which I was familiar as my father had thought it important to learn the tongue of most of his vassals. I noticed he was quite drunk. In contrast, I sipped my goblet of wine cautiously, despite its quality.

'We would like to gain an audience with the king,' Wilhelm said, 'but we do not know when he will return to London.'

'I cannot help you with that. He is still fighting in Normandy. No one knows when he will return to the city. Your wait could be a long one.'

'Thank you again for letting us stay here for a few days. I need to make some enquiries with my compatriots at the German Wharf.'

'Ah yes, the Easterlings. They keep themselves much to themselves as they always have – except for business. And of course, you are more than welcome to stay, however long you wish. In fact, I would be disappointed if you didn't.'

'I thank you for your hospitality,' Wilhelm said. 'I did not expect otherwise.'

'You have helped me in the past. Further to what you said earlier, I shall keep my ears open about your problem and speak with my colleagues. If I hear anything, I shall let you know.'

We slept in the hall next to the embers of the fire. I went to bed with the sound of a baby crying somewhere close, but I was so exhausted and heady from the wine that I fell asleep immediately.

The next morning, we rose early and broke our fast with bread and cheese before leaving. Wilhelm wanted to go to the German Wharf at Dowgate, which was close to where our host lived. Although cold, it was a fine day and the streets were crowded. We walked along the river and I marvelled at the sight. The Thames was the widest river I had ever seen and it was busy with boats and ships of all description. However, it was the bridge, a few hundred paces ahead of us that took my breath away. Although incomplete, it looked impossibly long, covered in scaffolding and swarming with workers. I counted nineteen arches and saw how a drawbridge had been built near the middle, presumably to allow ships access upstream.

A short time later, we reached the large stone building that Wilhelm explained was used by the German merchants, most of whom were from Cologne. There was a walled enclosure and courtyard busy with men stacking barrels from a ship that had just docked at the wharf. We passed into a capacious warehouse packed with goods of every kind: bails of cloth, barrels of wine, kegs of salt, wooden crates stacked with furs and pelts and much more. Everywhere I looked people were working. Wilhelm glanced around, heading towards a wealthy-looking man wearing a purple velvet doublet edged with fur. They spoke together but, of course, I didn't understand German. I strolled to the set of huge double doors that looked out onto the wharf. The docked ship was large and fat-bellied with a single mast. While I watched the stevedores unloading its cargo, Wilhelm joined me.

'I have spoken to a man I know and he will keep an eye out for anyone who might come looking for us. I cannot help but think that your uncle will pursue us, and this is an obvious place to look if they come to London – considering my past.'

We spent most of the day at the waterfront, walking along the river to the huge castle that marked the eastern end of the city. London was fascinating, and it seemed that around every corner there was something new to see. Wilhelm might have been wary about my uncle or his men finding us, but with so many people around I thought it unlikely. We returned to Edward's house before the curfew came into force.

The next day, I told Wilhelm that I wanted to see the city outside the gates of Edward's house.

'*Nein*, I really do not think that is a good idea,' Wilhelm said. 'If you are recognised…'

'We do not know that Gilbert or his men are even here. I have always wanted to see London. I will be careful.'

'But the city is dangerous.'

'Come, Wilhelm, let the boy look around,' Edward said. 'I will loan Alwin as a guide. He will make sure he keeps out of trouble.'

'He is the Lord of Cranham now,' Wilhelm said. 'I can only give him my advice. It is up to him whether he chooses to heed it.'

And of course I did not.

Alwin turned out to be the same red-haired youth who had let us in the gate when we had first arrived. He was only four or five years older than me, but he knew London like only a man born there could. He showed me everything, from the markets and food stores of Westcheap, to Saint Paul's Cathedral – the church that had impressed me when we had arrived and where dozens of masons were working to finish the tower, taking me through a gate and out of the walled city along the Strand, a wide road flanked by big stone houses, over the Fleet and along the Thames. We passed the distinctive round Temple Church of the Knights Templar and Westminster Hall, a huge structure used by the king for royal feasts and banquets. By the hall was another monastery complex and a large church, where the remains of King Edward were buried and the place where the kings of England were crowned.

The next day was All Hallows' Eve, the time when the ghosts of the dead walked the earth. Alwin took me to the Smoothfield, just outside the city's north-western gate, to a huge horse and cattle market alongside a priory. It was crowded, but I found watching the palfreys interesting and especially enjoyed the races, where the destriers were shown off. Alwin told me that on some days there would be a fair where tournaments and jousts would take place, but unfortunately this was not one of them. Despite the jostling and the sheer noise, we spent most of the time watching the action and it was late afternoon when we started back towards Edward's house. Before Aldersgate, the sound of a dog whimpering in the entrance of an alleyway seized my attention. I turned to see two men dressed in homespun fabric, laughing. One of them, a burly man with no neck and a face red with drink, was beating a puppy with a wooden stick while his friend encouraged him. Without thinking, I shouted and rushed at the man, pushing him from behind and causing him to stumble.

The man turned on me. 'What do you think you're doing, you little turd?'

'Leave the dog alone!'

'Are you going to make me? You're just a boy.'

'Maybe he wants to be beaten himself?' the man's companion said.

I shook with anger, but already some people had stopped to see what was happening.

'What a well-dressed boy,' a woman shouted. 'Must be good for a shilling or two.'

I felt Alwin pull at my sleeve but I shook him off.

'He looks like a rich merchant's brat,' said the second man. 'Better teach him a lesson.'

My hand dropped to where my sword would normally be, suddenly realising I had left it at Edward's house.

Instead, I quickly drew my knife and brandished it at him. The puppy had limped away and more passers-by were stopping. There must have been a dozen or more now watching.

'Nothing to say now, eh?' the man said. 'Dog got your tongue.'

I felt myself blush but I couldn't back down, despite the puppy having disappeared. The woman who had spoken cackled something to the man next to her. Around me, I could sense the crowd, watching, waiting in anticipation, eager for blood. I glared at them all before my heart stopped. Standing opposite and looking directly at me was my uncle's second-in-command, Gervase. The drunk man was saying something else, but I no longer heard.

I ran.

There were shouts behind as I pushed through the gathered people and dashed towards the gate some couple of hundred paces away, barrelling into a woman in my haste to get away. I could hear Alwin running to keep up and when I glanced back to catch sight of Gervase, I could not see him. Nevertheless, I was convinced he must be in pursuit. When I passed the priory gate and hospital with a Norman church, Alwin caught up and grabbed my arm, pulling me up short. 'Slow down! If the guards at the gate see us running, they will stop us, thinking we are thieves – or worse.'

I could see his logic and I paused, panting at the unexpected exertion. I scanned the faces around me but I could not see Gervase.

'We have to return to your master's house now. There is someone after me.' I could see Alwin's eyes light up in interest, but I didn't explain.

The guards at the Aldersgate barely glanced at us as we re-entered the walled city. Once inside, I pulled Alwin down an alley to wait. I knew Gervase had seen me but I needed to know how many men he had and whether my uncle was in London. We did not have to wait long. After watching the people passing on the main street, I caught sight of Gervase again. He was followed by four men-at-arms, all of whom I recognised from Cranham. There was no sign of my uncle. They walked past the alleyway where we were hiding without seeing us. Even now, I remember how hard the blood was pounding in my ears.

We waited long enough for me to recite three paternosters, before emerging into the street where I followed Alwin. We threaded our way through a market back towards where Edward lived. And then it happened.

I had just turned another corner when I was confronted by one of my uncle's soldiers. He was as surprised as me, but I was quicker, sidestepping around him and sprinting down the street with Alwin close behind. The soldier cursed and shouted for his companions as I swerved down another alley, scattering a pack of dogs who were nosing through a pile of refuse. At the next corner, I paused for Alwin who had dropped behind, scanning the street for signs of pursuit but not seeing any, wary of getting totally lost in the warren of narrow streets and lanes. Alwin was already panting heavily and I let him run past to lead the way as the first of my uncle's soldiers appeared at the end of the road. We kept running, down the alleyways and the less crowded streets, but we were attracting attention. So, around the next bend we slowed down to a fast walk. My mouth was sawdust-dry, my lungs burned and I could feel my heart thumping in my chest. Any moment, I expected to hear the clatter of boots on cobbles behind us, but there was no further sign of pursuit. Had we finally lost them?

A short time later, we were back at Edward's house by the river. I found Wilhelm sitting by the fire in the hall on the upper floor. He listened to my account of seeing Gervase with a grave face. 'It is as I thought. You are too dangerous to Gilbert alive. I warned you…'

I lowered my head in shame. He was right. I had been a fool, but we would both suffer the consequences.

'My old friend Conrad at the German Wharf also said that there was a man asking about us this morning,' Wilhelm said. 'This is not good. I think you should stay here in the relative safety of Edward's house and not go out anymore. Now they know for sure that we are in London, it will be harder to stay hidden.'

If I had to remain inside for any length of time, I would go mad – certainly with all the attractions of London so tantalizingly close. But his words were wise and this time I did not argue.

The door banged open and our host Edward entered with a grave face. He called for wine and when it arrived, he came and sat with us. 'I have heard some strange tidings,' he said. 'It seems the ghosts really are abroad this All Hallows' Eve!'

We looked at him expectantly. What could have happened now?

'I met a merchant from Suffolk with whom I have dealings. He told me he had it on good account that both Lord Roger Fitz Simon of Cranham, and his son Richard, were tragically killed in the last week.'

I looked at him in surprise. I felt very much alive.

'Apparently Lord Roger died in a hunting accident, and two days later his son and heir was killed by outlaws when returning to the castle from a short trip.'

'That was what he wanted to happen,' Wilhelm said.

'And the first part is true enough,' I added, 'except it was no accident.'

Wilhelm scratched his head in thought. '*Ja*, but that is what he is telling people. If everyone thinks young Richard here is dead, then it is easier for him to convince the king he should inherit your father's lands and estates.'

'So, we have to go and tell the king I am still alive,' I said. I thought for a moment. 'I also need to write a letter to Isabella and Alice. They must be distraught with grief.'

Wilhelm nodded. 'And you can write to the king at the same time. I do not think we should go to Normandy. It is too dangerous. Rather, we should wait for his return to England and attempt to obtain an audience. But we must be careful in the meantime. I have no doubt that if your uncle learns our whereabouts then it shall result in both our deaths.'

I was in no doubt about the truth of that either. We sat in silence as the wood on the fire crackled and popped, each of us engrossed in our own thoughts, mesmerised by the flames and savouring the warmth.

CHAPTER SIX

The next day was All Saints, but I remained confined to Edward's house and the courtyard, flanked by the several smaller buildings on one side, and a yard that bordered the river on the other. Most of the time I helped Alwin in the stables, mucking out the stalls and feeding Cobalt or one of the two palfreys that belonged to Edward. Cobalt's wound had healed and the courser seemed unaffected by her ordeal. She sensed my restlessness and nuzzled her head at me, whickering gently as I rubbed her down. Apart from Wilhelm, she was the only connection I still had with my previous life. After everything that had happened, I felt an even stronger bond with her. And, of course, I got friendly with the dog that had initially greeted us so ferociously, a grey Alaunt named Troy that I played with and fed whenever I got the chance. I also spent time on other menial chores in the hall and warehouse which occupied the entire ground floor of the main house. No one forced me to help, but I was used to working as a page at Cranham and it was only fair considering we were staying indefinitely as guests. Wilhelm also spent most of the time in the hall helping Edward with his ledger, occasionally donning a dark cloak to go and speak with his friends at the German Wharf in disguise. Sometimes, especially in the evenings, we would sit by the fire in the hall and play chess, but I had little patience. Suffice to say, Wilhelm always won.

I wrote three letters with ink and vellum given by Edward. The first was a formal account to Isabella of what had happened. She would probably have heard anyway but I didn't want her to think me dead, even though we had never been close. The second was for Alice, and this took me significantly longer. While writing, I had an overwhelming feeling of homesickness – I missed my little sister more than ever. Her life must have changed as much as mine and I wondered how she was coping.

My letter to the king was, of course, more formal. It was also short, letting him know that I was not dead and requesting an audience when he returned to the country. But the fact my uncle was one of the king's closest retainers worried me and I didn't want to say too much – not until I got the chance to talk personally to him. It took me most of the day to write the letters and when I had finished Wilhelm joined me, giving me a copy of my father's seal to stamp the wax. 'As your father's steward, I often sent documents in his name. Now I shall give the letters to Edward. He says he has someone trustworthy going to East Anglia who will deliver them to your sisters. He will keep the letter for the king and deliver it when he is again in the country.'

We ate our meals as honoured guests of Edward's family. Emma, Edward's daughter, was still shy, but she didn't seem as frightened as before, and on one occasion I caught her looking at me with her dark eyes across the table. She had very pale skin in direct contrast to her crimson-faced father, with freckles that I found alluring and red, full lips. But when I smiled at her she quickly averted her eyes again. Nevertheless, I felt strangely attracted, a sensation I had never had before for any girl. In the past, girls had always bored me. Edward's wife noticed our little exchange and she chuckled and said something to Edward that I did not hear, causing my cheeks to burn red, although I didn't really know why. I resolved to avoid Emma's glance in future and lowered my head, concentrating on my food and trying to hide my embarrassment.

As time went on, I found my enforced confinement increasingly difficult. Outside the doors of the small courtyard, there was a bustling city to be discovered. I would stand at Edward's wharf on the river side of the house and watch the ships coming and going, my head full of travel and adventure. The wine merchant had a small boat but when I asked if we might take it out on the river, Edward refused. 'I cannot spare Alwin to take you and the river is more dangerous than it looks.' And, of course, Wilhelm thought it a bad idea.

Three days after I had seen Gervase at the Smoothfield, the calm of our sanctuary was shattered. I was stacking barrels in the warehouse on the ground floor of the main building when I heard Troy barking and the sound of horse hooves on the cobbles. My stomach jumped into my throat as I realised what it must be. We had been found.

God knows how they had found us so quickly? I was sure we had lost them. Maybe they had followed Wilhelm on one of his short trips to the German Wharf; maybe they had been tipped off. But now they were here and we had to leave fast. I had to warn Wilhelm, who was upstairs in the hall, and get my sword. I clambered up the ladder that led to the hall above, shouting for Wilhelm. He was in the large chamber with Edward. They must have heard what was going on because they had both come to their feet and were heading for the door that led to the outside steps and down into the yard. Wilhelm looked scared, but Edward had a furious expression on his face. I grabbed my sword and bag, stealing a quick glance through the window. Gervase and his men were in the courtyard, all of them mounted with drawn swords. Troy was still barking and being restrained by Alwin. At a signal from Gervase, one of his soldiers dismounted and rammed his sword down the dog's throat, the blade emerging through the back of its head in an eruption of blood and gore. Alwin dropped the leash and stared in shock.

'You have to leave immediately,' Edward said. 'Take the small boat at the dock and go, otherwise there will be more bloodshed. I shall try and delay them until you are clear.' He flung the door open and strode out to confront them.

Wilhelm hurried towards the ladder that led down to the warehouse, but I continued to watch what was happening as if nailed to the floor.

'Come on, Richard.' Wilhelm's voice trembled with fear. 'We have to go now.'

I did not move. Edward was descending the outside steps, but I could see that his hands were trembling despite his outrage. I could not hear what he said, but Gervase's men dismounted. Wilhelm called to me again.

'Go to the boat,' I said, 'I will come in a moment.'

Wilhelm started to say something but I waved him away. He disappeared down the ladder and I looked back to what was happening outside. Edward was protesting, but Gervase marched up to him and punched him in the face, knocking him to the ground. He barked another order and his men started towards the house. It was time to leave.

I rushed to the trapdoor and jumped down the ladder in my haste to get out of the building. In the warehouse, the big double doors that faced the river were open and I could see that Wilhelm had reached the boat and was looking back to see where I was. My sword was still sheathed, and I was about to draw it when I spied the crossbow lying on top of some crates in the corner. Next to it was a small bag of bolts, and I grabbed them both, sprinting through the doors and into the backyard. Behind me I could hear shouting and realised that one of Gervase's men had seen us and was giving chase. Just as I reached the boat, the first soldier came charging around the corner. I shouted at Wilhelm to untie it and started to load the crossbow, bending over and putting my foot in the stirrup and pulling back the string. The soldier shouted to the others and rushed me. There was little time, but I carefully laid the bolt in the groove and levelled it at the running man. He was less than ten paces away when I pulled the trigger and, despite him twisting to avoid the shot, the bolt hit him high in the shoulder, slamming through his mail and causing him to career over into a stack of barrels that I had unloaded earlier. Wilhelm had untied the boat and was desperately trying to steady it with the oars. I jumped in, my momentum crashing me into Wilhelm and almost throwing me into the water. For a moment, I thought the boat would tip over and capsize before I regained my balance. Two more of Gervase's men came charging through the warehouse shouting in anger. I scrambled to the bench and grabbed the oars, elbowing Wilhelm out of the way, knowing that I was stronger than the German. I hauled with all my strength and the boat pulled away from the quay. It was not a moment too soon. The first soldier had reached the edge of the quay, but he was powerless to stop us now and I continued to row further out into the sluggish river. The other two soldiers had reached the edge of the wharf and they were joined by Gervase who raised his fist and shouted something I did not hear. One of the soldiers tended the man I had shot, and I considered loading the crossbow to fire again, but decided against it. It would only provoke them and I didn't want their anger taken out on Edward or his family. I paused, letting the river's current nudge us downstream.

My mind went to Cobalt, left in the stables and I felt a deep sense of loss. I doubted very much I would ever see her again. Father had given her to me on my seventh birthday and she was the only horse I had ever known or ridden. Another link to my past had been broken. 'Do you think Gervase will harm Edward or his family?' I asked Wilhelm. Emma's face appeared in my head.

The German looked up at me with resignation in his eyes. 'Who can tell? I wish now we had never gone there. We have only brought misery and danger to their lives.'

'But Gervase will only be making trouble for himself if he harms or kills anyone else. They are innocent. He wants to kill me. What would he gain in harming them?'

Wilhelm shrugged. I realised what the last week or so had taken out of him. He looked tired and old – defeated almost, but I felt a sudden affection towards him nevertheless. Without him, only God knew what would have happened to me. I was touched by his loyalty, and now understood why my father had trusted him so much.

'We are almost at the German Wharf,' he said. 'Row back towards the shore or we shall overshoot.'

When I craned my neck around, I saw the warehouses and wharves by Dowgate getting closer. I pulled on the oars again and the boat turned towards the wooden quays that jutted out into the river. We passed several small skiffs and a dead dog floating under the surface, steering around a moored cog that was being loaded. It loomed over us as we paddled past, finally blocking our view of Edward's wharf.

We had escaped again, although it had been a near thing. Until now, God had been on our side and our luck had held.

But how long would that last? It was only a matter of time before our luck would run out.

We moored the boat at the quay and I climbed up the ladder to the wooden wharf, pausing to look around the enclosure of large warehouses and other buildings. Like before, there were many people working, but no one paid me the slightest attention and I relaxed, bending to help haul Wilhelm up.

'We need to talk,' the German said. Despite the cold he was sweating. 'Before I speak again to my friend Conrad. We need to decide what we are going to do?'

'We know what we are going to do. We have to gain an audience with the king, whenever he returns.'

'I think the time has passed for that, Richard.' Wilhelm removed his red cap and mopped his head with a cloth. 'If we stay here in London, it is only a matter of time before your uncle's men find us again.'

His words made sense. 'Yes, then we have to go to Normandy and speak with him personally.' I saw the colour drain from Wilhelm's face. 'I do not think the whole of Normandy is in flames. However, I must speak with the king.'

'But there is a war... It is also the obvious place for your uncle to find us.'

I felt a rising anger. 'I am not going to give up Cranham so easily. And I am not craven. We have no other choice, Wilhelm. I wish it were different.'

There was nothing more to say. We entered the nearest warehouse and Wilhelm said something to one of the men working, who crooked a dirty finger behind him to another door. The next room looked like a refectory, with rows of trestle tables. On the far table sat the man Wilhelm had spoken to before, wearing the same purple doublet. He sat with two other men and they had just finished eating.

'Hello, Conrad,' Wilhelm said. 'Can we talk?'

'Come and join us,' Conrad said in English, which I assumed was for my benefit. We sat down and he poured us each a cup of ale from a jug, introducing his companions as Hartman and Rüdiger. 'What is the matter, Wilhelm? You are as pale as a ghost.'

'We had a visit from the people I told you about. We had to flee. There was no other choice but to come here.'

The man introduced as Rüdiger scowled and said something in German to Conrad. Despite the fact we were sitting down I could see he was tall, possibly over six feet, but also thin with a hooked nose and prominent Adam's apple. He was clearly unhappy about something and Conrad's explanation in German didn't seem to help. He turned to Wilhelm and spoke in faltering English. 'Why have you here come? You bring us danger.'

'I came here because we are the same folk and many here used to be my comrades.'

'You are not the same as we. The most here are *Kölner*, like I. Conrad says you come from Lübeck. Your city is not even in the Empire anymore.'

'But we share the same tongue and I traded from here, like you, for many years – albeit without the trading concessions the English give to people of your city.'

'And now you bring danger to us all,' Rüdiger repeated.

Conrad sighed. 'I am sure that Wilhelm would not do so if he had any choice, and I for one will always help if I can.' He looked at both of us. 'So, what kind of help is it that you require?'

Wilhelm looked at me.

'We need to take ship away from here,' I said. 'Anything going to Normandy.'

'Well, you have arrived just in time,' Conrad said. 'With winter almost here there shall be precious few more ships sailing. But there is a ship ready to leave at high tide today.'

'But it is only delivering weapons to Honfleur before sailing on to Dordrecht and then Bremen,' Rüdiger said. 'There is a war in Normandy. If you wish to return to England, then you will be out of luck.'

I shrugged. 'We will take it.' I looked at Wilhelm. 'There is no choice. We have to throw ourselves on the mercy of the king. We can but hope that the injustice of events will stir him.'

Wilhelm nodded, looking back to Conrad. 'But there is a problem. We do not have enough money.'

Conrad smiled. 'I think something can be arranged, for old times' sake if nothing else.'

Rüdiger looked angry. 'Old times' sake for you perhaps, Conrad, certainly not for me. If they wish to seek passage to Normandy, then they will have to pay like everyone else.'

'Leave that with me,' Conrad said. 'I shall pay the money needed for my old friend here…'

'And I thank you,' Wilhelm said. 'Of course, I will reimburse you when I can. That I swear.'

Conrad came to his feet. 'Good, then it is sorted. The *Christofer* is nearly loaded. She is carrying a cargo of wool, hides and arrows for the army in France. Her captain is a West Frisian, Hauke Herrema, a good man and very experienced. He is supervising the loading. Go and speak with him – tell him I sent you.'

We left, returning into the hive of activity outside. It wasn't hard to find Captain Hauke. He was a large heavyset man with a broken nose, no neck, and hands that looked like they could crush small animals. Hauke was on the rear deck of the cog shouting orders and he hardly glanced at us when we boarded the ship up the gangplank. We waited patiently as he berated one of the crewmen for not stacking the sacks of wool quickly enough, and although I could not understand everything he said, the language was similar enough to English for me to pick out some of the words. I could see that most of the cargo was already onboard, only the last few sacks were still sitting on the dock and the majority of the crew were covering them with oilskins to help keep them dry in the event of bad weather. Finally, satisfied at last, the captain turned his attention to us, his sun-beaten brow frowning as if we had just crawled out of the sewers.

'We have been sent by the merchant, Conrad,' Wilhelm said. 'We would like to book passage to Honfleur. He will arrange the payment due.'

Captain Hauke scratched his grey stubble. 'Will he now? I hope you have strong stomachs. At this time of year it will be a rough passage and no mistake.' He gave me an appraising eye. 'Pray God you are good at bailing out water, boy, as you will be spending most of the journey doing it.'

'I am no boy,' I said in a flash of anger. 'I am Lord Richard of Cranham and I would ask you to remember that!'

Maybe it was my frustration with everything that had happened that made me speak so and reveal my identity, maybe it was my natural arrogance – the arrogance of youth, but my words caused Wilhelm to wince and I realised I had made a mistake.

The captain looked at me and smiled. 'Well, you are a spirited one, *boy*. I do not care if you are a lord, lady, prince or even fuckin' King John himself. On *Christofer*, I am higher than all men and second only to God. As long as you remember that, I will not have to throw you overboard and feed your skinny arse to the fishes.'

I wisely kept my mouth shut, looking round at the ship and taking in as many details as possible. She was a strongly built craft, made of oak, squat and box-like and wide of beam, with high sides reinforced by crossbeams and a single mast with a square-rigged sail, which was lowered. She had a modest deck at the stern with a steering oar on the starboard side. Below, the cargo hold was open to the sky, with no cabin or any place to avoid any bad weather, and with running boards along the gunwales in order to reach the small area of foredeck at the front. I counted twelve crewmen and noted there were half-a-dozen soldiers, whose job I assumed was to keep us safe from any pirates. They were playing dice on the wharf, oblivious to the work of their companions. And we were not the only passengers. Two young Cistercian monks were also waiting patiently on the quay. One of them looked as pale-faced as I felt – probably, like me, contemplating his first sea voyage and uneasy about what the ocean would bring. I just hoped we would not run into any sea monsters.

But as well as the uncertainty, I felt another emotion too, the thrill of excitement. Some part of me was looking forward to this new adventure that had become my life. Despite my uncle's best efforts, we had managed to keep one step ahead, and with God's grace we would continue to do so. For the first time since we had left Cranham I felt an optimism. I turned to Wilhelm as the older man cursed.

And then I saw what he had seen. A group of armed men had entered the compound through the open gates. Gervase and his soldiers, now only three in number. They were grim-faced and spotted us immediately. I came to my feet and drew my sword. Hauke saw my movement and looked to see what had caused our alarm, resting his eyes on the armed men approaching and he frowned.

Gervase reached the gangplank and withdrew his own sword with a rasp. 'Now we have got you at last, you little shit.

I am going to make you pay for what you did to Miles, before I stick you like a pig!'

He took a step onto the plank as Hauke strode across the deck, pulling himself up by one of the shrouds and blocking his path.

'Get out of my way, sailor,' Gervase growled, 'or I shall cut that ugly head from your shoulders.'

'I am no sailor. I am captain of this ship and if you take one step further, I will gut you like a fish and strangle you with your own innards.'

Gervase paused and scowled, taking a measure of the Frisian. The crew had stopped working and several had now joined Hauke, some of them with makeshift weapons or tools. Gervase turned back to consult with his men and the rest of them drew their swords. It looked like they were willing to make a fight of it and my pulse began racing.

Hauke whistled and the half-a-dozen soldiers that had been playing dice on the wharf came to their feet. Two of them levelled crossbows at Gervase and his men. Hauke said something to them in his language and laughed. Gervase was now heavily outnumbered and I watched in satisfaction as he reluctantly sheathed his sword.

'I do not know where you are going, but it is easy to find out!' Gervase called to me. 'And when we do, we will kill you. Of that you can be certain.'

Anger surged up in me. 'And you can tell my treacherous uncle that one day I shall come for him. Tell him that God and all his angels shall not save him from my revenge!'

Gervase and his men turned and retreated through the main gate of the enclosure, leaving me shaking with anger. Wilhelm's face was white.

Captain Hauke looked over at me. 'Well, boy. You appear to be more interesting than you look. I do not want to know what that was about. It is your business. But when it interferes or concerns *Christofer* it becomes mine. As long as you remember that, we will get along fine.'

I remained silent, brooding on everything that had happened and pensive about the prospect of leaving my country of birth and going to Normandy. It still felt like I was running away, as if I was somehow betraying my father's memory. Sir Hugh de Burcy's words about picking your battles came back to me – battles that could be won, but it was only a slim consolation. I felt wretched about leaving and unworthy of the people who had died helping me escape.

Wilhelm went to speak with Conrad again, and he only returned when the tide was full and we were ready to sail. At least he was in better spirits, explaining that he had received word Edward and his family were unhurt. 'Apart from a few bruises and the death of the dog. One of Gervase's men smashed two barrels of wine in anger and frustration, but they got off lightly...'

I was glad, again remembering Emma's face and feeling relief that no one else had been hurt on my behalf. Hauke's bellowed orders snatched me away from these thoughts and the crew cast off. Several men used long polearms to push us away from the quay and we drifted into the current of the river. Others set oars and began rowing us downstream. I noticed a large wooden crucifix nailed to the mast and saw one of the crewmen kiss it. Once we were on the open sea we would be in God's hands and I mumbled a prayer myself.

Ahead, I could see that the drawbridge on the great span across the river was open to allow ships access up and downriver. Wilhelm told me this was only possible twice a day at slack tide, otherwise we would have to "shoot the bridge", something that was best avoided. A few moments later, the oars were brought in and we were passing underneath, some of the crew using the poles again to prevent the ship smashing into the pilings set into the riverbed. It was incredibly narrow and I held my breath for a moment until we were out the other side. Once through the arches of the bridge, the river was busier with small boats and ships but Hauke was not perturbed, even when we nearly collided with a small skiff that was too slow to get out of the way. I studied the stark stone of the castle again, noting how it dominated the gaggle of wooden houses around it like a mother hen surrounded by her chicks. Surely it was the greatest fortress in the kingdom.

Soon afterwards, the city and its stink had passed behind us and the landscape changed to miles of empty marsh and sandbanks. The wind picked up, tossing up whitecaps on the water, as the sky turned a dark slate-grey. Hauke yelled an order and the sail was raised, flapping and billowing as the crew brought it under control. I shivered in my cloak as seagulls screeched above us, smelling the salt on the breeze and enjoying the feel of the wind in my hair. For the first time in my life, I felt a sense of freedom, with no idea what the future would bring.

We were leaving and I didn't know when I would see my homeland again.

CHAPTER SEVEN

We sailed downriver towards the Thames estuary, passing several cogs and a galley, all of them struggling upstream towards London. The river was wider here, and the wind got steadily stronger as we approached the sea – the strength of the tide helping to sweep us out into a tumult of wind, rain and growing darkness. The crew fastened oilskins to act as a shelter on the open deck and the wind cracked and tugged at them like giant hands plucking strings. They struggled to lower the sail, to prevent it from being ripped to shreds, furling it in the belly of the ship. Hauke wanted to take shelter by the coast, but the looming storm was too great and we plunged forward into banks of waves that cascaded water over the prow, dousing everyone and tossing *Christofer* as if she was mere matchwood. The immensity of the ocean was like nothing I had ever seen and I was terrified – terrified of the howling wind, terrified of the angry waves and terrified of the approaching blackness. Hauke shouted to us to secure ropes around our waists to avoid being swept overboard and we needed no urging. My stomach was heaving like the sea around us. Then I was violently sick, vomiting over the side. Hauke, crouched at the ship's stern, to help the helmsmen control the steering oar, bellowed orders above the screaming wind. 'Get bailing, you useless bastards. If you value your lives, bail for all you are worth. Bail!'

I scooped out water, emptying my guts into the stinking bilge, convinced we were all going to die. I bailed until my arms were screaming at me to stop and I was drenched in seawater and vomit. Ahead of us, huge black ridges of waves rose up and continued to batter the ship relentlessly. The timbers of *Christofer* ground together in protest and I thought the ship would wrench itself apart under the pressure of the continual punishment. The wind screamed and howled like the coming of hell itself. Even now, some forty years later, I shall never forget that storm and I am still amazed that we survived. Maybe God heard the whimpering prayers from the two monks, for somehow, against all odds, the ship stayed afloat. I have no idea how long the storm lasted, but since that endless night I have always hated the sea. We fought for half the night and at some time we lost one of the crew, swept overboard so fast I never even heard him scream. At least for the poor man it must have been a quick death. I could not imagine anyone lasting longer than a few seconds in that furious sea.

But by the following morning, the storm had blown itself out and we were all exhausted, collapsed in the bottom of the ship, too weary to bail any further. The lightening horizon gradually heralded the beginning of a new day. The ship had been pummelled and some lines of rigging had broken and the bowsprit was damaged, but at least the mast was still intact. God help us if that had come down.

Hauke was still full of energy and he gave the crew no time to recover from the horrors of the night, shouting and kicking the men to get them back to work. They came to their feet reluctantly, moving around the ship like wraiths as they began the repairs needed. I looked at Wilhelm. The German looked dishevelled and was shivering uncontrollably. Everything and everyone onboard was completely soaked. The two monks did not look any better. They had helped all night with the bailing, mumbling prayers and beseeching God to save us, which thankfully the screeching of the wind had drowned out. The bilge-water was up to my knees and the cargo was half submerged, so I picked up the bucket and began to scoop out the water again.

The wind was fresh but at least the rain had stopped, so by the time the weak sun had risen in a sky the colour of pewter, I was feeling slightly better again. There was no land in sight and the sea was still choppy, although nothing compared to the night before. The crew raised the sail and it flapped and cracked as if in protest. I felt awful; my stomach was empty and my throat coarse from retching. I took a long swig of water to help wash the salt and bile from my cracked lips.

Hauke came over to me and grinned. 'Well, *Lord* Richard, you worked well last night, but there is still too much water in the bilge. Eilert will give everyone something to eat soon and in the meantime, start bailing again.'

I scooped up more buckets of water and poured them over the side even though my entire body protested. My arms felt like lead weights and all I wanted to do was sleep. Wilhelm looked even more exhausted than me and I managed three buckets to every one of his. The half-a-dozen soldiers were bailing as well, however, even with all of us working together we hardly made a difference. The sooner this voyage was over the better.

Eilert, a weasel-faced man, set up a bronze pot over a hearth, consisting of a narrow wooden chest filled with clay and covered by bricks. In a short time, he cooked up an eel stew, the first hot food since our escape from Edward's house.

He walked along the running boards alongside the cargo and gave it out in wooden bowls along with a hunk of hard bread, a small lump of cheese and some dried meat that tasted so salty it was hardly edible. Everyone got a mouthful of the tart wine from a skin that he carried at his waist. Despite its sharp taste, I savoured it in my mouth like the finest Bordeaux claret. After a short break we continued and the monotony was only broken when Hauke told me to stop. 'You are young with good eyes, Lord Richard. Get up front and keep an eye open for land.'

I could hardly repress my relief and I picked my way around the cargo to the front of the ship, climbing up to the platform at the bow. The fore-stays were ripped and tattered – *Christofer* had certainly been badly damaged by the storm. I scanned the horizon but I could not see anything.

It must have been late morning when I first saw land, a brown smudge between sea and sky that was difficult to discern at first, even with my keen sight. As if to confirm what I saw, a flight of gulls appeared, circling and squawking above us. I shouted back what I had seen and a few moments later Hauke joined me, the big Frisian squinting as he followed my finger. He roared for the helmsman to change course.

Sometime later, the white cliffs of what could only be France were clear to everyone on our left. I was now back with Wilhelm on the stern deck and an experienced sailor was at the prow. Relieved that land was in sight again, I spent most of the afternoon trying to sleep, the ship's pitching and rolling making it all but impossible. Eventually, as darkness fell again, I dropped off for another uncomfortable night.

I awoke the next morning, cold and hungry with clothes as stiff as wattle. It was windy, but at least it had stopped raining, and it was easy to make out the land on our port side. Not long afterwards, I saw the top of a church tower.

'Where are we?' Wilhelm asked the captain. He was shivering and white-faced.

'Dieppe,' Hauke said. He pointed to what looked like a fishing town on both banks of a river estuary, surrounded by hills and cliffs. 'If we were going any further than Honfleur, I would put in to repair the ship from the damage as it is a safe anchorage, but I think we'll make our destination without any more problems. We were lucky that the storm didn't blow us further off-course.'

I watched the distant shore, seeing smoke rising lazily into the air. Everything looked peaceful and it was hard to believe a war was being fought nearby.

The wind began to pick up and it started to rain again. A long time passed and we huddled underneath the oilskin covers as the ship rolled and pitched. Eilert cooked up a fish broth which was welcome, though I knew I would tire of it on any voyage longer than a few days.

With more gulls screeching and diving around us, we rounded a headland into the wide estuary of another river. 'The Seine,' Hauke said. 'Goes all the way to Paris and beyond.'

I watched as we passed several smaller ships and what looked like fishing boats with more flocks of gulls swarming in the air around us, hungry for fish. Even though it was my first time at sea, I could feel the ship was damaged. It moved sluggishly and had a list to starboard, something that had been absent when we had left London. I mumbled a prayer that she had stayed afloat. It could very easily have been otherwise. Hauke shouted commands to the crew as they ran to reef the sail. In the open hold, most of the men employed to protect us from any pirates were still bailing out the water, passing buckets up in a chain to their comrades. Ahead I could see another town on the other side of the estuary, several wharves jutting into the water with a tumble of half-timbered buildings and churches behind. We had reached our destination of Honfleur.

The harbour was a mass of ships and boats. *Christofer* docked at a long wharf alongside another ship and we made our farewells to Hauke while the crew secured the moorings.

'Good luck on your journey, Lord Richard.' The big Frisian grinned. 'We are stuck here repairing the ship for a day or two before we can continue. Maybe we will meet again.'

I doubted that. I was just glad to be back on solid ground again, although I was worried for Wilhelm who had picked up a rasping cough since the storm. It was still raining and I pulled my cloak tighter around me. I was wet, aching and miserable. 'Where do we go now?'

'We need to find out where the king is,' Wilhelm said. 'Probably in Rouen.'

We were at the edge of a square surrounded by half-timbered buildings. Due to the weather, there were not many people about, but I saw a soldier standing in the doorway of a tavern set back from the road, and the stalls of a small market by one of the streets that led up the hill. I suggested to Wilhelm he ask the man, while I purchased a few things for our journey. When I returned a short time later, having bought some cheese, bread and two skins of wine with the few silver pennies I still had, Wilhelm was looking a little brighter.

'We are in luck, Lord Richard. The king is much closer than Rouen. Apparently, he is less than ten miles away, strengthening an old Roman tower in a place called Trianon. The soldier I spoke to is from a party sent here to collect some supplies – probably the arrows that were on *Christofer*. If we leave now, we will arrive before it gets dark.'

This was the best news since fleeing Cranham. We asked directions and set off immediately, picking up the road that went south, quickly leaving the town and the sea behind us. Wilhelm coughed and spluttered and I was concerned about his health. Because of this our progress was slower than it would normally have been. Nevertheless, it was mid-afternoon as we walked the muddy track through heavy areas of woodland, passing several thatched cottages strung along the road. Ahead of us was the village of Hébertot, and I could see from the soldiers in the street that this was where the king was.

But when we entered the village, we had to jump out of the road as a large group of horsemen thundered past, showering us with water and mud from the puddles. I looked at Wilhelm and my heart sank. It was King John and his entourage. They galloped through the village and out of sight without stopping. When I asked one of the soldiers outside the church, he informed me that the king was returning to a nearby castle. 'However, he will be back tomorrow,' the soldier said.

We were disappointed to have missed him, but at least he would return. The night was spent in a farmer's barn that cost us a silver penny and my sleep was again disturbed, this time by Wilhelm's coughing. My father's former steward was in a bad way and I didn't know what to do.

At the church the next day, there was a small group of petitioners hoping for a chance to put their grievances to the king. He arrived on horseback with his full entourage sometime mid-morning, the soldiers clearing the people away as he strode into the church ignoring those waiting. As the largest building in the village, the king was using it as the base of his operations in the valley. I spoke to the man-at-arms in charge outside and explained who I was. He told me to wait while he informed the king that I wanted an urgent audience.

A while later, I was called, and led with trembling legs into the church, conscious of my dishevelled appearance. Wilhelm waited outside. King John sat on a chair in the nave deep in discussion with several other nobles, all of whom turned to regard me. The king was not a tall man, possibly shorter than me, but he was well-built and athletic, with a short, tidy beard and wary eyes. I gave a deep bow.

'So you are Richard Fitz Simon,' King John said. 'Are you related to my man, Gilbert?'

'Yes,' I said, 'I am the son of Roger Fitz Simon. My father is Lord of Cranham. Gilbert is my uncle.'

'I see. Your uncle is one of my most loyal captains. Do you have news about his return?'

'No... but it is of my uncle I wish to talk.' I took a deep breath and explained everything that had happened, from my uncle and his men arriving to the death of my father and the takeover of the castle. I was as brief as possible and the king listened without interrupting.

'These are very serious allegations,' he said when I had finished. He thought for a moment before looking towards one of his retainers, a tall, formidable-looking man in his late fifties dressed in mail. 'What do you think, Earl Marshal?'

'The allegations are indeed dire, sire,' the older man said. He looked at me. 'I knew Lord Roger. He was a good and honourable man and it pains me to hear of his death. But, from what you have said it seems to me there is no proof that he was killed by Gilbert.'

'I know what happened,' I said.

'Yet you were not there.'

I shook my head. 'No, but I was when he killed my father's chief knight in front of my very eyes.'

Earl Marshal grunted something I didn't understand.

'This matter will have to be discussed when I return to England and Gilbert can put forward his side of the story,' King John said. 'You are very young. Do you have money to pay the relief?'

Another man, thin-faced with a red nose, stepped in. 'It seems to me, sire, that Lord Richard here would qualify as a ward.'

'I am more interested in an amount of coin. We *are* fighting a war here.'

My heart lurched into my stomach. It was as Wilhelm feared. 'I… I have no coin.'

The king sighed and I saw the interest drain from his eyes. 'Then we must discuss this again at a later date. In England. With Gilbert present, of course.'

His words felt like a slap to my face. The men around began talking again and it was clear I was now dismissed. I bowed again before stumbling away in shock. The king did not care about justice or what had happened to me or my father. All he cared about was gold. He had no intention of helping me.

Outside, Wilhelm was not where I had left him. Another group of riders had arrived and they were dismounting from their horses, some fifty paces or so away. I glanced around and suddenly saw Wilhelm; he was hiding behind the wall of a shed. I followed his line of sight and froze. The riders who had just dismounted were Gervase and his men.

I pulled the hood of my cloak up and walked across to where Wilhelm was hiding. My heart was hammering in my chest. 'We have to leave now.'

His face was pale and he just nodded. I led the way down a small path that led away from the road, through a farmyard where a dog began barking and towards the forest behind.

It was only once we were in the trees that I explained to Wilhelm how my audience with the king had gone. 'His only concern was money.'

'I feared as much,' Wilhelm said. 'And with Gervase here we are in danger for our lives.'

My heart began to calm its frenetic beating. We headed back in the direction we had come, towards Honfleur but avoiding the road.

'What do we do now?' I said. 'We do not have much coin – can we even pay to return to England?'

'Barely,' Wilhelm said, 'but I don't think we should return. If we do, your uncle will kill us both.'

'Not return?' I felt a rising anger. 'You mean… run away?'

'We are not running away. We need to find a place where we can gather our strength. We shall return.'

He was right but I didn't want to see it. Tears came unbidden to my eyes. How would I ever regain Cranham if I was no longer in the country? 'Where would we go?'

Wilhelm hesitated. 'We could go to Lübeck – the city of my birth. I no longer have any property in the city but my brother is there… he may help us. If Hauke is still in Honfleur perhaps we can continue with him to Bremen. For that, we will need no coin.'

'And then what? I might as well be dead. My uncle will have won.'

'Only for now. In Lübeck we can recover, prepare and gather funds. You can finish your training and learning until you reach adulthood. And we will need gold. Then we return and challenge your uncle.'

'But that could take years?'

'Yes, it will, but there is no other course for us. This is the only way to thwart your uncle's plans.'

We lapsed into silence and trudged on, my mind reeling at the thought of not returning to England.

The journey back to Honfleur took half a day as we walked across fields and through woods, not daring to use the road and risk discovery from Gervase and his men. The moment Gervase spoke to the king he would find out we were here. It wouldn't take much effort to realise we would have returned to Honfleur. So there was an urgency to our movement. Nevertheless, the weak sun was already past its peak as we reached the town again, heading down the main street that led to the harbour.

To my intense relief, Hauke and the *Christofer* were still moored along the quay. When we arrived, they were loading crates but there was only half a dozen still on the wharf, so I assumed they were nearly finished. The ship sat higher in the water and looked to be in a far better condition than when we had arrived at the port – the bowsprit and shrouds now repaired. Hauke gave a beaming smile when he saw us. 'Decided not to stay here after all, Lord Richard. I said we would meet again!'

Wilhelm explained that we wanted to continue to Bremen. Hauke was surprised, but agreed. 'I will collect the fare from Conrad in London.'

We boarded the ship and waited as the last few crates were carried aboard. I watched the bustling on the wharves, my mind in turmoil at the prospect of leaving England and my home for good. I kept glancing along the quay to see if I could see Gervase and his men, but thankfully there was no sign.

Wilhelm joined me at the gunwale as the crew began untying the mooring ropes. 'It looks as though we have made it.'

The crew cast off, using the oars to push away from the shore. I felt no satisfaction. How could my uncle just usurp my family so easily without me being able to seek justice? Everything in my life seemed so dark – like the storm we had just survived leaving England. The only thing in our favour was that we knew the location of the deeds in Saint Edmundsbury. I had agreed that it would probably take years before I could return to Cranham to challenge my uncle for ownership. Little did I realise then that it would take a lot longer than that – decades even, as my tale shall tell.

In the meantime, I was a fugitive, forced into exile with no home or family. And no chance of recovering what had been stolen from me.

Yuriev Monastery,
Novgorod Republic,
May 1242

⸻

I paused in my recollection and Fergus looked up from the lectern, quill in hand and a scowl on his face. We were in the scriptorium at Yuriev with sunlight pouring through the high windows along with the ringing of bells from Saint George's Cathedral outside. Two other monks were busy scribbling at desks in the corner.

'Am I supposed to feel sympathy for what happened to you?' Fergus asked suddenly.

I looked at him in surprise. 'You are not supposed to feel anything. It is my story – nothing more, nothing less. Why are you so hostile?'

'If you understood the history of my country, you would not have to ask that question. You Anglo-Normans ravaged my land... From your King Henry to John, you butchered hundreds of people and destroyed countless villages. Families like mine dispossessed as your people made us adapt to your foreign customs and your foreign laws. My kinsmen were forced to bow the knee to the might of the Norman kings...' He looked away in disgust.

'What has this to do with me?' I said. 'I have never been to your land – nor would I want to.'

'But in you, I see the same high-born arrogance that I grew up with. The arrogance of Norman nobility. You complain about losing your castle and estates without a thought for the people forced into the same position by your kind. People like my family. By the grace of God, I thought I had escaped from all that shite, and then you turn up…'

'I see. So this is why you do not want to write this story. Because I am a Norman of noble birth?'

Fergus said nothing.

'But I have just explained it to you… I left my land many years before you were even born, when I was fourteen, and yet you choose to blame me for everything that happened in your land since.'

'It is clear that people like you will never understand.' Fergus shook his head, not bothering to hide the contempt in his voice. I could see the Irishman's hands trembling with indignation. 'But there is no getting away from it. You ran away, so you did. Aye, you let your uncle take everything that was dear to yourself and you ran.'

'Brave words from a scribe who knows nothing about honour or courage.' I felt my own anger rising. My recollection had brought up emotions and feelings that had lain dormant for a long time, but there was also truth to the Irishman's words that I had no wish to hear. 'I was fourteen years old with no possible way of challenging my uncle. Have you ever faced death with a sword in your hand, scribe? If you had you would not say such things.'

'What do you know of my life? It was a long path that led me here. I have seen enough in my time. I was not always a scribe.'

'But that is all you are now,' I retorted. 'A lowly scribe for the Prince of Novgorod. If I was fit enough, I would rip your head off and shit down your neck for such words! You are nothing but a pig's turd. You have not earned the right to judge me.'

Fergus came to his feet and hurled the ink pot at the wall. 'Jesus, that's it! I've had enough. I cannot do this anymore.' He stormed out of the scriptorium, leaving the two other monks whispering to each other. I closed my eyes. My shoulder pained me and I wanted to return to my room. I waited a short time before Dimitri and his young helper, Grigori, returned from praying to help carry me back to my bed in the infirmary.

It had been a week since I had started working with Fergus and it had not been easy. The Irishman's hostility had not diminished, and if anything, my account seemed to have fuelled his dislike of me, if such a thing was possible. Hardly a session went by without him making some caustic comment or an argument erupting between us, although this was the first time it had gone so far. Normally I tried to keep my control, but I had a bad temper and his comments about me running from my uncle had touched a nerve. Maybe I would speak to Prince Alexander the next time I saw him and tell him the arrangement wasn't working – although it would mean I could no longer finish my story. And I wanted to finish my story. It was important that my son learned the truth about his background.

Dimitri and Grigori returned and the two monks in the scriptorium complained to them about the spilt ink. Dimitri shook his head and ordered Grigori to clear up the mess, helping me back to my room alone. My limbs ached from the movement and my wound seared. Even though I had made progress on the road to recovery, I knew I still had a long way to go.

Fergus didn't come to Yuriev the next day, nor the day after. That night there was a storm. The wind whipped around the compound like an angry spirit, banging doors and slamming shutters, letting in the lashing rain in furious gusts. In the small room where I lay, the candles danced and gutted like demented apparitions, most blowing out with the force of the gale. At its peak, the storm was so strong that I heard a resounding crash from outside, but I did not know what it was. Despite the howling wind, I eventually drifted off to a fitful sleep, my mind dreaming again of that sea voyage from England when we had all nearly lost our lives.

The next morning everything was silent, eerily quiet, as if the night before had never happened. When no one arrived, I struggled out of bed alone, gasping in pain and feeling a dizziness come over me. After it had receded, I shuffled to the door, opened it and passed through the corridor outside. I limped into the bright light of the yard and saw the reason for the noise in the night. One of the buildings had lost its roof; piles of logs and shattered wooden planks were strewn everywhere leaving a gaping hole in the top. A group of monks stood looking at the damage, talking in subdued tones. One of them saw me and they all turned in my direction. Dimitri scuttled across with Grigori, his bearded face shaking in disapproval. He clucked around me like a chicken but I waved him off, although I allowed Grigori to help support me. I had wasted too much time in bed already.

Dimitri was talking and Grigori translated his words. 'You very bad... must wait for us to help. Not walk on own.'

I ignored him, looking at the group of monks gathered around the shattered building. 'I see the storm last night has caused you problems.'

Grigori translated the words to Dimitri as I awaited his reply. 'Yes... we make better later. Today is holy day – Saint Nicetas Day... come many people to Yuriev.'

Before I could reply, a shout went up and the gates at the other end of the yard opened. A procession of mounted riders entered the monastery led by Prince Alexander. I had not seen him for a week. He looked magnificent on his white charger. Alongside rode Fergus, who did not look at me, and a high-ranking priest dressed in a long black cassock, a tall hat and veil of the same colour. The priest wore a large golden cross around his neck on a thick chain and his long beard was almost entirely white. Behind them rode a host of other nobles, priests, soldiers and a number of women and children. Alexander displayed his usual good humour and he dismounted and greeted the abbot, turning to help the old priest dismount from his horse.

'That is Archbishop Spiridon of Novgorod,' Grigori said. 'He is very great man… was *hegumen* here before.'

'*Hegumen?*'

'Was lord of monastery… before.'

'Ah,' I said. 'You must mean the abbot.'

Grigori nodded. Dimitri led us over to the group and Alexander turned and bowed his head to me. Fergus reluctantly translated. 'Prince Alexander says it is good to see you looking better. He would like to talk with you after the service in the cathedral.'

I nodded in acknowledgement, wondering if he would chastise me for my argument with Fergus. Many of the new arrivals were looking at me curiously and I caught some hostile expressions, especially from some of the soldiers whom I assumed had fought at the battle on the frozen lake. As one of the captured enemy knights, I expected to attract attention and I was not disappointed – not that I cared what any of them thought. The archbishop himself gave me an inscrutable look as the procession proceeded into the cathedral of Saint George. A small boy stared as if I had just exited the gates

of hell themselves, sticking his tongue out at me. When I
growled at him, he rushed to hide behind his mother's skirt
and she gave me a scathing look.

Dimitri spoke to Grigori who then said to me, 'We all go
in now. Stay at back and keep quiet.'

I followed them into the cathedral. Inside, it was even
more impressive, stretching above our heads up to the three
cupolas that felt as if they were as high as heaven itself. The
walls were painted in frescoes that covered all the area in
between the long thin windows set in arched niches, some of
them so large they took my breath away. The frescoes depicted
figures from the Bible that I could recognise, and they were
even painted on the arches that split the church into bays. I
was impressed by the icon of a figure dressed in red holding
a spear, whom I assumed represented Saint George, and the
fresco of Christ at the top of the central dome. Hundreds of
candles on stands lit up the interior and bathed everything
in a warm yellow light, while one priest swung a censer filled
with incense. The people crowded before the altar and, like
in the Latin Church, everyone stood, although there were
wooden stools around the edge for the old or infirm. Some of
the monks began singing whilst others chanted. To my eyes it
seemed more chaotic than the ordered services I was used to,
as people moved around and others prayed openly, everyone
repeatedly making the sign of the cross, while some prostrated
themselves by touching the limestone floor with their heads.
The service was long and the archbishop gave a sermon but,
of course, I could not understand a word. It was a relief when
it was all over, and shortly before the end I could leave with
Grigori aiding me, walking back across the muddy grass
outside, still wet from the night before, towards the building
that had lost its roof. Nevertheless, it was a warm day and I
enjoyed the touch of sun on my face.

A few moments later, people started to stream out of the cathedral, milling around the entrance in small groups. Prince Alexander and the archbishop emerged together, surrounded by a gaggle of priests and courtiers. Several of the dogs waiting outside began barking. Dimitri came over to where I stood and said something to Grigori. 'You go back to room now,' the young monk translated. 'Prince Alexander wish to talk with you later... before he returns to Novgorod.'

I was summoned a while later to the scriptorium where I was left alone to wait for Prince Alexander. He arrived sometime later, just when I thought he had forgotten about me, along with Fergus who trailed behind like a whipped dog. In contrast to earlier, his joviality had completely vanished. He frowned. Alexander started talking quickly and Fergus struggled to translate. 'Prince Alexander is wanting to know why you threatened me last time we met? He is not happy that a prisoner should act in such a way...'

'Tell him,' I said, feeling my anger bubbling to the surface again, 'I do not react well when someone accuses me of being craven.' I looked across the room to the stain of ink on the wall where Fergus had hurled the inkpot.

Fergus translated my words and the two of them spoke more while I watched. It was clear the prince was berating the Irishman. Eventually, Fergus explained as Alexander watched. 'Prince Alexander says that... I should not have spoken to you in such a way. He says he too knows what it is like to be sent into exile.'

'He does?'

'Aye, he was sent into exile by the *boyars*, the nobles of Novgorod – some of whom are here today – and I accompanied him. He was only called back to fight you at the Battle of Lake Chudskoe, where you were captured.'

I knew the *boyars* were powerful nobles in Novgorod, but this information was new; I did not know they had expelled their own prince. 'Why would they do that?'

Fergus looked irritated at my question, but he answered nonetheless. 'There were a number of reasons. They were not happy about paying tribute to the Tatars, among other things. Ultimately, it was a power struggle between them and Prince Alexander, one that is still not resolved.'

Alexander said something more and I waited for the translation.

'But Prince Alexander also says that you must remember you are a prisoner. You cannot threaten… me or anyone else.'

'If you do not make witless comments about things you know nothing about then I would not need to threaten you.'

Fergus shook his head in exasperation. 'You are impossible now.'

'No, I am a knight and a soldier of Christ. If you insult me, I get upset. When I get upset, I'm inclined to threaten people. Are you really so surprised?'

Alexander interrupted and we both looked to him. Fergus examined his feet as the prince spoke with a rapid-fire staccato, reluctantly translating what had been said. 'Prince Alexander says that if you do not agree to his terms you shall be taken from here and put in a cell in Novgorod. He assures me you will not like this option. But if we are able to work together, we can continue without any further problems.'

'I have no qualms if you remember to keep your own opinions to yourself in future.'

Under the scrutiny of Prince Alexander, the Irishman swallowed a retort and I enjoyed watching his discomfort. He gave a curt nod.

'And I wish to know if Prince Alexander has yet agreed a price to ransom me back to my Order?'

Prince Alexander smiled and said something. Fergus translated. 'What are you thinkin' you are worth now?'

I laughed. Did he think I was feeble-minded? 'My Order does not like paying ransoms. I would be surprised if they would offer anything.'

'Yet they paid the ransom for your captured comrades.'

'Of which I know nothing.' I pretended the matter was of no interest to me.

'You do not, but Prince Alexander thinks your question is immaterial.' Fergus smiled maliciously. 'You are still far too wounded to travel and have yet to write your life's account.'

I held my tongue. After all, it was true. With my wounded shoulder I would not last two days travelling, even on horseback.

'Prince Alexander must be going now. He will not be able to return for a week at least. I am to come tomorrow and we are to carry on with your chronicle. Prince Alexander has made it clear that we are not to… be upsetting ourselves. Otherwise there will be trouble so. Prince Alexander will want to see some progress when he returns next time.'

I bowed my head to the prince, who nodded tersely, turning for the door. What choice did I have? I wanted to leave here, but I had no real desire to return to my Order. With my injury it was unlikely I would be able to fight again and a resumed life of prayer or meditation appalled me. Maybe when I finally left this place, I would try and return home to England and finish what I had left behind so long ago. My uncle would be long dead but Walter would probably still be alive. And I would gladly take my vengeance out on him. It was long overdue. But in the meantime, I wanted to write this account for my son. If I did not survive or was otherwise unable, he would be tasked to complete this in our family's name. Honour demanded it.

So, I had to finish my chronicle, which meant I had to hold my temper and not let the Irishman rile me so easily. I had to hold my temper in order to complete what I had started.

Because I had a story to finish.

PART TWO

LÜBECK, 1203–1204

CHAPTER EIGHT

It rained the entire next day and I spent a despondent time sitting under the oilskins with a wheezing Wilhelm, while the wind blew the rain and spray at us. Water dripped down my back and my sodden clothes chafed and felt as heavy as mail.

We always sailed within sight of land, a grey smudge on our starboard side, with the monotony only broken by the odd church spire. There were not many other ships and Wilhelm, in one of the few moments he was awake, explained that most captains were reluctant to sail in winter due to the bad weather – with the added risk of storms and shipwreck.

One night was spent anchored in the harbour of Dordrecht, but there was a war going on. Dirk VII, Count of Holland, had died and his brother, William I, was contesting his daughter Ada's succession. A coalition of enemies now besieged the castle just outside the walled town, so Hauke decided to forgo any business and we sailed early the next morning.

I sat under the oilskins with Wilhelm and the two monks, mostly in silence, watching the bleak, flat landscape of islands, shoals and sandbanks drift by. Wilhelm's health had not improved, he had a high fever and he drifted in and out of consciousness, mumbling in his sleep in his own language. When we reached Bremen, I would have to get him help, either from an apothecary or a physician. But with such little money, I was daunted at what lay before us.

We passed several villages, partially raised on terps, but they were miserable-looking affairs where the locals eked out a wretched existence among the swamps, reeds and mud. We saw several fishing vessels but no other ships. We spent another night moored up in the entrance to a tidal creek with only the numerous waterfowl as company. The darkness was disturbed by Wilhelm coughing and I spent most of the time unsuccessfully trying to sleep.

At least the next day was fine and free of rain, albeit cold with a westerly wind that drove the ship faster and whipped up whitecaps across the water. We gradually left the mudflats and islands behind and Hauke told me that we would soon be coming to the River Weser which led to Bremen. I could hardly wait to get my feet onto dry land again.

The *Christofer* reached the estuary of the Weser and we docked at a toll station built amid the marshland where Hauke went briefly ashore. The shore looked desolate, with a few stunted trees in infertile-looking heathland rising above the marsh and mud. There were several small ships, coasters and barges that plied the river, moored up along a long wooden wharf and we waited for the tide to change in order to make travelling upstream easier.

Hauke returned and we continued. Both the monks examined Wilhelm. The older one, Brother Nicholas, confirmed what I thought – he needed shelter, warmth and some hot food. 'It will help him the most along with prayer, of course. There is a Benedictine abbey by the *Ostertor*, outside the eastern gate, dedicated to Saint Paul. The monks there will help.'

We talked in Latin rather than English or French. At this time, my mastery of the language was rudimentary, but I realised that in the Holy Roman Empire I would need to improve my proficiency. No one would understand me otherwise.

'We shall be going there ourselves,' Brother Nicholas continued, 'so I can show you. I was there once, although many years ago.'

We spent the balance of the day moored at the toll station. Despite his earlier good humour, Hauke was in a foul mood, snapping at his crew as we settled down for a cold meal of dry fish and bread and our last night on board.

The next morning, we awoke to a pristine frost that coated the stark trees, highlighting the branches now etched in white. I sat wrapped in my cloak next to a shivering Wilhelm for the rest of the journey. We arrived in Bremen after middle day, rowing slowly into the small river known as the Balge that branched off the north side of the Weser and where docks lined the banks. Most of the quays were occupied with barges, but we also saw a couple of smaller cogs and several Viking-style longships.

We moored between two long barges, the *Christofer* swinging around and gliding in between the two vessels with barely a bump, demonstrating Hauke's skill on the steering oar. Beyond the wharves and warehouses, half-timbered buildings towered over the waterfront and the crowds of people going about their business. It reminded me of London, although here the houses were even taller. A crane on a large warehouse winched wooden crates from one of the river barges, a number of men pulling on the ropes and shouting in a harsh, guttural language that to my ears sounded like they were clearing their throats.

'Well, that is our destination finally reached,' Hauke said. He turned to me and smiled for the first time that morning.

'That was our last voyage before winter. May God guide you and keep you and your friend safe.'

I thanked the big Frisian and helped Wilhelm to his feet, supporting him as we descended the gangplank. The two monks followed us onto the quay and we waved goodbye to Hauke and his crew. Brother Eustace helped me with Wilhelm, and together we walked through the city.

We passed through the *Ostertor*, the eastern gate set in a wooden palisade that encircled the city on the landward side, crossing a flooded ditch and reaching the monastery of Saint Paul shortly afterwards. The monastery was close to the river and surrounded by a stone wall set amid an orchard. It was good to be away from the city crowds and I paused, listening to a group of sparrows chirping on a tree branch, enjoying the serenity while Brother Nicholas went to speak to the abbot. He returned a few moments later with a man of middle age who introduced himself as Abbot Segebodo von Uthlede. In a grating voice, Wilhelm spoke to him in German, before another monk helped him to the infirmary. The abbot spoke to me in Latin, explaining I was welcome to stay in the dormitory in the guest quarters until Wilhelm was well again. 'But we are expecting pilgrims from Lüneburg tomorrow on their way to the Shrine of the Three Kings in Cologne, so it may become a little crowded.'

I thanked him for his hospitality, before a novice monk showed me where I would be staying. The dormitory was full of pallets for sleeping and little else. I felt lost and alone.

Over the next few days I spent much of my time in Bremen, mostly in the large market square that was a hive of activity, dominated by the huge edifice of the cathedral with its two towers. The weather remained cold, colder than it had been in England, and I walked the narrow streets of the city taking in the strange sights, sounds and smells, as much to keep warm as anything else. On one occasion, I returned to where the *Christofer* was moored, but found the ship covered and deserted with no sign of Hauke or his crew.

I spent as little time as possible at the monastery. Brothers Nicholas and Eustace left early the morning after we had arrived, continuing their journey to Bursfelde Abbey. The guest quarters were full and I found it disconcerting sharing a room with the group of pilgrims who, despite being in a place of meditation, babbled constantly in their incomprehensible tongue. Luckily, they only stayed two days before departing again.

It seemed what Brother Nicholas had said on the ship was true: with rest, warmth and proper food, Wilhelm made rapid progress towards recovery. Two weeks later he was fit to travel again. We decided to leave the day after *Andreasnacht*, the night of Saint Andrew's Day, and I took one last walk into the city to buy some provisions at the market with the little funds we had left. Despite my lack of German, I bought a small loaf of bread, beans, dried meat, several sausages, some apples and a hunk of cheese, along with two flasks of beer. The vendor, a rosy-cheeked man with a red moustache, looked carefully at the couple of silver pennies I gave him, noting the short cross motif, before weighing them and biting them to check they were real. I didn't worry as Wilhelm had told me that English coins were of superior quality.

It was on the way back that I noticed a group of figures crowded around a man next to the entrance to the cathedral. The man was speaking to the crowd and he was tall, with a carefully clipped beard, wearing mail with a sword at his belt over a white tabard with a black cross, reminding me of a Knight Templar. To my youthful eyes he looked magnificent. Most of the people listening were young men, some barely older than me, and they jostled each other to get a good position to hear every word the knight was saying. I paused, fascinated, even though I could not understand anything. The man spoke for a while, finishing his speech and bowing to the crowd. He talked individually to some of the young men, which seemed to last for ages, before they dispersed, leaving me alone. The knight smiled at me and said something in German. I asked him to speak in Latin and he introduced himself as Matthias von Sulingen.

'Are you of noble birth?' the knight asked.

'I am, in my country.'

'Are you interested in joining the armed pilgrimage to the Holy Land?'

'I have... just arrived in Bremen. My friend is sick.'

'The Order of Brothers of the German House of Saint Mary in Jerusalem are always looking for men of noble birth. We need brothers to help safeguard our hospital in Acre, as well as our fortresses there. You are young, but you can become a half-brother – and train to become a knight-brother when you are older. But you need to speak German. Do you have any experience of arms?'

'I was trained as a page and would have been a squire now in England...'

Matthias went on to describe more about his Order's work. I listened, enchanted by his words and the exciting world of adventure he conjured up. He was so noble, the epitome of everything a knight should be – a hero, a true warrior of Christ. Even now, so many years later, I remember how impressed I was.

Of course, I was only a naïve fourteen-year-old who didn't know a rat's turd about anything.

The next day we continued our journey to Lübeck. Flurries of sleet and snow stung my eyes as we set out on the rutted track that led north-east and my cloak was stiff with frost. Of course, we were on foot, and Wilhelm told me that it would take at least five days to reach our destination. Despite the weather, the road was busy and we fell in with a group of twenty or so wandering pedlars heading for Hamburg that made us both feel more secure about travelling an unknown road. 'These are difficult times in the Empire,' Wilhelm said. 'There is a dispute between the Welf dynasty and Philipp von Schwaben from the House of Hohenstaufen. The struggle has lasted over five years and much of the country is lawless. It is more dangerous here than in England.'

Considering this information, I wondered whether coming to this country was the right decision, but I kept quiet.

However, by the grace of God, we saw no sign of outlaws or war. The countryside was open and relatively flat and we passed many small villages that looked like the ones in England, built predominantly of wood, wattle and thatch, with tendrils of smoke smudging the sky. I imagined the families sitting huddled around their hearths inside. Wilhelm began to teach me some basic German phrases that would be useful and the pedlars roared with laughter when I mangled their language trying to pronounce words that, to me at least, were unpronounceable.

By the middle of the second day my feet began to get blisters, nevertheless there was nothing for it but to plough on regardless. Wilhelm's health was significantly better. The fever was gone and he was bearing up well to the long hike. He continued to try and teach me the fundamentals of his language as we walked.

'Low German is also called Low Saxon,' Wilhelm explained. 'It is descended from Old Saxon, which was spoken in England when your King William invaded.'

I nodded absently, not really interested. I was more concerned about what awaited us when we reached Lübeck. 'You said your brother is still a merchant in the city. Will he be able to help us? You did not sound certain when we talked before.'

Wilhelm sighed. 'My relationship with Eberhard is a complicated one. I have had no contact with him for eight years. To be honest, Lord Richard, I do not know. There was bad blood between us the last time we saw each other. He is not... an easy man. Unfortunately, considering the circumstances, we have no choice.'

His words sounded ominous.

We spent that night in a stable in a small village where the pedlars shared a fiery liquid with each other and talked late into the night. The next afternoon we reached Hamburg, crossing the Elbe river by ferry into the city and spending the night on the floor of a cheap inn in the *Reichenstrasse*. The inn was a run-down wooden structure of three floors, across a stinking, offal-filled canal opposite the enclave that surrounded the brick edifice of Saint Mary's Cathedral and the bishop's castle. Wilhelm told me that the Danish king, Waldemar II, was now overlord of the city but I could see no sign of it. Despite my exhaustion, the sound of drunken singing and laughter from the neighbouring taverns was accompanied by the inevitable barking of dogs that succeeded in keeping me awake well into the night.

We did not stay long in Hamburg, leaving through the *Schulthor* early the following day in a blustering wind. For most of the morning we travelled alone. It was a relief to be away from the crowded city with its inevitable stench and the cold air helped to banish its memory from my mind. We trudged on and I told Wilhelm about the Teutonic knight in the market place in Bremen.

The German listened patiently. 'The Order was founded in the Holy Land, as far as I am aware. I can imagine that for someone of your age they must seem very impressive. However, do not let them distract you. Your fate lies in another direction.'

I remained silent, knowing he was right. How wrong we both proved to be on that point, but I must not get ahead of myself again. Suffice to say, fate was laughing at me that day.

As it was wintertime, dusk came all too soon and we were forced again to stop early, spending the night in a small castle situated in a forest, called Burg Arnesvelde, that was undergoing massive renovation and rebuilding. We slept in a small barn in the outer bailey and were fed a watery vegetable soup. That night, surprisingly, I slept better than I had since leaving Cranham. The next morning it was slightly warmer and we left before dawn, picking up the road north-east again. We joined a merchant caravan heading our way that welcomed fellow travellers. We were even allowed to ride up front on one of the ten wagons, each pulled by two oxen, and I was glad to give my sore feet a rest. The area was very flat and we passed more villages, areas of forest and heath, crossing several bridges that spanned half-frozen streams. By late morning, we topped a gentle rise and I caught a glimpse of the spires of the city of Lübeck through the bare trees. We paused for a moment, as one of the wagons had broken a wheel, and I scanned the city, noting the brick city wall under construction and the sun glistening off the water. It looked peaceful and at ease with the world and my earlier misgivings relented. Wilhelm gazed long at the city of his birth. I was certain he was thinking about his brother.

We left the caravan at this point, Wilhelm explaining that they would take the long route to skirt the city because there was no bridge over the Trave at this point. 'Although they have been talking of building one for as long as I remember. But do not worry, we can get a boat across the river and enter the city through the *Holstentor* gate that connects it with the harbour.'

In less time than it took to say the rosary, we found an old man willing to row us across the river to the bustling harbour on the other side. The surrounding land was marshy and waterlogged, and ducks glided through the reeds and a gull swooped and dived above the surface of the water. The man strained and heaved at the oars and I almost felt like helping him. Eventually, we reached the far side and walked the last few paces to the gate.

Wilhelm had said nothing since we had paid the ferryman and my feeling of apprehension returned. We were ignored by the Danish-liveried guards at the gate, their yellow shields emblazoned with three blue lions. Of course, I did not know then that I would get to know this city almost better than anywhere else in the world.

There was no point in worrying anymore. In a short time, we would find out what reception awaited us with Wilhelm's brother.

We proceeded up a hill flanked by tall wooden buildings to a market square that was bustling with people and activity. The square was fronted by narrow wood, plaster, and brick houses of obvious wealth, and a large Romanesque basilica constructed of brick reached up behind the town hall, which Wilhelm explained was dedicated to Saint Mary. We pushed through the mass and Wilhelm led me along another filthy street that led down the other side of the hill. After turning a few corners, we eventually came to a row of more modest buildings. Wilhelm rapped his knuckles on a green-painted wooden door, next to a small picket fence where chickens clucked in the dirt, explaining that this was where his brother lived. 'Or at least he did eight years ago.'

The door was opened by a middle-aged woman who squinted at Wilhelm suspiciously as he explained our business. After a brief conversation the door was closed and Wilhelm turned to me. 'Eberhard no longer lives here. The woman does not know exactly where he is living now, but she thinks it is near the *Petrikirche*, Saint Peter's Church. We passed close to it when we arrived, near the market square in the west of the town. If so, it means Eberhard has risen in the world.'

We walked back up the hill towards the tumult of the market before retracing our steps to the *Holstentor* gate and the docks that lined the Trave. The harbour was teeming with people, but Wilhelm knew his way and we threaded through the throng until we reached the double gates of one of the many warehouses. 'This used to be my brother's warehouse. If we are lucky, it still is.'

And lucky we were. We entered and Wilhelm immediately stopped as a tall man turned to him and said something in German. I could see the larger man's eyes widen as he realised who it was standing in front of him. For a moment there was silence, and I found myself holding my breath before Wilhelm started to speak. I watched as first one brother, then the other began talking, both raising their voices until I was sure they were having a terrible argument. It was strange; I had never seen Wilhelm raise his voice before and I wished I could understand what was being said. Eberhard did not look anything like his older brother. He had a large beak of a nose and the way he towered over Wilhelm made me think violence was about to take place. But nothing happened. Wilhelm paused and took me aside. 'Please wait for me outside,' he said. 'I need to speak longer with my brother and that will be easier alone.'

I shrugged and walked out into the yard that fronted the harbour, shivering as I watched the men around me working. After a short while, Wilhelm came out, wringing his hands, his face looking grave.

'What did he say?'

Wilhelm sighed deeply. 'My brother said many things – most of them unpleasant. It is complicated. Eberhard thinks I ruined our family, at least financially. And he is probably right, although that was far from my wish. Come and sit down. We have to wait until my brother's business here is concluded, so I might as well explain the situation to you.' We took a seat on two barrels.

'My father was a merchant who traded in salt from Lüneburg and herring from the Baltic. This had always been the family business and it is what my brother took over. I took another path… I wanted to forge my own future so I became a cloth merchant instead – I had always been more interested in fabric. Needless to say, this did not go down well with my father, Detmar, who thought me arrogant and ungrateful. This was a view readily supported by Eberhard.'

Arrogant and ungrateful were not two words I would ever have associated with Wilhelm.

'I had always been my father's favourite, so he took my refusal to work in the family business badly. Eberhard had always been jealous of our relationship. Everything he did was wrong in our father's eyes. He had been groomed for the church, something he had initially welcomed, but my refusal to take over the business changed his life too. However, even with my desire to build up my own, separate, business, my father supported me – financially at least.'

Wilhelm went on to explain that his father had funded the cost of buying a ship for him, almost impoverishing his own business in the process, and when the ship sunk in a storm Wilhelm's business ultimately failed. 'My father lost most of his money. As you can imagine, this caused great problems between us. I had a big argument with both my father and Eberhard the last time I was here. My father died shortly afterwards, although by then I was back in London and unaware of this for six months, until I received a letter from my brother. Eberhard blamed me, saying that the loss of money had driven my father to drink, to despair and to his death. After that letter, we had no contact – until now.'

'Is that what you were arguing about?'

Wilhelm removed his red cap and ran his hands through his thinning hair. 'Ja, partly. It is clear that Eberhard has made a success of my father's business, but he is still bitter about events of the past. Nevertheless, we are still family and he has not refused my request for lodging. But he will make it uncomfortable for us... or me anyway.'

'But at least we have somewhere to stay. It must have been a big shock for him to see you again?'

Wilhelm laughed unexpectedly, a sound so incongruous that I looked at him in surprise – gaiety was not something I was used to from the German.

'Ja, I think so too. It is not easy for me to return here.'

I was sure about the truth of that, but what choice did we have?

We waited for a long time before Eberhard was finished at his warehouse. He came out and scowled at us both before saying something to Wilhelm. They both looked at me.

'My brother tells me that you are an English lord,' Eberhard said in fluent Latin. 'Well, that might be the case in your land, but Lübeck is very different. Merchants like me run this city. I shall treat you like the boy you are and find work for you, so at least you can earn your keep and be useful. Under my roof you shall obey me in all things, is that clear?'

I nodded my acceptance – I was hardly in any position to dictate any terms. Apparently satisfied, Eberhard turned and strode towards the city gate leaving Wilhelm and me struggling to keep up with him. We walked back to the merchant's house in silence. The building was behind Saint Peter's Church, a smart, wood-and-plaster-built townhouse of four floors, with a small warehouse and counting room on the ground floor and a courtyard and another wooden-built house behind. I was given a tiny room in the eaves of the attic, accessed by a narrow staircase as steep as a ladder, and I cursed out loud when I banged my head on the rafter at the top. A small door led into my room, and I dumped my pack and sword on a chipped stool, opening the small window before sitting down on the low bed, little more than a straw pallet of dubious cleanliness. There was a musty aroma of damp and I looked up at the beams festooned with hundreds of cobwebs. It was obviously a long time since this room had ever been used. This was my new home and I could have wept.

I must have fallen asleep because a light tapping at the door woke me. Dark shadows across the rafters indicated dusk was approaching, which meant I had slept most of the afternoon. I opened the door to a servant who gave me an oil lamp and told me that supper was served in the hall on the first floor. The room was modest compared to our hall back in Cranham, with a low ceiling, wood-panelled walls, and a large table filling most of the space. A solid wooden cupboard displayed the family's plate and silver filled most of one side. Eberhard sat at the head with a fireplace behind and a demure, pale-faced woman, who I assumed was his wife, alongside him. To his right sat a burly, hard-looking man and another, aged about twenty, next to his wife. The younger man glared at Wilhelm and he barely glanced at me as I washed my hands in a bowl and took a place next to my father's former steward. A moment later, we were joined by a blonde-haired girl of roughly my own age who was red-faced and out of breath. Eberhard said something that was an obvious rebuke and she blushed further as she sat down opposite me. The first course was brought out and we began to eat. I was ravenous and I wolfed the pea soup down, causing the older youth, who by now I realised was Eberhard's eldest son, to sneer as he whispered something to his father. As the meal progressed and further courses of cooked fish and vegetables were put on the table by servants, I found my attention constantly drawn to the girl opposite me, the way she cut her food, the way she took only small bites of her meal. It was easy concentrating on her as the conversation was limited and I understood none of it anyway. She reminded me a little of Emma who had intrigued me at Edward's house in London. But, unlike Emma, she seemed uninterested in both me and Wilhelm, ignoring both of us for the whole meal and leaving me feeling even more downbeat than before. I did not belong here; I did not understand the conversation or what was going on around me. All I wanted was to be home again, sitting in my father's hall at Cranham, playing pranks with my sister Alice and completing my training to be a squire.

After the meal, the servants cleared the table and the rest of the family left, leaving me, Eberhard, Wilhelm, and the hard-looking man alone. For a short period the three men spoke German before Eberhard turned to me and spoke in his flawless Latin. 'This man is Henkel, captain of the mercenaries who safeguards my goods and caravans from Lüneburg and sometimes performing any other work I may have. He has been in my employ for the last three years and I trust him implicitly.'

I wondered why he was telling me this and felt Henkel's eyes drilling into me, but I avoided his stare, finding the man more than a little intimidating.

'You and my brother have shown up here without warning and I am obliged to provide hospitality,' Eberhard said. 'However, whilst you live under my roof you will be required to work. My brother...' he couldn't keep the bitterness from his voice, 'will do what he should have done years ago and help the family business. He told me that you were undergoing martial training in England. This could be useful to me, despite your youth. Therefore, starting tomorrow morning, you shall be in my employ under the command of my friend, Henkel, here.'

I turned and looked Henkel in the eyes for the first time and froze. The man's gaze was as cold as a winter blizzard. I felt the hairs on my arms stand up and a great feeling of foreboding descend on my shoulders.

CHAPTER NINE

The next morning was the Feast of Saint Nicholas. A servant woke me before dawn and told me to bring my pack and sword and go with him. I just had time to grab a hunk of bread, cheese and cold meat from the kitchen before the servant led me outside. It was cold, with a strong breeze that whipped around the narrow streets, rattling the shutters of the tall houses and harrying a small group of women on their way to collect water from the well and empty chamber pots of night waste. The servant led me down the hill to the stables near the *Holstentor* gate, where he left me. Here, a group of figures waited, silhouetted against a lantern that one of them carried. I saw the burly form of Henkel, who said something to the men in German and the others laughed, turning to look at me. I swallowed my nervousness, wondering where we were supposed to be going.

Henkel spoke in a low, deep voice as the group, half a dozen in number, huddled around to listen. All the men were armed, and I saw that under their cloaks some of them were wearing mail. One of the figures, a tall, well-built youth with blond hair only a year or two older than me, leaned close to me and spoke in broken Latin. 'We ride Lüneburg – pick up white gold. My name Otto… who are you?'

'I am Richard,' I said.

'You are from England. Welcome to Lübeck.'

And that proved to be the only welcome I would receive in this foreign city. Henkel led us into the stables and we were all given horses. Mine was a grey mare, but no one told me her name. We rode through the streets as the city woke around us, reaching the southern gate as a cold, wintery light brightened the horizon. The gate had just opened and the Danish guards let us through without any interference. We cantered along the road to the bridge, clattering over it and the Wakenitz, the tributary of the Trave that bordered Lübeck's eastern side. Henkel led the way and, as it got lighter, I saw that I was the youngest in the group. The other men looked a rough and ready bunch, but we rode so hard I had no time to let it worry me. We travelled all day, riding almost without a break and stopping the night in a small copse of trees off the road. Because I was new and the youngest, it fell on me to collect the firewood, although Otto helped me. The young German was good-natured and I was pleased to have him as my companion. And Otto was the only one of them who spoke some Latin, so it fell on him to convey Henkel's orders. It was a relief to be away from the baleful gaze of our captain, even if it was just for a short time. The other men ignored me, which was fine; I didn't understand what they were saying anyway. To tell the truth, I was wary of them all.

It took three days of hard riding to reach Lüneburg, crossing over the wooden bridge that spanned the Ilmenau before reaching the town, nestled in the shadow of the castle and monastery that looked down from the Kalkberg. It was a strange sight, unlike anything I had seen before. The salt mine was located south-west of the town, dozens of boiling huts surrounding the salt spring connected by channels and canals of brine, and busy with workers. It was clear that Henkel and his men knew the town well and we ignored the area, heading for a large tavern where we were given a dormitory on the second floor, before all of the men went downstairs to get drunk, leaving me and Otto alone in our room.

'I see you get the worst bed... next to shit bucket,' Otto said with a laugh. 'Where I normally sleep.'

'I think Henkel hates me,' I said. 'The way he stares makes me nervous.'

'That is just the way he is,' Otto said. 'But be careful, Richard. I see him fight and he is like devil. Do not cross him.'

I certainly had no intention of doing that, but I didn't want to talk about our cheerless captain. 'How did you come to be working for him?'

'A long story,' Otto said. 'My family are *ministeriales* – my father worked as Seneschal for Hermann II, Bishop of Münster. For me to learn my trade, I was sent to Lübeck to serve Bishop Dietrich, but it... did not work out. I was there less than six months before I work serving Eberhard. That was five months ago. But I am glad you are here now to take the shit instead of me.' He laughed and clapped me on the back. 'And what about you? What is a man from England doing in the Empire?'

I was reluctant to explain what had happened, but I looked into the big German's open face and felt trust immediately. Against my better judgement, I began to explain everything that had happened, from my uncle's arrival at Cranham, to my father's murder and our flight.

He looked at me in amazement. 'An incredible story – and you are noble birth like me. We are both working as *Dienstmänner* – retainers, with a group of outlaws as comrades and a merchant as boss! *Ach*, this talk makes me miserable. Let us go into town and find some girls.'

I was too exhausted from the ride to want to do anything apart from sleep. My arse and legs burned from three days in the saddle, but Otto must have been more used to riding because he decided to go out anyway. The next morning, I was the only one with a clear head. Henkel was grimmer than usual and the rest of the group were morose and argumentative. Only Otto was in good spirits, giving me a wink as we mounted our horses at the stables, demonstrating with a crude gesture what he had got up to during the night.

Henkel led us to a large sandy space at the edge of the town where a great crowd gathered. There was a market going on and lines of wagons pulled by snorting oxen were being loaded with sacks of salt. Groups of men, armed and armoured, stood around in small groups talking.

'This is where we meet the caravan and the other men that are to escort it to Lübeck,' Otto said.

Henkel strode through the crowd and we followed. We met another group of mercenaries that would help escort the caravan to Lübeck, and the way the men greeted each other made it clear that they had worked together before. Even Otto knew some of the men, and again I felt out of place. As we waited, I watched the merchants and pedlars selling their produce, the food vendors moving through the crowd offering sausages made from pork and grain. My stomach groaned and rumbled but I did my best to ignore it. I had no money anyway.

It seemed to take forever for the porters to finish loading the wagons, some thirty or so in number, to be escorted by approximately twenty-five armed men. I was eager to start, but there were further delays and it must have been almost Nones before we finally got underway. After an age, the caravan leader barked some orders and Henkel spurred his horse on, leading the six of us forward to take up position in the vanguard. The caravan rumbled out of the sandy market square and through the narrow streets and over another bridge that spanned the river, past a fish market and out of town, heading north. I rode alongside Otto, watching either side of the track for any sign of danger. The landscape around was a mixture of forest and heathland but the road was in poor repair, rutted and uneven, and the wagons regularly got bogged down in the mud.

I soon became bored and frustrated at the slow rate of progress. And I was not the only one. Although most of my compatriots had made this trip many times, the monotony of riding at a wagon's pace grated on everyone and nerves were ragged. It was already getting dark when we stopped the night at a small hamlet of five or six hovels set amid low-lying meadows and marshland where we would cross the River Neetze the following morning.

Next day, there was a fine drizzle in the air that reminded me of England. Henkel led us across the river, which was not wide, although it was deceptively deep. A ferry operated that would transport the wagons and it took the best part of the day for the caravan to cross. Progress remained painfully slow over the next two days, the crossing of the Elbe by Artlenburg, again by ferry as the river was swollen and the ford was impassable. On the north bank was the burnt remains of a castle that Otto said had been destroyed by Henry the Lion before either of us had been born. Now a new castle was being built nearby, and the chipping of masons' hammers rang across the river. We spent that night alongside the ruins and it rained most of the time. I shared a tent with a snoring Otto, listening to the rain pattering on the canvas, and despite my tiredness, it took me a long time to fall asleep.

The following morning was bright and crisp with a strong easterly wind. As usual, we rode vanguard, keeping sharp eyes on both sides of the track that had turned into a muddy quagmire due to the rain of the previous days. Up until now, no one had seen any sign of outlaws or brigands and to my young eyes I could not imagine anyone being daring enough to attack a caravan with over a hundred people, at least twenty-five of them armed and armoured. I was still being given the more menial tasks, fetching water and firewood every night, as well as looking after the horses, but if I had been squiring for Lord Bigod that would have been no different. And, of course, I jumped at any chance to be away from Henkel's cold stare.

But this day Henkel was in brighter spirits than normal and I even saw him laughing with Johann, his second in command, a small wiry man who had a long knife scar down the side of his jaw. Henkel turned and said something to the rest of us, riding slightly behind.

Otto translated his words for me. 'The village of Lütau is ahead. Henkel wants to go to scout out the route before us. It means we get to ride a bit.'

Henkel said something more in German and kicked his horse forward. The rest of us immediately did likewise and we galloped across the adjoining field, hooves tossing up clods of earth as we let the horses run a bit, enjoying the freedom of being away from the caravan. My horse dropped back a little, but I felt exhilarated for the first time since arriving in this country, feeling the wind in my hair and my heart banging in my chest. After a mile or so, Henkel pulled up his horse and scanned the land around until the rest of us caught up, our horses snorting in the cold air. He issued a few commands and three of the men were sent back to the ferry, leaving Henkel, Johann, Otto and me. Henkel pointed to a column of smoke rising from some trees another half a mile away from the road and said something more in German.

'Henkel wants us to check out where the smoke is coming from,' Otto said. 'He thinks it is more than just a woodfire.'

We followed Henkel in single file down a narrow track towards the trees. I rode with one hand on the hilt of my sword, prepared for any possible attack. We passed into the forest and I strained my ears to hear anything unusual. As we progressed deeper, it seemed ominously quiet and I felt increasingly nervous about what could be waiting. Henkel was leading and he must have heard something, because he raised his hand and stopped. After a moment, I heard what had alarmed him – the nearby sound of leaves rustling and the snapping of branches, like the passage of many animals.

Henkel motioned us to be quiet and dismounted, tying the reins of his horse to a tree. The rest of us did the same, and I drew my sword with a faint rasp. Henkel glared at me before disappearing into the undergrowth, leaving us to catch him up. We followed him for fifty paces or so before stopping on a rise overlooking a swiftly running stream. Down below I saw a girl of perhaps sixteen or seventeen sitting on a rock while a dozen or so sheep drank from the water. Her dog must have heard us because it looked in our direction and began barking. For a moment, we all watched her before Henkel spoke to Johann, who slipped off into the trees, before he turned to Otto and said something more.

'We are to wait here,' Otto said.

Henkel emerged from our cover and approached the girl, his hands outstretched to indicate he intended no harm. At first, she looked alarmed, but Henkel said something to her and she visibly relaxed, calming the dog down. She had a dirty face and there was something feral about her, but she was pretty with dark unkempt hair. I watched, wondering why we were wasting time here when we should have been protecting the caravan, when Henkel suddenly lunged towards the girl, trying to grab her arm. However, she was fast and twisted from his grip and darted away as her dog sprang forward to protect her. Henkel cursed, drew his sword in one swift movement and stabbed it into the dog's flank without any hesitation. The dog died in a splash of blood.

The girl started running for the trees but Johann appeared ahead of her. He caught her by the arm and threw her to the ground where she landed in a pile of leaves. Henkel threw himself on her and I watched appalled as he hitched up her tunic, fumbling at his hose as he mounted her. The girl was fighting desperately and Johann came to his aid, kneeling on her arms, using his weight to pin her to the ground as Henkel began to rape her. Johann punched her several times until her face was a bloody mess and her struggles stopped. I could not watch any more, I still had my sword drawn and I rose, intending to stop the atrocity taking place in front of me. Otto rose too, grabbing my arm and pulling me back down. 'Nein, Richard! He will kill you!'

I knew Otto was right but still I struggled against his vice-like grip. Eventually, I relented and we both watched in horror. After a short time, Henkel was finished and Johann took his turn. He was even quicker, finishing with a grunt of satisfaction only a moment later. Henkel approached us still lacing up his hose. He glared at me with an intensity, as if daring me to protest about what had just happened.

'Do not say a word,' Otto whispered.

Henkel said something to Otto before turning to me. 'Kill her,' he said, walking back through the trees towards where we had left the horses. Johann followed him, smirking at us both as he passed. The girl remained in a heap on the ground, trembling and sobbing. I stood shocked at the order I had been given.

Otto turned to me with a grave look on his broad, guileless face. 'He wants you to kill her,' he said. 'Otherwise I am to kill you.'

I looked at my new friend in surprise. 'And would you do that?'

'Of course not. But he will want to see proof. If she lives, she can identify us.'

I cursed, turning to make sure that Henkel and Johann were out of sight. 'As God is my witness, I shall not harm a hair on her head,' I said vehemently. I broke cover and walked down the rise towards where the girl still lay. She looked up at me in fear, seeing the drawn sword in my hand. Her lips and nose were crusted in blood. Oblivious to what had happened, the sheep continued to drink from the stream. I turned as Otto came up behind me.

'What are we going to do?' the big German said, panic in his voice. 'If we do not kill her then Henkel will kill us both.'

The girl looked at us with eyes wide with terror. I thought for a moment before approaching the nearest sheep. I lunged with my sword, piercing the animal in the side. It toppled to the ground and the other sheep scrambled away from me, bleating in fear. 'Tell her to go,' I said to Otto. 'Tell her to go quickly. If Henkel returns all three of us shall die.'

Otto said something to her in German and the girl struggled to her feet, limping slowly away into the trees like a wounded animal.

'Henkel will see blood on my sword,' I said. 'As long as he doesn't want to see her body, he should believe the girl is dead. He would not expect me to defy him.'

Otto didn't look convinced and I prayed I was right. But what else could we do? We walked back to our horses, untying the reins and leading them out of the trees to where Henkel and Johann were already mounted, waiting for us, the smudge of smoke above the trees and the original reason for our foray already forgotten. My sword was still unsheathed and wet with blood and I saw Henkel watching me, slit-eyed, reminding me of the way a falcon viewed its prey. He said something to Otto, who nodded before replying.

'I told him that you killed her,' Otto said to me as we mounted our horses. 'I think he believes me. He has no desire to go back to check the body.'

Henkel said something to Johann and they both laughed. I hated him then. Since that time, I have seen dozens of women, girls and even children raped and killed in front of my eyes, but this was my first. I knew that I would never forget what I had seen on that cold December morning in that woodland near Lütau.

And, whatever happened, I also knew that one day I would kill Henkel.

It took another week to complete the journey back to Lübeck, making laborious and gruelling progress in the mud and rain. Altogether it was a miserable experience. In time, I would make that trip on many occasions, but it was this first expedition that I would always remember most. We never saw any sign of outlaws. Otto and I never spoke about what had happened, as if by never mentioning it we could deny what we had witnessed. And when we returned to Lübeck I didn't say anything to Wilhelm either, reasoning that he had enough problems dealing with his brother and hardly needed any complications from me. And what would it have achieved? We had no coin and no other prospects, so leaving was not an option. So I relegated the memory to the back of my mind and got on with the work I was assigned.

Every morning I would wake with the bells for Prime, having a light breakfast before learning German under the tutelage of Wilhelm before his duties in the counting house took him away. My tasks involved guarding Eberhard's warehouse at the harbour, unloading and stacking the goods, escorting him or other members of his family on their business around the city, looking after the horses in the stables by the *Holstentor* gate and any number of menial tasks that were required of me. When possible, I would train in the yard behind the warehouse with some of the others in the service of Eberhard, practising my skills with sword and shield. Despite being the youngest, I found my training at Cranham held me in good stead and I could more than hold my own, despite all my opponents being older than me. After a particularly gruelling combat with Otto that left us both lathered in sweat despite the cold, we both clasped hands, Otto looking at me with a new respect. 'You fight well, Richard. *Ach*, I'm exhausted.' We were both pretty evenly matched, despite Otto being over a year older than me. But Otto was as good-humoured about it as usual. 'I pity any outlaws we may meet next time we go to Lüneburg.'

Henkel showed no interest and rarely attended any of our training sessions. I did not see him again at Eberhard's house, which was a relief. Sometimes, days would go by without meeting him at the warehouse. But then he would turn up, inevitably with Johann or another one of his cronies, forever watching, issuing his commands in a curt growl and making me very uncomfortable. Of course, he spoke no English, French, or Latin, but he would look at me with his glacial eyes and sometimes call me 'English Lord'. The way he said it made it feel like an insult.

The main mealtime was in the late morning, as in England, but because it was Advent we were fasting, so we ate an abundance of fish and vegetables rather than the usual meat. Meals were a soulless, miserable affair, with hardly any conversation and an icy atmosphere I could cut with my sword. Eberhard's daughter was named Elsebeth, and while she still intrigued and interested me, she remained aloof and arrogant, treating me with contempt, as if I was nothing more than one of the servants. But that would change the next day.

Eberhard spoke to me after breaking our fast three days before Christmas, accosting me when I was about to leave for his warehouse. 'You are to return to the hall after Terce. I want you to escort my daughter to the market. I would prefer to send someone more experienced, but everyone is busy. I am holding you personally responsible for her safety.'

I knew that Henkel had taken the others, including Otto, to the castle at Bucu, on the other side of Lübeck, located at the mouth of the peninsular upon which the city stood surrounded by the Trave and Wakenitz rivers. They had gone to see Albrecht von Orlamünde, the Danish governor and nephew of King Waldemar II, who resided there, and were then supposed to go on to the fortress at the mouth of the Trave, known as Travemünde, on an errand to which I was not privy. I was looking forward to spending some time with Elsebeth, despite her obvious disdain of me. I hoped the German I was learning was up to the task.

The bells were still ringing for Terce when I returned to Eberhard's house, climbing the narrow stairs to the hall on the first floor. Eberhard, Elsebeth and a maidservant were waiting for me, and I listened humbly as Eberhard lectured me again about looking after his daughter. A moment later the three of us were outside in the street.

'I want to buy some cloth in the market,' Elsebeth said in impeccable Latin, looking at me for the first time.

'I did not know you spoke Latin…' I said in surprise. 'I was expecting to have to practise my German.'

'Let us hope not,' she said, smiling for the first time. 'My father thought it important that all of his children were educated.'

Elsebeth led the way up the hill to the market place. It was not far, and the streets were crowded with all types of people; servants on their masters' errands, wealthy town burghers and their entourages, as well as the omnipresent beggars and animals nosing through the refuse. The babble of noise around us was incessant. I walked alongside her, armed with a dagger in my belt, keeping my eyes open for any sign of threat. Progress was slow in the narrow street as we negotiated our way through the crowds of people, but when we reached the market in the square near the top of the hill, it became a little easier. Elsebeth knew exactly what she was looking for and headed straight for the stalls that were selling cloth. She started inspecting a bolt of dark-blue wool, chatting casually to the vendor, asking her maidservant's opinion while I glanced around at the surrounding people.

'What do you think?' she asked me.

'Er... it is very nice,' I said, surprised to be asked my opinion.

'Nice? Is that the best you can say?' She smiled again. Her eyes were green. 'However, he wants too much money. But I do like the colour.'

For a considerable time we looked at various other examples and she ended up buying three bolts of cloth and some linen, arranging for them to be delivered to her father's house the following day. She paused at the edge of the square, saying something in German to her maid who then disappeared to buy something else, leaving the pair of us alone. Elsebeth turned to me. 'How are you finding working with Henkel?'

I was surprised by the question and it must have shown.

'That bad, is it?'

'Why do you want to know?' I said, irritated. 'You have hardly spoken to me since I've been here and now you act like we are friends.'

'I know... My father does not encourage it. He does not want us to get too familiar. He is still upset that my uncle has returned.'

'But what does that have to do with Henkel?'

She sighed, looking over her shoulder as if we might be overheard. 'Henkel is a good friend of my father... but he scares me.'

'With good reason.'

'You work with him... what is he like?'

I remembered what had happened in the copse only ten days earlier. 'You don't want to know.'

She saw the disgust on my face and frowned. 'But I do want to know.' She looked scared then and my heart reached out to her. 'I want to know because my future may depend on it. My father is considering... a betrothal.'

I looked at her in shock. 'In the name of Christ, no! He must be at least thirty, old enough to be your father!'

'Since when has that ever mattered? I am a woman – used as a bargaining piece for alliance or gain. Is it not the same in your country?'

'Of course, but Henkel? Is this what your father really wants?'

'My father needs Henkel. I don't know, but he seems to have a hold over him. Henkel has become very important to my father's business.'

Our attention was distracted as a man approached and said something to Elsebeth. I gripped the hilt of my dagger in readiness, but I saw that it was Eberhard's eldest son, Detmar. And he was not happy. He began haranguing Elsebeth in German before glaring at me. 'Why are you standing here in the street? You are supposed to be escorting my sister to and from the market, not talking like two fishwives. You have already missed dinner!'

I stared at him defiantly, unwilling to break eye contact. He might have been five or six years older than me, but he was only half a head taller and I wanted to punch him. With an effort I controlled my temper. Elsebeth said something to her brother before marching off in the direction of the house, only in the next street. I hurried along behind but she ignored me. I heard Detmar indignantly running to catch up. We reached the front door and Elsebeth went inside, climbing the steps quickly. I was about to follow when Detmar stormed through the open door behind me and grabbed me by the arm. 'What are you doing, *Arschloch?*'

All my anger and frustration exploded. I smashed Detmar into the wooden wall, banging his head, before driving my fist into his stomach. When he doubled over, I rammed my knee into his face, feeling satisfaction as I split his lip which immediately began to pour blood. 'Don't ever touch me again,' I hissed in his ear. 'Next time I will kill you!' I stormed from the house, leaving him in a crumpled heap at the bottom of the stairs.

CHAPTER TEN

I fully expected to be thrown out of the house when Eberhard found out I had beaten his son, but it did not happen. Nothing was said at the evening supper, despite Detmar's face and lip being swollen. I could only assume that Detmar had said nothing to his father, embarrassed at his own humiliation at being humbled by a mere child. Elsebeth gave me a sharp look but said nothing, and no one else seemed to notice the looks of venom Detmar threw at me. He would not forget or forgive, I knew that. He would try and settle the score.

But with Christmas only a day or so away there was plenty to do and I had no time to think more about it. Henkel and the others returned from Travemünde. Eberhard wanted the warehouse cleaned and refurbished and we spent most of the time there, restacking the barrels and crates, fixing the roof timbers that had partially rotted and the missing tiles on the roof. An entertaining time was spent one afternoon, rushing around flushing out the rats that were a perpetual problem.

As in England, much of Christmas was spent in church, starting with Midnight Mass. The entire family, along with

Henkel and the men working for Eberhard, were in attendance. We went to the cathedral, outside of the walled city but still on the half-island on which Lübeck was built, a huge barn-like building under construction, which was nevertheless packed with the city's most eminent burghers and decorated with foliage and flowers. I tried not to fall asleep, partly helped by a trapped sparrow that fluttered and flew around the dark recesses of the high roof randomly shitting on the congregation.

At dawn the next day we were in the church again, this time the Romanesque *Marienkirche*, Saint Mary's Church, for another dull service that I could barely understand. Elsebeth looked beautiful in a dark burgundy-coloured dress trimmed with ermine, and I spent most of the service covertly watching her from behind.

Eberhard had organised a big feast, inviting several of the city's top merchants as well as all the men working for him. The hall on the first floor was packed and I was glad to be excluded from the top table, sitting next to Otto and the other mercenaries that worked for Eberhard. After fasting for Advent, it was a relief to eat meat again and I drank too much wine, which I regretted the next morning. The next day was the Feast of Saint Stephen and there was another meal, this time with only the family, Henkel and myself. Elsebeth was seated alongside him and she looked very uncomfortable. Eberhard was in an unusually good mood, talking and laughing with Henkel and even Wilhelm. I listened, surprised that I could understand a little of what was said. Henkel showed obvious interest in Elsebeth and I could scarcely bear to watch, distracting myself by talking with Wilhelm, although I hardly heard what he said.

Why did it bother me so much that Elsebeth was to be betrothed to Henkel? It had nothing to do with me. And she was of marriageable age anyway. But Henkel? Perhaps it was knowing what he was capable of that upset me so much. Seeing him fawn and fuss over her was intolerable. I went to bed in my tiny attic room in a foul temper.

We had the next few days off and apart from continuing my morning German lessons with Wilhelm, much time was spent in a local tavern, *Zum Goldenen Hahn* – The Golden Rooster, a small hostelry down a back alley not far from Eberhard's house. It was a rough and ready place that stank of stale sweat and beer, but most of Eberhard's men drank there. One afternoon, two days before Saint Silvester's Day, I was sitting in the Rooster with Otto and another of my new comrades, Conrad, although everyone called him Kunz. Kunz was five years older than me with a pock-marked face from smallpox as a child. He had red hair, big jug ears, and was probably one of the ugliest men I had ever seen. Despite this, Kunz was easy-going and always telling jokes, and even though I could not understand most of them, he made the rest of the men laugh most of the time. But the subject we were talking about now was, for me at least, no laughing matter. 'I cannot believe her father would want his daughter to marry a man like Henkel,' I said.

'You need to keep your voice down,' Kunz said, lowering his own. 'If Henkel heard, he would kill you. You can gamble your life on that.'

'I know. He seems to have taken a particular dislike to me.'

Kunz nodded. 'I think it's because you are foreign.'

'*Ach*, Elsebeth is certainly very pretty,' Otto said, changing the subject back to the conversation. 'But if Eberhard wants his daughter to marry Henkel, I do not see what you can do about it.'

He was right. There was nothing I could do and it infuriated me. It was late afternoon, already dark outside, and I was feeling drunk and wanted to go home. I bid my comrades good night and staggered out of the tavern. The cold air slapped me in the face but it helped to sober me up as I wobbled up the deserted street. Behind me, I heard the door of the tavern open again as someone came out for a piss.

Maybe it was the amount I had drunk that made me careless, but I didn't see the shapes emerge out of the darkness from behind a wood pile until it was too late. Two figures suddenly confronted me, blocking my path, both armed with cudgels. Nevertheless, I was quick, despite my inebriation. I drew my dagger and slashed out at the figure directly in my path, taking my attacker by surprise and slicing into the man's hand. My vision exploded as something cracked me around the back of the head. I fell to the ground, dazed and bleeding, my weapon clattering out of reach, before the two men in front began laying about me with their clubs. I curled up, trying to protect my head as the blows rained down. It must have lasted only a few moments but it felt longer. I heard shouting nearby and the blows stopped. My mouth was full of blood, and the shit and mud from the street. Somewhere close, I could hear Otto's voice and the sound of running feet.

A few moments later I was pulled to my feet, my body screaming in protest. I caught a glimpse of running shadows disappearing up the street.

'Are you all right?' Otto said. 'You were lucky I came out for a piss.'

'Thank God you did. But I managed to wound one of them…'

Otto looked up the street towards where the attackers had fled. '*Ach*, where are the city watch when you need them? I shall escort you home. You look a right mess. You will have some nasty bruises when you wake up tomorrow morning.'

Otto helped carry me home, which was not far, and we saw

no sign of my attackers. I had not seen any of their faces, but I had a good idea who had attacked me. Detmar. Of course, I could have just bumped into the wrong people at the wrong time, but I didn't think so. And if I was proved right, I would make sure the bastard suffered for it.

The next morning, I awoke, crusted in blood – battered, bruised and feeling like Sir Hugh had flayed me with a morning star. When I appeared at breakfast, Wilhelm got upset, running around and fussing over me like an old woman. Eberhard looked shocked at my appearance. 'You must be more careful,' was all he said. 'The streets of Lübeck can be dangerous at night.'

I saw no sign of Detmar at breakfast, nor Elsebeth for that matter. After eating, Wilhelm took me to his room at the rear of the house and helped to clean my wounds. He was not happy. 'Richard, you should not waste so much time in that tavern. It has a bad reputation – no wonder you were attacked.'

'It did not happen in the tavern… it happened in the street. And I think I know who did it.'

'Who?'

I paused. What would it achieve by telling him? I intended to settle the score and knew Wilhelm would try and talk me out of it.

'Tell me, Richard.'

Still I hesitated. However, I could see Wilhelm would not let the matter drop. I sighed. 'Your nephew.'

'Detmar? How can you be sure? Did you see his face?'

I shook my head. 'No… and there were three of them. But I wounded one in the hand with my knife.'

Wilhelm thought for a moment. 'Do not say anything

about it, at least for now. My nephew is difficult... but we are in his father's house. Be very careful before you accuse him of anything. Eberhard is most likely to take his son's side, whatever the rights and wrongs may be.'

'I know, Eberhard hardly gives me the time of day. But if it was Detmar, I shall get my vengeance, however long it takes.'

The German lesson that followed was cut short because of my injuries. I rested for a while before joining the others for dinner. This time Detmar was there, and I saw immediately that his left hand wore a bandage. He refused to look at me and I knew. I knew it had been him that had attacked me in the alley. Elsebeth was also present and she gave me a look of concern but, under the watchful eye of her father, said nothing.

Afterwards, I needed to get some fresh air. It was still a free day for us and I considered going to the Rooster but decided against it. My body cried out in protest with each step, but I pushed on nonetheless. To my surprise, Elsebeth accosted me when I was halfway down the street. I waited as she caught me up.

'What in God's name happened to you?' she said. 'You look terrible.'

'I'm glad you noticed. I was attacked leaving the Rooster last night.'

'You should go back to bed and recover.'

'Why should you care?' I said, exasperated. 'You should be more concerned your father does not catch you talking to me.'

'He's at the warehouse. But I want to talk about Henkel again. We were interrupted by my brother last time.'

'What can I say? If your father says you are to marry him, then you are to marry him. Neither of us can do anything about that.'

'But I want to know more about him. I *need* to know more.'

I lowered my voice. Despite us speaking Latin rather than Low German, I did not want anyone to overhear. 'But it will make no difference.'

'My father has not finally decided yet if we are to marry. If I am strongly against it, he may change his mind, but I need to know.'

I found it highly unlikely that Eberhard would change his mind if his relationship with Henkel was so important. He certainly did not seem the type of man to be swayed by sentimentality over the happiness of his daughter, but I said nothing. The expression on her face was a mixture between hope and fear and I felt pity for her. 'He is not... not an honourable man.'

'Why not? What has happened that you should say this after being here for such a short time?'

I explained what had happened on the return trip from Lüneburg. When I finished, she was biting her lower lip to avoid crying.

'So now you know,' I said. 'And if you really do have any influence over your father you should try and change his mind. I cannot imagine marriage to such a man would make you happy.'

She looked so wretched at this news I had to stop myself from embracing her. God, she was beautiful.

'Well... now I know. I thank you for being honest, even though the news distresses me.'

'And I am sorry for having to upset you. But you cannot say anything to your father. If Henkel finds out I will probably die.'

'Yes... I can see that. I shall speak to my father about the betrothal but will not mention you.' She turned away for a moment, wiping what looked like a tear from her eye before turning back and changing the subject. 'Why did you hit Detmar that day we bought cloth at the market?'

'Your brother is a bastard. These bruises are a testament to that.'

'What do you mean?'

I told her about getting ambushed in the alley and wounding one of my assailants. She listened in silence as I spoke about the bandage I had seen on Detmar's hand at dinner.

'He said he cut it sharpening his knife.'

'Well, he did not.'

She thought for a moment. 'I hope you let the matter drop. Detmar is the apple of my father's eye. If he learns that you fought with him, he would probably throw you onto the street.'

'But what do you expect me to do, let him treat me like shit? I am a nobleman, son of a baron and heir to a castle and other estates. I have been trained to fight ever since I could pick up a sword. It is a matter of honour. If your brother wants more trouble with me then I shall gladly give it to him.'

'Well, I hope that does not happen. I will speak with Detmar and tell him to leave you alone. We used to be close and maybe he'll listen to me. But I must go now. Thank you for talking so honestly.'

She turned and walked away and I watched until she was out of sight. My heart was beating with excitement. When I look back at the memory of that day, so long ago now, I think it was the first time I felt love. Love is not something of which most warrior monks have any experience, but I am convinced that it was real. Now I am old, but I can still remember every detail of her – the way she laughed and the habit she had of tugging at her hair as she brushed it from her face. In the subsequent weeks, I found it hard to get her out of my mind. She would haunt my dreams, haunt my waking moments, jumping into my head at the most inappropriate times. Of course, being a merchant's daughter, she was far beneath my noble station – or at least my old station. And without a doubt, my father would never have approved. But I did not care. I was young and I was in love.

And the thought of her with Henkel was enough to make me scream.

We returned to work a few days later after Saint Silvester's Day and the Feast of the Circumcision of Christ, and to be honest, it was a relief to be busy again. I was recovering from my injuries and I no longer got strange looks every time I left the house. Eberhard sold a large consignment of salt to a Danish trader who would transport it to Falsterbo in Scania, Sweden, to be used in packing herring when the trade began the following summer. It was rare for sea-borne trade to take place in the winter but the weather, although cold, was relatively peaceful and some ships were risking the crossing from Scandinavia. Our job was to guard the cargo as his men worked and stamped the barrels with Eberhard's brand – dreary and tedious work. The amount of salt stored in the warehouse was running low and I knew that we would have to make another trip to Lüneburg soon to pick up more, a prospect that appalled me after the last time.

It was two weeks later when we made that trip again. On the second day of the journey I celebrated my fifteenth birthday, sharing a skin of wine with Otto and Kunz and speaking in whispers after everyone else had retired to their tents. I looked older than my years, many people thinking I was at least sixteen, mainly due to my size. I was bulking up as well, putting on layers of muscle due to our training and physical work and I was proud of the thin line of down that graced my upper lip and chin, thinking, naively, that I was finally a grown man.

Despite Henkel and his obvious disdain for me, I was feeling more secure with most of the other men in Eberhard's employ. With the exception of our captain and Johann, I felt that I was at last being taken more seriously, and I was slowly finding it easier to understand the conversation around me, with Otto helping to translate when I could not. Due to the mud of the roads, it took half a day longer to reach Lüneburg. The caravan we helped escort back to Lübeck was twice as large as the previous one and took two full days longer. But we saw no sign of any outlaws and thankfully there was no repeat of the experience of my first trip. However, there was one unpleasant incident. Johann and one of the mercenaries from another group had a fight over a chicken found along the road, the other man losing an eye as knives were drawn. There was a tense standoff between us and the man's comrades that nearly descended into a pitched battle before Henkel finally calmed the situation down by offering the wounded man a small bag of silver for his injury. Johann laughed about it later but Henkel cut him off with a sharp word, telling him that the money would be deducted from his purse. That shut Johann up and I felt a tremor of satisfaction. After Henkel, Johann was the colleague I liked least – a vicious, vindictive little man if ever there was one. We arrived back home the next evening – wet, tired and saddle-sore.

The following day we received no respite. Otto and I had to escort Eberhard as he called on various other merchants in the city on business that he did not share with us. However, Otto had overheard a little of what had been said and let me know as we waited in the main square outside of the town hall. 'Eberhard is in dispute with another merchant about the price of goods paid on a shipment of salt from last year. I do not know any more than that.'

I was not really interested and I looked around the main square, busy with people as usual. My attention was drawn to a man in the white habit of a Cistercian monk preaching about a pilgrimage somewhere, but I found it hard to understand and soon lost interest. Eberhard was inside the town hall and we had no idea how long he would be, so we both wandered around the market. I had a little silver in my purse but nothing interested me enough to buy and we returned to our position outside of the town hall just as our master emerged. He had a face of fury and Otto looked at me quickly, raising his eyebrows.

'Home,' Eberhard growled. We took up positions either side of him and marched the short distance back to his house, where he stamped up the stairs giving us the rest of the afternoon off.

'I am going to the Rooster to find a nice little girl I know,' Otto said. 'Are you coming?'

I declined, wanting to see Wilhelm. We bid each other goodbye and I went into the counting house on the ground floor. Wilhelm was bent over a ledger in the back room, surrounded by parchments and clutter. In the corner was a narrow pallet where he normally slept. His fingers were stained black with ink and smudges dappled his forehead but he looked up and smiled wanly at my appearance. I asked him how his work was going.

'Eberhard gets me to do the paperwork. In his opinion that is all I am good for...'

'That does not seem very clever considering your experience.'

The small German gave a shrug. He looked tired and worn out. 'Clever does not come into it. Working with Detmar is the hardest thing. He uses every chance to discredit and belittle me.'

'Well, he's a pig's turd so I wouldn't expect anything else.'

'He certainly hates me for what I did to the family. I think he resents me even more than Eberhard. To be fair to him,

Detmar does seem to have a good head for business, despite his laziness. My brother prefers his advice over mine anyway.'

'Advice, like what?'

'Perhaps you will see. He is angry with another merchant. A man called Klaus Gerber. They did some business last year without an official contract – it was all based on mutual trust. Gerber disputes the amount of money he owes. I advised Eberhard to contact the merchant guild and then take legal action with the *Rat*. They would put the case to the *Ratsherrn*. Unfortunately, I fear that my brother has other, more nefarious plans…'

'He did not seem very happy when he left the town hall.'

Wilhelm thought for a moment. 'That is interesting… maybe he did try and follow my advice after all.'

We talked briefly of other matters and I thought no more of it. It was another three days later before I learned the relevance of that conversation. I had overslept and was late to meet Henkel and the rest by the stables after dawn. I arrived out of breath sometime after the bells rang for Prime, in streets thick with fog to find Henkel, Johann, Kunz, Otto and a giant of a man from Hamburg called Makko. Makko was not the sharpest sword in the armoury and was normally only used for heavy lifting work, so I was slightly surprised to see him. Otto gave me a wink as Henkel turned and glared at me. 'You are late, English Lord. When I say be here at Prime, you are here at Prime. Do you understand?'

I mumbled an apology, not wanting to look him in the eye. After a moment he turned his attention back to the others. 'We are going to pay someone a little visit – someone that owes money to our master. It should be easy. I'm not anticipating any opposition. But stay aware and be ready for anything. Let us go.'

To my surprise we did not take any horses. We followed Henkel through the early morning streets that slowly filled with people. There was an otherworldly feeling, with all sounds muffled by the seeping fog that entangled its tendrils around everything and reduced visibility to fifty paces. We trooped across the market square and followed the ridge of the hill for a couple of streets before taking one of the roads that led down to the poorer part of town, towards the Wakenitz river where the fog was even thicker. In front of me, Kunz was telling Johann a story about some girl he knew, although I could not understand most of it, and after a while Henkel snarled at him to shut up. We carried on in silence. A few moments later we turned down a small alley with refuse littering the ground. Two dogs bickered over a piece of rotten meat. One of them turned and growled at Henkel and he gave the animal a hefty kick in its flank, sending the creature off whimpering into the fog whilst the other dog snapped up the meat and disappeared with its prize. I clenched my teeth in anger at his unnecessary brutality, but did not dare say anything. Nearby, I could smell the putrid stench of offal. I had never been to this area of the city and I found myself gripping my knife as I glanced around nervously, imagining dark figures looming out of the fog. But a moment later we emerged into a wider street with more people, passing the monastery of Saint Johannis.

A blind man approached us holding out his alms bowl with skinny arms. Henkel stopped and gave him a pfennig. He saw my expression of surprise.

'I know what it's like to be poor,' he said grimly, 'not all of us are born into money!' He led us onwards down the street, reaching the boarded-up shutters of our destination shortly afterwards. Henkel signalled Johann to take up position opposite and rapped his knuckles on the wooden door.

A moment later there was the scraping of a bolt and the door opened, revealing a man of middle age with a drooping moustache and grey unkempt hair. He tried to slam the door, but Henkel gave him no chance, kicking it open and forcing himself inside. He grabbed the man by the arm and threw him to the ground. The rest of us followed him in. Johann pulled the man to his feet and propelled him through the next doorway and into the main counting room and warehouse, throwing him to the ground again where he collapsed against a barrel. There was no one else in the room as we entered and spread out, covering the doors. Henkel said something to Makko and the big Hamburger strode over and pulled our victim to his feet, pinning his arms behind his back.

'I think you know why we are here, *Herr* Gerber.' Henkel drew his dagger and ran his finger over the sharp edge. 'We want the money you owe our master.'

The man stammered something I could not understand. Henkel approached him and held the dagger to the man's face, the point pricking him just beneath his left eye until a droplet of blood formed. I watched, uncomfortable. What in Christ's name was I doing here?

'I do not... I do not have it,' the older man said.

Henkel withdrew the dagger and slammed his other fist into Klaus Gerber's stomach. The man gasped as he doubled over and vomited all over the floor. Henkel said something to Johann and laughed. He walked to the table that occupied one side of the room. It was covered with dozens of parchments, wax tablets, an oil lamp and abacus. With his free hand, Henkel upended the table, scattering everything across the floor.

Alerted by the noise, the door at the other end of the room opened and a girl, about sixteen years old, stood there. Her eyes widened when she saw us and she was about to scream when Johann lunged forward and grabbed her, pulling her into the room.

Henkel turned his attention to the girl. 'Now what do we have here? A nice little *Mädel*. I wonder what we are going to do with you?'

I looked towards Otto in alarm. He stared at the scene with the same consternation as me. A picture of that small copse and the shepherd girl jumped into my head.

The Bible is full of stories of saints and disciples doing godly and brave things. However, real life is very different from the scriptures. Some men do bad things and many more men allow bad things to happen without doing what they know to be right. I was *that* man that day. Henkel grabbed the girl's dress and in a quick movement ripped away the cloth at the front, revealing a pert, white breast. I watched, stunned and appalled as he ran his fingers across the girl's body as Johann gripped her tightly, grinning lasciviously. Gerber tried to get to his feet but Makko held him down with ease. And, through it all, I did and said nothing.

'I have the money,' Gerber said, coming to his knees. 'Please do not hurt her... I have the money you seek.'

'Ah, so you suddenly remember now, do you?' Henkel said. 'It's strange what effect the sight of a nice tit can do to a man.' He strode back to where the old man cowered on his hands and knees. Dribbles of vomit and saliva hung in strands from his mouth.

Henkel turned on me. 'Look at our English Lord. What's the matter, Richard? Never seen a girl's tits before?'

Johann laughed. 'Not at his age. He's just fresh from his mother's tit himself.'

I kept quiet, feeling a rising anger but knowing I could do nothing.

'*Papi!*' the girl cried. She was trying, and failing, to cover her nakedness.

'Please leave my daughter alone,' Gerber said. 'She has

nothing to do with my dispute with your master. Please let her go... I will give you the money. Anything you want.'

'Anything we want. Do you hear that, Johann? Maybe it's your daughter I want! Did you think of that, you dried up piece of gristle?'

'Please... I will give you all the money I have here. Just leave my daughter alone.'

Henkel motioned to Makko to let the merchant up. He came to his feet, wiping the vomit from his mouth.

We waited as he shuffled to get his strongbox with Makko as escort. The rest of us stood there for a few awkward moments, Henkel staring at the man's daughter as if he was considering taking things further. She sobbed gently, refusing to look at any of us. I stood, hardly daring to breathe, throwing looks at an uncomfortable-looking Otto. Kunz kept swallowing repeatedly, something he did when he was nervous. After a very short time, Gerber stumbled back. Makko carried a big wooden strongbox that the older man opened with trembling fingers. Henkel strode over, looked inside and ordered Kunz and Makko to empty everything onto the floor. 'There should be enough to pay the debt,' he said. 'We will split the rest of the money between us... a finder's fee, if you like.'

The sacks of coins were put into a bag that Makko had brought and, to my relief, we left without any further violence, leaving Gerber and his daughter in tears, but alive.

'Even Henkel is not crazy enough to rape another merchant's daughter,' Otto whispered to me as we left. '*Gott sei Dank.*'

We walked back through the busy streets, still cloaked in fog, to Eberhard's house. When we returned, our master was jubilant, inviting us all for a celebratory drink in his hall. We were given a glass of wine and a small purse of pfennigs from what had been stolen, but it felt like Judas's thirty pieces of silver. I was sickened by what I had taken part in.

Eberhard looked happier than I had ever seen him. He clasped Henkel around the shoulder and raised his glass to the rest of us. 'This is as good a time to announce some special news to you all. Your captain, Henkel Kistner, has been a good friend of mine for over three years now. And friends should be rewarded, should they not?' He smiled broadly at us.

A strange feeling fluttered in my stomach like a trapped bird.

'And what better way to reward my good friend than to offer my daughter Elsebeth's hand in marriage. I have decided to accept Henkel's request for betrothal, the wedding to take place after Easter.'

The words struck me like a crossbow bolt. I should not have been surprised, but somehow, I was. Henkel beamed, his victory complete. Despite my prayers, my greatest fear had now been realised.

CHAPTER ELEVEN

The next time I saw Elsebeth was two days later at the late-morning meal. She was pale and drawn, with dark rings under her eyes. There was a deep sadness about her, although she was doing her best to hide it. She averted her gaze for the entire meal. At least Henkel was absent. Eberhard spent most of the time talking with Detmar about expanding the business by building a permanent warehouse in Lüneburg, while his wife sat in demure silence next to him. I was not sure whether Elsebeth had honoured her promise and spoken to her brother, but Detmar did not look at me. Nevertheless, I watched him out of the corner of my eye, noting his petulant, arrogant manner and feeling another urge to stick my fist in his face again. As usual at mealtimes, Wilhelm was very quiet.

My German lessons with my father's old steward were coming along well. I could now understand most basic conversation and my own spoken German was getting better, although everyone said my accent was atrocious. Kunz regularly pulled my leg over it – doing what even I thought was a fair imitation of me. It was the grammar that I found the hardest, but it did not worry me too much because I knew this would improve in time. I had always found learning languages relatively easy and didn't think Low German would be any different.

The weather was warmer than it had been but it rained almost every day, the dark clouds rolling low across the sky, ready to drench everything in moments and turning the streets into a muddy morass. Two weeks after we had recovered the debt from Klaus Gerber, Makko, Otto and me were required to load a trading vessel with salt that Eberhard had sold to a merchant from Rostock, another town along the coast to the east. There was a vicious wind that cracked and billowed the sails of the ships and skiffs on the River Trave and chased whitecaps across the water. It was precarious work, the wet weather making everything slippery and more difficult. The trader was also buying various goods from some of the city's other merchants, bales of cloth and kegs of beer for the most part, so we were not alone in loading the ship with the barrels and crates needed. A crane on the quay winched the heavier cargo into the ship's fat belly and Makko nearly had a fight with a short bull of a man, whom he had accidently bumped on the gangway, but the merchant from Rostock came running, shouting at both men before anything serious could happen. It took the best part of a day to finish the work and afterwards we were all exhausted. Otto wanted to go to the Rooster, but I wanted nothing more than to get to sleep, so I left the two of them and went home.

When I climbed the stairs to my room, I heard sobbing from behind the door as I passed Elsebeth's chamber on the second floor. For a second, I stood there, unsure what to do, but I knocked lightly on the worn wood. I heard scrambled movement and the door was opened. Elsebeth stood before me, wiping her face.

'Are you well?' I said.

She glanced over my shoulder. 'Come in, but keep quiet. If my parents catch you here there will be big trouble.'

I crept into the room. It was only a little larger than mine, with a window overlooking the small yard at the back opposite the house where Detmar lived. There was a big bed heaped with a fur blanket, along with a desk, a stool, and an iron-framed wooden casket that presumably held her clothes. I turned to face her.

'I assume you know about my betrothal?'

'Yes,' I said. 'Your father announced it after we recovered some money for him. I am sorry...'

'It was as you said. My father did not listen to my objections... I am scared of what awaits me.'

I did not know what to say, I was scared of what awaited her too. She looked at me, chewing her lip, before bursting into tears. For an awkward second, I just stood there before taking a step forward and embracing her.

It was what anyone would have done – a show of compassion, a show of sympathy to a girl in need. But I was in love, and although I didn't know it then, so was she. She hugged me back and I could smell her hair. It smelt of lavender. We clung to each other for an awkward moment before I broke away.

'I have to go,' I said. She looked at me with moist eyes, but nodded. If I stayed there a moment longer, I was scared of what might happen. I would lose my honour and bring disgrace down on both of us. I pushed past her and opened the door, climbing up the stairs to my room as quickly as possible, only relaxing when the thick wood of my own door was safely closed behind me. My heart was thundering in my chest and I felt confused and close to despair. In only two months, Elsebeth would marry Henkel and there was nothing I could do about it.

The next day I awoke in a foul mood. Outside, I could hear the steady pattering of rain again as I broke my fast in the hall on the first floor with only Wilhelm as company. My father's former steward scrutinised me carefully, asking if everything was well.

'Why should it not be?' I was more curt than I intended.

'Anything to do with Detmar?' Wilhelm had lowered his voice in case we were overheard.

'Not this time.' I refused to say any more.

Afterwards, I was distracted during my German lesson. As we were finishing up, there was a knock at the door and Eberhard appeared. 'I have to go to Lüneburg to personally sort out some business. I shall be escorted by Henkel and most of his men and will be away for several weeks. While I am absent, Detmar will be in charge.' He looked at me. 'You shall stay in Lübeck. I am expecting a delivery of furs and flax within the next day or two from a Novgorod trader who wintered in Wismar. You will work with Otto and Makko, unloading and protecting the shipment. You shall obey my son, Detmar, in everything. Is that clear?'

I nodded. Eberhard dealt almost exclusively in salt, but if the price was right, he would occasionally buy other goods, so although unusual, it was not entirely unprecedented. Nevertheless, this was mixed news. While it would be good to have Henkel gone, the thought of having to obey any commands from Eberhard's son would be unbearable. Wilhelm did not look too happy about it either. Eberhard said something more to Wilhelm and then he was gone.

Wilhelm sighed and ran his hands through his thinning hair. 'This could be an uncomfortable few weeks. You will have to try and keep your temper, Lord Richard. Detmar will be looking at ways to provoke you. This must not be allowed to happen, otherwise...'

He didn't have to say any more; we would be kicked out of Eberhard's house and become homeless.

It was two days later that the ship, a cog bigger than *Christofer*, appeared in the Trave at the end of its journey. I was working in the warehouse along with Otto and Makko but in truth, there was little to do, and we gathered in the entrance of the yard to watch as the cog was towed slowly into the harbour. The rigging looked ragged and the half-furled sail was battered and holed, testament to the bad weather encountered on its long journey across the Baltic. Soon there would be plenty of work to do and it was already early afternoon. 'We've got our work cut out now,' I said to Otto. 'I will let Detmar know that the ship is docking.'

In the warehouse, emptier than I had ever seen it, Detmar was stocktaking with another young man, a blue-eyed youth with hair the colour of straw that I had seen him with several times previously. They were laughing and drinking wine, in fact it seemed to me they were drinking more wine than actually working. Detmar sneered when he saw me, saying something to his friend who giggled like a child. I remembered Wilhelm's words about keeping my temper. 'The ship is docking now,' I said. 'But we will need help unloading it. The three of us will not finish it by nightfall.'

'Then you will have to spend the night guarding it on the wharf,' Detmar said. 'There shall be no more help.'

I waited outside with Otto and Makko until the ship was properly moored. It took an eternity until it was ready for us to unload and Otto grumbled, impatient like me to get started. Only Makko was unperturbed at the time and the thought of sleeping the night outside. 'He's too simple-minded to realise how cold it will be,' Otto whispered to me, making sure that the big Hamburger didn't overhear.

The ship's master, a short man with most of his teeth

missing was just as anxious to get the ship unloaded. 'We have to clear the hold today as we are taking on a new cargo tomorrow morning at first light.'

For the rest of the afternoon we worked relentlessly, stacking the bundles of furs and flax with the help of the twelve-man crew. It was wearisome work. The goods stacked up slowly on the quay but we had no time to transport any of it to the warehouse. 'That bastard, Detmar, is too miserly to spend some silver and employ some much-needed help,' Otto complained. 'Even Eberhard wouldn't leave us to do this alone.'

When the bell rang from inside the city for Vespers, we were far from finished. Detmar came to check our progress and seemed pleased to order us to spend the night with the unloaded cargo on the quay before disappearing for home. The docks slowly became quieter. We carried on working until it was totally dark before finally collapsing in exhaustion. Only Makko was untired, but he was an ox so he didn't count. Otto made a small fire with some driftwood, but we had to keep it hidden behind the stack of goods as it was forbidden and we did not want any trouble from the watch. One of the crewmen on the ship felt sorry for us and gave me a small flask of wine that eased our thirst.

'It could be worse.' Otto took a hefty swig of the wine and smacked his lips greedily. 'It could be raining.'

I grunted. It might have been dry but it was damned cold. Even the fire did not make much difference. We sat and talked in soft tones. Otto spoke about his childhood growing up near Münster and I wrapped myself in my cloak and listened, feeling homesick for England. After a while, I felt the cold creeping into my bones. The small amount of driftwood was almost consumed and the fire, never large to start with, was already dying down. I volunteered to go and look for some more, thinking the movement would warm me, so I walked the length of the empty quay, passing several moored ships and skiffs rocking on the swell, enjoying the quiet, apart from the creaking of the wooden hulls and slapping of halyards in the wind. Normally bustling, I had never seen the harbour so deserted and at peace. I remembered there were some broken barrels in the yard of Eberhard's warehouse that we could use for firewood, so I headed past the gate and stopped.

Through the small window I could see the glow of an oil lamp. That was strange. There was no reason why a light would be left burning and it was an obvious fire hazard. Perhaps there was an intruder. I drew my dagger and cautiously approached the main door. To my surprise, it was unlocked. Surely Detmar would have locked it before leaving for the night?

I slipped in. Most of the warehouse was sheathed in darkness, with the only light coming from the lamp placed on a barrel near the double doors. I paused to let my eyes adjust to the gloom, but I was aware of a grunting noise coming from one end of the warehouse. My heart was thumping in my ears as I tiptoed along the wall towards the sound, clasping my knife tightly. The hairs on my neck were standing up – there was someone here. Ahead was the partition that split the main warehouse from the small office at the back. I turned the corner and saw what was making the noise.

Detmar was bent over his young blond friend. Both men had their breeches around their ankles and Detmar's face was red and lathered with sweat. It was obvious what they had been doing. What they were still doing. My arrival stopped everything. For a moment we stared at each other in shock as the enormity of the situation became apparent. Detmar was at a loss for words and in that moment, I realised I had him.

I looked in his eyes and slowly smiled. Still he said nothing. Then without saying anything myself, I turned and slowly retraced my steps back out of the warehouse. I felt stunned about what I had witnessed, but also a strong sense of elation.

Because I knew that from that day onwards, I would never have any further problems with Eberhard's son.

After an uncomfortable night, the three of us were awake well before dawn. We were tired and cold, but when I remembered what had happened in the warehouse it made it all worthwhile. I had not told either of my comrades about what I had witnessed. I could always tell them later, but if they said something, it could jeopardise the new-found power I had over Detmar.

It took all morning to load the cargo into the warehouse, and while we sweated and struggled, we saw nothing of Detmar or his friend. I was not really surprised after the night before. He must have been terrified about what I would do. And that was just it. After thinking it over during the night, I knew I was not going to do anything. But of course, Detmar did not know that. Afterwards, the three of us decided we had worked enough for the day and so we went down the Rooster and got pissed all afternoon. Detmar never showed up.

The next day, I was summoned to the hall by a servant where I met Otto who had been given the same instructions. After a while, we were joined by Eberhard's wife and Elsebeth. Elsebeth's mother spoke in a quiet voice and I found myself straining to hear every word she was saying. One of us was required to escort Elsebeth to the market and the other to accompany Eberhard's wife to the church. I prayed I would be given the former job, but she told me that I would be escorting her to the church. Otto's face lit up and I cursed silently to myself. Elsebeth said nothing. She looked distracted.

I was to escort Eberhard's wife to Saint Mary's Church, where she spent some time praying and then more giving alms to the dozens of beggars outside. I knew the slight, demure woman was very pious, and she seemed to spend most of her time in worship. There was even a tiny chapel in an alcove next to the hall on the first floor. I rarely saw her at Eberhard's house. She ran the household efficiently but she barely spoke a word to me and spending half the day in church at prayer was not my idea of a good time. But of course, I had no choice. I wondered how Otto and Elsebeth were getting on.

We returned to the house after Nones and Eberhard's wife disappeared upstairs, probably to pray again. In the yard at the back, the servants were beating blankets and furs on a rack to clean them. I paused and looked towards the two-storey house on the other side of the yard where Detmar and his wife lived. Wilhelm had told me he had married only four months before we had arrived, but I had only ever seen her at the feast on the first day of Christmas. I wondered if Detmar was at home, but I doubted it. With no instruction from Eberhard's son, I decided to go and speak to Wilhelm in the counting house on the ground floor.

'Have you seen Detmar in the last two days at the warehouse?' Wilhelm asked the moment he saw me.

'Not since we started unloading that ship from Novgorod,' I said. 'But why concern yourself? Surely you are pleased not to see him.'

Wilhelm smiled. 'I cannot pretend it does not make my life easier. But it is strange... he has completely disappeared. His wife Brigitta hasn't seen him either.'

That did not surprise me at all. No doubt he was tucked up somewhere with his pretty friend.

There was nothing for me to do, so I decided to go to the warehouse yard and practise my sword-craft, striking a wooden post that we used and then sharpening my sword and knife with a whetstone. After a short time I was joined by Otto, who turned up with a smile on his face.

'*Ach*, that Elsebeth is certainly a charming girl,' Otto said. 'I can see why you like her.'

I was not sure if he was trying to rile me so I scowled at him.

'But to be honest, I think I prefer her maidservant, Agnes. She has a nice little arse and she could not take her eyes off me all day. She has good taste, that is for sure.'

'Is that all you think about?' I said. 'I hope you had a better day than me. Eberhard's wife does nothing but pray. I think even God must be weary of hearing from her.'

Otto laughed and we practised with sword and shield until it began to get dark. I returned to Eberhard's house as the bells rang for Vespers, going straight to the hall for supper where I was joined again by Wilhelm, while Otto predictably went down the Rooster. After a meal of lamb stew, I climbed the stairs to my room, intending to get some sleep. I was about to strip off when I heard the creaking of footsteps on the stairs, followed by a gentle, tentative tap at the door. Of course, I was in no doubt who it would be. Elsebeth.

'I need to talk to you.' She slipped past me and into the tiny space, deftly avoiding the beam on which I usually hit my head.

I closed the door quickly, inviting her to sit down on the bed whilst I perched on the stool.

'Have you seen Detmar?' she said.

'You are the second person who has asked me that today. No, I have not seen him for two days.'

'Has anything happened? Between the two of you, I mean.'

'Why would you think that?' Whether she knew about her brother's tendencies I did not know, but I was not about to tell her.

'Because of your earlier fight. And because you spend most of your time at the warehouse.'

'He has not been there since we last unloaded. He ordered us to sleep the night on the wharf to guard the goods, just to save a few pfennigs.'

'That does not surprise me. He has always been miserly. But I am concerned about him...'

'I am sure he will turn up.' I wanted to change the subject. 'But it is certainly nice not to have Henkel around.'

An awkward silence followed and I was aware of my heart thumping in my chest.

'I do not want to talk about Henkel,' Elsebeth said.'I wish I was to marry someone like you.'

We embraced, and all my resolve and notions of honour were swept away like flotsam on the tide as I kissed her. When she parted my lips with her tongue I didn't care anymore. Everything that had happened and my life that had been turned upside down suddenly did not matter. All that mattered was her.

CHAPTER TWELVE

The next morning, I awoke thinking I must have been dreaming, my mind mulling over the events of the night. I could barely believe what had happened. Of course, Elsebeth had left shortly afterwards, with only a quick kiss to remind me of what we had just done. When I broke my fast there was no sign of her, but we needed to talk, so afterwards I went to her room. She was not there. I considered going to see Wilhelm, but I was concerned the canny German would take one look at me and guess what had happened, so I decided to skip my class and go to the warehouse at the docks.

When I got there, I found Otto and Makko in the yard sitting on some barrels talking, although Otto had a bored expression on his face. There was still no sign of Detmar. My big friend was pleased to see me and he suggested we did some practising with sword and shield again. 'Anything to get away from that Hamburger lump,' Otto confided, out of earshot of Makko. 'Talking with him is more tedious than going to church.'

But after only a short time training, he could see that my heart was not really in it as he caught me a stinging blow on my sword arm. 'You seem distracted this morning.' He looked at me with raised eyebrows. 'Has anything happened?'

I led him further away from where Makko sat carving a figurine out of a piece of wood whilst whistling a tune. I told him about the night before with Elsebeth.

He looked at me incredulously. '*Mein Gott*, Richard! If Henkel or her father were to find out…'

He did not say any more. If they found out, I was dead.

'What are you going to do?'

'I do not know yet. But I think I love her, Otto.'

My friend shook his head in exasperation. 'Love? But this is madness. You should come down the Rooster more often and meet some of the girls there. You are on thin ice, Richard. This makes me very nervous.'

'Me too,' I admitted. My mind was in turmoil. The truth be told, I did not know what to do.

'Was it your first time?'

I felt my cheeks blushing and I was about to lie when we were interrupted by the arrival of Detmar. He strode in as if he had never been missing, ordering us to move the goods from the ship to another part of the warehouse, and make room for the salt expected back with Eberhard from Lüneburg. He was alone, without his friend, and I noted he refused to look me in the eye, giving me a spark of satisfaction.

After explaining what he wanted, he disappeared into the office at the back where I had caught him with his friend. But thankfully, he didn't stay long, leaving as quickly as he had arrived, allowing us to get on with our work unmolested. It took the rest of the day to finish our task and afterwards the three of us decided to go to the Rooster to quench our thirst. As usual, it was busy with labourers, apprentices and artisans, and the air was thick with the stink of sweat, stale ale and the fried sausage that was the establishment's favourite. A group of stevedores on a table near the door started singing. Despite the crowd, we managed to get seats on the end of a bench. I could see that Otto wanted to talk again about Elsebeth but Makko's presence made that impossible. I was glad. There was nothing more I wanted to say about it.

Three beers later, I was beginning to get bored. All Makko ever talked about was food and Otto was more interested in one of the serving girls, a busty brunette named Eva who grinned at him every time she passed our table with flagons of beer. We had just ordered our fourth drink when the door opened and a girl, no more than sixteen, came in tentatively, pausing as she scanned the tavern. I recognised her immediately. It was Agnes, Elsebeth's maidservant.

One of the stevedores made a lewd comment to Agnes and both Otto and me got angrily to our feet, but Hilde the landlady, a woman as wide as she was tall, stepped in and shouted at the man to shut up, threatening to throw him out if he continued. Poor Agnes stood looking flustered and out of place, before she noticed me and Otto. She came over and Otto immediately perked up, all interest in the serving girl lost.

Agnes looked at me. 'My mistress is outside. She wants to talk to you.'

I needed no second invitation, thanking her before pushing the door open and going out into the cold air. Elsebeth was waiting, dressed in a long, grey cloak with the hood pulled up to hide her identity. I resisted the urge to take her in my arms.

'I must talk with you,' she said.

'I tried to find you earlier but you were not at home,' I said, looking at her. 'I have been thinking over last night. I want to do the honourable thing. I want to marry you.'

Her eyebrows raised in an expression of surprise. 'But my father will never accept that. And Henkel…'

'I know this, of course. That is why we will have to leave Lübeck.'

'And go where?'

'I do not know. But it hardly matters... as long as we are together. I can find work. A man with a sharp sword is always in demand.'

She shook her head firmly and my heart dropped. 'It would never work,' she said. 'They will come after us. I do not want to spend the rest of my life living in fear.'

'But we can go far away from here, somewhere they will never find us—'

'No, Richard. It would bring disgrace and ridicule upon my family. It would kill my father. I cannot do that. Family is everything to him. And what about your friend, my uncle. If we were to disappear, he would be thrown out – or worse. This decision would affect more than just us. It would destroy my entire family.'

I had not thought about Wilhelm and I shuffled uneasily, but I was not going to give up. 'Wilhelm could come with us.' Even as I spoke, I knew my father's steward would never agree. Could I reward his loyalty to me by abandoning him, running away like a thief in the night?

She shook her head. 'This is madness, Richard. I am a woman and must live the life preordained for me. My mother believes that all women are condemned to their fate because of Eve eating the apple in the Bible. We are unclean and sinful – the physical manifestations of lust. Perhaps she is right...'

I turned away and cursed, feeling a rising despair. 'But I love you,' I said, realising how pathetic I sounded.

'And I love you too. But we both knew the situation. I am to marry Henkel and neither of us can change that... we have to accept the paths laid out for us. Love is something only found in bards' stories. This is the reality of our situation. I am sorry, Richard, I really am. I wish it were otherwise.'

'Me too,' I said with resignation. 'So, what happens now? I suppose you will meekly marry Henkel and put up with everything he does to you.'

'What choice do I have?' She shuddered. 'Running away with you is hardly a solution, however much I would like it to be.'

I turned, hearing the door of the tavern open. It was Agnes.

'I have to go,' Elsebeth said. 'My mother might spend most of her time talking to God, but even she will notice my absence if I am away too long.'

My stomach lurched as if I'd been punched.

'Do not worry about Agnes,' Elsebeth said, noting my look at her maidservant. 'You can trust her completely.'

I said nothing.

'I am sorry, Richard. I know this is not what you wanted to hear. By God's grace, perhaps we can talk again later. I hope you do not hate me…'

'Of course I do not hate you… I love…' The words stuck in my throat.

She took my hand and gave it a quick squeeze before disappearing into the darkness with Agnes running to keep up.

I stood there for a moment, fighting back tears before turning to go back into the tavern, determined, if nothing else, to get as drunk as possible.

For the next few days I only saw Elsebeth at dinner times, late morning in the hall. While she was friendly, she was also distant, without any meaningful conversation taking place between us. Although I never spoke to him about the matter, I caught Wilhelm looking at me strangely one morning and worried that he might suspect something. If he did, I was sure my father's old steward would not have approved. The only person who knew what had happened was Otto, who did his best to cheer me up, always trying to drag me down the Rooster whenever he could, where he said I could have my choice of girls. I was not interested. I wanted Elsebeth, nobody else. Instead, I chose to stay in most evenings, hoping that Elsebeth might change her mind and come to my room again. But she never did.

There was enough work at the warehouse to keep us all busy. A small caravan, only six carts, had been sent on earlier by Eberhard. It arrived on Saint Perpetua's Day with news that our master himself was expected back within the next three days. The thought of Henkel returning to Lübeck put me in a sour mood. And with Eberhard back home there would be no chance of spending more time with Elsebeth, even if we both wanted.

I was feeling downcast and miserable when I wandered home from the warehouse in the approaching darkness. There was no hurry to return to Eberhard's house and my soulless attic room, so I decided to take a short detour to the market in the city's main square, despite not having much money to buy anything more than a sausage or fruit pasty from one of the food vendors. Although most of the stalls had started to pack their produce, there were still plenty of people around, trying to haggle a bargain or on their way home. I ambled aimlessly through the booths with their coloured awnings, oblivious to the noise and smells of the crowd, before spying Agnes at a stall some thirty paces ahead. A moment later, I saw Elsebeth, wearing a plain grey cloak over her gown. She was talking animatedly to a cloth seller but there was no sign of anyone else. I was sure that Eberhard would not have approved of his daughter being abroad without an escort. As I approached, I noted a youth standing behind her, scruffily dressed and dirty. Another boy, younger but as unkempt as the first, confronted her with his hand out for alms. Elsebeth reached for the purse concealed by her cloak, before giving the younger boy a coin. The youth behind, seeing where she kept her money, pulled something from under his rags and I glimpsed the flash of a knife as he quickly cut the cord to her purse. It was done so fast and deftly that no one noticed, certainly not Elsebeth herself, Agnes or the stall-holder to whom they were talking. But I noticed, and I dashed forward, determined to stop the thief.

The youth walked away calmly as if he had done nothing, bumping into a thin, middle-aged man. If I had not been watching him like an eagle, I would have missed him thrust the purse into the older man's hand. He immediately hid it under his cloak. When the youth disappeared into the crowd, I accosted the older man, now also walking away, grabbing him by the arm and pushing him back towards the stall where Elsebeth and Agnes, still unaware, continued talking with the fabric seller.

'*Was ist los?*' the man spluttered. He tried to pull his arm free.

I held on firmly, calling out to Elsebeth who turned around, surprised to see me. 'Richard, what are you doing here?'

'This man has stolen your purse. We need to call the city watch and have him arrested.'

'Let me go. I have nothing to do with any theft!'

We were beginning to attract the attention of those around us. I lifted the man's dark-green cloak and saw he had several other pouches hanging from his belt. However, Elsebeth's distinctive red purse was still clutched in his other hand. I grabbed it and ripped it from his fingers, lifting it up to show Elsebeth who was walking over to us.

The man punched me in the face. It was so quick and unexpected I immediately released my grip on his other arm. For a second, I was blinded by pain. Then he ran, darting through the crowd, narrowly avoiding another stall-holder who made an unsuccessful attempt to grab him. By the time I had recovered he was gone. I rubbed my sore eye as I gave Elsebeth her purse back.

She looked at me gratefully. 'We should get you home and seen to. You are going to have a bruise tomorrow.'

I shrugged, trying to look nonchalant. 'It would not be the first time.'

'Thank you,' she said. 'If my father knew I was in the market without an escort he would be angry.'

'I agree. I looked over the heads of the people around us but saw no sign of the thief. 'I would understand his concern.'

'But you were all busy in the warehouse. And I am not a child anymore. This is my city. I will not be scared to go where I will.'

I nodded. It was not my business and I did not want to argue with her. I was just glad I had been there to stop the theft. We walked home together, Elsebeth's reason for coming to the market forgotten. Once back in Eberhard's house, she insisted on examining my injury, sitting me on a stool in the kitchen, clamping a damp cloth to my face as she ushered the cook and servants away. We had seen no sign of her mother, but I assumed she must be praying.

And then, of course, the inevitable happened. She kissed me and I responded. Despite everything she had said the previous time we had spoken, love triumphs over all. I knew she felt the same love for me as I had for her and what was wrong with that? As we fumbled and groped like two moonstruck young lovers, I forgot about the sin and the fact I would be condemned to hell. I forgot about the risk and what would happen if we were caught. I even forgot the danger of Henkel finding out. Nothing else mattered. I took her on the wooden table in the middle of the room. Her gasps of pleasure seemed loud enough to wake the dead. Even now, some forty years later, I still remember it so clearly, despite it only lasting a few moments. On many a cold, windswept night in Livonia, when the snow piled up to the eaves of the dormitory I shared with my fellow warrior monks, I would savour every detail of what happened between us, the memory helping to boost my spirits when everything else was so dark. Of course, God sees everything, and He knew our sin. It bothered me later. I would spend many sleepless nights worrying about God's judgement, when I knew I would be found wanting. Now, I do not care. Why would the Almighty, in all his power, care about what a mere boy of fifteen was doing? It is the priests that care. Always was and always will be. They are jealous of anyone who might be having any pleasure. Damn them all. Damn the whole miserable, dried-up, cheerless lot of them.

Afterwards, Elsebeth readjusted her dress and all but fled from the room, leaving me alone for a moment. I left the kitchen shortly after, passing several servants who looked at me questionably. Did they know what we had been doing only a few moments earlier? I felt their eyes on me when I passed before slowly climbing the stairs up to my lonely room.

As we had been warned, Eberhard and the others returned three days later from Lüneburg at the head of a large caravan transporting the white gold. It was a day of driving drizzle that soaked everything and cut visibility to a few paces. As usual, Makko, Otto and myself were in the warehouse and we stopped working as the dozen or so wagons rattled through the gates into the yard, their wheels thick with mud. All the riders that accompanied them were soaked and weary-looking. I looked on despondently as Henkel rode behind Eberhard, sharing a comment with Johann. Now it was too dangerous for anything to happen between me and Elsebeth again.

With only a perfunctory greeting, Eberhard and Henkel left quickly, leaving the rest of the men to help us unload the wagons. It was good to see Kunz again and I realised I had missed his easy smile and ready humour. When the warehouse was finally filled, we all went to the Rooster. Next to the roaring fire over a beer, Kunz explained that they had run into outlaws near Juliusburg and there had been a brief fight. 'We saw them off, though, without too much trouble – mainly due to Henkel.'

'Henkel?' I asked.

'Yes, he fought like a demon, killing two attackers before the rest of us even knew what was happening. The man is certainly someone you want on your side in a fight.'

I reflected on that while I gulped my beer. That night I drank more alcohol than I ever had in my life, having to be carried home by Otto and Makko, neither in a better state than me. The next morning, I awoke in beer- and vomit-stained clothes with no idea how I had made it upstairs to my room. I overslept again and, after a change of tunic and quick wash in the yard, I was late getting to the warehouse. When I turned up, I was met by a smirking Johann who told me Henkel wanted to see me in the back office. With my head pounding like it was being struck by a hammer, I followed him through the warehouse, feeling uneasy. Henkel was sat behind the wooden desk, cleaning his nails with a dagger.

Henkel fixed me with his stare. 'You look terrible, *Lord* Richard. I hope your night of debauchery was worth it.'

I nodded, feeling my heart begin to beat faster.

'Elsebeth says you recovered her purse after she was robbed in the market. That is good. That is your job. What I want to know is how did you let a thief get so close?'

I didn't know what to say. If I told him it was just chance, he would tell Eberhard and Elsebeth would get into trouble about going to the market alone. But otherwise it was as though I had not been doing my job properly. 'There were too many people...' Even to my ears it sounded weak. And although I had done nothing wrong, I felt guilty.

Henkel said nothing and I felt my apprehension grow. After an awkward silence he spoke again. 'But that is not the reason I wanted to see you.'

I waited, feeling Johann's eyes boring into the back of my head.

'I have been told that you saw something – something you should not have seen.'

I thought for a moment, not understanding. My confusion must have been written across my face.

'*Det-mar*,' Henkel said, as if I was simple-minded.

I thought back to when I had caught Detmar in this very room. 'What about it?'

'Let me make this clear, *Ausländer*,' Henkel said. 'You did not see anything. Detmar was not here that night.'

'I have not said anything to anyone. Why would I?'

'You tell me,' Henkel said. 'Just as long as you understand the reality of the situation. I do not want you thinking you can use this information for your own gain.'

I felt myself flush as anger welled up in me, but I fought to contain it. 'Why do you hate me so? I have done nothing to you...'

Henkel looked at me in surprise. 'It is true I do not like you, English Lord. I do not like you because you are arrogant. You think yourself better than the rest of us due to your noble birth. Everything you say and do makes this obvious – the way you look down your nose at us lesser mortals. And I do not know why you are here. This is not your land. This is not your city. And this is not your home. You and Wilhelm are only trouble – here to benefit off the goodwill of my friend and patron. Let me make one thing clear... If you ever cross me, Detmar or any other member of Eberhard's family, then I will take great pleasure in breaking you like the young colt you are. I shall make you regret you ever decided to come to the Empire. Now get out of my sight and return to your work.'

I fled the room, pushing past Johann back into the main room of the warehouse. Otto, stacking barrels at the other end, looked over with an expression of concern on his wide, guileless face.

My mind raced. Obviously, Detmar had spoken to Henkel, which meant that Henkel already knew about his penchant for boys. Maybe this was what Elsebeth had meant when she had feared Henkel had a hold over Eberhard. It was certainly true that Detmar's punishment would be dire and the family disgraced if it was made public. And Henkel had just confirmed what I already knew. He hated me. Any tiny suspicion that there was something between me and his future wife would produce catastrophic results. There would be no benefit of the doubt or mercy. Somehow, I could not help but think that things were drawing towards an explosive conclusion for me here in Lübeck.

A conclusion that would probably lead to my own death.

CHAPTER THIRTEEN

With Eberhard home, Elsebeth adopted a polite aloofness with me, much like she had when I had first arrived. I became sick four days after Eberhard's return, with a raging fever that confined me to the pallet in my room, where I tossed and turned in a sea of sweat. Considering my illness, I had hoped that perhaps she would come and visit but I was disappointed. She was probably preparing for the betrothal party that Eberhard had declared at the first meal since his return. The betrothal would take place in the main hall of the house, with most of the city's eminent merchants and officials invited.

I was tended by Wilhelm, who would come and see me twice a day with an awful concoction that he assured me would help. It tasted so bad it made me feel I would throw my guts up. On the day of the betrothal party I was still ill – and glad of it, having a good excuse to avoid attending the party going on two floors beneath me. Of course, I could still hear the voices, music and sounds of revelry as I lay in my room and, however hard I tried to ignore it, I could not help but think of Elsebeth down below with Henkel. My only company was the mice that scurried around in the eaves of the roof, but I was well used to them by now and I hardly noticed anymore.

Sometime into the party I was visited by Wilhelm, this time with a flagon of wine rather than his foul potion, and he sat down on the stool at the end of the bed.

'You should be enjoying the party,' I said, 'rather than being upstairs with me.'

He smiled, looking tired. 'They will not miss me. I'm as popular as a leper at the Christmas feast. And now you are feeling a little better I would talk to you.'

'About what?'

The German sighed deeply, as though in pain. 'About my niece... Elsebeth.'

'What about her?'

'I am not *blind*, Lord Richard, and I hope I am not a fool either. I have seen the way you look at her.'

His words struck me as hard as any blow. I thought I had been extremely discreet. 'Does Eberhard suspect?'

'I do not think so. My brother is not known for his sensitivity and he would have said something if he knew. But, Lord Richard, please listen to me... Nothing can be allowed to happen. Do you understand?'

I dropped my gaze.

'*Gott im Himmel*,' Wilhelm said. 'Something has already happened, hasn't it?'

'I love her, Wilhelm,' I blurted out. 'I wish it was not true, for both of us, but I do.'

Wilhelm seemed to deflate, lowering his head and covering his face with his hands. He mumbled something in German I did not understand.

'But nothing will happen again,' I said with more aggression than I meant. 'How can it? With Eberhard and Henkel back home, I have no chance to even speak with her. And she will not go against her father and refuse to wed Henkel. So you have nothing to worry about!'

Wilhelm looked at me and shook his head. He came to his feet slowly and paused at the door. 'I hope you are right, Lord Richard, because if you are wrong it could finish both of us. I have to return to the party, although I wish it were otherwise. My brother is easy to take insult – especially where I am concerned. It is good timing that you are ill... it would prove difficult for you at the party. But please get well soon.'

And with that he left me to my misery.

It was two days later before I was well enough to leave my room and another day before I returned to work. I detached myself as much as possible from everyone around me, withdrawing into my own despair, concentrating on the work I was assigned and disdaining the camaraderie of Otto, Kunz and the rest. Wilhelm did not mention our conversation again.

There was no sign of Elsebeth at mealtimes. It was as if she had disappeared after her betrothal. The wedding was now only four weeks away and I wondered how she was dealing with the prospect of marrying Henkel. I worried about her and wondered if she thought about me. But if she did, I saw no sign of it.

There was plenty of work to do at the warehouse, but I avoided the usual arms practice with my comrades as well as choosing to shun the Rooster afterwards. Every night I would retire to my room alone, revelling in my sorrow as if it was justly deserved. As the days counted down to the wedding, I became even more downcast, until Otto pulled me aside late one sunny day, with our work finished. His wide, honest face was creased in concern.

'Are you well, Richard? These past weeks you are hardly talking. Everyone has noticed – even Henkel. Can I help, we are friends, *ja?*'

'Just because we are friends does not mean I have to tell you everything, Otto. Can you not understand that I do not want to talk? Leave me alone.' I saw the flicker of hurt cross his face, hating myself even more for taking out my frustrations on my friend.

'Well, I am sorry to be concerned,' Otto said. 'I know it is a hard time for you... what with the wedding—'

'Did I not just say I had no wish to talk about it? Why not piss off to the Rooster with the others and leave me alone!'

Otto's face darkened. 'I am sorry, Richard. I thought friends were supposed to help each other in difficult times. I am sorry if I was mistaken. Maybe some of the others are right... maybe you do think you are better than the rest of us.' He turned and left me staring at his back as he rejoined the others, some of them looking at me warily.

I let him go. I cursed myself, but my natural pride prevented me from apologising for my hastily spoken words – words I had regretted the moment they were uttered. I have never been a patient man and my natural self-confidence makes many consider me arrogant and unapproachable. And they are probably right. That was pretty much what Henkel had confirmed in the warehouse. Now, at my venerable age, I do not give a rat's turd what people think of me. Anyway, arrogance is not the worst sin and I have long since learned to live with it.

But the next few weeks proved to be some of the loneliest of my life. My comrades all but ignored me – even Otto, and neither of us could summon up the courage to talk and reach a reconciliation. The only person who spoke with me was Wilhelm, and after our previous conversation about Elsebeth, I was cautious about bringing up the subject again. To pass my time alone, I wrote another letter to Alice, informing her I was in Lübeck and asking for any news from home. My plan was to give the letter and sufficient coin to anyone at the harbour who was travelling to England, and hope it was delivered. When I finished it with only a little spilt ink, my sister's face came into my head and I felt a grief descend like a downpour of rain. I hoped she was well.

However, with the arrival of Easter, things improved, at least as far as food was concerned. With Lent over, we could eat meat again and, after a long service in Saint Mary's Church, there was a feast in Eberhard's hall. Everyone who worked for him was invited. Elsebeth was there, but she sat at the top table with her father and Henkel and I had no chance to talk with her. Instead, I remained subdued, ignoring the chatter of my comrades around me, picking at my food despite relishing the meat again. Eberhard had spared no expense, and along with the rich meal of pork, lamb and various dishes of eggs and vegetables, he had laid on some entertainers and we watched a play depicting the crucifixion, replete with children running around dressed as angels. A couple of times during the performance, I caught Otto looking at me, but he turned away every time our eyes met. Afterwards, Kunz told a long story about a whore named Hedwig he had once nearly married, boasting about her being the best hump to be had, but I retired to my room before I heard the end, glad to be away from the stifling atmosphere and my comrades' apathetic glances.

With Easter over, it was only a matter of days until the wedding and I became even more melancholic. I was given the night shift with Friedrich, a new worker a few years older than me. It was our duty to guard the warehouse and ensure that the valuable salt was safe. One of us would sleep while the other kept watch, the time measured by a burning candle marked at intervals to show the passage of time. I was happy with the task – Friedrich was a man of small words and I could spend hours thinking and mulling over my ill luck. Our work was over when the city bells rang for Prime. I could return home, just as the city around me started work, retiring gratefully to my room to sleep.

My night shifts finished three days before the wedding, so unfortunately, I had no excuse to avoid the occasion. I dreaded the thought of seeing Elsebeth. The day dawned bright and warm and, with a heavy heart, I prepared for the ceremony, dressing in the best of my two tunics, a black garment of what had once been good quality wool but was now beginning to look threadbare. The wedding was to take place at Saint Peter's Church and I walked the short distance with Wilhelm in virtual silence. Outside the doors of the church, a large crowd had already gathered. I recognised some people, my comrades, of course, and any guests who had been invited to the house, but most were strangers to me. Although there was no sign of Eberhard himself, Henkel was waiting with the rest of the family, as well as several of Eberhard's wealthy merchant peers. Wilhelm told me he would have to stand with the family but I had no intention, or need to do so, so I lost myself in a group of well-wishers near the back. I could see Otto talking to Kunz, laughing about something trivial, no doubt. While I was watching, he turned and met my eye, giving me a tentative smile. I nodded curtly and looked away as the murmur of voices around me rose. Elsebeth and her father had arrived.

She looked stunning. Emotion welled up in me as she glided through the crowd on the arm of her father. Her face was veiled, which meant I could not see her expression, and she glanced neither left or right as they reached the circle of people at the door of the church, where Henkel waited with the priest. Elsebeth took her place on the left side facing the church and I remembered a lesson from Father Bertram – it seemed so long ago now – where he had explained that this was because women were created out of Adam's left rib. I wondered how my old tutor was managing in a Cranham run by my uncle or whether he was even still alive.

I didn't even really listen to most of the ceremony. However, my attention was wrenched back when the priest addressed the crowd asking if anyone knew any reason why the two should not be married.

Yes, I wanted to scream at the top of my voice. Yes. I love her and she is no virgin. But of course, I said nothing. I felt Otto's eyes on me but I refused to look at him.

After the brief pause, the ceremony resumed, culminating in Henkel giving Elsebeth a ring. A few more words were said and they kissed. I looked away as people clapped, before the priest blessed them and led everyone into the church. I was one of the last to follow and I paused as I reached the door. Did I really want to go inside and help celebrate the marriage of the woman I loved to the man I hated?

I decided I did not, turning away as the last of the crowd filed in and the door closed behind them.

It felt awkward standing outside on my own, but a moment later the thick door of the church opened again and Otto came out. 'Are you coming in?' he said.

'I don't think so.'

'But you will be missed.'

I sighed. 'Not in the church – they will be too busy praying to notice. But I will have to attend the feast. I am dreading it.'

'I can imagine. It cannot be easy for you…'

'No, it's not.' We looked at each other in awkward silence for a moment before I spoke again. 'I do not suppose I have been easy to work with either.'

Otto smiled. 'Not really…'

'I am sorry. It was not fair taking out my problems on you.'

'But I understand… Does that mean we are friends again?'

'I suppose so.' The truth be told, I had missed his companionship far more than I would have thought or admitted.

'We can drink on it at the feast,' Otto said. 'But I had better go back in.'

I nodded and he pulled open the creaking church door, disappearing back inside. It was sometime later before the doors opened again and everyone emerged. I mingled with the people, oblivious to the buzzing of conversation as I waited for Wilhelm to come out, before the whole procession proceeded up the street to the market square. The wedding feast was in the town hall, the half-brick, half-wood building that dominated the city's main square, taking place in the main hall on the first floor. It was far bigger than Eberhard's hall at home and it seemed that most of the city was packed inside as the guests spoke in small groups before taking their places at the trestle tables. I was about to take a place on the same table as most of my comrades when I heard my name called. It was Eberhard, with Henkel and Elsebeth standing behind.

'I do not believe you have given the happy couple your best wishes, Richard,' Eberhard said. He moved aside, motioning me towards the newly wedded pair.

I congratulated them clumsily in my faltering Low German, noting that Elsebeth refused to look at me. Henkel just stared with his icy eyes. Eberhard ushered the pair on to speak to a middle-aged merchant in a bright-blue tunic edged with fox fur. I was left to stare after them, my heartbeat pulsing in my head and my stomach churning like a storm at sea.

Now all I wanted to do was get drunk, as drunk as possible to forget what had just happened. When I took my place at the table next to Otto shortly after, that was exactly what I did. The lavish meal of many courses went by in a haze as I drained one goblet of wine after another – so many in fact that even Otto warned me to slow down. By the time the leftover food was cleared away and the tables removed for the evening's entertainment, the hall had started to spin and I was having trouble keeping awake. When I left the hall to take a piss in the privy, I decided to take the opportunity to go home.

The walk back was not far but with my head reeling it took me longer than normal. At the corner of Eberhard's street, I had to pause and empty my guts, throwing up in the open sewer that ran down both sides of the muddy lane. A passing woman muttered something but I didn't understand, or care. After vomiting, I felt better and staggered the rest of the way to Eberhard's house, lurching up the stairs to my room where I passed out.

So ended one of the worst days of my life.

And that was it. It was done. But somehow it snapped me out of the melancholy I had been feeling for the last few weeks. Things slowly returned to normal, as normal as my life had been since fleeing England. The summer came, and we were up to our throats in work. We travelled twice more to Lüneburg and, to my disappointment, we saw no brigands, outlaws or sign of any other enemy we could fight. And fight was what I wanted to do. I wanted to experience something more dangerous than training in the warehouse yard. I was a big, strapping fifteen-year-old who desperately wanted to prove himself in battle.

Of course, following her wedding, Elsebeth moved out, setting up house with Henkel in a small building behind the street that ran along the ridge of the hill upon which the city was built. I had hardly ever seen her when she had lived at Eberhard's; now it was as if she had disappeared from the city altogether. Henkel, too, spent less time with us. He didn't even come on the second trip to Lüneburg, leaving Johann in command, which was almost as bad as far as I was concerned.

Things improved with my comrades. I was still stung by Otto's words and so I worked as hard as I could to not appear arrogant. I knew that sometimes my manner and temper worked against me and I tried harder to control them, at least when I was at work. I made an effort not to complain about whatever chore or task I was assigned, even helping to dig a new privy by the warehouse without grumbling. I even started going down the Rooster again more often. Despite my youth, I had developed a taste for drinking, although far less than most of my comrades.

One fine sunny morning in early June, Eberhard appeared at the warehouse in an uncommonly good mood. Most of the men who worked for him were unloading another three wagons that had arrived from his new warehouse in Lüneburg. He called everyone over to him in the yard outside and informed us that he had just purchased a ship.

'She is a cog and is in the harbour now,' he said proudly. 'We shall be sailing to Falsterbo for the herring market.'

This joyous announcement was greeted by virtual silence. I was horrified at the news. After our journey here from England and the storm of storms I would never forget, going to sea again was the last thing I wanted. And looking at the faces of the dozen or so of my comrades, I saw that most of them agreed. And who could blame them? A trip to Denmark, even in the summer, would only mean more work and more danger.

But our lack of enthusiasm did not dampen Eberhard's spirits. He beamed at us before speaking to Henkel. 'I have decided to call her the *Elsebeth*, like my beautiful daughter. As you are my daughter's new husband, so will you be my captain.'

Henkel didn't look any more pleased than the rest of us. 'And like my daughter she will require a strong hand. In August, we shall sail to Falsterbo together. It will be good to get some sea air into our lungs.'

'Good for who?' Kunz whispered next to me. 'Certainly not good for any who cannot swim – most of this company, I'd wager...'

'Eberhard always wanted his own ship,' Wilhelm told me later. 'Normally, he would charter a ship when needed, but now he can afford his own. That's one better than our father. He nearly bankrupted his business buying me one.' We were in the counting room on the ground floor of Eberhard's house. It was the next morning, just before our usual German lesson.

'Did you know beforehand?' I asked. 'I'm not sure I could go to sea again after our last experience.'

'Detmar told me yesterday. He thought it would make me jealous.'

'And does it?'

Wilhelm gave me one of his rare smiles. 'I cannot pretend that seeing my brother more successful than I ever was makes me feel good. Look at me... I am a fugitive living on the goodwill of my younger brother. But, despite everything that has happened between us, he is still family. A bigger part of me feels proud. Our family are no longer minor merchants. I wouldn't be surprised if my brother is not asked to join the *Stadtrat*, the council made up of the city's leading merchants. In normal times, they run the city.'

I nodded absently, my mind wandering, as it often did, to Elsebeth.

Wilhelm sighed deeply. 'You are thinking about my niece. You have to get her out of your mind.'

'Is it that obvious?'

'To me it is. You forget, Richard, we have had quite an intense time in the last eight months or so. I have learned to know – and to respect you – quite well.'

I was unused to praise and deflected his compliment. 'And you have proven to be a true and loyal friend to me, as you were to my father. I probably would not even be alive without your help. I want to return to England and confront my uncle. Every day we remain here he has won. He has taken everything from me. I would take vengeance for the death of my father and Sir Hugh. That bastard has gotten away too long—'

'But we have talked about this, Richard. If you go back you will be killed. We need to bide our time.'

Despite knowing he was right, I felt my familiar anger rise. 'I am fed up of biding my time – skulking away in exile while my uncle does as he pleases. What about the letters we wrote to the king when we were in London?'

'I have heard nothing from Edward. I wrote to him after we arrived here last year, but he has not replied. I hope he and his family are well.'

I thought of Emma and immediately felt guilty. 'I hope so too.'

'We agreed we would wait. When you are an adult grown and we have more money, then we can consider returning. Otherwise it is futile.'

I succumbed into silence, feeling the usual dark gloom descend over me. We ended our conversation and concentrated on learning German.

The next weeks passed quickly. These were days of hot weather and we all sweated loading and unloading more cargo in the warehouse. Eberhard was eager to take the *Elsebeth* for a sea trial and we all spent one long day onboard, Wilhelm included, learning how to sail. She was a grand ship, slightly larger than *Christofer*, but with a proper deck and a raised stern.

As the Trave at Lübeck was far narrower than the Weser, we were towed downstream from the harbour to where the river widened, well past the island on which the city was built. From here we could travel alone and we unfurled the sail, hauling at the ropes to raise it aloft. I was relieved that the weather was good; a balmy day with hardly a cloud in the sky, far different from the time we had set sail from London. Once the sail was up, there was time to take a break and I joined Wilhelm at the rail, looking out at the flat landscape that drifted past, soaking up the smell of salt in the air as seagulls dived and shrieked above us.

Wilhelm pointed to the remains of several buildings on the left bank, including what looked like an old church, interspersed with hovels that were still occupied. 'That is Alt-Lübeck or Liubice in Slavic, the site of the original town. It was destroyed by the Rani – a pagan tribe, when I was a boy.'

I looked at the pack of dogs nosing along the waterside along with half-a-dozen sullen, dishevelled-looking people. A group of women washed clothes at the riverbank. It looked a forlorn place, prone to flooding, unlike the lofty houses and towers of the new town.

'I don't know what you were complaining about, Richard,' Otto said with a laugh. 'Sailing is not so bad. I think I could even get to like it.'

'It is easy in the summer,' I said. 'Wait until you are sailing in late autumn, being lashed to pieces in a storm with the waves as high as the mast and water up to your knees. You will not be so happy then, I promise you.'

But it was a good day, with the work not too arduous and the sun on our faces. Eberhard was like a child, deliriously happy with his new purchase, which must have cost him much of his fortune, discussing with Henkel and another man I did not know, the ship's handling abilities and the work he wanted done before we were to sail to Falsterbo in August.

And that was our work for the next few weeks. On one bright day the cog was hauled out of the Trave, where the ships were built beyond the harbour and the city walls. Nearby, narrow channels ran down the hill where they were irrigating the land so that more of the half-island could be built upon and the city allowed to expand. It was quieter here, away from the bustle of the warehouse and harbour, but the work was so gruelling I thought my arms would never recover. Afterwards, we spent days scrubbing off the green muck that coated the hull. It was boring work, scraping the algae and chipping away at the barnacles, sometimes relieving the tedium by throwing it at each other, though generally left alone from interference by both Eberhard and Henkel. Nevertheless, working outside all day was uplifting, especially in the warm weather, and the harbour nearby was an interesting place with ships and people constantly coming and going. There was always something to see. One day, I saw several ships leave, flying the banner of a red cross over a red sword. I didn't recognise the flag, and neither did Otto when I asked him, but he said they were probably men on their way to bring Christ to the heathens who lived further east along the Baltic. I watched for a while as we took a break, munching on my bread and cheese, wondering about the adventures that awaited them. I remembered meeting the knight in Bremen and how impressed I had been. If my own situation were different, I would have considered joining them. But Wilhelm was right; my destiny lay elsewhere. I had to prepare for the day when I would return to England and recover all that was mine.

After careening *Elsebeth*, we recaulked the hull with the help of an old man and his two sons who had been doing it all their lives. They showed the rest of us how to press the tarred moss into the grooves between the planks, covering it with wooden laths secured in place with caulking clamps called sintels. The old man sealed several other cracks and splits in the hull with more caulking. I laughed, watching Otto try and emulate him, but far less competently. He was so poor that the old man sent him off to help redistribute the ballast, a mixture of rock and sand that sat in the bottom of the hold to stabilise the ship. That was harder work and I was glad that my own efforts did not disappoint. I tried to put Elsebeth out of my mind and I was generally successful, the easy camaraderie of my comrades certainly helping, until I glanced up to see Agnes standing nervously some twenty feet away. She was looking directly at me and my heart caught in my throat. I dropped my tools and went over to her.

'My mistress sent me,' Agnes said. 'She wants to speak to you about a matter of importance.'

'Where is she?'

'She cannot come here. She would like to meet you tomorrow... outside the city.'

'Where?'

'Near the *Falkenwiese*, on the half-island by the Wakenitz. It is near where they fly the birds of prey. You must leave the city through the south gate, go across the wooden bridge by the mill and turn left, following the road through the forest. You will come to a small hut just off the road on the right that belongs to an old healer woman. Elsebeth will meet you there at Terce. It is important that you are not followed.'

I nodded, barely able to talk, I was so excited. But my elation was tempered with trepidation. Was something wrong? Why would she want to talk to me so urgently?

CHAPTER FOURTEEN

arly the next morning, I went to the shipbuilding yards along the Trave to work on the *Elsebeth* again with the rest of my comrades. In a short break, I told Otto about my planned meeting with Eberhard's daughter. He didn't think it was a good idea, but he agreed to cover for me if anyone wondered where I had gone.

When the time came for me to leave, I felt a quivering in my throat and my palms were damp with sweat. I had not seen Elsebeth since her wedding over two months before and wondered whether marriage had changed her and, of course, why she wanted to talk to me. After collecting my sword from the warehouse, concerned about the potential danger that might await me outside of the city, I walked back through the *Holstentor* gate. My destination wasn't far enough to warrant collecting my horse from the stables and I walked the well-trodden streets, passing out through the southern gate and across the open ground on the south end of the half-island, where pens of pigs squealed and grunted. Here, the land was also being drained and ditches crossed the ground running down to the Trave. I passed the cathedral and the windmill by the bridge, where more houses were now being built, and across the *Mühlenbrücke* as the bells from the town behind me began to ring for Terce. Nearby, animal skins were stretched on racks. I wrinkled my nose at the pungent smell of shit and piss emanating from the tanning pits that lined the river, increasing my pace as I passed another wooden windmill, before reaching the welcome cover of the trees and leaving the hovels and stench behind. I paused briefly to check that I was not being followed and, when satisfied, I continued into the woods. After a short time, I saw a small wooden hut partially hidden by trees in a clearing some fifty paces to my right. This had to be where the healer lived.

I approached the shack cautiously, my hand on the hilt of my sword, but before I got within ten feet of the wooden door it opened and a figure, wearing a grey cloak with the hood pulled up, stood framed in the doorway. I knew at once it was Elsebeth, and it took my entire self-will not to embrace her. There was no sign of the healer woman.

'Richard,' Elsebeth said. 'Thank you for coming. I was not sure you would.'

'Of course I would come if you asked. Are we alone? Where is this healer – the one who owns the hut?'

'She is picking mushrooms in the forest. She has left us alone to talk and will not return until we are both gone. I have known her most of my life – my father has employed her on several occasions. Even my mother would attest for her competence.'

'Lower your hood. I cannot see you properly.'

She was reluctant, but after a brief hesitation she complied. I gasped in shock when I saw her face. Her mouth was swollen and her eye and cheek were black and purple.

'How did this...?' I felt my anger rising. 'Henkel? Did Henkel do this to you?'

She lowered her head. 'You were right... he is not a good man.'

'He is a bastard!' I raged. 'I shall murder him for this.' I strode around the clearing, fuming.

'You cannot. If you even say anything, he will kill us both.'

'Unless I kill him. Have you thought about that? What does your father say? Surely he cannot be happy his precious daughter is being treated so.'

She lowered her head. 'My father does not know... I have not seen him for a few weeks. But please, Richard, this is not why I wanted to talk to you.'

'Don't tell me there is more?'

'I'm afraid so.' Elsebeth now had tears in her eyes. 'And I am not sure you are going to like it.'

I wasn't sure either. In fact, I was sure I wouldn't. 'What is it?'

She hesitated and then blurted it out. 'I am with child.'

I looked at her for a moment before shaking my head. 'Well, I wish you and your husband all God's blessing. Why are you telling me this?'

She hesitated again, not daring to look me in the eye. 'Because it is yours.'

It felt like she had slapped me. All my belligerence drained away and I staggered back in shock, my legs feeling like dough. I sat down on the trunk of a fallen tree. 'How can you be sure?'

'Because Henkel cannot make love to me. He cannot even get aroused without violence.'

'But how can you be sure it is mine?'

Her eyes flashed in sudden anger. 'Because I have not slept with him – with anyone, apart from you!'

'I am sorry,' I said. I went to embrace her but she recoiled from me and I sat back slowly on the tree, putting my head into my hands.

'No, Richard. I am sorry to have to tell you this. I do not know what I should do, but I do know that I will take no potion to rid me of it.'

'But if Henkel finds out?'

'I don't know... I shall worry about that later. But I shall have the baby, if God wills it.'

'And what about me?' I said. 'We could still run away. It is not too late. We could start a new life somewhere else...'

She shook her head. 'We spoke about this before and I gave you my answer then. I am sorry, Richard, but that has not changed.'

'So, if you will not run away with me, why trouble yourself to tell me at all? What do you hope to achieve apart from ruining my life again?'

'God knows that has never been my intention. I thought you had the right to know. You are the father of my unborn child.'

'But what do you expect me to do with this information? You are a married woman now. If you will not run away with me there is nothing I can do.'

'I do not want you to do anything. I just think you have the right to know.'

I heard a whinny and saw that a horse was tied to a tree next to the house. Elsebeth saw my glance and pulled her hood up again, covering her bruises. 'I have to get back to the city, otherwise I shall be missed. Please wait a short time before following. It would not be appropriate for us to be seen together...'

'No,' I said. 'That would not do at all.'

She looked at me for a moment before shaking her head, either in exasperation or pity, I was not sure. She turned and walked to her horse. I watched her climb up into the saddle, feeling a chasm opening between us. There was no sign she was with child, although we had last fornicated over four months previously. Of course, wrapped in the loose cloak she wore it was hard to tell, but it would not be long before it was obvious. Elsebeth walked her horse over to where I stood.

'I am sorry, Richard. I would change things if I could. I hope you can forgive me.'

And with that she nudged her horse forward, back through the trees in the direction of the road. I watched her go, my mind paralysed by what she had told me.

I followed a few moments later, walking dejectedly back through the trees and the city beyond.

The next day we finished the recaulking of Eberhard's ship and most of us spent the following morning in the back-breaking job of manhandling it back into the water. It was a hot day again, and we dripped with sweat as we tugged and strained on the ropes under the watchful eyes of the old man and Eberhard. Eberhard was insufferable, bawling at us to be careful, worried we would damage his precious ship. 'Maybe if the bastard shut up and helped instead of just shouting it would be easier,' Otto said between clenched teeth as his biceps bulged with the strain.

Luckily for me there was no sign of Henkel, and I was unsure how I would react on seeing him. He seemed even less interested in the ship of which he was nominally captain than the rest of us. Nevertheless, the hard work helped to take my mind off what Elsebeth had told me, but I was still as short-tempered as ever, snapping at my comrades until Makko threatened to throw me in the river after I called him a fat Hamburg donkey. Otto managed to calm us both down and with so much work to do we had no time to argue or fight.

Finally, to everyone's relief, we managed to ease the cog down the rollers and back into the Trave with a splash. A ragged cheer rang out and I even found myself grinning. Eberhard, who only moments before looked like he would have a seizure, visibly relaxed and even allowed himself a smile of relief.

After we finished work, we were all exhausted and hungry. Otto and I decided to get something to eat from one of the numerous vendors in the market square. 'It is typical that Eberhard did not put on a feast for us,' my friend complained. 'After such a hard day, he should roast a pig for everyone who helped get his damn ship back into the water without even so much as a scratch.'

In the market square, a crowd had gathered to listen to a speech. I suggested to Otto that we buy our sausages and go and see what the man had to say. He wore the robes of a bishop and was flanked by several lesser priests. We wandered across, pushing our way through the crowd. The bishop was a tall, well-built man of middle years, with the stature of a warrior more than a priest. Although I did not realise it at the time, this was the first occasion I was to see Bishop Albert von Buxhövden, a man who would wield a great influence on my life and would cause me many problems in the future. He spoke with passion, in a clear voice that resonated across the heads of the surrounding people. I found it hard to understand exactly what he was preaching, but I was also surprised that I could follow the gist of much of what he said. He was speaking about travelling to a foreign land to fight the pagan unbelievers. At first, I thought he meant Outremer, but it rapidly became clear that he was talking about somewhere else and I turned to Otto for clarification.

'He is talking about a land called Livonia,' Otto explained. 'I have heard of it. It lies far to the east.'

The bishop continued his rant against the pagans, berating the crowd one moment and lowering his voice and pleading the next. The man's charisma was apparent and he had the crowd entranced. 'Even now, we are building a great city called Riga,' Albert said, 'a city of light in the middle of the heathen darkness. We need more settlers and we need more warriors to bring the gospel of Christ to the pagans. Livonia is the land of Mary and we must fight to impose her rule. I spent last winter there and we need more people – colonists and those willing to take the cross. Pope Innocent III himself has declared a bill granting papal privileges to anyone willing to go on crusade to Livonia. This means your sins shall be forgiven if you come and fight for God.'

There was a ragged cheer from the crowd.

Albert raised his hand for silence before continuing. 'There will be ships sailing under a Cistercian monk called Theodoric of Treiden in a month or so. There shall be room for anyone wishing to implement God's will. Theodoric will preach again here in Lübeck before he sets sail. Anyone of you willing to take up the sword against the enemies of God should finalise their affairs and be ready to sail by the beginning of September at the latest. Come and fight for the Lord. Come and fight for the Land of the Blessed Virgin!'

His sermon was finished. The bishop conferred with the group of priests before leaving the square with the majority of them in tow, while another priest began to speak to the crowd. Unfortunately, he lacked the power of the bishop and people slowly began to disperse. But I was interested in a young knight dressed in mail and holding two horses behind the priest. On his shield was the same emblem of a red cross over a red sword that that I had seen on the ships when we'd been recaulking Eberhard's cog. I pulled Otto over to him, and whilst the priest carried on his uninspiring speech, we talked to the knight. He was not much older than me and explained he was not a knight but a sergeant, similar to a squire, named Stephan, and his Order was the *Fratres militiæ Christi Livoniae*, better known as the Livonian Brothers of the Sword – or Swordbrothers. They were newly created and were based in Riga, in Livonia. I had never heard of either the Order or the place, but he explained Bishop Albert was building this new city in a wilderness of pagans. Both Otto and I were interested. 'You should think about joining us. It is a hard, but Godly life.' Stephan explained a little about life there. 'If only it were not so cold.'

'I could not imagine having to pray seven times a day,' Otto said after we had taken our leave, echoing my own thoughts. 'Their knees must be red sore. And can you believe they go without women? The life of a monk is not for me – even if they get to fight sometimes.'

'What do you know about Livonia?'

'I hear there are dragons and giant birds and the pagans sacrifice humans to them,' Otto said. 'No end of strange things, anyway. And Livonia is damn cold. Better go to the Holy Land – at least there it is warm.'

'But the Saracens fight well, I hear,' I said. 'And what is happening there now? The armed pilgrimage last year didn't get further than Constantinople…'

'Better the Holy Land anyway,' Otto repeated. 'I hate the cold. Let's go down to the Rooster. I want to hear about your meeting with Elsebeth.'

So, we went down to the packed tavern and I told him. He looked at me in shock and shook his head. 'You surprise me all the time, Richard. I do not know what to say. If Henkel ever found out…'

'I do not care about Henkel. I care about Elsebeth. You should have seen her, Otto – she was battered blue. I shall kill him for this!'

'She is his wife. He can do as he wishes. The law is on his side.'

'Damn you, Otto, you sound more like Wilhelm every day.'

'Well, I am sorry about that, but it's true.'

I fell into a glum silence, but in Otto's company it was hard to remain miserable. I thought about everything Elsebeth had told me. The thought of becoming a father – especially as the child would probably never know, was heartbreaking. 'I am scared for her, Otto,' I said. 'When Henkel finds out she is with child he will know it is not his. Only God knows what he will do then. He might murder her.'

'I cannot imagine he would do something like that to Eberhard's only daughter,' Otto said. 'Even with the best reason in the world...'

'We do not know. That's just it, we do not know! He is dangerous enough, that is for sure. If he can beat her so badly for virtually no reason, imagine what will happen when he finds he has justification.'

'*Ach*, you will drive yourself mad thinking about everything that might happen, Richard. It is out of your control. You cannot worry about something you have no control over.'

I saw Kunz come in the door, looking around the packed tavern for us. We had to change the subject. 'I do not want to talk about it anymore. Talk solves nothing. Let's get drunk and forget them.'

Otto agreed and Kunz joined us. We all got drunk together. I had no idea then that things were rapidly coming to a head and were about to spin out of control.

The next few days we worked in the warehouse. Henkel was seldom there and when he was, I ignored him, although it took every ounce of control I possessed. Wilhelm suspected something was wrong. I caught him looking at me strangely a couple of times, but he never asked and I never told him. That was until one morning.

We were in the counting house on the ground floor when I questioned him about Livonia. 'What do you know about the country?' I said. 'Otto says there are dragons and giant birds, and I have heard the pagans there eat Christians alive.'

'I know nothing about that,' Wilhelm said. 'But I have heard that the East Baltic is infested with pirates. It is not a place I would wish to go to.'

'I never want to set foot on a ship again.' I studied my father's old steward and now my friend. Large dark bags hung under his eyes. He looked pale and weary, as if he had aged five years since we had fled England.

'Do not forget my brother's planned voyage to Falsterbo...'

'How can I forget it? I hope he doesn't pick me to accompany him.'

Wilhelm gave a tired smile. 'And I have no doubt that if he does you will distinguish yourself again.'

I felt less sure. I had not distinguished myself very well with Elsebeth. And how would I be able to put up with being in such close proximity to Henkel on nothing larger than a cog? Only one of us would return, and it would probably not be me. 'Hopefully, he will hire a proper crew again... and he will still need men to safeguard his warehouse here in Lübeck.'

Wilhelm shrugged. 'If I spoke to my brother, it would not aid your cause. He would probably select you to spite me.'

That was likely true enough.

'But why are you suddenly interested in Livonia?' Wilhelm said. 'Have you been listening to that bishop preaching in the square?'

I nodded. 'So you've seen him too. We spoke to one of the knights, or sergeants, that accompanied him. It sounds like a noble cause. Better than working under Henkel anyway.'

'I can believe it. Henkel is a very intimidating man and he certainly scares me to death.'

'Me too.' A thought came to me. 'Would you have any idea whether Henkel has a hold over your brother?'

Wilhelm frowned. 'He would not tell me anyway. A hold over my brother? Why would you think that?'

I hesitated because until now I had kept it to myself. But there was no reason not to tell Wilhelm. I explained about catching Detmar at the warehouse with his friend when we had slept on the quay.

Wilhelm's eyes widened in shock at the news. 'I had no idea... although it would explain a few things.'

'I was warned later by Henkel not to say anything otherwise he would exact retribution. He was very clear about that. I wondered if this knowledge gave him some hold over Eberhard.'

'If it became public knowledge it would certainly bring humiliation down on our family,' Wilhelm said. 'And Detmar would face catastrophic punishment. Sodomy is considered unnatural by the Church with stiff punishments, which can range from castration to being burnt at the stake. Have you told anyone else? Your friend, Otto, perhaps?'

'No. I thought the knowledge would possibly prove useful against Detmar.'

Wilhelm sat back, pondering everything I had just told him. 'But there may be something in what you say. I always wondered why my brother would marry Elsebeth to a man like Henkel. He has only known him for three years, and Henkel is unsavoury to say the least.'

At the mention of Elsebeth, I turned away lest he saw my dark expression. I walked to the table where Wilhelm worked.

It was heaped with manuscripts and various pots of ink, quills, wax tablets and the ribbon and seal used for sending correspondence. I thought about Elsebeth's bruised face and what she had told me. 'Henkel is beating her,' I said in a low voice. I heard Wilhelm take a sharp intake of breath and I turned back to him.

'When did you see her?' he said.

'That does not matter. He is beating Eberhard's daughter.'

Wilhelm sighed deeply. 'To be honest, it does not surprise me. And as far as I am aware Eberhard does not know. I do not think he has seen her for some time – he is too busy with his new ship and expanding his business.'

'Elsebeth said as much.'

'But Richard, there is nothing you can do about it. Henkel is her husband and can do as he chooses. Especially if he does indeed have some kind of hold over Eberhard.'

Otto had said much the same thing. I considered telling him the entire story, but something stopped me. It would destroy him. After Wilhelm's loyalty, advice and friendship, I could not do that.

'You have to put this from your mind,' Wilhelm said. 'She is not the first woman to be treated badly by her husband. If you get involved it will destroy everything we have achieved here.'

'And what exactly have we achieved here?' I said, feeling the familiar anger gnawing at my guts bubble up. 'We are living here on the goodwill of your bastard brother and we have no power over our lives. We should never have left England!'

'There was no choice, remember? If we had stayed, we would likely both be dead now. We have talked about—'

'Enough, Wilhelm. I am tired of hearing it!' I shouted. Of course, he was right, Wilhelm usually was. But I was still angry.

Wilhelm just looked at me for a few moments.

My anger subsided almost as quickly as it had appeared. 'I am sorry. It is not your fault. Please forgive me. You have been a loyal companion and do not deserve my rage.'

Wilhelm gave a small shrug. 'I can sympathise with your frustration. I would also rather things were different. But Richard, you will have to watch your temper. It worries me. You have just demonstrated how quickly you can become enflamed.'

'But I just feel so powerless.'

He nodded. 'I understand. However, you must be patient. We agreed that you needed to finish your training and gather coin before returning to England.'

'But every day I spend with Henkel is a torment. He tries his hardest to belittle me and after what he's done, I want to rip his head off.'

'You must ignore all the provocation.' Wilhelm got to his feet, approached me and looked into my eyes. 'You are a brave young man who has suffered much. And I know you care a lot for my niece. Maybe I can try to convince Eberhard to give you other work or perhaps you could seek different employment in the city, but that might mean you need to find new lodgings. That would be preferable to crossed words with Henkel or worse. But know one thing, Richard… if you fail to control your temperament it will lead to nothing good. It could very well destroy the both of us.'

CHAPTER FIFTEEN

Now that his boat was finished, Eberhard wanted to use it, not just wait for the herring market in Falsterbo the following month. Ten days after we refloated her, on the eve of the Feast of Saint Mary Magdalene, he announced to us in the warehouse that Henkel would sail with a cargo of salt and local beer to Bornholm. He would take a proper, trained crew of eight men accompanied by half a dozen of us to act as an armed escort. Not to my surprise, but to my relief, I was not among those picked. Otto neither. The prospect of a week or two without Henkel was very appealing.

They sailed the morning after the feast, leaving the rest of us to carry on working at the warehouse. Eberhard bought some furs and hemp from a trader from Visby in Gotland and we, of course, had to unload the cargo. We spent the next day loading the trader's ship again with salt he had bought from Eberhard and barrels of Lübeck beer. The salt stores in the warehouse were still half-full and Wilhelm told me that no more would be sold, because Eberhard wanted to restrict supply so that prices would rise before the herring market.

He expected that we would make one more trip to Lüneburg before sailing for Scania.

The weather remained good, the long days sunny and hot. Over the next week or so, we worked continually, loading and unloading several ships that docked in the harbour. It was hard work but without the scowling and disapproving Henkel watching over us there was a more light-hearted atmosphere, at least when Eberhard or Detmar were not there.

One afternoon, on the way back from Eberhard's warehouse with our work complete, I left the others on their way to the Rooster, choosing instead to go to the market as I wanted to buy a new belt. I was looking at the wares of a leather stall, the noise and bustle loud around me, when I spied Agnes through the crowds carrying a basket of bread and eggs. She looked to be in a hurry.

All thoughts of purchasing a belt were gone. Perhaps Elsebeth was also in the market. I decided to follow her maidservant. But the way she deftly darted through the crowd made it clear almost immediately that Agnes was without her mistress. I continued to follow her anyway, pushing through the people, ignoring the tumult around me, intent on not losing her. If she was travelling home, I would learn where Elsebeth lived. Perhaps I could take advantage of Henkel's absence and talk to her again about becoming a father.

Agnes left the market, heading towards the ridge of the shallow hill and the street that led to the fortress at the other end of the island. All I knew was that Elsebeth and Henkel were supposed to live somewhere close. I was about twenty paces behind her, but as the crowds thinned, I had to drop back and keep more distance between us, otherwise she might see me. A man kneeling at the edge of the street was shouting at passers-by that God was judging us for our sins. He held his arms out, clutched at the hem of my cloak, imploring me to accept the Lord into my heart, but I shook myself loose and pushed past him, slowing down as Agnes suddenly paused as a man accosted her.

It was Johann, and I watched as he angrily jabbed his finger at her but I was too far away to hear what was said. After he berated her, they both turned, heading further up the road. For a moment I was undecided. Obviously, with Johann keeping an eye on his master's new wife and maidservant, there was no chance for me to talk to Elsebeth. But I still wanted to know where she lived. I continued to follow them.

They turned right down an alleyway between a wooden shack and a smithy. I paused at the corner of the street as they disappeared into a courtyard. My heart was beating in my chest like the blacksmith's hammer that I heard from the workshop. I crept along the side of the wall, momentarily distracted as a boy appeared from the shed, fetching more charcoal for the forge. He glanced briefly at me before breaking up the burnt branches with a small axe. I carried on, reaching the end of the wall to look into the courtyard behind.

I just caught a glimpse of the back of Johann going through a door into a single-storey wooden building. So this was where Elsebeth lived. I looked at the house, very tidy but unassuming, with a tiled roof and a woodshed against one wall. For a moment I stood watching when the door suddenly opened again and Johann appeared. He saw me immediately.

'What the hell are you doing here?' he snarled, striding over to where I stood.

I cursed under my breath. 'Nothing… I saw Agnes in the market and—'

'What has Agnes got to do with you?' He stopped in front of me. I was slightly taller than him but he looked very threatening, the scar down the side of his jaw almost pulsating in repressed fury.

'I just wanted to talk with her...'

'You keep your filthy hands off her. She is mine, do you understand? Go and get your own girl down that shitty tavern you always go to.'

I dropped my eyes. 'It was nothing like that... I just wanted a quick word.'

'Well, she wants nothing to do with you. So get lost, before I lose my temper.'

I turned and walked down the alley to the main street, feeling his stare drilling into the back of my head. The boy was still chopping the wood charcoal and he looked at me and smiled. I nodded to him before reaching the main street again.

That had been close. I cursed my ill luck at getting caught as I walked back the way I had come, passing through the market again as the stall-holders began to pack up for the day.

The encounter whirled around my head. Johann was nothing but a turd. And Otto would not be pleased to learn that Johann considered Agnes to belong to him. And what was I thinking of anyway? After all, Elsebeth had made her position abundantly clear. Nothing more I said would make any difference. She wanted no more to do with me and the sooner I accepted that the better.

I did not want to return home to Eberhard's soulless house and I had no wish to go down the Rooster. So I wandered the streets of Lübeck, deep in thought over my predicament, oblivious to the noise and stink of the city. The crowds were thinning as people made their way home and the tall houses threw long shadows across the market square. When the bells began to ring for Vespers, I decided to go to the church to pray. Maybe God would provide the answers I could not.

It was almost dark now and I went to Saint Mary's Church, just behind the town hall. It was a brick-built church with semicircular arches and I joined the townspeople queuing to get in the door. I had been here before many times, and preferred it to Saint Peter's Church or the barn-like cathedral just outside the walled town. I particularly liked the murals on the walls, especially *The Last Supper*, which was painted with such skill that the figures almost climbed off the wall on which they were portrayed.

I knelt on the straw-covered floor in the nave and mumbled my prayers with everybody else, but afterwards I remained with my eyes closed, ignoring the movement of people and the mumbling of the paternoster around me. What was I going to do? Everything Wilhelm had said was right. It was true that my temper was dangerous and when ignited, almost uncontrollable.

Memories of Cranham jumped unasked into my head. It had been nearly a year since I had lost my home, and the bitterness I felt was unabated. My oath to recover everything that had been stolen from me was unfulfilled. The deaths of my father, Sir Hugh and the others were still unavenged. Not only that, my chances of ever returning and speaking with King John seemed further away than ever. And I had received no reply to my letter to Alice written nearly three months previously. I wondered how life was now for my little wildcat. She would be settled in now. I would have given everything in that moment to see her again. Perhaps she would know what had happened to our old home?

What was I to do about my more immediate situation here in Lübeck? Perhaps my knowledge of Detmar could persuade Henkel to stop beating Elsebeth. Surely having this information must help my dire predicament? But despite hating Eberhard's son, could I reveal what I knew and let him face the horrendous punishment that would ensue? He was still Wilhelm's nephew. I knew that I could not.

But of course, there was more than just Elsebeth. There was my unborn child to consider. If I did nothing, I was putting it at risk. What was I going to do?

I did not know what I expected from praying. I opened my eyes and looked towards the altar and the painting of a huge Christ on the cross behind. I prayed for Him to help me. To guide me. To advise me.

I prayed for my soul. But God was not listening.

Of course, this time of peace could not last. Three days before the Feast of Saint Lawrence, Henkel and the crew of the *Elsebeth* returned. I was bitterly disappointed, harbouring a secret hope that the ship would be lost in the unpredictable waters of the Baltic. That would have solved many of my problems. But Henkel always seemed to have the luck of Satan. I wondered how long it would take him to realise that his new wife was with child.

My child.

I did not have to wait long. Two days after they returned, I was helping Wilhelm complete a stocktake of everything stored in the warehouse. Detmar was also there, cooped up in the small back office going through the ledgers.

'You missed a keg of salt in your tally,' Wilhelm said in the disapproving voice I had come to know well. 'This is not like you, Richard. Are you still worried about what we talked about?'

'Of course I am,' I said. 'I cannot think of much else.'

Wilhelm started to say something but paused, looking towards the big double doors behind me. He frowned. I turned to look at what had grabbed his attention. It was Agnes, and I had never seen her look so wretched. She was out of breath and red-faced, crying and her hair unusually unkempt. She saw me and ran over.

'You *have* to come,' she sobbed.'Before he kills her.'

'What are you talking about? What has happened?' Wilhelm said.

But I knew what she was talking about. She was talking about Henkel.'I have to go,' I said quickly.

'But Richard—'

'There's no time, Wilhelm!' I started for the door when I heard a voice behind me.

It was Detmar.'Where do you think you are going?'

'Why don't you just piss off,' I snarled, not even bothering to look at him and not slowing my pace. I ignored his snort of indignation and went outside into the yard, intending to collect my sword from the chest in the corner where we kept our arms for practice. When I retrieved my weapon, I could hear harsh words between Wilhelm and Detmar behind my back. I turned to see Detmar about ten feet away, striding towards me, leaving Wilhelm standing with a concerned expression in the warehouse doorway.

'How dare you speak to me like that, *Arschloch!*' Detmar shouted. His face was red and his fists were clenched.

My temper exploded in me. I dropped my sheathed sword and took three quick steps, punching him in the face as hard as I could. He went down and my momentum caused me to fall on top of him. I smashed him in the nose I'd broken in our last altercation with my elbow. He lay whimpering and bloodied and I came to my feet, giving him a hefty kick in the stomach. I spat on him and picked up my sword, dashing to the main gate of the yard followed by a distraught Agnes.

Otto and Makko were working, stacking barrels near the gate.'Where are you going?' Otto called.

'Henkel's beating Elsebeth again,' I said, 'and I'm going to stop him.' I waved off Otto's protests and ran into the street. Almost immediately, I realised that the sight of a man running through the streets waving a sword around would cause alarm, so I slowed down to a fast walk, allowing Agnes to catch me up. My heart pounded in my chest and I could not help thinking I was hurrying to my own death.

In the market square, crowds of people delayed our progress and I pushed through as quickly as I could, receiving some nasty looks and comments from people I'd elbowed out of the way. I ignored them in my haste, leaving the market with Agnes panting behind me as she struggled to match my pace. We moved on and reached Elsebeth's street, picking up speed now that we were close to her house.

We reached the narrow alley next to the blacksmith's workshop. Now I could hear shouting and the sound of breaking pottery. I began to run, leaving Agnes behind, rushing into the small courtyard and reaching the wooden door of the building that I had seen Johann enter before. Henkel's shouts of rage from within propelled me on and I tried the door, but it was locked. Behind me, I heard Agnes puffing as she ran into the yard.

'The door is locked. Do you have a key?'

She shook her head as I heard a chair breaking inside. I hammered on the wood, but it remained unopened. There was nothing for it, I took a step backwards and shoulder-barged the door, which exploded inwards with a splintering of wood, throwing me forward onto my face. As I scrambled to my feet again, I saw I was in a small anteroom. The shouting came from the next room. It was Henkel and he sounded like he had lost his mind, oblivious to the noise I had made breaking into the house. I drew my sword and pushed the next door open, peering into the main room.

Henkel stood over Elsebeth, who was curled up in the far corner covering her head. The room looked like the site of a pitched battle, with the table lying on its side and stools and smashed pottery littering the floor. Oil from a broken lamp puddled on the floor before me. For a second, I watched, too stunned to move.

'Who is the father?' Henkel screamed at his wife, incoherent with rage. 'Tell me or I shall kill you!' He turned and looked at me for the first time. 'What the fuck are you doing here?'

'*I* am the father,' I said.

His eyes widened in shock.

Behind him, Elsebeth looked up, her face covered in blood with one eye swollen shut. At the sight of her I felt my familiar anger rise.

'You?' Henkel said, incredulous. 'But you are just a boy.'

'It is still true.' I lifted my sword.

'Richard,' Elsebeth said. 'Why are you here?'

'Shut your mouth, bitch!' Henkel turned back to her. 'Is this true? Is this foreign runt the father?'

Elsebeth lowered her face and whispered something. Henkel bellowed in rage and struck her around the head with the palm of his hand.

I had seen enough. I charged at him, screaming at the top of my voice, swinging my sword, intent on killing him while he was still unarmed and unprepared. But he moved as fast as a viper, springing to the side and grabbing one of the fallen stools. I ducked as he threw it at me. It narrowly missed my head, but caused me to lose my footing and I careened into the debris on the floor.

Henkel used the time he had gained to dash to a hook on the far wall, grabbing his own sword. He unsheathed it and grinned at me malevolently. Now my advantage was gone and a chill like icy rain ran down my spine.

He sprang at me, sweeping his sword around in a feint before slashing directly at my head like the stroke of an axe. He was unbelievably fast and it took all my training to get my own sword up to block the attack. Even then, the strength of his blow drove my sword downwards, the point of his blade gouging into my upper left arm.

I backed away, keeping my sword raised to deflect the next attack. Blood poured down my arm from the wound, but I hardly felt it, concentrating all my attention on my opponent. I was shaken – I had crossed swords with Henkel and felt his strength. And his skill. Henkel was the better swordsman and I knew he was going to kill me.

As if he could read my mind, Henkel smiled again. He knew it too. I had withdrawn behind the overturned table, and he moved around to block me from getting to the door. Now I would have to get past him if I wanted to escape. Not that I did, of course. Despite knowing I was outmatched, I was determined to go down fighting. Maybe, if I was lucky, I would be able to wound him before I died.

The sound of running footsteps from the doorway distracted both of us for a split second. I looked to see Wilhelm come through the door, out of breath, looking shocked as he quickly surveyed the destroyed room. 'Gott im Himmel!' he said. Wilhelm turned to look at Henkel just as he sprang at him, thrusting his sword forward.

I watched in horror as Henkel's blade sank deeply into Wilhelm's stomach. My father's steward looked at it protruding from his body with an expression of complete disbelief before blood spurted from his mouth. Henkel twisted and withdrew the sword with a horrible sucking sound. Wilhelm collapsed to his knees, vainly trying to hold in his guts with both hands before falling onto his face into a puddle of blood.

The sight of my loyal friend dying in front of my eyes spurred me into action. I charged at Henkel, slashing at him with short strokes like Sir Hugh had taught me at Cranham, driving him back to the wall with my sheer aggression and savagery. Out of the corner of my eye, I caught a glimpse of someone else in the doorway, but I had no time to look properly as Henkel counter-attacked with a flurry of blows that forced me back across the room. I fought desperately, using every piece of skill I had learned, but it was not enough. I winced as Henkel's blade sliced into my sword arm, just below the elbow. It was not a deep wound, but blood flowed copiously down my arm with every subsequent movement, dripping into the palm of my hand and making my grip on my sword slippery.

But now, over Henkel's shoulder, I could see it was Otto in the doorway. My friend looked stunned by the death of Wilhelm, but only for a second. A moment later he snapped out of his shock, drew his own sword and dashed into the room. But Henkel missed nothing, spinning around from me to swing a vicious blow at Otto, which would have decapitated him if my friend had not slipped in the pooled oil and fallen backwards onto his arse. Otto was totally vulnerable to Henkel's next attack, so I sprung forward to distract him, sweeping my sword around in an arc, forcing Henkel to parry and give Otto a chance to recover and regain his feet.

We faced off against each other. There was a calmness about Henkel that had been absent when I'd first entered the room. A calmness in contrast to my rising panic. He was enjoying this.

'Do either of you two boys really think you can win?' Henkel taunted, looking from me to Otto. 'I grew up in the gutter. I've learned every dirty trick there is, and two on one is no problem.' He feinted towards me before flicking his sword back to Otto who only partially managed to parry. My friend howled as Henkel's sword cut into his waist. The wound did not look deep from where I was standing, but Otto sagged and took a step backwards, lifting his own sword to ward off another onslaught.

I attacked again, raining blows on Henkel's sword using my entire strength. Henkel parried them all, but at the end of the exchange he was breathing heavily. I felt my spirits rise, maybe my youth and training were beginning to wear him down. But Otto was in visible pain. His wound was worse than I thought. Nevertheless, I needed his help. We needed to assault Henkel at the same time.

Henkel attacked, a series of short quick lunges that forced me back again. I felt the side of the overturned table against the back of my legs and Henkel's next lunge forced me back again, except there was nowhere to go. I managed to parry his blow, but then the worst thing that can happen in a fight occurred: my sword broke, shattering with a clang, jarring my arm and leaving me with a stump of a blade barely longer than a dagger. The momentum caused me to fall over the table and onto my back. Now I was completely defenceless.

Henkel smiled again, knowing I was finished. He loomed over me, bringing his arm back for a final strike. I could see that he intended to put all his strength into it. I looked desperately for Otto but he was near the door, too far away to help me.

And then Elsebeth appeared above me. She threw a wooden cup at Henkel as he was bringing his sword down. It hit him full in the face and he roared in pain, causing him to miss me, his sword slicing into the wood of the table edge.

'You cheating bitch!' Henkel screamed, back-handing her in the face with his free hand. Elsebeth's head snapped back and she tumbled to the floor. He turned back to me, tugging at his sword that was stuck in the table. It was embedded so deeply that he couldn't extract it with just one hand and he tried with both, his face straining with the effort. For a split second I was forgotten.

I saw my chance and I sprang up, thrusting the sharp stump of my sword upwards into Henkel's throat as hard as I could. He staggered backwards, clutching at the wound as blood gurgled and sprayed everywhere. I stabbed him again, feeling a frenzy coming over me. He crumpled to his knees and I stabbed yet again, repeatedly driving the remains of my sword into the soft flesh of my enemy. After a moment it was over. Henkel lay at my feet, a bloodied, butchered, mutilated mess.

My enemy was dead.

CHAPTER SIXTEEN

If I thought I had problems before, now they were only beginning. I had killed a man, and if caught I would die. We had to escape, but Otto was badly wounded and in a great deal of pain. He slumped against the wall as Elsebeth, who had brushed my aid away, helped to bind his wounds, using an old tunic that had belonged to Henkel. I was concerned that the sound of our fight would have attracted attention, but Elsebeth said that the noise from the blacksmith would have masked it. I hoped she was right.

After attending to Otto, the two girls bound my own relatively minor injuries. Everyone was in shock and I could see that Elsebeth was trying desperately not to cry. Agnes was not as controlled and she sobbed openly, refusing to look at the two dead men just feet away.

'You saved my life, Richard,' Otto said, trying to smile but wincing instead. He was deathly pale. 'But what are we going to do now?'

'We have to leave the city – and get you to a physician.'

'Go to the healer's hut in the forest,' Elsebeth said. 'Her name is Tekla. Tell her I sent you. I do not think she will turn you away and you can trust her. I shall come when I can and we can talk further.'

'But what will you do now?' I said.

'I will have to tell the truth. People will know you came here, so I have no choice. You will both be fugitives. You will never be able to return to Lübeck.'

'That thought does not distress me,' I said.

Agnes fetched water from a well in the yard and we did our best to clean ourselves of the blood that was everywhere. It was time to go. Elsebeth gave us two long cloaks that had belonged to Henkel to cover our own bloodstained clothing. The problem would be getting past the guards at the gate. An idea came to me and I quickly seized an unbroken flagon of wine, taking a long draught before pouring some over the front of Otto's tunic. 'Drink some,' I ordered him. He looked perplexed before my meaning became clear to him.

My sword was a broken mess and I did not want to flee Lübeck unarmed, so I took Henkel's, a fine blade, slightly broader than mine but clearly of excellent workmanship and one I had admired before. I quickly cleaned it using the rest of Henkel's tunic, left over from binding Otto's wound, ignoring Elsebeth's disapproving look. It did not fit into my old scabbard so I took Henkel's, noting the superior leather and the eagle motif that decorated the top.

'If you get caught with that you will be in big trouble,' Elsebeth said. 'There are many people in this city who would recognise it immediately.'

I shrugged. Better than being unarmed.

We left shortly afterwards, passing through the shattered door and back into the courtyard. I half-carried Otto, expecting to see the city guard appear and arrest us, but there was no sign of anyone. We stumbled past the blacksmith's workshop without receiving so much as a glance. My hopes began to rise.

We struggled down the hill towards the city's southern gate. It was open with several Danish guards talking in the entrance. They were stopping anyone wishing to enter but ignoring the few people wishing to leave. My hopes rose further but, nonetheless, I avoided eye contact as we approached, Otto leaning on me for support. We were almost through the gate when one of the Danish soldiers suddenly blocked our path. My heart sank.

'What is the matter with your friend?' the guard asked in reasonable German.

'He's had too much to drink,' I said. 'I am taking him home.'

'A bit early in the day, don't you think?' The guard came closer then wrinkled his nose when he smelled the wine on us. Otto began to sing a song and the man waved us through irritably. We continued down the road that led past the cathedral, passing the pens of animals and wooden huts that stretched to the bridge and Otto grinned through gritted teeth at our subterfuge. After what had happened, I was in no mood to celebrate.

I could smell the tanning pits before we came to them, but our progress was painfully slow. To my dismay, we were getting odd looks from many of the people we passed. But thankfully, we were soon in the forest and alone. Otto was weakening and his wound had begun to bleed again through the improvised bandage. Up ahead, I saw the small track that led from the road to the healer's hut, hidden in the trees. It was not a moment too soon. Otto was putting more weight on me and I feared he was going to pass out. And he was bloody heavy. I hoped the healer woman was home.

Luckily, she was. We were about fifty paces from the hut when the door opened. She rushed out and lifted Otto by the other shoulder, helping me carry him through the wooden door and inside. We manhandled him onto a straw pallet that occupied one side of the room. My own wounds were hurting and I was exhausted, so I slumped down on the dirt floor next to the door, watching the woman attend to my friend. The hut was a basic affair with a firepit in the centre and rafters festooned with bundles of medicinal herbs and dried plants. Despite the strong smell of woodsmoke there was a musty aroma that hung in the air like a cloud. The woman collected several pottery and glass bottles from a shelf on the wall, quickly mixing up some herbal concoction in a pestle on the table, before returning to a now unconscious Otto, bending over him as she examined his wound. She was probably close to forty, with greying hair tied back and a kind, not unhandsome face. And there was something else as well; a strength or stubbornness that indicated she didn't suffer foolishness lightly.

'How did your friend receive his injury?' she asked, not looking at me. She had undone the makeshift bandage and was cleaning the wound with water, wine and a thick liquid that looked like honey, before applying a dark, viscous substance to the edge of the incision.

I hesitated, not sure if I could trust her. She turned and looked at me, and for a split second I got the uncanny feeling that she could read my mind. Elsebeth's words about being able to trust her came back to me. 'There was a fight at Elsebeth's house. My friend was cut with a sword. Will he recover?'

'He is young and strong but he has lost much blood. But with rest he should fully recover, if the rot does not set in.' She turned back to Otto, finished applying the substance before quickly rebinding the wound. Otto remained unconscious.

'So you must be the young man she has spoken about.'

I explained what had happened and she listened in silence. When I had finished, she looked at me with pity in her eyes. 'Boys do so like to play with swords.'

I felt my face flush. 'It was not like that. Henkel was going to kill her. We saved her life.'

'And now she is with child and without husband. Poor girl.'

'She is better off without a husband like Henkel.'

'Spoken like only a man could,' she said. 'She will be the one that has to pick up the pieces of her life when you are long gone.'

'That is unfair.' I felt my anger rising. 'I wanted to run away with her. She was the one who refused!' Who did this woman think she was?

'Very gracious of you. You don't know the meaning of unfair – you are noble born. You can thank your God for that. Now let me look at your wounds.'

'They are nothing,' I said, but in truth they bloody hurt. When she insisted, I did not resist. Nothing further was said as she applied the same brown substance that stung, although I did not show it.

After she had rebound my arm, she spoke again. 'I have to go out. But you and your friend must stay here. Do not leave the hut. And if anyone comes do not answer the door. I shall not be long.'

And with that she left, leaving me with an unconscious Otto and my own contemplation. I immediately thought of Wilhelm. My father's old steward had proven a loyal and dependable friend and braver than I would ever have believed. Without him I would never have made it this far. He had trusted and followed me, acting as both confidant and advisor, his humility and calmness proving to be a good counter to my natural arrogance and impetuosity. And it had cost him his life. A deep despair settled over me and I felt tears coming. Despite trying to fight them they flowed freely and I finally gave in, revelling in their misery. I cried for Wilhelm, and I am not ashamed to admit that I also cried for Elsebeth and everything that had happened. I had lost my friend along with the last connection I had with Cranham and my previous life. As the tears streamed unheeded down my face, I clenched my eyes shut, willing things to be different.

Despite what she'd said, Tekla was gone the whole afternoon, returning only as the hut was becoming gloomier with darkness not far off. I was napping, slumped against the wall where she had left me. Otto was still unconscious but his rising chest confirmed he was not dead. She swept in like a summer storm, jerking me awake, causing me to grab my sword, ready to fight again. As the door banged shut behind her, I saw she was carrying two dead squirrels which she dumped on the table, barely glancing at me, before briefly checking on Otto. She began to skin the red fur from the animals before putting it in a cauldron that hung from a tripod over the fire. She stirred up the glowing embers, added more wood, and soon the sweet aroma of cooking meat filled the hut, reminding me of how hungry I was.

Tekla did all of this in silence, only speaking when she had finished the preparation for the meal. 'You can stay here until your friend has recovered, but then you must leave. If you are found here, I shall be severely punished. Many people rely on my healing, therefore I cannot allow this to happen. If you were not friends of Elsebeth, I would have turned you away already. As long as you are here you shall do as I say. Is that understood?'

I agreed to her terms. There was no other choice and I needed time to think about what we would do anyway.

And that was what I did for the next two days. Otto awoke, still in pain and confined to bed. Tekla was away most of the time, leaving instructions for me on how to administer the herbal concoction to ease Otto's agony. I was not allowed to stray far from the hut and under no circumstances was I to go near the road that cut through the forest. I spent my time cleaning and sharpening the sword I had taken from Henkel, chopping wood and fetching water from a secluded spot on the Wakenitz where I also washed our bloodstained clothing. When he was awake, I spoke with Otto, but he was far from his usual cheerful self. It made me feel guilty – he wouldn't have been in this situation if not for me. I owed him for his help. But what in the name of God were we going to do?

The answer came to me in a dream on the third night in the hut. I awoke, cursing myself for not thinking of it earlier, but now at last I had a clear plan in mind. As usual, Tekla left early for the city to perform her usual house visits. She had told me the night before that she was expecting to deliver at least one baby. 'That's how I know Elsebeth,' she had said. 'I delivered her fourteen years ago.'

When she was gone, I told Otto my plan. He listened to me as I explained my idea. 'I do not know why I didn't think of it before.'

'But Livonia?' Otto said. 'Did I not tell you I hated the cold?'

'What choice do we have?' I said. 'I would rather go home – home to England, but that is impossible. If we join that order of warrior monks then at least we can finish our training and get to fight.'

'But as a monk?'

'Yes, we do not have enough money otherwise. Do you have a better idea?'

Otto didn't.

'We need to find out what day they sail. The bishop said that a Cistercian monk called Theodoric of Treiden would be sailing at the beginning of September. He also said that this Theodoric would talk again in the market beforehand. We need to find out.'

'But we dare not go into the city,' Otto said.

'Maybe we could ask Tekla?'

'She is an odd one, is she not?' Otto said. 'Living all alone here in the forest. Do you think she's a witch?'

'She is a healer – and she has done a pretty good job on your wound, so I would not worry. As we are stuck here, she is the only one that can find out what we need to know.'

'I should ask her,' Otto said. 'With my natural good looks and charm she would not be able to refuse me.'

I shook my head. 'She is old enough to be your mother... maybe even your grandmother.'

'Any port in a storm,' he said with a laugh, before wincing. 'Anyway, she would not understand your atrocious accent.'

I punched him playfully on his arm. Otto's appetite for the opposite sex always amazed me. Of course, he was tall, blond and broadly built – and I suppose he was handsome too, although I did not want to admit it. Certainly, most girls seemed to think so. For him, the thought of living a monastic life of celibacy must have been appalling. It was far from what I wanted, too, but being an outlaw, always on the run and fearing arrest, was even further.

'We can ask her,' I said. 'She does not want us around any longer than she needs, so she might be willing to find out when they sail.'

'But what if they do not accept us?'

I had not considered that possibility. 'Then we will have to flee. Go south. But you heard the bishop's speech... they're desperate for people to take the cross.' I hoped I was right.

As it was, we did not have to wait for Tekla to return. In the early afternoon it began to rain and there was an abrupt knock at the door. Both Otto and I looked up from our game of dice and froze. I put my finger to my lips and crept to the door, peering through the small hole at eye level to see who had interrupted us. A second later, I wrenched it open to see a startled Elsebeth. She quickly entered the hut, and after scanning the trees to make sure she had not been followed, I closed the door behind her.

She stood, dripping wet, and for a second, we stood looking at each other in silence. Her face was still bruised.

'I am glad you came,' I said.

'I was in two minds. But I said I would come and I keep my word.'

'What happened after we left?'

In a faltering voice, she explained that after we had left, she had gone to her father. Not unexpectedly, Eberhard had taken it badly, ranting and raving in a fury. 'He is devastated. I've never seen him like this before. He has promised a bag of silver to anyone that either kills you or helps bring you to justice. I explained you were only trying to protect me but he wouldn't listen.'

'And what did he say about Henkel killing Wilhelm?'

'Nothing... he did not say anything.'

'He did not say anything about the murder of his own brother?'

'Not really.'

I looked at her intently. With the rain dripping down her face it was hard to tell if she was crying or not. 'What do you mean *not really*? Then he did say something?'

Elsebeth hesitated.

'Tell me Elsebeth, please...'

'He said, "good riddance". He did not like his brother, Richard. You know that.'

'Then he should be ashamed of himself. I thought your father believed in family above everything?'

'Not with Uncle Wilhelm. I do not know much about what happened in the past – I was only a small child. But my father never forgave him. I am sorry… I know he was your friend.'

'Yes, he was.'

She changed the subject. 'Where will you go?'

'We talked about taking the cross and going to Livonia… But we do not know when they set sail. Would you be able to find out for us?' I explained how she could ask in the market square. 'They seem to be there recruiting most days.'

'I can try,' Elsebeth said. 'But if my father starts watching my movements it may be difficult. I could send Agnes if there are any problems.'

I looked around to see Otto watching us, his interest piqued by the mention of her maidservant's name. I wanted to talk to Elsebeth alone but there was nowhere private in the small hut. I led her outside, where we stood under the overhang of the thatched roof as the rain continued to stream down.

'How are you?' I said. 'Is everything well with the…?'

'With the baby? Yes, I think so. Henkel never hit me in my stomach.'

'Does your father know?'

'Yes… it is getting obvious now. He believes it belongs to Henkel. My father will help me look after it.'

'Elsebeth… it is not too late, we can still—'

She raised her hands. 'We have talked about this, Richard. Why can you not accept my answer?'

'But things have changed. I want to be with you. I want to help bring up our son.'

'How do you know it will be a boy? Would you be so interested in the child if it were a girl?'

'Of course,' I said, but the truth was I hadn't even considered it might be a girl.

'I can see from your face you have not even thought about it. No, Richard, I am sorry but I will not leave Lübeck. What kind of life would our child have as a fugitive?'

'Can I write to you? At least allow me that.'

She closed her eyes and nodded. 'I have to go now. If I can find out when the people you spoke of set sail to Livonia, I will let you know. Goodbye, Richard. May God protect you.'

I watched as she disappeared into the rain.

CHAPTER SEVENTEEN

Two days later, on the eve of the Feast of the Assumption of the Virgin, we had another visitor. It was not Elsebeth; it was Agnes. I was disappointed, but at least Otto was happy. His wound was healing and he could move around with only a little pain. We were both outside and he was watching me cut wood with the axe, when she appeared through the trees.

She looked scared, but wasted no time explaining the reason for her coming. 'My mistress was not able to come herself, for which she sends her apologies. She has a message.'

'Which is?'

'The people you are interested in sail in two days' time, after the feast tomorrow. They leave at dawn in three ships.'

I had heard enough. Otto wanted to talk to Agnes and after saying my goodbyes I went inside the hut to give them time alone. In order to reach the harbour by circumnavigating the city, we would have to leave early the next day. I peered out of the window and saw Otto and Agnes in a deep embrace, and felt a pang of jealousy. Women were only trouble – a lesson I had learned to my cost. Maybe following another path as warrior monks was the best thing for both of us.

Agnes left and Tekla returned from the city. No preparations were needed to leave, we had nothing apart from our weapons and the still bloodstained clothes we wore. After eating, the healer woman changed the dressing on Otto's wound and proclaimed herself satisfied at his progress. 'He shall be fit enough to travel tomorrow. It is not far. As long as you do not move too fast and his wound doesn't open again. I will accompany you on the first part to show you the best path. You should have no problem reaching a point near the harbour by tomorrow night.'

We went to bed before dusk. The next morning, Tekla woke us in darkness, giving us some bread and cheese as well as two hares she had caught and cooked the previous day. Dawn was lightening the sky when we left, Tekla leading us further into the trees away from the road that led directly to the city. Already, I could see that it was going to be another hot day and the air was fragrant with a woody incense as squirrels scuttled up the trees that surrounded us. We travelled in silence, passing close to the Wakenitz, where I could see the city walls through the foliage on the other side of the river. A group of women were washing clothes and they chattered to each other, their voices drifting across the sluggish water as the bells of the city's churches began to ring for Prime. We eventually came to a narrow track that wound through the tall beech and oak trees heading south. After a short while, the vegetation thinned, and through the undergrowth I could see another, bigger road that crossed from left to right. It was the same road we had traversed many times escorting the salt from Lüneburg.

Tekla stopped. 'This road passes through the village of Saint Jürgen and enters the city across the *Mühlenbrücke*. But you need to ignore it, keeping to this path, until you come to the Trave. There you will find a wooden bridge that spans the river before joining another road where you must turn right, keeping the river on your right-hand side. You will then reach the city from the south-west. I wish you both God's blessing.'

We barely had time to thank her before she slipped back into the trees, leaving us alone. We crossed over the Trave and joined the road. There were other travellers abroad, mostly heading towards the city, but no one took any notice of us. Otto was bearing up well, but we both welcomed the rest when we stopped off the road in a copse of ash trees for a light meal of bread and cheese. The sun was now high in the sky and it was another sweltering day. Sweat dripped down my face and back.

We continued, the road winding through the valley with the river just out of sight to our right. Soon we were in the trees again and we stopped to help an old pedlar and his family whose cart had overturned on the uneven road. Afterwards, we were both drenched in more sweat, but the old man gave us a flask of beer which helped quench our thirst, although he looked alarmed when he saw the bloodstained clothes under our cloaks. We carried on. The city was close now and the number of people was increasing. Despite the peace around us and the good weather, I felt apprehensive as we emerged from the trees with the city now in full view ahead of us. A crow hopped around at the edge of the road and cawed at us. Otto grimaced, declaring it a bad omen. My apprehension grew as we passed a collection of hovels towards the forest of ship masts to the west of the city.

We found a stand of oaks, away from the road but still in sight of the city, and we settled down. We could get a boat to ferry us across and reach the harbour in the same time it would have taken to walk to the warehouse from Eberhard's house.

We spent the rest of the afternoon napping and talking in the sun. From where we lay, we could hear the festivities taking place in the taverns and streets of the waterfront. The church bells rang for the Feast of the Assumption of the Virgin and we shared the beer as the sun began to cast long shadows. As it was getting dark, we made a small fire and ate the hares. Otto volunteered to take the first shift on watch after declaring that his wound did not pain him too much. Wrapped in my cloak, I curled up and fell asleep to the sound of drunken laughter drifting through the trees.

Despite one of us always being awake during the night, we both slept well, although I was eaten alive by the flying insects and awoke covered in bites. It was still dark, but a slight brightening of the sky to the east indicated that dawn was not far off. A brisk wind made it clear the good weather of the last few days was over. We kicked over the embers of the fire before descending the rise to one of the many skiffs that plied the river, ferrying people across to the harbour. I paid the man when we climbed out, entering the labyrinthine tangle of wooden buildings. There were already plenty of people on the move or starting work. We were close to Eberhard's warehouse and I felt a constriction in my throat, pulling up the hood of my cloak to cover my head. Thankfully, the gate to the surrounding warehouse wall was still closed. Nevertheless, I breathed easier when it was behind us. It did not take long to reach the dock where we had been told they were to sail. Three cogs were tied along the quay and a small crowd of people were gathered. Two men in white surcoats with the red sword and cross motif of the Swordbrothers stood talking. I steered Otto over to them while other men continued to load the ships with the last supplies. We asked the older of the two Swordbrothers how we could join the order.

'You need to speak to Abbot Theodoric.' He pointed to a stocky man in the black and white robes of a Cistercian monk who was deep in conversation with two other men.

We approached the group and stood patiently while the abbot finished his conversation. While we waited, my eye was drawn to one of the men he was talking to, a tall, elderly man who must have been at least fifty. Despite his age, he had a long mane of black hair with scarcely any grey, framing a strong face with deep-set eyes. He wore a light-blue tunic edged with the darker blue-grey of fur above black striped breeches and leather boots. Around his neck was a large golden cross that looked expensive. He was clearly not German, and he was relaxed and at ease. Theodoric was younger, but not by much, and he was no taller than me, even if he was twice as wide. He finally noticed us and stopped talking. 'What can I do for you, boys?' He had an open, honest face and I liked him immediately.

I bowed my head. 'We would like to join the Swordbrothers, father. We want to fight the pagans.' I didn't really give a damn about pagans, but I thought it was something he would want to hear.

Theodoric ran a practised eye over the both of us, noting our swords and clothing with a raised eyebrow. 'Well, you are both too young to be knight-brothers, but you look fit, and by the swords you carry I assume you have received martial training.'

'I am of noble birth and was training to be a knight,' I said, 'and Otto is *ministerialis*.'

'The Order normally only accepts men that are already knighted as full brothers – but considering your age there could be an exception. And we also need sergeants, so you can learn to support the knight-brothers until you reach your majority. We are a new Order and need everyone we can get. Do you belong to any other religious Order?'

'No,' we answered together.

'Are you married? Have you any hidden disabilities?'

We both shook our heads.

'Are you in debt? Are you serfs?'

We both answered no again.

'Good. Are you prepared to fight in Livonia, or elsewhere if commanded?'

'Yes,' we said.

Then he asked us a series of other questions. 'Are you prepared to help care for the sick? To practise any craft you know as ordered? To obey the Rule?'

We replied yes to all.

'Well, that is a start anyway.' Theodoric beamed. 'You shall have to swear to these things formally in an initiation ceremony before you are accepted as brothers, but that is some time off. It is normal for a gift of coin to accompany new recruits. Do you have any money?'

I looked at Otto before opening my purse, showing him the few pfennigs I had.

'I see,' Theodoric said. He looked disappointed. 'Give it to me anyway, you shall have no need of coin in the commandery.'

We both gave him our last few coins, before Theodoric told us to join the other volunteers, some twenty or so already waiting on the deck of one of the cogs. We had just reached the gangplank to board the ship when I froze, hearing a familiar voice behind me calling Otto's name. It was Makko.

'*Scheiße!*' Otto mumbled.

I turned to see Makko standing on the edge of the quay, looking at us with a moronic grin on his face. My heart nearly stopped when I saw Detmar just ahead of him, in conversation with another merchant. He had not seen us yet.

Otto started to wave Makko away as I pulled my friend up the gangplank and onto the deck of the ship. For a moment,

Makko continued to stare in confusion before turning to Detmar and saying something. I slipped the hood of my cloak up to cover my head, but not before Detmar glanced over and stared directly at us. For a moment he looked at me incredulously, before saying something to Makko and quickly disappearing into the crowd.

'Well that Hamburger ox has dumped us in it,' Otto said.

'We should have been more careful,' I said. 'Makko is so feeble-minded, he does not even know what he has done. But they will be back.'

'Hopefully after we have sailed,' Otto said. 'What shall we do, Richard?'

I was thinking. There was no doubt that Detmar would return, probably with the city watch. We could run, slip away in the bustle of the crowd before anyone knew we had gone. But how far would we get with no money and supplies? Not far at all.

'We should speak with the abbot,' I said. 'Maybe he will help?'

Otto looked unsure, but I walked the gangplank again back to the quay where Theodoric continued his talk with the two men. Otto followed reluctantly.

Theodoric looked surprised when I asked him if I could speak privately, nevertheless he led me a few paces away out of earshot of the others. 'What can I do for you?'

I explained what had happened at Elsebeth's house without telling him about our relationship. He listened as I told him about the fight and the deaths of Henkel and Wilhelm, with a frown that only deepened when I finished my story.

'But you say you killed this man in self-defence?'

'Yes,' I said. 'I swear on the Bible that it is true. Otto can confirm my words. Henkel killed Wilhelm before I killed him. He tried to kill both of us too.'

Theodoric looked to Otto, who nodded before lifting the edge of his tunic and showing the abbot the bloodstained bandage of his wound.

'This is not good. Now I see why you wish to escape to Livonia. You say this other man saw and recognised you?'

'Yes. I think he will make trouble.'

Theodoric thought for a moment. 'Well, we have nearly loaded the last supplies.' He looked at the sky. 'There is a good wind. We shall be able to sail shortly. Maybe nothing will happen before then. Go and wait with the others.'

Otto and I returned to the already crowded ship, watching as the crew began loading crates of trussed chickens, stowing them under the deck. As time passed, I began to relax. The preparations to sail were almost done and the tender that would tow us downriver was already alongside. I overheard a sailor telling one of the passengers that the journey would take two to three weeks, making this journey many times longer than the voyage from London. My hands became clammy at the prospect. Give me an enemy with a sword any day. How could you fight the sea?

It was then that I saw a group of men pushing through the crowd, with the tall figure of Eberhard at its head. I groaned and considered hiding behind the other recruits but dismissed the idea immediately. I walked to the gunwale towards where my accusers stood on the quay. I would face my enemies openly.

'There they are!' Detmar shouted to his father. His face was still bruised and his nose a mess from the beating I had given him. I looked at them defiantly, my hand on my sword.

Detmar's shout had attracted attention and I watched Theodoric, still accompanied by the two men, stride the length of the wharf to where Eberhard stood near the gangplank that led to our ship. Eberhard was accompanied by Johann and some of my old comrades, including Makko and Kunz.

'What appears to be the problem here?' Theodoric said.

Eberhard pointed at me. 'The problem is there. Standing on the deck of one of your ships.'

Theodoric turned and gave a theatrical sweep of his arm in our direction. 'I see only new recruits ready to do God's work in Livonia. Please explain yourself.'

'That man,' Eberhard said, almost apoplectic with rage. He pointed at me again. 'That young man killed a dear friend of mine and the husband to my daughter. I want to see him dancing on the end of a rope. You must hand him over immediately so that justice can be done.'

'Must I?' Theodoric folded his arms across his chest. 'On whose authority? Why would I hand him over to what looks like nothing more than a group of brigands?'

'I am one of the most prominent merchants in Lübeck! The *vogt* is on his way to make the arrest. This man is a murderer. I demand that you hand him and his accomplice over at once. This is not a religious matter.'

'The boy in question swears that he acted in self-defence. What is more, I believe him. We are about to set sail on God's work. The pope himself, when I last saw him a little over three months ago, has declared a remission of sins to those who take the cross. Therefore, as far as the Church is concerned, both boys are innocent.'

I watched the exchange with interest. Johann was staring at me and I could see he was itching for a fight. I held his gaze. Johann was a good swordsman but I felt no fear. I had killed his master and would happily do the same to him if he wanted. He was nothing but a rat's turd. Detmar, in contrast, refused to look me in the eye.

'The boy is a murderer,' Eberhard pronounced. 'The

authorities have been hunting him since he committed his atrocious crime. You cannot sail until this matter has been settled. The *vogt* shall be here soon...'

'We are ready to sail now and every moment we waste here could cause the wind to change,' Theodoric said. 'And that must not be allowed to happen. If you are unhappy, I suggest you take it up with the Danes or Bishop Albert. He is somewhere in Westphalia preaching God's message.' Theodoric said something to his two companions and they prepared to go up the gangplank. As far as Theodoric was concerned the matter was decided. Eberhard stood red-faced on the quay, while Detmar looked like he was going to be sick. Kunz appeared confused, as did Makko, although that seemed to be the big Hamburger's only expression. Johann continued to glare at me and I knew he would do something. He would not let the death of his master and friend go unavenged. And I was right.

He screamed a challenge and drew his sword, elbowing past Theodoric in his haste to get to me. He charged up the gangplank as everyone else looked on in shock.

I drew my sword swiftly to block Johann's frenzied attack as everyone else scattered out of the way. My arm jarred in pain as I again parried Johann's next strike, catching his blade with mine and driving him away. Johann responded with a furore of blows that forced me back across the deck. I managed to block each attack without striking back. My enemy finally relented and we circled each other warily.

'That is Henkel's sword you have!' Johann's scarred face was a rictus of hate. 'I see you are a thief as well as a murderer!'

'And you are nothing but a piece of shit!' I spat back at him.

Above us, I could hear Theodoric shouting but we both ignored him, continuing to circle each other, each looking for an opening or weakness.

Johann swung his sword towards my head, and when I raised my own sword to parry, he changed direction, flicking his weapon back to slash down towards my stomach. But I had learned this feint from Sir Hugh and I was ready, blocking the blow before breaking contact and taking a step back. I grinned at him.

In comparison to Johann, I was young and inexperienced. He had spent twenty years learning the art of swordplay and he was good. But I had one distinct advantage I knew would prove crucial. I was fast. Lightning fast.

And I used that speed now, lunging at my enemy, catching him completely unprepared. He tried to raise his sword to deflect my thrust but he was too slow. My sword pierced Johann in the middle of his unarmoured chest. For a moment he looked at me in shock, before falling backwards to the deck of the ship, blood seeping from his wound.

I did not need to look at him again to know he was dead. Around me I heard an audible sucking in of air. Blood pounded through my veins and fury exploded in me. I strode to the gunwale and pointed my sword at Eberhard. 'Johann is dead. Now he can join his master in hell. Henkel killed your brother in cold blood. But then again, you cared nothing for your brother, did you, Eberhard?'

Eberhard looked at me aghast before breaking eye contact. He turned to Theodoric. 'He just killed my man. Do you doubt now what he is capable of?'

'He acted in self-defence before a hundred witnesses, you fool. Your man attacked him and got what he deserved. I shall pray for his soul.'

But I was not finished berating Eberhard. I felt Otto tugging at my arm but I shrugged him off. I had kept all this anger bottled up for the last few months and now was the time to let it all out. 'You are nothing but a bastard. Your precious friend Henkel was a murderer and a rapist that beat your own daughter until she was blue. Did you never notice, Eberhard? Did you never notice her swollen face or did you choose not to see? Henkel was a piece of rat's dung and the world is a better place without him.' I stood with my arms extended, brandishing my bloodied sword high for everyone to see. 'Here I am, Eberhard! If you want me so badly, you whoreson, come and get me... Any of you!'

Of course, no one moved. I felt Otto next to me again and the mist of anger slowly began to clear. Theodoric stepped onto the gangplank followed by his two companions and I finally lowered my sword. Eberhard and my old comrades continued to look on in shock and I saw the two Swordbrothers both had their own weapons drawn. They followed Theodoric up the gangplank.

Otto put his arm around me. 'It is over, Richard. No one else wants to fight you.'

I relented, letting him lead me across the deck to the opposite side of the ship. The other passengers watching in silence made room for us, moving away as if we were lepers. Theodoric said something to the two Swordbrothers and they picked up the corpse of Johann, carrying him down the gangplank and depositing him on the quayside, directly in front of where the others stood, before returning to the ship. The tender was already in position in the Trave and at a shout from the captain the crew began to push the ship away from the dock with long poles. The bow was pulled round by the tender until we were facing downstream. Behind us, the other two cogs were likewise pushing away from the quay. A large crowd had now gathered, lining the harbourside. Eberhard and his group hadn't moved and I saw a rider draw his horse up next to them. He must have been the *vogt*, or sheriff, but he was too late. We were already being towed downriver.

Theodoric came over to us. 'I cannot believe what I just witnessed. Where did you learn to fight like that?'

'Back home, in England. And then here in Lübeck.'

'Well, you are very good.' He indicated the strange-looking man I had seen him talking to earlier. 'Caupo knows a bit about fighting. He was particularly impressed. But I fear you have not heard the last of this little incident. I do not like merchants – the love of gold burns brighter in their chests than the love of God, and there will be problems. I must say though, I did enjoy seeing the look on his face when I refused to hand you over.'

'Eberhard is used to being obeyed,' I said.

'Well, not this time. But you are lucky you are sailing with me rather than Bishop Albert. He would have handed you over without compunction to avoid upsetting the money men. Almost all the crusaders needed in Livonia sail from this port and he cannot afford any disruption. The merchants could make things difficult. I should probably have handed you over too. But I have faith. Faith that you shall prove to be a worthy soldier of Christ.'

I nodded, not sure what to say. Theodoric went to speak to the captain while I walked over to the gunwale, looking at the wharves and quays slowly falling behind. I wondered if Elsebeth was in the crowd – at least she had not been with her father. Otto joined me and we scanned the harbourside. Then I saw her, standing with Agnes away from the bulk of people. My breath caught in my throat as she gave a small wave. I could feel Otto's excitement next to me as Agnes gave a heartier one. Would we ever see them again? Would I ever see my son... my child?

So, I had been chased out of another city. Always moving further away from my goal: Cranham, the only place I really wanted to be. Always running away. I made a vow there and then that I would return one day to this city. I would return to Lübeck, regardless of the risks or dangers involved.

Now, I was heading for a country I had never even heard of only a month before, off to fight for the God I questioned daily in my head.

Now, as Theodoric had said, I was to be a soldier of Christ.

Yuriev Monastery,
Novgorod Republic,
June 1242

—————

The scratch of the quill opposite stopped abruptly as Fergus realised I was no longer talking. He looked at me expectantly, before reverting to the sneer that now seemed permanently fixed to his face, as if he knew something I didn't. Since Prince Alexander had spoken to us, his outright hostility had receded to a sullen silence, punctuated by the odd ironic comment and his perpetual sneering. This change in behaviour infuriated me even more than when we were exchanging barbed insults.

'I've had enough for the day,' I said. I glared at the Irishman as I came to my feet, daring him to say something. My shoulder burned, but I was damned if I would tell him that was the reason.

There were no farewells when I hobbled from the scriptorium and into the warm air outside. At least now I could move around without any aid, but I often had to pause for flashes of sudden pain. I sat down on the stone seat built into the side of the well, enjoying the sun on my face.

Recounting my story was proving to be more difficult than I imagined. It was hard for two reasons. The events I was recalling had occurred so long ago it was hard to remember exactly what had happened, despite my good memory. And secondly, I had trouble with some of the feelings it evoked – feelings buried for so long I had forgotten they existed. Talking about Elsebeth was the most difficult.

And thinking about Cranham always brought up my anger, despite the events being so long ago. I knew I would never return to the land of my birth and the thought still frustrated me. Remembering the death of my father, Sir Hugh, and the men who had shown their loyalty, Wilhelm included, rekindled feelings that had been suppressed for forty years. And, of course, there were the doubts. Maybe if I had returned to England after Lübeck and confronted my uncle, things would have been different. Maybe if I had been more persuasive with Elsebeth... There were always so many maybes, questions only God knew the answer to.

I awoke in the infirmary the next morning hearing voices outside through the shutters of my window. It was relatively rare to hear people talking loudly; the monks moved around the monastery in virtual silence. My interest was immediately roused. I sat up and struggled into my clothes, not so easy with one arm in a sling and my shoulder swathed in bandages. Sharp pain stabbed at my wound and a wave of dizziness swept over me, but I managed to keep on my feet, waiting patiently for it to fade. When it had passed, I shuffled outside into the early light of the dawn. Across the grass, I noticed a group of figures near the entrance to the cathedral. Even in the poor light I could see they were not monks. As I approached, I saw they carried weapons and wore the distinctive conical helmets of Russian soldiers. They turned to regard me before I reached them, and I recognised Prince Alexander, who said something that made the others laugh. Fergus nodded curtly before translating the prince's next words. 'Prince Alexander bids yourself good morning,' Fergus said as Alexander continued talking. 'Things have changed. You are to pack your things and come with us to Novgorod.'

'Novgorod?' I said. 'Why? I am supposed to be recovering here.'

'You are a prisoner and you go where you're told,' Fergus said with obvious relish. 'Prince Alexander shall be busy for the next few weeks and needs myself by his side, so I can no longer come daily to Yuriev. Therefore, he has decided we must continue the chronicle at Gorodische, his palace south of the city. The prince wishes to pay his respects to his dead brother buried here, so he does. Meantime, you can make any preparations to leave. The journey shall not take long.'

Alexander entered the church, followed by Fergus and several other men. I returned to the infirmary where I said goodbye to Dimitri. His eyes sparkled with amusement and his beard trembled as he chuckled aloud. He gave me back my sword but my mail-coat from the battle was damaged beyond repair. I thanked him with heartfelt emotion; this man had undoubtedly saved my life by his diligence and skill. We couldn't speak each other's language, nevertheless I clearly conveyed my respect for him. And gratitude.

Outside, the sun was rising slowly in a cloudless sky, heralding another fine summer's day. The bell began to ring and the yard quickly began to fill up with monks, all heading for the cathedral. Prince Alexander emerged with his entourage and I joined them. He said something to Fergus.

'Prince Alexander wants you to swear on your honour as a Christian you will not try and escape. If you refuse, you will have to give up your sword and be manacled.' He looked like he wanted me to refuse.

'I agree,' I said without hesitation. Where would I escape

to? I was also curious to see Novgorod, a city I had heard so much about.

Alexander seemed satisfied. He led us away from the stables and main gate, heading towards a long, perpendicular wall at the other end of the monastery. We passed some fruit trees and reached a smaller gate, which opened to a patch of grass by the riverbank. The river was wide and I could see Lake Ilmen, sparkling in the early morning light. We walked across a narrow beach to where a barge waited. Not far away, a group of women from a nearby village washed clothes while children played in the sand. Everything was peaceful, far from the threat of war. We climbed aboard the barge and I was given a seat near the bow. Behind me, under an awning, sat Prince Alexander with three priests and the rest of the men and soldiers crowded onto the rear of the boat. Half-a-dozen men manned the oars and they pushed off into the sluggish waters of the Volkhov, disturbing a multitude of geese in the reeds that took flight, flapping and splashing across the water. The men began to row and we headed slowly downriver, the oars gently pulling the barge towards the other side.

Up ahead, on the opposite bank, I saw a stockaded settlement on a low rise, with the onion-domed cupola of a church within. A path led from the gate down to a wooden jetty and I realised this was our destination. A short time later, the oars were banked as we came alongside the jetty and moored. After we had climbed out, the prince said something, clapping me on my good shoulder and pointing up towards the palisade.

'Prince Alexander says that this was the original city of Novgorod. Now it is his palace. It will be your home until you are ransomed back to your Order.'

I said nothing, following Alexander up the path to the gate. I gave the settlement a critical eye. It was well located, on a small hill surrounded by a partially flooded ditch and embankment, topped by a stout palisade of long logs laid horizontal in the Russian way. On top of the palisade were soldiers, which meant it had a fighting platform, although I could not see if it encircled the entire settlement. It was the only defensible site I could see in the predominantly flat, marshy terrain.

Before we reached the gate, it swung open, revealing half-a-dozen soldiers who greeted Alexander and his men warmly. Although I no longer wore mail or my white surcoat with the black cross of the Teutonic Order, it was obvious I was not Russian and I could feel the people watching me, although more with curiosity than hostility.

Inside, Gorodische was packed with wooden buildings, making it more of a village than a palace. And it was busy. People crowded the shops and shacks buying whatever goods were for sale while children and chickens ran between their legs. Alexander was at his affable best, a quick word to a man here, slapping the back of a street vendor there, laughing and chatting with the people we passed on our way towards a larger stone and wood-built building alongside the church I had seen from the river. We reached the main palace and climbed the wooden staircase to the front door on the first floor. Alexander led us into a large hall. He began talking earnestly to two men sat at a long table and I was taken away by Fergus and a guard down a short corridor to a windowless, cell-like room, with whitewashed plastered wood, as in the monastery, and lit by an oil lamp that hung from a peg on the wall.

'This shall be your room.' Fergus pointed towards the narrow bed that filled most of the space. 'The physician will come and examine your wound later. You are not allowed to leave the palace without an escort. Now, I'm sure you must be tired, so we'll be leaving you to rest. There shall be a guard stationed outside your room.'

'The guard is unnecessary. I gave my word I would not try and escape. Anyway, where do you think I would go?'

'The guard is for your protection, so he is.' Fergus gave one of his now familiar sneers. 'And anyway, we all know your kind cannot be trusted.'

I fought the desire to punch him and they left, closing the door behind them. I felt exhausted and my wound throbbed. I reclined on the bed and quickly fell asleep.

A bell ringing from the church next door woke me. I had no idea how long I'd slept, but I could hear raised voices in the hall speaking Russian. I lay listening and not understanding. Nonetheless, I was sure one of the angry voices belonged to Alexander. A moment later there was a gentle knock at the door. It was the physician, another monk in black, at least thirty years younger than Dimitri.

'Good afternoon.' The monk spoke impeccable Latin. 'I am Miroslav. I have been assigned to tend you back to health.'

He was tall and slim, with a short, tidy beard and bright blue eyes. I let him change the dressing and he inspected the wound carefully. As he moved around the room, I noticed he wore a piece of cloth on the back of his habit that contained a cross and other Biblical images, as well as a crucifix around his neck. He prodded and poked but seemed satisfied with my progress. Nevertheless, the examination was agony for me and I clenched my teeth to avoid screaming out loud.

'It seems Brother Dimitri has done his usual good work again.' Miroslav smiled, and rebandaged my shoulder. 'The wound is inflamed but you should recover, although there may be permanent damage. I doubt you will hold a shield for long with this arm again.'

I knew this, of course, and I'd already come to the realisation that my fighting days were over. I was simply too old. But it didn't distress me. I had killed my first man at the age of fourteen and I had seen enough death to last a hundred lifetimes. If I never saw another corpse again, I would be happy.

'You need to get plenty of rest,' Miroslav's voice was soft and his Latin was superior to my own.

'I've had plenty of rest,' I said. 'Now I'm starving. I am going to get something to eat.'

Miroslav didn't object and he helped me down the corridor to the main hall. From the fading light through the open shutters, I estimated it was late afternoon or early evening. At the top table, Alexander sat deep in conversation with half a dozen of his close advisors and I could see from the grim expression on his face that he was not happy. My arrival with Miroslav went unnoticed and we took seats at one of the lower tables. Miroslav said something to one of the servants who disappeared, returning a few moments later with two steaming wooden bowls of cabbage soup with pieces of mutton floating in it and a hunk of black bread.

'This is called *shchi*,' Miroslav said. 'It is rather tasty.'

'What are they talking about?' I nodded my head towards the prince and his advisors in between mouthfuls of food. 'The prince isn't happy.'

The monk looked at me, then smiled. 'It is quite complicated. Prince Alexander was at a meeting again of the *veche* – a public assembly – in Novgorod. He argued again with some of the *boyars* and the *posadnik* – the city mayor.'

'Argued about what?'

Miroslav sighed deeply. 'About what terms of peace to offer your people. Prince Alexander would like to be generous because he wants peace on our western frontier so he can concentrate on the more dangerous threat.'

'And what is the more dangerous threat?'

'The Tatars, of course,' Miroslav said, as if it was obvious. 'They have raided and sacked many settlements to the south and east. Two years ago, they even sacked Kiev.'

'I remember. Were there any Mongols at the battle on the ice?'

Miroslav smiled. There was a calmness about him I found reassuring. 'I really have no idea. You will have to ask Prince Alexander that question yourself. I am but a modest monk, not a man of war.'

I looked up from my bowl as more men came into the hall to eat. Some of them looked over at me warily and none sat at our table.

'They are the prince's *druzhina*, his retainers,' Miroslav said in explanation. 'Most of them will have fought in the battle where you were captured.'

They certainly knew who I was. I noticed one of the men glaring at me and I met his gaze, refusing to turn away. I grinned, hoping to goad him. If it came to a fight, I would be barely able to defend myself, but a warrior must have pride. Without pride we are nothing.

One of the man's comrades said something to him, jerking his thumb towards where Alexander sat behind. The man continued to hold my gaze and I was damned if I was going to break eye contact first. After a moment more, he looked away reluctantly, obviously convinced by his comrade's words. I turned back to Miroslav.

'Prince Alexander warned his men not to try and pick a fight with you,' the monk said. 'You are to be treated with respect.'

'So I see,' I said ironically. Fergus had entered the hall with several other bookish-looking scribes, but they also sat away from us. Everyone was eating now, and the murmur of

Russian voices had dropped noticeably. I finished my soup and a servant came and offered me a cup of *kvass*, which I knew from my time in Estonia. It was a fermented drink made with rye and was mildly alcoholic. To me it tasted like goat's piss. Our main course consisted of a variety of freshwater fish caught in the lake, some fried, some baked, and accompanied with peas and more cabbage, turnips and steaming bowls of carrots. It was all served with more bread.

I saw that Alexander had been joined at the top table by a young, very attractive woman who Miroslav told me was his wife, named Paraskeviya but now called Alexandra since their marriage. She was tall and slim and her hair looked like gold in the light of the candles, and I observed how many of the men in the hall watched her closely, if somewhat covertly. The prince was still deeply involved in his discussion and barely picked at his food. He hardly noticed his wife.

When the meal had been cleared away by the servants, most of Alexander's retinue drifted off, leaving less than twenty people in the hall. Alexander called me over, waving me to join him at his table where he still sat with most of his advisors. I took a seat, feeling everyone's eyes on me. Fergus also joined us and Alexander began speaking quickly to him. After a short moment Fergus began to translate.

'Prince Alexander wants yourself to accompany him to Novgorod for the next *veche* in ten days' time.'

'Why? I don't speak Russian and I doubt anyone would want to hear what a vanquished enemy has to say.'

'On the contrary,' Fergus said. 'They will be very interested in what you have to say now. You know better than anyone what terms of peace your Order would accept.'

'Why would I help an enemy parley for better terms? I am a knight of the Teutonic Order. I shall not betray my own people.'

Alexander frowned and said something to Fergus.

'You are not being asked to betray anyone. Prince Alexander wants yourself to help convince the *veche* towards a lasting peace. That is in the interests of your Order as well as Novgorod the Great. Some *boyars* want us to take advantage of our victory and attack Livonia. We know your forces are spread thinly and would need time to assemble, certainly after your defeat at Lake Chudskoe. An attack would have a high likelihood of success. If the *boyars*, supported by the archbishop, win the argument, that shall be the fate that awaits your people. Prince Alexander wants to avoid this. He believes nothing can be gained by raiding Livonia again.'

'Yes,' I said. 'You already raped and pillaged much of Ungannia last time.'

'As did you at Pskov,' Fergus retorted. 'We saw the evidence in the burnt monasteries and destroyed icons. It was disgusting, so it was.'

'Don't be so naïve,' I retorted. 'Disgusting things always happen in war. Some of the things I've seen would make your nails curl.'

Fergus snorted. 'But why will you not answer the question? Will you speak at the *veche*?'

'Do I have a choice?' I looked at Alexander.

The prince said something and everyone around the table laughed. Of course I had no choice. If Alexander wanted me to speak at the assembly then speak I would. I didn't object to attending the *veche*. It might even be entertaining. But my shoulder was throbbing and I was tired. It was time to rest again. I came to my feet, bowed my head to Prince Alexander and asked his leave. Miroslav helped me to return to my small room.

I continued my story with Fergus in the scriptorium the next morning.

PART THREE

LIVONIA, 1204–1205

CHAPTER EIGHTEEN

Despite the fine summer weather, the ship pitched and tossed in the rolling waves as seagulls screeched high above the deck, circling and diving around the sail that billowed and cracked in the stiff wind. I stood at the raised stern, watching the two other ships in line behind us and the smudge of land that stretched across the horizon, breathing in great lungfuls of salty air. I was alone. Most of the other passengers kept their distance, wary after what had happened in Lübeck, but I felt their eyes on me when they thought I wasn't looking. Let them look. I had done no wrong and had nothing to hide.

The ship was named *Saint Maria*, after the mother of Christ. She was larger than *Christofer*, both in length and beam, with a proper deck and a raised stern. From the mast flew the banner of a white cross on a black background that I found out later was the new flag of Riga. And she was crowded, with a dozen crew and approximately forty or fifty passengers: Theodoric and his entourage of priests and monks, the two Swordbrothers, Caupo and another two men who were not German. Otherwise, there were a dozen prospective recruits for the Sword Brethren Order and twenty or so men who had taken the cross to go to Livonia, most of them armed. There was also a girl of roughly my own age, accompanied by her father and a maidservant, but I paid her no further attention. The ship was also packed with supplies, urgently needed according to Theodoric, to help bolster the forces and fledgling settlement of Riga. When I peered down the hatch below deck, I saw there was hardly any room, with barrels, kegs and crates jammed into every available space, and linen hammocks hanging or stretched in the few gaps between.

I joined Otto, who squatted forward of the mast trying to keep out of the crew's way, as he played dice with three of the other youths who wanted to join the Swordbrothers, all of them several years older than me. The first, crouched next to Otto, was a thickset, almost fat, boy of sixteen or so with short blond hair and bad acne. His name was Gerhard and he was from a small town near Lübeck I had never heard of. 'My father was a poor knight – a *ministerialis*,' he explained after Otto had just won the last round of dice. 'But he died a year ago.'

I nodded absently, preoccupied with my thoughts and hardly listening. One of the other youths, a taller boy who was almost a man, was watching me carefully. 'That was some fight you had in Lübeck,' he said. 'Where did you learn your skill with the sword? I thought the other man would cut you to ribbons. Why did they want to arrest you?'

I felt my irritation rise again. 'Those are too many questions. I have no desire to speak about this. And who are you anyway?'

'My name is Hinz. My father is a merchant in Lübeck.'

'Oh God… so he's a bastard then.'

He looked hurt. 'Why do you say that? I meant no disrespect.'

My anger collapsed immediately. 'I'm sorry,' I said. 'I have endured much of late, but that is no excuse. I worked for Eberhard Weber.'

'I know of him. His son, Detmar, is an arsehole.'

I smiled. 'Yes, that's the truth of it. But he shall not forget me in a hurry.'

He nodded, satisfied. 'I think there will be ordeals ahead for all of us. I have heard that life in Livonia is not easy...'

'And damned cold,' Otto said.

'God's work is never easy,' the third boy said. He wasn't playing dice despite sitting with the others. I looked at him with interest. He must have been sixteen or seventeen, as tall as Otto although not as muscular, with a pale, feminine face that girls would probably find attractive and his straight black hair grown long and tied at the nape. He introduced himself as Emich. 'I look forward to helping bring the pagans to the Lord.' Around his neck was a chain with a finely crafted silver cross.

'I'd rather let the priests do that,' Otto said. 'I'm just glad to get away from Lübeck. But I am looking forward to fighting the pagans.'

I nodded in agreement. My friend had echoed my own thoughts exactly.

'Of course, if they resist our efforts...' Emich conceded. 'But it is our duty to try and save their souls, not just kill them.'

Otto shrugged and grinned at me. We didn't care either way.

'We have to train first with sword and shield,' I said. 'Working as sergeants to obey every wish of our masters. We will be virtually slaves. I have no illusions that it shall prove easy.' Opposite me, I noticed Gerhard had turned pale. Beads of sweat prickled his brow. Without any warning, he jumped to his feet and dashed to the side of the ship to vomit over the gunwale.

'If he is sick now,' Hinz said with a chuckle, 'imagine how he'll be when we're in a storm. I don't want to sleep next to him.'

'If there is a storm,' I said, 'then you will not want to sleep next to anyone. And don't let the good weather fool you. It could change in a moment.' I spoke like a veteran despite having hardly any experience of sailing – only the time when we had all nearly drowned.

'Have you noticed that girl onboard?' Otto said. 'She's quite pretty but her father guards her like a gaoler. I tried to talk to her but he immediately whisked her away... but not before she told me her name. Margret. I feel sorry for her with a father like that.'

'I've hardly noticed her,' I said truthfully. 'I want no part of any women.'

'Well. That's why we're going to be monks. There'll be no women for either of us...'

On the raised deck at the stern of the ship I saw Theodoric in conversation with the captain. The captain was a short man with a bushy grey beard that looked as though it might have small animals living in it. I listened as he paused in his conversation to berate one of the crew for not working fast enough.

'Are you playing, Richard?' Otto held up the dice.

'There doesn't seem much point without any money.' I looked back at Theodoric, remembering how he had taken our last few pfennigs.

At the bottom of the steps up to the stern deck, the two Swordbrothers were talking quietly, looking over at the assembled passengers. One of them was young, but the other man interested me more. He was older, at least in his mid-thirties, with a bushy, bleached beard and a face that looked like it had been hewn from stone. He saw me watching him and gave a small nod, almost imperceptible, before looking away towards the empty sea. I wanted to talk to him but there was no haste. There would be enough time on the long journey. I spent the rest of the day playing dice, keeping out the way of the crew and getting to know my new companions.

The next morning the weather was also fair, with light clouds scudding the sky and a fresh breeze that filled the sail and drove us on eastwards. We had spent the night sleeping in our cloaks on deck, along with some of the crew under some oilskin covers in the bow, but we were still soaked from the spray that washed continually over the high sides of the ship. Everything was permanently wet and water dripped from the shrouds and the sail, puddling on the deck, but I was glad we hadn't slept in the hold with most of the other passengers, as the smell of vomit and shit was overwhelming. Food was served in wooden bowls, a watery soup with pieces of fish in it, while others queued up to relieve their bowels at the two seats that projected precariously out of each side of the prow. I walked away from the others and ate my soup, staring at the distant shoreline to our left, which I had been told was Denmark. A few moments later the elder of the two Swordbrothers joined me.

'Abbot Theodoric says that you have consented to join our Order,' he said. 'That is good. We need new blood and you have proven you can fight.'

'I thank you for your words, although it was not a fight I looked for. I am Richard. Richard Fitz Simon.'

'Dieter von Stammen.' The man spoke slowly in a deep voice, realising my knowledge of Low German was limited. He explained he had been in the Order of Swordbrothers from its inception in 1202. 'It was founded by Theodoric, although it was sanctioned by Bishop Albert. Knights and men are needed to provide a year-round defence of the colony. It is our duty to build and garrison castles to protect the mission and help convert the local pagans from their evil beliefs. We are few in number – less than fifty full brothers – but our task is a great one. And we are a young Order. You and your friends shall be welcome and much needed.'

Of course, I didn't know it then but I would grow to know Dieter well. In an Order with more than its fair share of sinners and criminals, Dieter would prove to be one of the best men ever to wear the white mantle with the red insignia of cross and sword, a man I would happily follow and trust with my life.

My attention was interrupted by booming laughter and I looked over at the elderly foreign man who was again talking and laughing with Theodoric.

'That is Caupo,' Dieter said, noticing my glance. 'He is a chief of the Livs and a good friend of both Theodoric and Bishop Albert. He was one of the first pagans to be converted to Christianity, over ten years ago, I believe. We have returned from Rome, having been entertained by Pope Innocent III.'

'What did the pope say?'

'He was impressed. We have travelled far over the last year, but it has been very beneficial for our cause.'

I found out later that it had been very beneficial indeed. Pope Innocent III had agreed to allow Albert to move the fledgling bishopric from Uexküll down the Düna river to Riga. He also agreed on the formation of a Cistercian monastery at the mouth of the same river, at Dünamünde, a few miles from Riga and to be administered by Theodoric himself. And of course, the pope's agreement on the foundation of the Militia of Christ (*Fratres militiæ Christi*), better known as the Swordbrothers and given the Rule based on that of the Templars and of which I was now a member. 'What is it like in Riga?' I asked.

'It is precarious. There are simply not enough of us. In the summer it is better because pilgrims come from the Empire, but they normally go home for the winter – before the sea freezes. The winter is harder.'

'And colder.' I remembered Otto's complaining.

'And colder,' he agreed.

I returned to my friends, answering their eager questions about what I had found out. After listening, Otto suggested we play dice again. I settled down, sitting with Hinz, Gerhard and Emich. It was going to be a long journey.

Thankfully the good weather held over the following days. Life onboard *Saint Maria* settled down into a tedious routine that hardly changed. During daylight hours there was nothing to do but sit and talk, sleep or play dice. One day, we spent an afternoon fishing from the stern deck but none of us caught anything. I would like to have trained in swordplay, but the ship was so crowded it was clearly impossible. 'Don't worry,' Theodoric said. 'There will be plenty of time when we reach Livonia. And you might get a chance before then. The Oeselian pirates are always active. Ask any captain who sails the route to Novgorod.'

His words would prove prophetic. It was something I learned the longer I knew the burly monk. Theodoric always seemed to have the uncanny habit of being right, as if the Lord personally confided the future to him.

We were now out of sight of land, which was no great problem considering the good weather. At night, progress was harder; but with clear skies the captain had no trouble navigating by the stars. However, on the fifth day out from Lübeck a wind picked up, churning the grey waters into whitecaps and billowing the sail and slapping the shrouds. I felt a tremor of apprehension when I looked up and saw dark clouds pushing oppressively down over the horizon. It was still warm, but there was no mistaking the storm on its way.

At the stern, the captain barked orders and the deck thumped to the sound of rushing feet as the crew responded, reefing the large square sail. The faces of my comrades mirrored the same fear I felt. Memories of the previous storm crossing the English Channel came unbidden to my mind and I felt a rising panic. I considered going to the hold, but the stink and the rats dissuaded me. No, I would rather take my chances out in the open, but many of the other passengers went below. Emich kissed his cross, mumbling prayers and Hinz began tying a rope around his waist. Otto and Gerhard just looked terrified.

As it was, we needn't have worried. The storm passed to the east of us and we watched the lightning flash on the horizon, feeling the wind in our hair and the salt on our faces. It was exhilarating as darkness fell and the heavens were still lit by jagged bolts of lightning that split the sky. But the storm came no closer. After watching well into the night, I eventually joined the others, settling down in my cloak in our usual place in the lee of the stern deck for another uncomfortable night of disturbed sleep.

For the next few days the weather was not so hot and there was even rain one afternoon, although little more than a brief shower. In the second week after leaving Lübeck, we put into the harbour of Visby on the island of Gotland to refill our water casks and take on a dozen stonemasons who were to help build a church in Riga and the castles that would be needed to keep control over the land. Theodoric refused to allow any of the volunteers to leave the ship, no doubt fearing some of us may have second thoughts and try to desert. Unfortunately for us, we lacked a favourable wind thereafter and had to spend a further three nights in port before the wind picked up again, allowing us to set sail at dawn on the fourth morning, heading directly east into the rising sun.

By now, everyone on board was thoroughly bored with the monotony and both the captain and Theodoric had trouble keeping tempers under control. A group of warriors on crusade argued over a game of knucklebones. One man accused another of cheating and it quickly escalated into a full-blown fight. Within seconds, all six men involved were throwing punches and the man accused drew a knife. Theodoric, aided by Caupo, Dieter and some of the crew, rushed in and banged heads together, the abbot lashing the men responsible with his tongue while Dieter used the flat of his sword. A moment later, several men were bloodied and the man who had cheated and drawn the knife was bound and thrown into the hold to calm down.

Everything settled back to normal. Just before darkness, our small flotilla of three ships was overtaken by a smaller cog, heading in the same direction, with a grey sail and flying the red and white flag of Lübeck. It passed close enough for us to see the figures on deck and several people waved. I wondered if they were also bound for Riga, but by the time the sun set behind us the ship was just a speck on the horizon.

It was early the next morning that the words spoken by Theodoric became reality. I had just taken my turn at the prow to relieve my bowels, a precarious morning routine, and was waiting for the usual fish broth when there was a shout from one of the crew. Ahead, a pall of smoke hung over the horizon. Everyone stared as it dissipated in the sky, wondering what awaited us. The captain barked some orders and the crew ran to tie the mainsail forward to the stem-post, trying to catch every gasp of what little wind there was. The ship turned slowly towards the source of the smoke.

Theodoric descended from the stern deck, his booming voice telling everyone to prepare for a fight. 'It is probably Oeselian pirates,' he said. 'They plague the waters of the eastern Baltic. Give out all the crossbows onboard to anyone who can fire them. All of you prepare any weapons you have. If you have need, Brother Dieter will give you something from the stores.'

My heart beat quicker in my chest at the prospect of a battle. In the years since, this sensation has become as common as cold on a lonely night's vigil, but at the time it was new. And I relished it. There was nothing like the thought that soon my life would be in the balance – dependent on God's grace and my own skill at arms. Otto felt the same and we grinned at each other as we fetched our swords, returning to our place at the gunwale, where we began sharpening them, although they were already as sharp as they ever would be.

'Can you see anything?' I said to Otto. I had learnt in Lübeck that my big friend's eyesight was as good as any eagle.

Otto shook his head and we were joined by Hinz, cradling one of the crossbows.

'You don't look like you know what end to point at the enemy,' I mocked, laughing at the expression of nervousness on his face. 'I don't suppose there was much need to shoot at people as a merchant.'

'How can you be so calm?' he said.

I laughed, more out of bravado and arrogance than anything else. The truth was, I wasn't calm – my palms were clammy and my mouth was dry. Everyone feels fear before battle but the trick is hiding it. You must hide the fact that your stomach is churning and your bowels feel like water. This is something I have always been able to do. Some people quite literally shit themselves, others vomit out of sheer terror or weep like women. I am lucky – I have never suffered from these problems. Instead, I feel the excitement. It is the feeling of anticipation that soon you can unleash your fury on the enemy, matching your sword skill in the ultimate contest.

The wind was scarce and our speed was agonizingly slow. It took much laboured sailing before the lookout shouted that he could see several ships now, one of which was on fire.

'There are four ships,' the lookout called.

'There are five ships,' Otto contradicted, squinting into the rising sun. 'Four are close together and the fifth – the one on fire – is a little apart, to the left.'

'You have good eyesight, boy,' Theodoric said from behind us. 'If you fight as good as your friend here,' he nodded to me and winked, 'then we shall have no problems.' He turned and bellowed, 'They are pirates – preying on some poor trader, no doubt! We shall be the instrument of God's displeasure. We shall bring down His divine justice! We shall smite the pagans as David smote Goliath!'

There was a ragged cheer and we were joined by Caupo, the Liv chieftain who had accompanied Theodoric to Rome. 'Now we kill pirates, yes?' he said. 'Stop boredom.' There was something comforting about the foreign chieftain. Despite his age, he cradled a wicked-looking axe in his arms and looked as though he could use it. Behind him, I saw that most of the other passengers were ready, brandishing spears, swords and the crossbows Dieter had given out. I imagined the scene was the same on the other two ships to windward, astern of us.

Now we were close enough, I could see the sun glinting off the enemy spearheads. One of the ships was a cog, the same one that had overhauled us at dusk the previous evening. It was under attack from two longships, on either beam, but the high sides of the cog loomed over the pirates and the Oeselians were having problems climbing the side. The cog's crew were fighting desperately to keep the boarders at bay, throwing spears and firing arrows down at the attackers amassed below them. A third longship, a little further away, was still burning but it looked as though the crew now had the fire under control. Precious moments passed by and we slowly drew closer. Sounds of screaming and the clashing of steel drifted across the water as we bore down on them.

Next to me, men began firing their crossbows and the air was alive with the thwack of strings as a barrage of bolts were fired. Hinz fired his, cursing when it went wide, before struggling to reload. I had practised many times with the weapon in the Northmead at Cranham, so I snatched it from him and showed him how to reload it, putting my foot in the stirrup and pulling back on the string, before adding the bolt and thrusting it back into his hands. 'Just point it at them and don't snatch at the trigger.' He aimed the crossbow and fired again, this time the bolt at least struck the hull of one of the longships.

The nearest Oeselian ship had seen our slow approach and a man wearing a bright-blue cloak waved in our direction, calling back the men who had began to scale the sides of the cog. We were now only a hundred paces or so away, but already some of the crew were pushing away from the cog, attempting to flee. I saw that the prow was painted like a sea monster and it reminded me of what Viking dragon ships must have looked like from lore. The Oeselian ship banked its oars and they swung away, some of the pirates jeering at us. Ahead now was the stern of the cog, being assaulted by two longships on the other side. Whilst we had the height advantage, allowing our crossbowmen to be able to shoot down into the open longships, they were faster and more manoeuvrable. A couple of pirates were hit by bolts, but the ship was already sweeping around abeam of us and then we were bearing down on the cog we had come to save, where a battle already raged on deck as the pirates were pushing the crew back towards the stern.

'We have to help the crew on the cog!' Theodoric shouted. 'When we come alongside, we must cross onto the other ship and do battle with the pagans!'

I pushed my way through the people behind me, crossing the deck to the opposite side where we would come alongside the other vessel. The *Saint Maria* was a foot or so higher than the other ship and it wouldn't be hard to climb over as the screech of voices and clash of swords on the deck intensified. An arrow whisked over my head and the crossbowmen kept firing, although their rate of fire had slackened, highlighting most of their inexperience. A few seconds later our ship collided alongside the other cog; the impact of the hulls scraping together nearly knocked me off my feet.

'Come on!' Theodoric bellowed, pulling himself up the gunwale by the shrouds. Apart from a wooden staff he was unarmed. 'For Jesus and for Saint Mary!'

Dieter, the elder of the Swordbrothers, led the attack, jumping up and over onto the deck of the cog, swinging his sword at a nearby pirate. Caupo was just behind him and, not wanting to be outdone, I followed, losing my footing in my haste and almost falling down the narrow gap between the two ships. I managed to keep hold of my sword as I swung on one of the shrouds and jumped over. There were approximately twenty pirates already onboard, with more still climbing the grapnel ropes and netting that hung down the other side to their own ship. Our approach must have surprised them because, unlike the other pirate ship, they hadn't seen us coming until we were alongside. The pirates had pushed the crew back to the stern deck and a furious fight was taking place there.

We attacked and I was suddenly faced with a large, hairy pagan who was all beard and fury. He snarled something before swinging his sword directly at my head. I ducked underneath and drove my own sword upwards, slicing the blade into the man's thigh. He howled in agony and dropped to the deck. Next to me, Otto parried an axe, smashing the hilt of his sword into the Oeselian's face, crushing his nose and showering me with blood and teeth. Around us, everyone was fighting and the crew, facing death only a few moments before, now fought with a renewed vigour. I saw one bare-footed sailor strike a pirate down with an axe blow that cleaved his skull. Behind me, I could hear shouting coming from our own ship, and to my shock I saw our people fighting. The *Saint Maria* had itself been boarded while we were attacking the pirates. I shouted out the danger and immediately climbed the gunwale to get back onto our ship to repel this new threat.

There were already at least half-a-dozen pirates who had reached the deck and more were climbing the grapnels. Ahead of me, I saw Gerhard and Hinz, fighting desperately with two pirates. The air rang out with the clash of swords and the shouts of anger and pain. Many of the people on *Saint Maria* were still armed with crossbows and they had to drop these hastily and grab weapons for close quarters fighting. The knucklebone-playing group that had caused problems the previous day were battling desperately near the bow. I jumped down from the gunwale and launched myself at the two pirates, slicing my sword across the back of one while Hinz thrust a spear into the guts of the other. Both dropped to the deck and I thrust my sword down, impaling the man I had sliced. He made gurgling noises as he died, soaking the deck with his blood. An arrow thudded into the mast next to me. Everything was chaotic. I could hear Theodoric shouting and men screaming. Another pirate climbed over the side of the ship and hurled himself at me, screeching a war cry, his wide-bladed sword held in front of him. Before he reached me, he was engaged by a sailor with a boarding axe and I had a few moments' respite. Near the stern deck, there was a savage struggle with men stabbing and slashing at each other. I saw a pirate hack a crewman down with his axe, before he noticed the girl Margret and her father cowering under the stairs that led up to the stern deck. He took three strides and grabbed her. The father tried to help, clutching his daughter by the arm, but the Oeselian kicked him back down and dragged Margret to the gunwale where their own ship was tied, no doubt thinking her good war plunder.

I charged across the deck and the pagan only saw me at the last moment, pushing Margret away and raising his axe to block my blow. But I was faster and I stabbed him in the ribs, twisting the blade to avoid it getting stuck. I wrenched it out and he looked me straight in the eyes in shock. I realised just how young he was – barely older than me. He collapsed to the deck and I pulled Margret up, shoving her away as another Oeselian, hanging on to the outside of the hull, tried to grab her and throw her down into their longship. I smashed my elbow into the man's face and felt a thrill as he lost his grip and fell between the two ships.

'Don't cut the boarding ropes!' Theodoric bellowed. 'Shoot the pagan dogs down!'

The last few pirates on our deck were being killed. A moment later, I was joined by Otto, who was bleeding from a head wound.

'It's nothing.' He grimaced at my unasked question. 'The man who did it died for the pleasure.'

'What is happening on the other ship?' I said.

'The pirates are running. The survivors fled back to their ship. I didn't even know we had been boarded…'

Around me, our people were firing crossbows again at the longship still lashed together with *Saint Maria*. I looked over the gunwale at the chaos on the Oeselian ship. Men were screaming in pain and half the crew were dead or wounded. Blood filled the bilge. The pirates had lost the will to fight and the few still alive and unwounded were trying desperately to cut their ship free from their own bindings. But the crossbow bolts rained down relentlessly, thudding into pirates and wood alike, and by the time the lashings were cut and she was drifting away there must have been less than a dozen men still alive.

The Oeselians were masters at hit and run attacks. Our arrival had surprised them and prevented them from overpowering the merchant ship. After putting up a stiff fight they were now scuttling away.

'Kill them!' Theodoric bellowed encouragement to the crossbowmen. He looked like he wanted to fire one as well. 'Rain down God's retribution on the unbelievers.'

I had never seen a priest so warlike or keen on killing people. I continued to watch the Oeselian ship as several men attempted to bank oars and row to safety, but the second cog in our small fleet, the *Abenteuer*, was bearing down, crossbowmen crowding the bows as they poured even more bolts into the longship. The Oeselians had no chance and the cog ploughed through the oars, snapping them like a wattle fence. The impact forced one side of the longship underwater and she began to sink.

The battle was over. There were pirates screaming and drowning in the water and the ship was so full of blood it looked like it was bleeding. I felt no pity for them – they would have killed the innocent crew of the merchant cog without mercy or remorse.

'Throw the pagan bodies overboard!' Theodoric shouted from the stern deck. 'They can go straight to hell.'

I felt movement behind me and I turned to see Margret standing with her father.

After a moment's hesitation it was her father that spoke. His lip was bleeding and he had a bruised eye. 'I saw what happened… I want… I want to thank you for saving my daughter.'

I nodded to him, not sure what else to say. Slightly behind, Margret was staring at the ground before she raised her head and I looked into her eyes. She gave me a smile so quick, that when she looked down immediately afterwards, I thought I had imagined it. She was a pretty little thing with an oval face framed by strands of dark hair that protruded under her bonnet and the hood of the cloak she wore. She must have been about twelve or thirteen.

I would have liked to have talked to Margret, if only briefly, but I didn't get the chance. After her father thanked me, he turned and ushered her away. I felt sorry for the girl and wondered why her father would take his daughter to a frontier wilderness like Livonia, with all the dangers that entailed. Nevertheless, apart from a brief curiosity, my mind returned quickly to the destruction around us. I still meant everything I had said to Otto about wanting nothing more to do with girls. Not after Elsebeth. Not that it really mattered – we would be in Riga soon, where I would take up my new life that demanded celibacy and obedience above everything. And anyway, it was not that I would ever see her again.

There is a Bible verse – I forgot from where – maybe Romans, that says, *O the depth of the riches both of the wisdom and knowledge of God! How unsearchable are his judgements, and his ways past finding out!* Well, that was certainly true. All I know is that the ways of the Lord are mysterious. No one can predict the future or know what will happen, nor the fate that awaits them, and we are ever fools to think otherwise. Nevertheless, in hindsight something now is clear.

God must have been laughing at me that day.

Four days later, on the Nativity of the Blessed Virgin Mary – very apt, as Mary was the figurehead of the crusade – we finally approached the mouth of the Düna river upon which Riga was built and there was no one aboard who didn't feel relief that our long journey was almost over. The morale on the ship had risen considerably after we had defeated the pirates and the continual good weather contributed to a carnival atmosphere, with frequent bouts of laughter as people recounted their own stories of the battle. Of course, the captain of the merchant cog we had saved was very grateful, as he should have been. He gave each ship a barrel of beer, which was drank on the night following the battle. His ship was on the long voyage to Novgorod and he was rightly concerned they would be attacked again further north. Nevertheless, he declined Theodoric's offer to sail with us to Riga.

Our losses had been light, with only our ship taking any casualties: two crewmen and three pilgrims. Several people were mildly wounded, Otto included, but none were in any life-threatening danger. At least with my friend, the wound he had taken fighting Henkel was all but healed and his new head wound was only superficial – although with the amount of blood it looked worse than it was. The captured Oeselian weapons were collected into a large pile and the dead pirates, over twenty in number, had been thrown overboard. And that didn't include the men from the longship that had been sunk. Three Oeselians had been fished out of the sea and Theodoric declared they would learn the error of their ways and be converted to Christianity. Despite this assurance, they were still put in chains and sat glumly by the mast for the rest of the journey.

Now it was our final day at sea and everyone was excited and apprehensive about what awaited us when we reached Riga. The day was cloudy with glimpses of sunshine and a sharp wind that buffeted the sail. I stood at the gunwale studying the shore of Livonia. The land was flat and featureless, similar to the entire journey, the sea fronted by a long sandy beach with dunes and forest behind. Ahead of us, the mouth of the Düna could be seen, a wide break in the sand. A shout from the lookout halfway up the mast brought my attention back to what was happening onboard. I found Otto at the bow, scanning the horizon ahead and the approaching ship.

'It looks like a cog,' Otto said. 'It has a cross on its sail. Maybe a trader?'

Dieter joined us, shielding his eyes as he stared at the oncoming ship. 'It could be the pilgrims that stayed over the summer.'

We waited as the ship drew closer. It was another cog, but larger than any of the three in our small fleet. People waved as we passed each other near the mouth of the Düna river.

'It is Arnold von Meiendorf and Bernard von Seehausen – the remaining knights who took the cross last year,' Dieter said. 'They must be returning to the Empire. That means there cannot be many pilgrims left in Riga, if any. The people shall be pleased to see us.'

And these words proved true. After the cog had passed, we steered into the estuary of the Düna, the *Saint Maria* rolling as the river ploughed into the sea, making the brackish waters treacherous. On our left, I could see earthworks and a half-completed palisade and Dieter explained this was the new Cistercian monastery of Dünamünde that was being built. 'Theodoric will be the abbot when it is finished,' Dieter said.

The river was huge, probably the widest I had ever seen, but progress was difficult in the tumultuous water as the ship pitched and heaved. Eventually, we managed to sail the short distance upstream until we reached our destination. I crowded the side with most of the other passengers, looking at the city it had taken so long to reach. Except it wasn't a city, more like a modest town, partially ringed by a wooden palisade. The crew reefed the sail and we moored in the main river, waiting for several boats pulled by oars that appeared from a much smaller river that flowed around the town and into the Düna. There was another village, just a couple dozen wooden huts and sheds outside of the stockade between us and Riga itself, where people from the shore watched us. I saw a few children wave before running through the gate of the town, presumedly to spread the word about our arrival.

Our crew tossed ropes to the men on the boats and we were towed slowly into the protected waters of an anchorage in the narrow lake created by the smaller river. A short jetty jutted out from the shore and we slowly turned towards it. A bell began tolling from inside the town and more people joined the crowd onshore. By the time the *Saint Maria* was towed alongside the jetty, most of the town must have been watching and waiting. A ragged cheer went up.

We had finally arrived in Riga.

CHAPTER NINETEEN

We collected our things before disembarking, slightly bemused by the growing crowd. Dieter von Stammen led the dozen of us who intended to join the Militia of Christ. After we had descended the gangplank, Theodoric stopped and began addressing the throng, while behind they began to unload the ship. Dieter didn't give us a chance to listen to the abbot's speech, leading us through the wooden hovels and shacks along the road that led towards a gate in the stockade. There was a smattering of applause and some of the crowd dropped to their knees as we passed, thanking God for their salvation. I looked back to see the other two ships begin docking at the jetty. There were now at least two hundred people waiting on the shore – a significant part of the population, mostly Livs and Letts but also some Germans.

Dieter led us across some boards that bridged a shallow moat and through the open gate and into the town, passing a guard who leant slovenly on his spear. We picked our way along a muddy street, fouled by the dogs that glistened with slime and ran wild. Like most towns or cities, it stank, and

I felt my heart sink, though to be honest what else did I expect? Riga was a primitive affair; every building made of wood – horizontally laid and rough-hewn, unlike the timber-framed structures whose walls were filled with clay and daub and plastered with limewash found in Lübeck. It looked a miserable place, but at least everyone was happy as news of our arrival spread. Some cheered, some clapped, while others thanked God and intoned prayers. One man even prostrated himself in the mud before us, beseeching God to crush the unbelievers. We walked around him.

'It's nice to feel wanted again,' Otto said. We had reached an uncobbled square fronted by a large wooden church with a small market. I found out later this was Saint Peter's Church, where the stonemasons with whom we had shared our journey were to work. It was from the tower of this church that the bell was ringing and dozens of people in the square cheered as Dieter led us onwards across another street and a set of gates set in a stone wall – the first stone construction I'd seen since we had entered the town.

At the gate there were two armed guards wearing mail and dressed in the white surcoats emblazoned with the sword and cross motif of the Swordbrothers. In contrast to the guard at the main gate, they looked alert and ready for trouble. Both were surprised to see us and we paused as Dieter and his comrade greeted them. After a brief conversation, the guards opened the gate and we were allowed into the commandery of the Swordbrothers.

Inside, it looked more like a construction site than the quiet contemplative space I had imagined. Workers were building a large stone building which Dieter explained would be the Order's headquarters, castle and Saint George's chapel. They were using both bricks and stone, though he told us that the stone had to be transported from Germany as the nearby dolomite caves were too dangerous to quarry. 'Most of the cargo aboard *Abenteuer* was stone for this building, as well as the church we passed earlier,' Dieter said. 'Although additional food and weapons would have been more useful, in my humble opinion.' Nearby, a group of masons were working, sitting on a patch of mud next to the new building, chipping at the stone. The rest of the yard was surrounded by wooden buildings, some of them two-stories high and, from a door in the long building opposite the new construction, three men emerged, all unarmed and unarmoured but in the robes of Swordbrothers.

'Brother Dieter, you have returned with God's providence,' the first man said. He was well-built with a dark, bristling beard and a weather-beaten face.

Dieter bowed his head. 'Master Wenno. I have more recruits for our Order. Theodoric has spoken to them and they all meet the conditions of acceptance.'

'How was your visit to the Holy See?'

'It was very successful. His Holy Father has sanctioned our Order.'

'That is excellent news, but we expected no less.' Wenno looked the dozen or so of us over, nodding in satisfaction. 'I am Wenno von Rohrbach. I am *Heermeister* of the *Fratres militiæ Christi Livoniae*. Unfortunately, as you can see, things are a little crowded here at the *Jürgenshof*. We were not expecting your arrival this year and we have no room at present. Some of our brethren are in the field but they shall return soon. In the meantime, we will erect tents in the yard to house you. I will speak with Brother Dieter and then with you all individually. In the meantime, I suggest you go to pray in the chapel and reflect on your circumstances. Your new lives shall be hard and filled with adversity. Living here on the frontier of civilisation is not easy and death is an ever-present risk. Pray to God to lighten your load and help guide you through the dangerous times ahead. Welcome to the *Jürgenshof*. Welcome to Riga.'

He turned to speak with Dieter as the rest of us looked at each other. It was no big thing to sleep in a tent for a while, despite the stink from the nearby latrines, but the winter wasn't far away and then it would be different. I hoped that the construction work would not take long, but they still had much work to do and there was no question it would be finished by the arrival of the cold weather.

'Not quite what I imagined,' Otto said in a low voice.

I wasn't sure what I had imagined, but we couldn't change anything anyway.

So, we went to the chapel, not much bigger than the one at home in Cranham, built against the outside stockade that ringed the town. It was more like a small barn with an altar on one side surmounted by a cross and a candle holder burning three candles, but otherwise empty. I knelt on the packed-earth floor and pretended to pray. In front of me, Emich was praying so loudly I moved away in irritation and knelt again near the door, next to Gerhard. He was not praying at all, but rather looking around the empty space with big, scared eyes, probably wondering what he had let himself in for. I had no idea how long we were left in the chapel, but it was a long time. Eventually Dieter arrived, picking each of us out one by one to speak with Master Wenno. I was the third to be singled out, after Otto, and was led out of the chapel across the yard to the same two-storey, wooden building from which Wenno had emerged from earlier.

'Just answer any of the Master's questions honestly,' Dieter advised. 'He knows what happened in Lübeck, but will still want to hear it from your own mouth.'

Inside was gloomy and it took a moment for my eyes to adjust. Behind a large desk sat Wenno, with several open parchments before him. The room was lit by a small oil lamp that coughed and spluttered like an old woman with the white plague. Two other men stood next to the desk: one of them wore a large cross around his neck and had the tonsure of a priest; the other was short and stocky, looking more like a thug to be found in any waterfront town rather than a monk – albeit a warrior one. He was also old, over forty and at least ten years older than Wenno. A scribe stood behind a lectern, quill in hand, ready to write what we discussed.

'I want to introduce you to the men standing next to me, as you shall have much to do with them in the future,' Wenno said. He indicated the man with the tonsure next to him. 'This is Priest-brother Berthold. He is our chaplain and one of the few priests we have at present and a great blessing to us. If you have any spiritual questions, he is the man to ask.' He paused for a moment, looking at the other man. 'Then there is Knight-brother Sighard. He is responsible for all the sergeants in Riga and is also the quartermaster.'

I nodded towards the bull-necked man.

'Knight-brother Dieter told me you are from England and of noble birth,' Wenno continued. 'Why did you leave your land?'

After a moment's hesitation I answered. 'My father was killed and my claim on the barony that belonged to my family was usurped by my uncle. I fled rather than be killed. Together with Wilhelm, my father's steward, we escaped to Lübeck.'

'Is that where you learned to speak German?'

I nodded.

'Well, you speak the language reasonably well, but you have an atrocious accent. We are a German order and it is imperative you understand all instructions given to you – in the field, lives may depend on it. I shall assign a tutor to continue your learning.'

I mumbled my thanks.

Wenno paused for a long time, making me nervous as he stared at me with an unfathomable expression. 'I have also heard there was an incident on board the ship that brought you here, in Lübeck. What happened?'

I hesitated before remembering Dieter's words in the yard. 'I was attacked on the ship by someone I used to work with – an... evil man.' I recounted what had happened in Lübeck, with the death of Wilhelm and Henkel to the fight with Johann on *Saint Maria*. 'But he attacked me first, I swear it was self-defence...'

'Knight-brother Dieter said as much – at least regarding the fight on the ship that was witnessed by many people. There could be problems, but we will worry about them when they occur. I'm told you fought well against the Oeselian pirates on your journey here. Our Order is a new one, and as yet very small. It seems you may prove an asset as long as you follow the discipline needed. We are monks as well as knights. Do you agree to respect the Rule and obey your commanders and any knight-brother above you in rank?'

'I do.'

'Considering your age, you cannot yet be initiated to become a knight. In the meantime, you shall work as a sergeant and squire for one of the knight-brothers. Do you have any suggestions, Knight-brother Sighard?'

'Knight-brother Rudolf von Elsdorf is without a squire at present,' Sighard said.

'Ah yes...' Wenno said. 'Knight-brother Rudolf is with our forces in the field at the moment. They are not expected to return for about a week. In the meantime, you shall learn your new duties from Knight-brother Sighard. He will conduct your training and ensure you learn and respect the Rule. Priest-brother Berthold will oversee your spiritual education. Do you have any questions?'

I shook my head.

'Good. You may leave. Knight-brother Sighard shall speak with all of the sergeants later, after Vespers.'

I bowed my head and followed Dieter back out into the yard.

'Knight-brother Rudolf is one of our Order's most noble and high-born members,' he said. He put his hand on my arm and briefly drew me aside. 'He is also treasurer, which makes him one of the most important men in our Order, third only to the Master and Volkwin, the vice-master and marshal. But be careful. He can be a difficult and demanding man, known for taking any slight as an insult. Just remember to obey your instructions, train hard and take comfort in prayer. Give him no reason to be displeased with your efforts. I wish you God's grace.'

He left me, heading back to the chapel to fetch the next recruit to speak with the Master. I looked around the yard for Otto, who I saw on the far side of the chapel, next to the outside wall, helping some other men pitch the tents that would become our home. As I walked towards him, a cold gust of wind made me shudder; it was noticeably colder here than in Lübeck and I wondered how long we would have before the full onslaught of winter.

I thought again of Dieter's words. I was ready to adapt to my new life but his warning made me uncomfortable. Apprehensive even. Things were going to be hard here in Riga anyway, I knew and expected that, but somehow, I had the unpleasant feeling they were now going to be harder still.

Over the next few days, we settled into the routine that would become our lives. We were woken at what seemed like the middle of the night, donning our clothes before trudging half-asleep to the chapel for Matins. Afterwards, we were allowed to return to our tents to sleep before we were summoned at dawn for prayers again in the chapel at Prime, followed by Mass conducted by Priest-brother Berthold. With the first set of prayers thankfully over, Berthold took me aside to learn German in the tiny scriptorium next to the chapel. The priest-brother was a calm and patient teacher, better even than Wilhelm and far superior to Father Bertram in Cranham. During this time, my comrades started their chores. With my lesson complete, I was assigned to work in the stables, mucking out the stalls and feeding the horses hay and oats.

This was followed by the chapel again for Terce and then my favourite part of the day: sword practice in the yard under the harsh gaze of Sighard. We joined the other twenty or so sergeants who wore dark tunics and mantles, in contrast to us newcomers who were still dressed in the clothes we'd arrived in. For the rest of the morning, we sweated and grunted with the effort as we were put through our paces. Afterwards, we filed after each other again to the chapel for Sext before breaking our fast with dinner in the refectory, a low wooden building by the main gate, taking our places in silence after the knight-brothers, numbering only some dozen or so in number, had finished. All mealtimes were taken in silence, accompanied by a reading of the Rule or passages of the Bible. We were all hungry after our exertion and it was hard not to gorge on the bowl of steamed vegetables and bread. In addition, we received a platter of different meat, mostly cuts of lamb and pork, along with cheese and washed down with beer. I was glad to see that even in a commandery on the frontiers of Christianity we ate reasonably well, although I knew that three times a week we would fast when no meat would be available.

Our training and drills continued in the afternoon before we were given more duties to perform. Sighard put us to work helping unload the stone for the masons; back-breaking toil that left us all lathered in sweat. In the mid-afternoon, we attended the chapel for Nones before having to continue with more chores for the rest of the day. Otto was given work in the blacksmith's forge whilst I was sent to the kitchens to help prepare the food for supper and the next day. Vespers at dusk was followed by supper, this time accompanied by wooden tankards of wine rather than the normal beer. We then had a short amount of free time before again attending Compline, followed by another tankard of wine before checking the horses in the stables again. Then it was finally time for bed, which was welcome after the labour of the day.

I shared a tent with Otto, Hinz, Gerhard, Emich and a quiet, shifty-looking youth of my own age called Ulrich, although everyone called him Uli. Unlike most of the other new recruits, Uli was from the south of Germany and spoke with a strange accent I had trouble understanding. He was also of low birth, which meant he would always remain a sergeant. But that wasn't the only reason I disliked him. It was the way he slyly watched everyone when he thought no one was looking, reminding me of the way a fox or wolf would watch its prey. I wondered if he was a thief and was glad I had nothing worth stealing apart from my sword. If he ever tried to take that I would be happy to give it to him – blade first.

The day after we finished unloading the supplies, we were practising with wooden swords in the yard. I was paired against Otto, but we were used to fighting each other. Otto was stronger than me, but I was faster and our bouts were always balanced, if slightly in my favour. On this occasion, both of us were tired from our interrupted sleep and our bout was lacklustre. A cold wind whipped around the yard as we halfheartedly parried and struck each other's shields, sweating and grunting while Sighard watched us critically.

'Get your shield up, Sergeant-brother Otto!' he bellowed. 'You move like an ox.'

I feinted a blow to his head, then swept my sword round and struck Otto on the shoulder. He grunted. I was aware that many of the others now had stopped their own practice and were watching us. Otto raised his hand in acknowledgement of my blow, hefting his shield for the next round. Behind him, I saw the group of longer-serving sergeants watching. One of them, a blond-haired youth, whispered to his comrades as he pointed at me.

Sighard marched up to us, clearly unhappy. 'I thought you two were supposed to have some experience! You fight like two old washerwomen.'

I felt my face begin to flush. It was true we were not fighting to the best of our ability but we were only training.

Some of the others began to snigger and Sighard turned on them. 'What are you laughing at? Most of you are no better. And did I tell any of you to stop practising?'

The sergeants immediately returned to their training. Otto rolled his eyes and grinned at me.

But the gesture did not go unseen by Sighard. 'And what do you think you are smirking at, Sergeant-brother Otto? Extra duties after Nones.'

The bell from Saint Peter's Church, just outside the commandery, began to ring for Sext. Despite enjoying the training, I felt relief to be away from Sighard, even if it meant praying again. Afterwards, I went to the stables next to the main gate to begin my work grooming the dozen or so horses. I was not alone, Gerhard had also been allocated the same work, as well as a quiet, skinny youth called Emil, who predated us, but both were outside in the yard exercising the horses. I was brushing down a magnificent brown stallion when I heard movement behind me. Three youths, all of them older and wearing the black tunics of sergeants, were standing in the doorway staring at me. I recognised them as the same boys who had been laughing at me and Otto in the yard.

The first one was tall, with blond hair and the wisp of a beard. He had been the one who had pointed at me during training. Despite being very good-looking, he had a petulant expression on his face. 'Well, hello, Richard. So you're the new sergeant we've all heard so much about?'

'And who are you?'

'I am Wolfgang and these are my friends, Gabriel and Reinhart. But it's a little rude we already know your name and you don't know ours – especially as we've been here longer. Don't you think, Gab?' He turned to one of the others, a youth who was big and broad, larger even than Otto, and at least eighteen years old.

'I think so,' the boy called Gabriel said. 'And I heard he's not even from the Empire.'

Wolfgang pulled a face of mock shock. 'Really? You mean an *Ausländer*? Why would an *Ausländer* want to come to Livonia? Could he be hiding from something?'

'What do you want?' I said.

'See what I mean!' Wolfgang took a step into the stall. 'These foreigners are very rude. I don't like rude people, do you, Gab?'

'No, I don't. And I don't like foreigners either,' the large youth said, following him into the stall. I backed up, looking for anything to use as a weapon, but the only thing was a pitchfork leaning against the wall by the door. I would have to go through all of them to get it – clearly an impossible task.

295

'Is it true you killed a man in Lübeck?' Wolfgang sneered. 'After watching you in the training yard it is hard to believe. Were you fighting a blind old woman?'

'Maybe it was a washerwoman,' Gabriel said.

Now they were all in the stall and they moved closer as I took another step backwards. There was no chance getting past them and when I backed into the flank of the stallion, I quickly ducked down and darted underneath. Now at least I had the horse between us. On my right, Reinhart lunged around the horse, trying to grab me and I kicked him in the groin, jumping over his body as he thudded to the ground. I dashed for the stall door but Gabriel grabbed my tunic and yanked me backwards.

'Now you are going to regret that,' Wolfgang said.

Then the beating began. A shower of kicks and punches rained down on me. I did my best to fight back but I had no chance against the older boys and I curled up into a ball, shielding my head with my arms as the blows continued. It seemed to last forever but then I heard shouts and suddenly it was over. Although barely conscious, I recognised Gerhard's nasal voice. Strong hands lifted me from the floor and I groaned. My lip was bloody but my face was relatively unscathed, unlike the raging bruises on my back.

'What happened?' Gerhard asked, as if it wasn't obvious.

'Nothing happened,' I snapped at him.

'But those sergeants…' There was confusion on his flabby face. 'Who were they?'

'Nothing happened!' I repeated. 'I was kicked in the back by the horse, fell over and hit my face on the ground.'

'If you say so. But you need to go to the infirmary. You are in no condition to train, or work.'

I reluctantly had to agree with him. Emil joined us but he didn't ask what had occurred. I suspected he already knew

– maybe even beforehand. Nevertheless, he helped Gerhard support me and I hobbled across the yard to the infirmary, behind another door in the long building constructed against the outside city wall. It was a small room, occupied by eight pallets but otherwise empty, and a mouse scurried away as my comrades lowered me down on the nearest bed. Emil went to fetch Brother Burkhardt, the infirmarer, and thankfully in the meantime Gerhard asked no more questions. Emil returned a few moments later with the monk. Brother Burkhardt was aged in his mid-thirties, short, brusque and impatient. He shooed Gerhard and Emil out of the infirmary before disappearing through a low door, where I heard him mixing something with a mortar and pestle. He returned a short while later and applied a salve of calendula on the bruises on my shoulders and back. The coolness of the cream immediately eased the pain.

'How did you receive these injuries?'

'A horse kicked me in the stables. The brown stallion – I forgot his name.'

'You mean Blitz, Master Wenno's warhorse. Did you upset him?'

'I don't think so.'

'Well, he didn't kick you very hard otherwise you would have several broken ribs. You were lucky.'

I didn't feel lucky. Everything in my life had gone wrong and now I was on the very frontier of Christendom, to fight for a god to which I was ambivalent, against a people I had never met and bore no ill will. And to make matters worse I had new enemies on my own side – people I hardly knew.

However, I was sure of one thing: I couldn't allow what had happened to stand. Even though it would have to wait, I was determined to get back at my attackers. I would make sure they lived to regret this day's work.

CHAPTER TWENTY

I spent the next two days recovering from my beating but I wasn't without visitors. The first, of course, was Otto, who came on the evening of the day I was attacked.

'Who did this?' he demanded. He was careful to keep his voice down to avoid Burkhardt from hearing.

'Some of the sergeants. Three of them. The leader was called Wolfgang.'

'Wolfgang… tall with blond hair?'

I nodded.

'I know who you mean,' Otto said. 'The bastard. I didn't believe a horse kicked you. We'll have to get them back.'

I nodded. 'But not without me, do you understand? Wait until I am out of here.'

Otto wasn't the only one not to believe my story about getting kicked by a horse. On the morning after I was attacked, on the day of the Exaltation of the Cross, I was lying on my pallet, dozing, when Master Wenno and Knight-brother Sighard strode into the infirmary. Wenno whispered something to Brother Burkhardt and the three of us were left alone.

'Brother Burkhardt informs us that you were very lucky not to be more severely hurt,' Wenno said. 'Tell us what happened in the stables?'

I explained about the horse getting agitated, forcing me away before it kicked me in the back, knocking me into the wooden wall of the stall where I received the injuries to my face. They listened before Wenno asked to see the wound on my back. I lifted my undershirt and rolled onto my stomach so they could see the bruises.

'It looks painful,' Wenno said. 'But it also looks like you were kicked several times. You have bruises on your right shoulder as well as your lower back.'

I held my tongue.

'Blitz has never been known to kick before. What did you do to make him so angry?'

'Nothing... I have experience with horses... I did nothing.'

'Your story makes no sense,' Wenno said. 'And your injuries look more like you were beaten. And probably by several people. Now tell us again, what happened?'

'I was kicked by your horse,' I said stubbornly.

Wenno shook his head and left the room, leaving Brother Sighard looking down at me.

'We are not feeble-minded,' Sighard said. 'We know you are lying. Who beat you? Tell me and I shall make sure they are properly punished.'

'No one beat me.'

'Why are you covering up for them? Are you afraid of retribution?'

'I am not afraid of anybody.'

'I will not tolerate any fighting among my sergeants. And I don't want you thinking that you can get revenge. We are all brothers here together. There are enough pagans to fight to keep anyone happy.'

'Yes, Brother Sighard.'

'And I am not happy that you are lying. It is not a good start for you. You would do yourself more favours by being honest.'

'I am being honest,' I lied.

'I will be keeping my eye on you – on all of you sergeants. I shall find out what happened, believe me. And when I do...'

He left the room, leaving me to my thoughts.

The following day, I was allowed to leave the infirmary and I hobbled back to the tent I shared in the yard, settling down to listen to the masons' hammers chipping stone outside. A few moments later my comrades returned from the chapel. I explained about the visit I had received from Wenno and Sighard.

'I knew it,' Gerhard said. 'I knew those other sergeants had attacked you.'

'Do you have a plan to get them back?' Otto asked.

'Not yet. It will have to wait, considering what Sighard said yesterday. I will have to be careful. He will be watching like a hawk – he said as much.'

'Maybe you could get paired against them in practice,' Hinz said. 'You are good with a sword. Accidents always happen in the practice yard.'

That was true and it had already crossed my mind, but Brother Sighard interrupted our conversation, sticking his head through the flap of our tent.

'All of you outside, now!'

We all looked at each other, fearing he had overheard our conversation, but when we emerged into the yard our worries were unfounded. More equipment had arrived and we were taken to a room next to the chapel where we were issued with the dark-grey mantles of sergeants, each with the insignia of the Swordbrothers on the breast. Some of us were also given a coat of mail, but there were not enough to go around so Gerhard from our group, along with half a dozen more who had sailed with us, got nothing. Mine was an old *hauberk*, some of the rings were rusty and it was only one layer of chains rather than the double layer I had back in England, but at least it had a *coif* that I could pull up to cover my head. And it fitted me. We were also given a padded jerkin to wear under the armour, an open-faced helm and a shield, painted white with the sword and cross motif, a *cappa* – a long tunic of black cloth to wear around the commandery, as well as a habit, also black, and a pair of breeches, undershirt and a cap. We looked at each other in our new attire and grinned.

'Now our new life suddenly feels more real,' Otto said. 'I was hoping to wake up and find out it was all a nightmare.'

My life certainly felt like a nightmare, but the following day at weapons practice, things took a turn for the better. I was paired with Reinhart, one of the boys who had attacked me in the stables, to fight without shield. Now, if I was a better swordsman, Hinz's words from the previous day would come true.

'Now you'll suffer for that kick in the balls you gave me,' Reinhart growled, quiet enough for only us to hear. He must have been roughly seventeen, only slightly taller than me, with a wide face and protruding teeth.

'Try your worst,' I hissed, clenching my sword in clammy hands. I was still stiff and sore from the beating but I was confident my speed would help me get the better of him.

And it did. As soon as we began, he launched himself at me, slashing wildly with his practice sword while the other sergeants fought in pairs around us. I parried his blows easily before sweeping my sword around and striking him on the upper arm. It was a hard blow despite the padded jerkin he wore and he shrieked.

Then it was my turn to attack. I lunged at him, causing him to take a step back, and darted to my right, feinting a blow to his leg before flicking my wrist and striking him full in the face. He dropped to the ground clutching his bloody nose.

'Stop!' Sighard shouted at us from across the yard. 'What do you think you are doing? You are not supposed to kill him.'

I lowered my sword and stood there defiantly while Reinhart stared up at me through the blood seeping through his fingers. The others around us continued their own practice, wary of Sighard's displeasure, but I was aware some of them were still watching.

Sighard marched up to me and leaned in close so no one else could hear. 'Now I know who attacked you in the stables,' he said in a low voice. 'And who the others are likely to be.' He looked towards Wolfgang and Gabriel who were paired together across the yard. 'I shall speak with you after Vespers. And if you ever lie to me again, even for a good reason, you shall be severely punished.' He turned to Reinhart. 'And you can get up too, beaten by someone two years your junior. You had better go to the infirmary.'

I looked across to Wolfgang and Gabriel. Now, they had stopped fighting each other and were glaring at me. I ignored them, turning to see Dieter stride across the yard to speak with Sighard. Reinhart staggered past me towards the infirmary and I was glad to see that his nose looked broken.

Otto looked over and raised his eyebrows. Sighard, still in discussion with Dieter, shouted to everyone to carry on with training. Now that I had no partner, I watched the others. Otto was pitched against Uli, the shady-looking boy who shared our tent. Uli might have been low-born but he was quick, and in his first attack he clipped my friend on his leg, although the blow was without force. Otto didn't seem to mind, saying something as both boys laughed. However, I was particularly interested in watching Wolfgang and Gabriel. Who knew when we would have to fight each other?

They both fought well: Gabriel fought more with brute strength, although he was far more agile than he looked. But Wolfgang was fast – perhaps as fast as me. And they were both older, stronger and with more experience than me. In comparison, Reinhart was not in their league.

It would be a tough contest if I ever had to fight either of them. A contest I was far from certain I could win.

True to his word, I was apprehended at the door of the chapel after Vespers by Brother Sighard. He put his hand on my robe and yanked me out of the file, pushing me to the side and telling me to wait. I was not the only one. A moment later he tapped Wolfgang and Gabriel on the shoulders and jerked his thumb to indicate they should wait too. Both looked surprised, throwing hostile looks at me before complying. The rest of the sergeants continued out into the yard, heading to the refectory for supper.

'You three come with me,' Sighard said. He headed in the opposite direction, past the tents where we lived, towards the far corner of the courtyard.

Wolfgang glared at me with narrowed eyes and Gabriel nudged me with his shoulder as I went past him to follow the knight-brother.

Sighard stopped at the corner of the courtyard, next to the latrines. He pointed to a patch of earth against the wall and three spades. 'We need a new latrine. You three will dig where it's already marked out until Compline. You shall not finish it today, but you can make a start. So what are you waiting for?'

I picked up a spade and began to dig. After a moment's hesitation Wolfgang and Gabriel followed reluctantly and for a short while we worked in silence under the grim scrutiny of Sighard. Then Wenno joined the knight-brother, watching us for a moment before drawing Sighard aside to speak out of earshot. I paused for a moment, sweat trickling down my face and back, my new undershirt chafing uncomfortably against my skin. Wolfgang stared at me and I scowled back at him.

'You told Brother Sighard about what happened in the stables,' Wolfgang accused, keeping his voice low. 'Which makes you a *Petze* – an informer!'

'I told him I was kicked by the horse.'

'Do you expect us to believe that?' Wolfgang said. 'How else would he know what happened?'

'He didn't believe me. He already knew what happened and my injuries confirmed it.'

'So you say,' Wolfgang sneered. 'How could he know...? You must have told him.'

'Because I beat your friend Reinhart in the practice yard. He said as much.'

'I do not believe you...' He looked quickly behind him. Sighard and Wenno had finished their conversation and the knight-brother was coming towards us. Wolfgang glanced back at me. 'And don't think we are finished either. Next time we will really mess you up!'

'The next person I catch talking will be fasting on bread and water for a week!' Sighard said. 'Get on with your work.'

We began digging again, working until it started to get dark and we could hardly see what we were doing. Finally, the bell from Saint Peter's Church rang for Compline and we were allowed to return to our quarters. I was exhausted and I ignored the questions from Otto and the others, falling asleep on the hard ground in our tent almost immediately.

Next morning we awoke to the patter of rain on the canvas. As usual, we got up bleary-eyed before shuffling to the chapel next to where our tents were pitched for Matins. The day continued with my German lesson in the scriptorium with Brother Berthold. The room felt crowded with just the two of us, with only enough room for a narrow desk, stool and lectern. Next to the door was a small shutter to let in natural light but, due to the bad weather, it was closed and we had to make do with an oil lamp ensconced in a shallow alcove cut into the timber wall. Contrary to his usual easy-going demeanour, Berthold looked serious.

'I hear you were attacked in the stables by some other sergeants,' he said. 'Do you have any idea why?'

I shrugged.

'So, you *were* attacked and not kicked by a horse?'

I kept quiet.

Berthold looked me directly in the eye. 'Do not forget what is written in the Book of Proverbs… *The Lord detests lying lips, but he delights in people who are trustworthy.*'

'No one believes me anyway,' I said. 'Wenno and Sighard didn't.'

'Because they are not simple-minded,' Berthold said. 'Contrary to what you seem to think.'

'What am I supposed to say? I'm not a *Petze*.'

Berthold smiled. 'I see you are learning some new words. No, I appreciate your position and I saw you were punished with extra duties yesterday evening.'

'I think Brother Sighard hates me.'

'No, he doesn't. Brother Sighard is one of the best monks we have in our Order. He is hard on those under him but even harder on himself. I promise you that when you finally face the enemy it is Brother Sighard you want fighting alongside you.'

'I can believe that.'

'It is true he doesn't suffer fools. And he hates dishonesty, but he is fair and a good soldier of Christ. We are lucky to have him.'

'If you say so.'

'I do, and your appreciation of him may come soon. The Master wants to make a last raid this year before the snows come. Towards Lennewarden. During the summer, Livs from Lennewarden and Ascheraden raided Riga and stole flocks of sheep. They are still pagan and we can't let them go unpunished. When Brother Volkwin returns, we shall begin preparations. I expect most of the Order will take part.'

I felt my pulse quicken. The thought of putting our training into practice would take the edge off my anger. Of course, I was young and craved the thrill of battle. It was all I thought about. Now it seems so foolish how eager I was to throw my life away – like so many others. War is not what the minstrels or poets say; it is not glorious; it is not honourable. War is blood, war is shit and war is death. And that is only the half of it. I would go on to see far worse things than the rape of the girl by Henkel on the return trip from Lüneburg, which already seemed a lifetime ago. I would see things I shall never forget until the day I die.

'My advice to you, Richard, is to restrain yourself. Do you think I cannot see the anger bubbling under the surface? What happened before you joined our Order does not interest me. Now you are a Swordbrother and everyone here is your kin. You need to restrain yourself, do all that is asked of you, obey the Rule and avoid strife with your peers. Remember, you are now one of God's chosen. And a monk. Always a monk. Now, let us get started on today's lesson.'

Later that same day, I was working in the stables, feeding oats to the horses that belonged to the knight-brothers. It was strange: I found myself looking continually over my shoulder, half-expecting to see Wolfgang and his friends and suffer another beating. But I was left alone, apart from Emil and Gerhard working in the next stall. Outside, I heard the scrape of the commandery gate opening and the sound of many hooves. I realised that it had to be the return of the expedition that had been in the field. Emil and Gerhard heard the commotion as well and we all went to look out into the yard.

Our suspicions were confirmed when it filled suddenly with horsemen. Two men led the column, both dressed in mail and wearing the surcoats of the Swordbrothers. They looked weary and the horses blew through their nostrils and snorted in the cool air. It was obvious they had seen fighting, some of their shields were chipped and battered and several of the men were lightly wounded.

'The first rider,' Emil said, 'is Volkwin, marshal of our Order.'

I watched the man as the horses came to a halt. He had a bristling beard, beginning to turn a salt-grey under his mouth, which made him look distinguished, and a natural authority that invaded the yard. Nevertheless, I found my attention drawn more to the second man. He looked superb – the archetypal knight; raven-haired and strong-faced, aged in his early twenties and wearing a white cloak draped rakishly across one shoulder. But he was having trouble with his horse. The stallion was skittish, stamping its feet and stepping sideways, tossing its head and obviously in distress. At Emil's prompting, we rushed forward to hold the horses so they could dismount and I went and grabbed Volkwin's reins, while Gerhard dashed towards the black-haired man's stallion, intending to seize the bridle and help calm the horse down.

To my horror, the black-haired man began whipping at the stallion with his riding crop and he snarled something as Gerhard approached, before slashing it at him. Gerhard reeled back, blood bright on his cheek, as the man finally got his horse under control. From the building across the yard, Wenno came out and frowned as he surveyed the scene. Volkwin swung his leg over the saddle and dismounted, not even noticing me. He was angry and he said something to the black-haired man I didn't hear, before turning and bowing towards Wenno. I glanced at Gerhard. He was shocked and just stood there, blood running from the cut on his face. For a moment, I thought he was going to cry, but he controlled himself and turned instead to the next man's horse.

The black-haired man dismounted. He had calmed down from his initial fury and now seemed to have already forgotten the incident, saying something to the knight behind him, who smiled. When I led Volkwin's horse to the stable, I felt my own anger rise at the black-haired man's behaviour. Back in the stables, I turned to Emil. 'Who is the man who struck Gerhard?'

'Knight-brother Rudolf. He is known for his temper.'

I groaned. This was the man I was supposed to squire for. I should have guessed the moment I saw him. I should have known that with my luck, he was the man I would have to serve. Dieter's warning came back to me. What had I done to upset God so much? Was it because of my lack of faith, my lack of conviction? Why did everything always go wrong for me?

Whatever the reason, there was now little doubt that with Rudolf back in the commandery my new life was only going to get harder still.

CHAPTER TWENTY-ONE

I t was not until the next morning that I met Brother Rudolf properly. Matins had just ended and where previously we had been allowed to rest, most of my compatriots choosing to sleep, we now had to serve our masters. I reported to Brother Rudolf in the common room shared by the knight-brothers next to their accommodation. The room was not large, mostly filled by a long table with a dozen or so stools scattered around, one of them occupied by my new master, reading a parchment on the table in front of him by candlelight. Next to him on the table was a sheathed sword and a coat of mail. He glanced up and scrutinised me with his hard, blue eyes. I got the feeling he didn't like what he saw.

'So you are to be my new squire. Are you of noble birth?'

I was slightly surprised at the question. 'Yes.' I nodded. 'My father was the Baron of Cranham.'

'And where the devil is that?'

'In England.'

He grunted something under his breath that I didn't catch. 'Well, at least you are not a *ministerialis* like most here. Or even worse, from a lowly merchant family. Now tell me, where is the honour in that? Honour is not something to be acquired, it is bred from birth. Everyone knows this. This is the fundamental basis of our world. Most of the men here would not know honour if it slapped them in the face.'

I listened, wondering where this conversation was going.

'Nevertheless, I am the nephew of the Duke of Lorraine and you do not come more noble than that. You are new here. I expect you to obey every order I give without question, as if it comes from Almighty God Himself. Do I make myself clear?'

I nodded.

'Do I make myself *clear?*' he repeated.

'Yes, master,' I said.

'Good. Now here is my sword to sharpen and my mail to clean. Make sure you do it well. I expect it to be finished after Sext. And do not forget to feed and groom my warhorse.'

And that was that, with the wave of a hand I was dismissed. I picked up the coat of mail and sword and left the room. That was my work for the early morning, using sand to scrub the armour and a whetstone to sharpen the sword. It was a fine blade, well-forged and balanced and still relatively sharp, with a bone handle and the symbol of the cross embossed in red on the pommel. I sat outside our tent, next to Otto, who was doing the same for his new master, another of the brothers who had just returned. The mail *chausses*, worn to protect the legs, were covered in dried blood, although I hadn't seen any wounds on Rudolf so I assumed it belonged to someone else. I used a barrel, filled with sand and rolled and scraped the iron rings before covering the coat with lanolin oil. It was dirty work and took a long time, but finally it was finished. We spoke in low voices as we worked, watching as the masons arrived for another day, building the new castle that would occupy almost half of the space in the commandery. They were making good headway and already the walls reached up over ten feet, although, with winter not far off, that would slow or stop altogether. However, we were not finished yet with our chores. I put the cleaned mail and sword in our tent and bid goodbye to Otto while I went to attend to Rudolf's destrier, Rabe – which meant raven in German – in the stables.

The stallion was a magnificent beast, tall and strong and as black as pitch. Rabe tossed his head and moved away when I entered the stall and, sensing his unease, I approached slowly, carrying a large handful of hay to feed him. I stroked his mane and spoke gently in his ear, feeling the horse noticeably calm as he became accustomed to me. I frowned as I studied his flank. It had been heavily raked by my master's spurs, and when I looked closer, I saw a mesh of old scars on both sides, some of them quite deep, and his neck and shoulders were also scarred with old cuts from a whip. I remembered Rudolf's behaviour when he had returned and I felt a rising anger. What a pig! What bastard could do this to such a majestic animal?

By the time Saint Peter's Church bell rang for Prime, I had finished rubbing down and feeding the stallion. With my early chores finally done, I emerged into the yard and joined the line of knights and sergeants heading for the chapel. Afterwards, I waited outside the refectory with the other sergeants as the knights broke their fast.

'I heard that the Master has convened a special chapter today,' Hinz said. 'They are to discuss the coming expedition.'

'Not before time,' Otto said. 'This place is slowly beginning to feel like a prison.'

Gerhard nodded. 'That's true. It will be good to get outside again.'

'And we will not have to go to chapel,' I said.

'But we will still have to pray, even in the field,' Hinz said. 'That should please our friend, Emich, anyway.'

We turned as the main gate nearby was creaked open by the two sergeants on duty. Half-a-dozen priests and Cistercian monks entered on foot led by Theodoric. One of the sergeants ran to inform the Master and the abbot strode over to where we waited outside the refectory.

'Ah, young Richard,' the monk said to me. 'It is good to see you again. I hope you have recovered from the journey and are settling into your new life here in Riga.'

'Yes, father,' I said.

'And you, Sergeant-brother Otto,' Theodoric continued, smiling. 'Have you killed any more pirates recently.'

Otto laughed as Wenno came out of the main building and strode towards where we stood with the new arrivals.

'Father abbot,' the Master said. 'It is good to see you. I hope the journey here was not too troubling.'

'From next door!' Theodoric laughed. 'I am not living at Dünamünde yet. I am currently at the bishop's palace.'

'I see,' Wenno said. 'It is good that you have arrived early. We will have a chance to talk before chapter begins.'

Theodoric and the monks disappeared into the main building with Wenno. A short time later the knight-brothers filed out, allowing us to enter the refectory.

Afterwards, because Priest-brother Berthold was attending the chapter meeting, there was no German lesson. Instead, I continued my work in the stables, helping to rub down and groom the other horses as well as taking them for a few laps of the yard. Now that the expedition had returned, there were many more horses than before, both the destriers – the big warhorses used in battle, and the palfreys used for daily riding. There was even a dozen or so of the local breed, smaller in stature than the other horses that had come from the Empire. Because of this, we were joined by half a dozen more sergeants and two Lett servants to help with the extra work. But there were still not enough horses for all the sergeant-brothers in the Order. I suspected that, as with the accommodation, clothes and armour, we newest sergeants would be the ones that went without. Maybe we would capture what we needed raiding in the field.

We attended the chapel again for Terce and then it was time for training. But on this occasion Sighard led us to the armoury, next to the infirmary against the outside wall, where we were each given a crossbow and some bolts. Otto pointed out that Wolfgang and Gabriel were giving me evil looks and I glanced over, wondering why Reinhart was not with them as usual. I thought no more about it. At the time I didn't realise the significance, an oversight that would cause me problems later.

Sighard led us out of the main gate of the commandery into the city. We were accompanied by a cart pulled by two of the local shaggy ponies and passed along a street where the wooden shutters of the shops and stalls were thrown open for business. Most of the people we saw were local Livs or Letts, dressed in hues of blue and brown, haggling with the shopkeepers in a strange tongue as chickens clucked around their ankles. The air rang with the sound of hammers used in the building of the new wooden houses around us. To our right was Saint Mary's Church and priory, a barnlike timber structure that was the city's cathedral and pre-eminent house of worship. The street led to a gate and tower in the stockade, passing through and over a bridge spanning the moat that helped protect the north side of the town. On the other side, a large sandy hill reached up and dominated the landscape around. We followed a sand road to an area of pasture that had been cleared of trees and given over to agriculture. Flocks of sheep grazed on the grass between the tree stumps and a young shepherd watched us warily. Further off, the dark forest of tangled oaks looked ominous and threatening. At a command from Sighard, we pulled up in the meadow and some of the sergeants fetched the targets from the cart, setting them up some hundred paces or so from where the rest of us stood. We were split into small groups and that was how we spent the balance of the morning, firing the crossbow bolts at the targets. In our group, to my surprise, Hinz was the best and he was very pleased about it.

'That's unbelievable,' I said. 'When we were attacked by the pirates you couldn't hit anything.'

'I learn quickly.' Hinz grinned. That was true but to be honest there was little to learn. The crossbow is a weapon that can be used by any idiot; you point it at the enemy and pull the trigger. Unlike the Welsh great bow.

It was time to return to the commandery. The targets were collected and put in the cart and Sighard ordered me and another sergeant to go and check the ground for any loose bolts that could be used again. I walked towards the line of trees and began picking up those I could see in the grass. Behind me, Sighard began to lead the rest of the sergeants back towards the town stockade. Two figures near the back hesitated and I assumed it must be my friends waiting for me. As I finished they approached. My heart dropped. It was Wolfgang and Gabriel.

I stopped and prepared for the coming trouble. Behind, several more figures detached themselves from the main group and Otto and Hinz were among them.

'Now we're going to have our little talk,' Wolfgang said, unaware of the people behind him.

'Do your worst, bastard.' I was ready to fight.

'Yes,' Otto said, as my two friends came past them and stood with me. 'Do your worst.'

Wolfgang and Gabriel both hesitated and looked at each other. 'There'll be another time for our little chat,' Wolfgang said. 'Come, Gab... I think it's time to go and pray.'

'Not so brave now when the odds are a little fairer, eh?' I said. My two antagonists walked away, following the other sergeants who had already reached the gate. They said nothing more. Ahead, I saw Sighard had paused and he frowned as he looked back towards us.

'Thanks, but we'd better go,' I said to Otto and Hinz. 'Otherwise Sighard will be upset.'

'Yes,' Otto agreed. 'It doesn't take much.'

We hurried back to the city as the bell rang for Sext. By the time we reached the commandery gate we had caught up with the slower sergeants, but I saw no sign of Wolfgang and Gabriel. Since the bulk of the Order had returned, the chapel was always packed and we managed to squeeze in at the back for the brief service. I caught a glimpse through the crowd of Reinhart. As if he could feel my eyes on him, he glanced back and looked at me before smiling and turning away.

Afterwards, we all filed out. Now was the time to give back my master's armour and sword, so I walked the short way to our tent with Otto, ducking under the flap to grab the sword and mail that I had cleaned earlier. When I was greeted by the foul stench of shit, I knew at once that something was wrong. I retrieved the sword and froze in horror when I saw the mail. It was smeared in dung and excrement. I grabbed the mail *chausses* and backed out of the tent.

'What is that awful smell?' Otto said.

I threw the soiled armour to the grass in front of him in disgust.

'How... who could have done that?'

I thought for a second. 'I think I know.'

'Who?'

I remembered the smug smile Reinhart had given me in the chapel. 'Reinhart didn't come with us when we were training outside of the city. Where was he exactly? It must have been him – the mail was fine before we left.'

I looked back to see more knight-brothers streaming from the chapel. One of them was Rudolf, and he looked across at me before walking over to our tents. Behind him, the last brothers were still leaving.

'Have you finished cleaning my sword and armour?' Rudolf said. He looked down at the pile of mail on the ground before me and wrinkled his nose. 'Is this some kind of jest?' he said coldly. 'Do you think to make a fool of me?'

'No, of course not,' I said. 'It wasn't—'

He took two quick strides and slapped me hard across the face. The blow took me by surprise and I staggered backwards, my head ringing, falling over the guy rope to our tent and landing on my arse. Otto looked on in shock as Rudolf came forward to strike me again.

A shout from behind interrupted him. 'Brother Rudolf!'

My master spun round and I looked in relief to see Berthold striding towards us.

'That is not behaviour becoming of a knight,' Berthold said. 'And even less for a monk.'

'This is not your concern, Priest-brother Berthold,' Rudolf said. 'This boy is my squire and I am his master. I shall discipline him as I see fit.'

Berthold pointed to the soiled mail still lying on the ground. 'And why do you think your squire would deliberately soak your mail in the latrine? Surely he would expect you would punish him for such action?'

'I don't care about his reasoning. He is an impudent young pup, and a foreigner to boot. Why he did this does not interest me. He has made me a laughing stock.'

'You seem to have managed that quite well yourself,' Berthold said, looking round at the group of knights watching from outside of the chapel. 'And pride is one of the cardinal sins, as I believe you have been warned of before. Remember Isaiah 2:12 – *The Lord Almighty has a day in store for all the proud and lofty, for all that is exalted (and they will be humbled).*'

'Keep your bloody Bible quotes to yourself,' Rudolf said. He turned back to me and pointed a finger. 'That was nothing. If my mail is not properly cleaned of this filth by Compline, I will beat you to within an inch of your life. Do not doubt me.' He stormed away, past the knights watching at the door of the chapel towards the knight-brethren's quarters.

'Are you well?' Berthold said.

I came to my feet. 'Yes,' I said. 'But I cleaned the *chausses* this morning. Someone must have dropped them in the latrine while we were training. And I think I know who.'

'Who?' Berthold said.

'Reinhart.'

'But he is ill. He was in the infirmary while you were training. I saw him there with my own eyes. It must have been someone else.'

An idea came to me. 'Maybe that was why we were delayed after target practice – to give him time to perform his sabotage.'

'Sabotage?'

'Never mind. Are you going to talk to the Master?'

Berthold shook his head. 'I will not have to. Enough people witnessed what happened. He probably already knows and if he doesn't, he will soon.'

'I don't want any more trouble,' I said.

'No, I am sure you don't. Let me have another word with Rudolf… somewhere not so public. And if he will not listen to me then maybe he will listen to Master Wenno.'

I wasn't convinced he would listen to anyone. Berthold smiled and walked back towards the other knights, leaving me alone with Otto.

'I am glad Rudolf is not my master,' Otto said.

No, he was *my* master. And now I knew what that entailed. Whatever I did would not be good enough for him. Would he ever be satisfied? I did not think so.

Rudolf von Elsdorf was an arrogant bully and I had no doubt he would do his utmost to make my life a misery for as long as I served him.

CHAPTER TWENTY-TWO

That same evening I gave Rudolf back his cleaned mail *chausses*. It had taken most of the afternoon to clean off all the faeces, but when I delivered it to him, he barely acknowledged my presence. For the next week or so I had no further trouble. Every morning I would report to him for chores and he never mentioned the incident in the yard, nor lost his temper with me again. Whether this had anything to do with Brother Berthold or Master Wenno, I had no idea.

There were no further confrontations with Wolfgang or his friends, but then again, we were too busy preparing for the expedition to find time to argue. That meant that my revenge on Reinhart would have to wait as well. There was so much to do as supplies arrived daily: food for the men, fodder for the horses, crates of horseshoes made from smithies in the city and boxes of crossbow bolts. The blacksmiths in the small hut next to the latrine worked all hours, repairing coats of mail, making spearheads and steel points for the bolts, as well as forging additional tools and any necessary repairs to helmets and other equipment. Otto was busy at the smithy much of the day, even working shifts during the night, while I spent most of the time in the stables. Sighard told us that the sergeants without horses would carry crossbows and fight on foot. This included all of us who had arrived on the three ships with Theodoric. Nevertheless, most of the knight-brothers and many of the sergeants would fight on horseback, the knights as heavy cavalry and the sergeants in a supporting role. And despite almost the entire Order taking part, the bulk of our forces would be made up of local Letts, already converted to Christianity, who would fight under our command. The plan was to meet them outside the city the day after the Feast of Saint Michael.

Next to the smithy, against the far wall, several workmen had begun building another wooden block for accommodation and I assumed this would become our quarters when finished. It was a relief to know we wouldn't have to brave the winter living in tents; by the time we returned from our raiding it should be finished.

On the eve of the Feast of Saint Michael, I was in a maudlin mood. Back home it was called Michaelmas, and I couldn't help but remember the same day, only a year before, although it felt much longer. That was when my life had begun to turn into a nightmare. That had been when my aunt Cecilia and my cousin Walter had arrived at our castle to change things forever. A familiar resentment rose like bile in my throat. Would I ever be able to get my revenge and reclaim what was rightfully mine? Now it was more unattainable than ever.

That evening, we were split into groups, each having to keep a vigil for a few hours in the chapel during the night. After Psalms and a sermon from Brother Berthold, we were left to our own prayers. It was cold and uncomfortable and, of course, we were forbidden to speak. The time seemed to last forever. When we were relieved and able to return to our tents, my knees were stiff and sore.

Much of the next day was spent in the chapel, but at least we ate well at dinner as Berthold read stories of the Archangels: Saint Michael, Saint Gabriel and Saint Raphael. We ate dishes of chicken and pork, bowls of steamed vegetables followed by fruit and cheese and all washed down with an abundant supply of wine. But alas, I was not destined to enjoy the wine as I received a tap on my back from Sighard, along with the others who worked in the stables, to take delivery of a long line of local pack ponies that would carry most of our supplies. We topped up the troughs outside the stables with water and fed them with hay and oats. The plan was for us to leave the following morning and there was a discernible excitement in the air. Gerhard was quiet and obviously nervous about what faced us, but I had my own fears to contend with and I could find no words of consolation for him. The afternoon was spent preparing our equipment and loading the dozen wagons that would accompany us with spears, shields, crossbows and boxes of bolts, as well as the canvas tents that would provide our shelter. This work kept us busy for the rest of the day.

The next morning there was a stiff wind with the threat of rain. In the chapel at Prime, there were so many people that many had to wait outside in the light drizzle that began just after Berthold started his sermon. My German tutor gave an impassioned speech about going forth to convert the Beast and bring them into the warm embrace of Christ. He spoke well and everyone left the service invigorated about the coming mission.

In the busy yard, horses were brought from the stables while grooms checked saddle straps and bridles, and knights made their last preparations before riding. The wagons and packhorses were already loaded and they formed up as the knights finally mounted their chargers. I helped my master, Rudolf, climb into his saddle, but once mounted he nudged

Rabe away from me without a word. Abbot Theodoric, along with half-a-dozen priests who were to accompany us, had come again and talked to Wenno and Sighard before saying a blessing and a prayer for the success of our raid. Everyone listened as his words drifted over the yard before he led the paternoster. Afterwards, I returned to the large group of sergeants who would fight on foot, finding Otto and Hinz in the column, adjusting my sword and slinging my shield across my back. In the group of mounted sergeants, I saw Wolfgang and his cronies laughing and I felt a flutter of irritation. Maybe when we were in the field, I would find an opportunity to get them back.

We were now ready to march and the gate opened. Wenno led the column into the street. Our army numbered just under two hundred men, led by the fifty or so knight-brothers, with us sergeants walking directly behind, followed by the baggage train and the mounted sergeants bringing up the rear. People cheered us as we passed through the muddy streets and I felt an uplift of spirits for the first time since arriving in Livonia. There was a pride in wearing the sword and cross motif emblazoned on our surcoats that I hadn't felt before. Perhaps it had something to do with the togetherness I felt with my comrades around me. We would be relying on each other in the next few weeks and all our lives would depend on it.

We left the city through the same gate we used to reach the meadow for crossbow practice, clomping across the moat before following the Great Sandy Way, under the *Kubsberg* or Old Mountain, to cross the bridge over the Rigebach, the stream that protected the city's east side. We then picked up the rutted track that doubled back and followed the stream south-east where we met the local Lett tribesmen who would fight as auxiliaries. They numbered roughly two hundred and fifty, some of them mounted on their small, shaggy horses, but most on foot. They were large, fierce-looking men, but looked more like a rabble, armed with spears or javelins, axes, and even a few with swords. Almost none of them wore any visible mail, although many wore fur and hides and carried shields. After Wenno and the Lettish chieftain spoke, the tribesmen on foot joined the column behind us, following the baggage train, while their mounted warriors would act as scouts.

'I wonder how useful they will be if we give battle,' I said to Otto.

Otto watched the group of Letts as they took up position. 'They look a wild bunch anyway. I'm glad they're on our side.'

'As long as they don't run,' I said. 'Berthold told me that sometimes happens.'

It started to rain harder but, thankfully, we soon entered the forest, marching in silence. Under the tangled branches it was eerily quiet, with only the noise of our stamping boots, the dripping of water from the branches, and the crunching underfoot of fallen autumn leaves. We had to stop often because of the slow progress of the wagons that kept getting stuck, and I was convinced we were too slow to catch any enemies we might come across. Sometime late morning, we stopped in a small grassy clearing to eat and pray before pushing on through the trees that spread endlessly around us.

On the first night, we reached the village of Holm, located on a small island in the Düna river. There was a rectangular stone-built wall with a tower in one corner and I spied the wooden spire of a Christian church amongst the yellow and green of the neighbouring trees behind, but we stayed in the shamble of huts and wooden buildings on the north bank of the river. The village chief greeted us. He was a short man with a long moustache named Ako, who arranged for the Order's leading half-a-dozen or so knights to be rowed across to the island to be personally entertained in his hall. My master was one of those honoured and I was relieved he was away, watching the black-haired figure climb into the barge at the jetty. The rest of us were allowed to make fires in order to cook warm food and Brother Wickbert, a red-headed, lanky man who had been in Livonia from the beginning of the Order, spoke to us. He was the most senior knight who had not accompanied the Master and the others to the island and he explained that this area was one of the first to be Christianised under the previous bishop, a man named Meinhard, who had built a stone fort here as well as another further upriver at Uexküll. 'Bishop Meinhard was a good man but he met his Creator about eight years ago,' Wickbert explained while the rest of us listened. 'However, Bishop Albert is better. He's a true man of God and takes no foolishness from the locals.'

'What do you mean?' Emich asked. 'I thought Meinhard was a good Christian. Didn't he convert many of the pagans?'

'Meinhard baptised many of the local Livs and Letts, that is true. In this very village even. He promised them he would build two stone forts, one here and one in Uexküll, to protect them against the Lithuanians and Semigallians – other more warlike tribes not far from here. But afterwards, they recanted their baptism, thinking they could wash off Christ's embrace in the waters of the Düna.' He shook his head at the folly of it. 'The Livonians are a stubborn bunch. Believe me, you cannot trust any of them. Ask Abbot Theodoric if you don't believe me. He was here during that time. I just wish we were fighting alone. We should be killing them, not converting them!' He turned and looked towards the fires of the Lett tribesmen spread out towards the trees of the forest. 'Better an enemy in front than a knife in the back from a friend behind.'

'I heard a story that the local tribes had never seen a stone building before,' Wolfgang said. 'What barbarians they must be.'

'The Semigallians attacked Uexküll and tried to pull down the stone walls with ropes.' Wickbert laughed. 'They didn't realise the stones were held together with cement. Suffice to say, they were seen off with heavy losses.'

Wolfgang shook his head. 'Barbarians, like I said.'

The conversation continued but I listened with only half an ear as I was tired from the march and looked forward to getting some sleep. Luckily, we managed to get a space on the earth floor of a rickety hay barn that kept the worst of the rain out. However, when it got dark and we went to bed, I lay curled in my cloak for hours, unable to sleep as the rain pattered on the wood-shingle roof and my comrades snored and fidgeted around me. Close to dawn, I was woken for a turn on guard duty and I came to my feet with weary and aching limbs to spend the last hours of darkness shivering on the perimeter set around the village.

By the next morning it had stopped raining, but there was a mist that hugged the ground, twisting and hovering around the wood buildings of the village and dampening the trees of the forest around. Sounds were strangely muffled as we gathered and prayed in the small field that led down to the river, before collecting our gear and preparing to move out. The few locals we saw either stared at us with curiosity or ignored us altogether, concentrating on starting their work for the day. I fetched Knight-brother Rudolf's equipment from the house where he had slept and helped him mount Rabe, passing him his lance which he took as usual without comment. The other knights climbed into their saddles, aided by their own squires, and at an order from Master Wenno they led us out, heading into the forest again.

We marched most of the day, only stopping to pray and eat. The baggage train struggled to keep up, particularly after the rain of the previous day, and after stopping for Nones they were left to be guarded by the mounted sergeants of the rear guard while the rest of us pushed on. It was late afternoon when we came to the village of Uexküll, another Christianised settlement, just a collection of wooden huts that surrounded a stone enclosure on the banks of the river with several buildings within, including a stone church. This had been the seat of the first bishop of Livonia, the same Meinhard that Wickbert had talked about the previous evening. Now, it had been given over to a secular knight called Conrad von Meiendorf, who was a vassal of Bishop Albert but had not yet taken up his fief. Nevertheless, a dozen or so of his retainers were already here. There were also several missionaries and monks in the original stone enclosure that consisted of a chapel and main quarters, along with a small hall and stables.

Sighard rode back from the head of the column to where we waited at the edge of the forest. 'There is no room in the village for all of us,' he declared. 'You sergeants are to spend the night here, but I have other duties in the fort. When the baggage train arrives, erect the tents there.' He pointed to the grassy area that led down to the river. 'And build a latrine… not too close to the tents. Emil, as the most senior sergeant here, you are in charge.'

My colleague from the stable nodded in acknowledgement. It would be dark soon and it would take all that time to complete the work assigned to us.

Sighard picked me out from the crowd. 'Sergeant-brother Richard, Knight-brother Rudolf requires your presence. He has a special job for you. You shall find him in the hall of the fort. I would not keep him waiting too long if I were you.'

He pulled his horse around and cantered back towards the village. Otto looked at me in sympathy while I shrugged and followed in Sighard's wake, wondering what awaited me.

The village was a collection of wooden huts, sheds and barns strung along the main track that led to the walled fort on the riverbank. The fort, for it could hardly be called a castle, was small, and if it had been in England or elsewhere in Europe it would have attracted little attention. However, it was the most impressive building I had yet seen in Livonia. The crenellated stone wall enclosed two small courtyards separated by a narrow span of water, connected by a bridge, and overlooked by the largest of the stone structures – the main building flanked by a church on one side and stables on the other, all of them forming one side of the defences. The main building was three stories high and crowned by a tiled roof. Behind, in the cleared meadow at the edge of the forest, there were wattle animal pens containing cows and sheep, along with a vegetable patch. At the gate, I spoke with one of the guards and he led me through the busy courtyard to an open door in the building that led up to the first floor.

The hall was approximately the same size as Cranham, with most of the space filled with rows of tables and benches, all of them occupied by the knight-brothers. The smell of smoke and meat cooking hung in the air, making me hungry. For a moment, I stood in the doorway scanning the faces for my master, the buzz of the conversation drifting around me. Sitting at one of the nearest tables was Rudolf, surrounded by half a dozen of his usual cronies, all of them young knights of his own age. On a table behind, I noticed Dieter talking with another knight I did not know.

'There you are,' Rudolf said. 'You took long enough.'

'I came as soon as I heard you required me.' I tried to keep the insolence from my voice.

'Well, it matters not. You're here now. The Master wants someone to check up on the baggage train and I volunteered you. Requisition a horse from the stables and go and find how long until they get here. Report back to me when you return.'

'One moment, not so hasty,' another knight said when I turned to go. He was tall, despite being seated. 'We have heard about you. Is it true you killed someone on the ship that brought you here from Lübeck?' All of them looked at me as I hesitated.

'Well, answer the question, boy,' Rudolf said.

'Yes, it is true,' I said. 'He was my enemy and no man of God.'

'It is difficult to believe.' The tall knight turned and laughed with the man next to him. 'You barely look old enough to be away from your mother's teat.'

'He was not the only man, either,' I said, feeling my face redden under the scrutiny. 'I also killed a few pirates.'

'That is hard to credit,' Rudolf said, shaking his head. 'You are so young. It seems more likely to be lies, or exaggeration at the least.'

I clenched my fists, bristling at being called a liar. Behind Rudolf and his cronies, I saw Dieter had come to his feet and had approached the table.

'I would be careful what you say,' he said. 'Brother Stephan and myself witnessed Sergeant-brother Richard in Lübeck. He acted in self-defence and killed his attacker with an extraordinary display of swordsmanship. The boy is not lying.'

'Pah,' Rudolf said. 'How is it possible? I heard that the man killed was an experienced swordsman.'

'He might well have been, but it did not save him. The boy is a formidable fighter and you would be wise to remember that if we engage the pagans in battle.'

A rising anger rose in me at being referred to as a boy, even by Dieter. Everyone was talking as if I was not there.

'Well, anyway, you had better get going.' Rudolf took a swig of the wine in front of him and ignored Dieter. 'It will be dark soon.'

Dismissed, I left the hall seething, returned down the staircase to the courtyard and crossed the small bridge to the other part of the fort where the stables were. The stablemaster was an older man who became surly when I told him I needed a horse, only allowing me to take one of the local shaggy ponies. 'And make sure you bring her back.'

I felt ridiculous when I mounted the horse, my feet almost touching the ground. The young guard at the gate, the same youth who had shown me to the hall, turned away smirking as I rode out back into the village. I continued down the muddy track, not daring to look at my comrades busy digging the latrine. If Otto and the others saw me now, they would piss themselves laughing. Luckily, they didn't notice, and soon I was riding past the encampment of Letts who didn't even glance at me. A few moments later I was in the trees, retracing the same steps from before, my horse crunching through the piles of leaves still fluttering down on the breeze.

Luckily, the baggage train was not far behind. I had been riding a short while when I encountered the first outriders from the mounted sergeants of the rear guard, two youths a few years older than me that I had seen around the commandery. They grinned openly at seeing me on the Livonian horse, before leading me back to where the wagons were labouring their way along the rutted track. Here, I met the knight-brother in charge, an old man named Ludger who pulled his horse up on a patch of grass to speak with me. 'It will be nearly dark when we reach Uexküll,' he said. 'I hope there will be hot food ready when we arrive.'

I had no answer to that and I turned my horse around to return to my comrades, just as another group of sergeants galloped up to us. When I saw Wolfgang and Gabriel among them, I groaned.

'Ha, what do we have here?' Wolfgang said as they pulled their horses up. 'Look, boys, it seems Richard has found his station in life.'

'A donkey would be more suitable for him,' Gabriel said, and the other sergeants laughed.

Humiliated and ears ringing with their mirth, I dug my heels into the horse's flank and she trotted forward, as eager as me to return to our camp. A moment later I had left the column behind and was alone in the trees again. I slowed down and patted the horse's neck. Maybe I had been wrong about her. She might be smaller than her European counterparts but she was sturdy, strong, and had borne me without complaint.

The forest around was quiet and still and becoming gloomy as late afternoon turned into early evening. I wasn't unduly worried; in a short time I would be sitting around the fire with my comrades. Behind me, I heard the pounding of horses' hooves and assumed it was the outriders taking up station again. Hearing them approach, I swung round to look and saw three riders almost on top of me. Too late, I realised it was Wolfgang and his friends. As Wolfgang thundered past, I felt a sharp wrench of my mail hood as I was yanked out of my saddle. A moment later I was falling, my shoulder impacting a tree root in an explosion of agony. My breath was knocked from my body and branches whipped at my face, filling my mouth with earth, leaves and blood. I lay dazed, momentarily blinded as I heard them rein their horses in.

'We have no time.' Reinhart's voice was unmistakeable. 'Ludger is only just behind. We can get him properly another time.'

'It won't take long.' The second voice was Gabriel's. My vision cleared slowly and I could see he was still mounted. A sudden excruciating pain erupted in my side as Wolfgang's foot slammed into my ribs. I curled up in a ball, expecting to receive a flurry of more kicks but none came. The reason became clear a few seconds later as the rumble of more hooves on the track heralded the arrival of the main column.

'What is happening here?' Ludger said, pulling his horse up to where Reinhart and Gabriel, still mounted, waited.

It was Wolfgang who answered. 'Sergeant-brother Richard has fallen from his… horse. We were just helping him.'

Ludger frowned and looked at me for confirmation.

'I am unused to these smaller, local ponies,' I said, grimacing. My ribs and shoulder were on fire and droplets of blood dripped from the scratches on my face. 'I will do better next time.' Ludger gave me a look suggesting I was a complete simpleton and I wasn't sure if he believed me, but that was his problem. Playing the role of the helpful comrade, Wolfgang guided me to my feet, supporting me to my horse.

'If you say a word…' he hissed at me, his back to Ludger.

'Fuck off,' I said through gritted teeth. I put my foot into the stirrup and pulled myself up into the saddle.

'You had better get back as soon as possible,' Ludger said. 'Tell the Master we shall not be long. And try not to fall off your horse again.'

I dug my heels into the horse's flanks and she trotted forward, gaining speed as I sought to put as much distance between myself and the column. I rode, seething and plotting, the soreness in my ribs gradually subsiding to a dull ache although the cuts on my face stung badly. Once again, I had been humbled by Wolfgang and his friends and it made me furious.

The sun had dropped below the tops of the trees when I came out of the woods at the edge of Uexküll. I lowered my head again while I passed through the armed camp of the Letts and my comrades. By the time I had reached the main settlement, the bells of the church had begun ringing for Vespers. I had no desire to go and pray, so after giving the horse back I hung around the stables, despite the questions my scratched face elicited from the grooms and stable-boys, before crossing the bridge to the other bailey where I waited outside the door of the church. A few moments later, with their prayers finished, the courtyard filled up with knight-brothers, but it was easy to pick out my raven-haired master and I made my report.

'What happened to your face?' Rudolf asked.

'I had a small accident… it is nothing.' I could see he wasn't really interested. 'Do you require anything else, master?'

He didn't, so I returned to my comrades, now eating an evening meal of beans and fish around one of the many small fires.

'What in God's name happened to you?' Otto said, looking shocked at my appearance.

I explained what had occurred in the forest.

'The bastards,' Otto said. Our conversation was interrupted by the arrival of the baggage train and its escort of mounted sergeants. Ludger led the column with Wolfgang and his friends not far behind. 'We should sort this out.' He came to his feet.

'No!' I said, more loudly than I intended. Several sergeants at the next fire turned to look. 'Now is not the right time,' I said in a lower voice.

Otto sat down again reluctantly. 'But you cannot let them get away with it. You will need help and we are behind you.' He turned to Hinz, Gerhard and Emich who all nodded, although I noticed Emich frown shortly after.

'It has to be a time when no one else is around,' I said. 'But this is my problem – and I shall solve it.'

For a moment we sat in silence as the carts of the baggage train rumbled past.

'We could get a servant to give them a message telling them to go somewhere,' Otto said, thinking aloud, 'but instead we would be waiting for them...'

'Somewhere quiet, where no one else is around,' Hinz said, jumping on the plan.

I listened in silence as my friends bandied around different ideas but I said nothing, just brooding. When I look back on it now, nearly forty years later, it seems so trivial, although of course, it wasn't at the time. However, it was my friends' reaction to me being attacked again that touched me the most. Without me asking, they were ready to help me, eager to hit back at my tormenters despite the risk to themselves and probable dismissal from the Order if caught. Wolfgang and his friends had done nothing to any of them, but they were my friends and it didn't matter – an attack on one of us was an attack on all. I had never had this before in my life. My companions in Cranham had been the sons of my father's retainers and, despite us getting on well, they had never been my social equals, let alone friends, not even John de Vere and Robert Percy. My comrades here were the only positive part of my new life. In a world with little or no contact with women, these relationships became even more important. When I look back on my time with the Teutonic Knights and the Swordbrothers beforehand, it is the friends and comrades that have come and gone over the years that stand out for me: their courage, their heroism and their humour. That, of course, and the battles.

Always the battles.

CHAPTER TWENTY-THREE

Over the next few days, we pushed on south-east through the forest, marching in file while the scouts probed ahead. We came across several unstockaded small villages, but the Livs had learned we were coming because they were all deserted. The people had taken their livestock and valuables and disappeared into the forest long before we arrived. We burned their wooden buildings anyway. I remember thinking at the time it was a mistake – the plumes of smoke would warn the tribesmen for miles around. Near one village, we came across an ancient grove of oak trees, festooned with fabric and offerings to whatever pagan gods the local people believed in. Faces and patterns were carved into some of the trunks. We chopped down the trees and destroyed everything.

The next night, we camped at the edge of the forest by a swamp, erecting our tents between stunted bushes of thorns and brambles. We were forbidden to make any campfires. Conversation centred on our inability to confront the enemy and the pittance we had seized in plunder to take back to Riga.

'Some of the scouts have had glimpses of the enemy, but by the time our knights arrive they have always fled,' Sighard told us as we ate our cold rations. 'Lennewarden is not far ahead and there is a wooden fort. This time we are going to do it differently. All sergeants on foot will move out during the night in order to attack the village at dawn. This way we hope to take them by surprise.'

There was a buzz of excitement but, as it started to get dark, we prepared to get what little sleep we were allowed. I needed to relieve myself and as we had built no latrines, I went into the nearby trees. I hadn't gone far when I heard whimpering coming from behind a tree. Drawing my sword, I peered around the trunk and saw a figure hunched over with his back to me. When a branch crunched under my foot, he turned abruptly and looked up at me. It was Gerhard.

'What is the matter?' I said. Even in the gloom I could see his cheeks were streaked with tears.

Gerhard came to his feet. 'I'm… well, I just feel a little sick.'

He tried to move past me but I put my arm out to stop him. 'No, tell me. Is it because of tomorrow?'

He looked down and nodded. 'I'm so scared…'

'We all are.'

He looked at me in surprise. 'But… you're not. The way you killed that man on the ship. You were so calm – so in control.'

'No, I wasn't. I was trembling all over.' That was true.

'But you couldn't have been scared… the way you shouted at those men on the quay. You *wanted* to fight more of them – I could see it.'

'That doesn't mean I was not terrified. The important thing is beating your fear and doing what you must.'

'But I cannot,' Gerhard said. 'I'm scared I will be killed… or wounded. I'm not good with pain. My father always said I was craven…'

'You will be fine. The tribesmen don't have a chance. They will not get anywhere near you, that's why we have crossbows.'

'But I'm scared that I will freeze when we join battle... that I will let you all down.'

'Stick close to me. I will keep an eye on you.'

'But everyone else... they seem so confident, some of them are even looking forward to battle.'

I certainly was. 'Most of that is just bravado, they are all shitting themselves. The important thing is not showing your fear. You have to control it.'

I am aware now, so many years after the event, that everything I said to Gerhard that evening was true. But at the time I was thinking aloud, saying what came into my head. I had little personal experience myself. It was the eve of my first proper battle as well, and I wanted to be alone with my own thoughts, but I also remembered the support my friends had given after I was attacked by Wolfgang. I took Gerhard by the shoulders and looked into his eyes. 'Everything will be all right. Believe me. You will not be wounded or killed.'

He nodded, desperately trying to regain his composure. 'But please... please don't say anything...'

I could see that my words had helped. I squeezed his arm. 'Now, go back to our tent and let me take a piss. I shall not say anything to anyone.'

He smiled in gratitude before disappearing back towards our camp.

Despite everything I had said, I found Gerhard's inability to hide his fear undignified. He was the son of a knight and would have been training all his life for this moment – and he was older than me. And the fact that his own father thought him a coward did not bode well. If my father had ever said such a thing, I would have died of shame. Gerhard knew what was involved before he had come here. And he knew what was expected of him. Like me, he had to come to terms with that. And part of that was learning to conquer the bone-numbing terror that turns your limbs to lead and your guts to slush.

Nevertheless, he was my friend and I would do my utmost to protect him like I had promised. I returned to our tent to find the others waiting for me before going to bed.

'Emich wants us to pray together before we sleep,' Otto said. 'Who knows what tomorrow will bring...'

It was the last thing I wanted, but I swallowed a retort when I saw the hope on Gerhard's face. If it would make him feel better then what was it to me? And it was not as if I didn't need God's blessing either.

We all knelt next to the fire and Emich recited a prayer. He looked mesmerising in the fire, the light dancing across his shadowed beauty. I bowed my head, marvelling at his piety, although I quickly lost interest and hardly heard most of his words. My mind was more focussed on what the morning would bring. When he had finished, Emich kissed his cross and then insisted we all do the same. Otto pulled a face but he kissed it along with Gerhard, Hinz and myself, the ritual strangely making me feel closer to my new friends. 'I think he has a direct connection to God,' Otto said afterwards, before we retired to our tent to get a few precious hours of sleep.

We were woken in the dead of night and prepared our equipment before moving out into the forest again, guided by several of the local Lett scouts. It was a clear night, partially illuminated by a half moon that seemed to hang above the trees, throwing pale shards of light that penetrated the diminishing tree cover. It was still incredibly dark, however, and we stumbled into each other as we tramped along the track, making enough noise to wake the dead for miles around. It took a long time, but finally we reached the edge of the village just before dawn.

Everything was confused. They must have been warned of our approach shortly before our arrival, for when we broke through the trees there was already panic. People were running in all directions in their haste to get away and dogs barked and women screamed. The knights charged, and a few moments later they were riding through the village, hacking at the fleeing figures. I saw Rudolf cut down a running pagan, chopping him in the back before wheeling his horse around while the man writhed on the ground in agony. Rudolf laughed, leaning out from his saddle and casually stabbing down, withdrawing his sword and spurring Rabe forward down a track between two wooden shacks to chase another group of people.

We moved slowly into the village, following Sighard, pushing through the cluster of wood huts and outhouses. The Lett auxiliaries were in the village as well, and I saw one pulling a cow by a rope while another was herding two terrified sheep away. A building was burning to our left and the flames were vivid in the grey half-light of the morning. On the ground lay the corpse of a man with his guts hanging out of his lacerated belly. I paused for a moment, looking at him, strangely both repulsed and attracted by the scene. My view was interrupted as three Letts stalked past, heading towards a thatched hut behind another house. They had drawn swords and at least one had blood on his blade, arousing my curiosity, and I watched them kick in the door of the hut and disappear inside. The rest of my comrades had passed further into the village, apart from Otto who waited with a quizzical look on his face. 'Why are you so slow, Richard?' he called to me. Behind him, I saw that Gerhard had stopped as well.

A moment later, I heard a scream coming from the same hut and I dashed towards the sound, drawing my sword. I burst through the doorway and saw the three Letts standing over a woman who was sprawled on the earthen floor, whilst a small boy stood crying in the corner. It was obvious what the three men intended. I shouted and shoved the nearest man away, knocking him to the ground, before swinging my sword in an arc to drive the other two back. The man I had knocked to the ground came to his feet brandishing his own sword and he snarled something in his language before pausing as Otto appeared in the hut's doorway with Gerhard just behind.

'Get out!' I screamed at the men, pointing to the door. Whether they understood my words I don't know, but they understood my gesture. They pushed past Otto and Gerhard and disappeared back outside.

'Are you hurt?' I said to the woman, but of course, she couldn't understand. She looked at me with eyes filled with terror. The small boy, probably no more than five or six, ran to her and she swept him up in her arms, clutching him tightly to her chest. What more could I say? I shrugged and headed for the door, followed by my two comrades. I would like to have stayed longer to guarantee her protection but there was no chance of that. We would be missed.

'What happened?' Gerhard asked. 'Who were those men?'

'Bad men.' I strode down the road to return to the other sergeants. Thoughts of watching Henkel rape the shepherd girl on the way back from Lüneburg came into my mind and when I looked at Otto, I could see he was thinking the same.

In the open space in the middle of the village our forces were gathering. Wenno was directing groups of brothers and he dispatched Rudolf with a dozen other mounted knights to finish securing the village. This time we had caught the enemy unawares and there were prisoners; a group of approximately twenty, mainly old men, women and children, knelt in a huddle guarded by several sergeants. One of Theodoric's priests berated them for their sins, but I doubted any of them understood a word. Most of the other sergeants in our group were listening to the Master's instructions. 'When we attack the fort, I want the sergeants with crossbows to sweep their ramparts with bolts. It is not necessary to kill everyone, but keep their heads down so we can assault the walls. The Letts have ladders to get over the stockade. Kill only those that put up any resistance. Remember we want souls to convert to God's will.'

We pushed through the rest of the village towards the river, through a stand of linden to the open ground that had been cleared of trees around the enemy's fort. The stockade was on a shallow hill. Though it wasn't much higher than a man, it would still be a challenge to assault, with arrows, spears and rocks raining down. It was also surrounded by a flooded ditch, with a rickety-looking wooden bridge leading to the entrance overlooked by a timber gatehouse with a fighting platform above. We lined up, unshouldering our crossbows, but I could already see the Livs in disarray and the gates to the fort were not even closed yet. Streams of people were still fleeing the village for the dubious security of the fort, but there were armed men behind the parapet and a few arrows whistled past our ears.

Leading the majority of the mounted knights, Wenno saw his opportunity in the chaos and charged forward. We loaded our crossbows and began firing bolts at the defenders on the walls. In front of the gates everything was in pandemonium as the knights rode across the bridge through the people still seeking safety. Three Livs were desperately trying to push the gate shut, but they weren't quick enough and the first knights, Wenno among them, were already in the entrance, slashing at the defenders in their path.

'Stop watching the gate and keep firing!' Sighard shouted.

A Liv defender leaned out from the top of the fighting platform above the gatehouse and threw a spear that hit one of the knight-brothers in the back, toppling him from his saddle. I pointed my crossbow at him and pulled the trigger, but the bolt missed, hitting the wood-shingle roof that protected the defenders. The gateway was narrow and the fighting was intense and, although I couldn't see from where I stood, I assumed the defenders were rushing men to repel our incursion. More knights were stuck on the wooden bridge, unable to get past and join the battle and making easy targets for the Livs in the gatehouse and on the walls. Wenno and the men with him were in trouble. Their momentum had been checked. The Master blocked an axe with his shield, stabbing his sword into the chest of his attacker, but there were too many people in the gateway and the knights couldn't punch through. Another knight-brother was struck by a spear and fell from his horse.

We carried on firing our crossbows but there were only a couple of Livs still behind the parapet. A group of Letts ran forward with two ladders, and Sighard drew his sword, shouting at us to follow him. I dropped my crossbow and picked up my shield, drawing my own sword and charging after Sighard, who was already running towards the ditch and the ladders that were being thrust against the palisade.

By the time I had crossed the flooded ditch and clambered up the hill to the base of the stockade, I was breathing heavily, my lungs burning. Behind me, the other sergeants were splashing through the water, but Sighard had already reached the bottom of one ladder. He said something to the Letts, elbowing them out of the way as he began climbing, closely followed by me and Uli, the sly boy who shared my tent in Riga. No missiles were aimed at us and a few seconds later we were over the top. To my surprise, the walkway was empty of any enemy, only one corpse with a crossbow bolt protruding from his forehead. The interior of the fort was a jumble of wooden buildings around a yard and I looked down at the melee in the gateway, where most of the Livs were fighting. I heard a shout from the gatehouse and an arrow thudded into the wood crenellation next to me.

Sighard waved to the Letts, who had climbed the other ladder to attack the tower nearest them, before turning to us. 'We have to take the gatehouse. Follow me!'

I dashed after him along the walkway and a moment later we were under the platform over the gate. A ladder led up to the enemy above, but when Sighard prepared to climb it with his shield raised above his head, a spear was thrown at him that deflected off, clattering to the floor. He cursed and stepped back as a man appeared at the top of the ladder, thrusting another spear down. Sighard dropped his shield and grabbed hold of the spear, pulling it as the man above held on desperately, fighting to prevent it being wrenched from his grasp. I saw my opportunity and grabbed a rung of the ladder, hauling myself up as I lunged above my head with my sword, feeling the tip pierce flesh. The man let go of the spear and fell back, blood pouring from a wound in his groin.

'Now let's get them!' Sighard shouted. He pushed me aside and bolted up the ladder to the platform above. 'For the Virgin Mary!'

I followed, but it was not easy climbing with a shield on one arm and a sword in the other. A clash of swords and shouting erupted above me and when I emerged, I saw Sighard fighting with two Liv tribesmen. I stood up, ready to help, but the knight-brother didn't need it. He stabbed one of the Livs in the neck. The stunned tribesman dropped his axe and took a step backwards, clutching at his ruined throat as blood spurted in a wide arc. Sighard withdrew his sword just in time to parry the slicing sword of the other Liv, pushing his enemy away, before taking a stride forward and skewering the man against the wood of the platform's parapet with a thrust to his body. The Liv died in a splatter of blood on Sighard's sword. Behind, the man I had stabbed was still rolling around in agony, bleeding profusely, his breeches soaked in blood and gore.

But I ignored him, looking down over the parapet to see that the knight-brothers had managed to fight their way through the Livs at the gate and the tribesmen were now beginning to yield. One moment, the mass of people below were fighting desperately, and the next they were throwing down their arms and surrendering. A couple of the Livs continued to resist, but they were isolated and killed with brutal efficiency. Wenno, his sword and lower body drenched in blood, shouted orders for the enemy to be disarmed and herded together.

Sighard joined me. 'You fought well,' he said, 'now help get this man bandaged before he bleeds to death up here.' The man I had wounded was still whimpering and moaning and we went to his aid, binding his wound with the man's own cloak before manhandling him down the ladder with the help of Uli and Otto. On the walkway, I looked back towards the village to see thick smoke fill the sky. They were burning the buildings. We had won.

Lennewarden was burned and the fort destroyed. Despite our success we had taken casualties: three knight-brothers had been killed and another two wounded, one of them seriously. No sergeants were lost – hardly surprising since we had played an insignificant part in the battle, but one youth, a quiet boy named Hans, stabbed himself accidently whilst cleaning his sword after we had taken the fort. We captured over seventy Livs and the priests began their task of converting them. On the cold and wet day after the battle there was a mass baptism in the waters of the Düna, although after what we had done to their village, I wondered how willing their conversion would turn out to be. Bringing people to God at the point of a sword has always disturbed me. I was eager to be away from this place of death, but destroying the fortress took time and we stayed three days before moving on.

Over the next week we carried on, burning villages and raiding cattle. We captured more Liv pagans, but like before, by the time we arrived in a village most had already fled, leaving only the old and infirm. There was a skirmish involving the mounted sergeants near Ascheraden, but only two of our men were slightly injured seeing off the Liv horsemen.

Before Ascheraden itself, there was another hillfort near the river, but this time far larger and more formidable. The fort was situated along the crest of a steep hill that, burdened as we were with arms and armour, would be difficult to assault.

Wenno, Volkwin, Rudolf and Berthold, rode to inspect its defences and they weren't happy with what they saw. When they trotted back, the defenders who crowded the walkway of the fort jeered and whistled. Acting as Rudolf's squire, I was close enough to hear what was said between the knights. 'We don't have enough troops,' the Master said. 'The way their ramparts are packed, they must have most of the able-bodied men in the area inside.'

'We could send in the Letts,' Rudolf suggested. 'Let them take the casualties. If they manage to secure a breach, we can exploit it.'

'Sacrificing our most recent converts in a pointless attack is hardly the best course of action,' Berthold said. 'Master Wenno is right. There are too many of them. Even if we succeeded in taking the place, our losses would be crippling for an Order our size.'

So we ignored the fort, skirting it to reach the settlement beyond. The Letts made no move to stop us burning their village, watching from the ramparts in silence as we fired the huts and crops. Anything of value had already been taken to safety or hidden, so we found virtually nothing in the way of plunder. But I did find a kitten in one of the huts – a tiny creature that followed me while I searched the building. I looked down when it snuggled up around my ankles and started purring. It would now be doomed to a short, brutal death, so in a moment of sentimental weakness I picked it up. I had no idea what sex the kitten was or if I would be allowed to bring it back to the commandery, but I went outside holding it in my arms.

'It's as white as snow,' Otto said. 'Like the mantles of the knight-brothers. That's a good omen.'

Some of the other sergeants came to see what I had found and we quickly attracted the attention of Sighard. 'What do you have there, Sergeant-brother Richard?'

'I found it alone in the hut. It will die if left here. Can I bring it back to Riga?'

'It will die long before we get back to Riga.'

'I will look after it. I'll feed it from my rations.'

Sighard shrugged as if it didn't matter to him. 'Well, cats are always welcome to catch rats and mice.' Since the fight at the fort in Lennewarden, Sighard's manner to me had softened. 'I won't object if you want to take care of it yourself. But don't let the Master see. He hates all animals except his horses.'

As we left the village it began to rain heavily and this weather persisted for the next four days, almost without stopping. By now, we were all thoroughly wet and tired of the whole expedition. We had punished the Livs from Ascheraden and Lennewarden for their attack over the previous summer, stealing what we could and burning everything else, and now our mission was coming to a close. We started on the journey back to Riga.

The kitten didn't die. I kept it in my pack during the march, where it slept most of the time. I fed it with milk I managed to get from one of the goats we had captured. Hinz, who said he knew about these things, determined that the kitten was male and approximately two weeks old. I named him Oskar. He soon became popular with some of my compatriots. When we made camp in the evening and I let him out of my pack, many of the other sergeants would come and look. One of them even brought a piece of fur to wrap him in. I saw Wolfgang and his friends sitting around their fire, occasionally looking over and laughing. I tried to ignore them but found it difficult. Otto still wanted to pay them back. 'This is the best time,' he said. 'Once we return to the commandery it will be much more difficult.'

'I can wait until the right time, even if it takes longer than planned.'

By Saint Luke's Day, we were back again in Uexküll. Thankfully the rain had finally stopped and several cows were killed and roasted, so we ate better than we had since leaving Riga. The Lett auxiliaries took their leave, melting back into the forest to return to their villages and farms, their departure being welcomed by many of the knight-brothers. Our spirits were high: we had taken plunder, we had gained valuable experience that would stand us in good stead for the future – and we had punished our pagan enemies. Even Rudolf was more pleasant than normal.

It was noticeably colder than when we had left, especially at night, and according to some of the older knights, winter would soon be upon us. Two days later, we reached Riga in the early afternoon, entering the town to enthusiastic applause from the townsfolk. More people came out of the houses and shops, cheering and clapping our return as we marched past on our way to the commandery. My eyes were drawn to a girl in the crowd of about fourteen or fifteen who looked somehow familiar. Small with an oval face and snub nose, she looked directly at me. When our eyes locked, she smiled and I realised with a start it was Margret, the girl I had saved in the fight with the pirates onboard the *Saint Maria*. There was no sign of her stern father. A moment later, we were past where she stood and I craned my neck, but she was quickly lost in the crowd. Seeing her again left me with mixed feelings. She was certainly a pretty girl and I felt strangely protective towards her, which was ridiculous considering I was now a member of an organisation that demanded chastity.

I tried to push her from my mind but I was still thinking of her when we reached the gates of the commandery.

CHAPTER TWENTY-FOUR

A week after returning to Riga, the first snows came. We awoke one morning to a smattering that coated everything, blanketing the buildings and yard in a carpet of white crystals and freezing over the water in the well. Luckily for us, the new wooden block they had started building when we had left for our raiding was now finished, so we no longer had to live in improvised tents in the yard, but there was no heating and it was still bitterly cold. The new building was on two floors with outside stairs that led up to a gallery, with the inside split into bare rooms that could sleep eight and reeked of freshly cut wood. I shared a room with my friends, including Uli who I still did not trust, but the shared experience of storming the gateway had tempered my dislike of him. There were also a couple of other youths whom I barely knew.

Life continued as it had before our expedition and I felt an anticlimax after tasting the thrill of battle. The weeks went by and a deep monotony and boredom settled in, only relieved with our training in the practice yard. December brought more snow and our chores now included shovelling paths free and breaking the ice in the well – an unpleasant job that entailed climbing down the rope and chipping away at the surface. The masons had stopped coming to the commandery as it was too cold for them to continue their work, and it seemed eerily quiet without the constant tapping of hammers on stone. Now, the half-built walls of the new castle and chapel stood stark and grey against the snow like broken teeth.

Not surprisingly, along with the snow, the temperature dropped, especially at night. We had undergarments in which we slept, and one blanket, but it was still freezing. 'Why can't they allow us a brazier at least?' Otto complained. 'The winter here is even colder than in the Empire – even colder than I had imagined.'

'It helps focus our minds on Christ,' Emich explained. 'Remember His suffering was far greater. Hardship brings us closer to God.'

Suffice to say, Otto was not satisfied by this explanation and neither was I. Apart from when we were working or training, we were cold all the time. Praying in the chilly chapel was particularly uncomfortable, especially for Matins in the early hours of the morning, and my feet felt like perpetual blocks of ice.

Over the years that I served with the Swordbrothers and the Teutonic Order, I gradually became accustomed to the cold and even began to enjoy it. And compared to some later winters I endured, that first one of 1204 wasn't even that bad. As an Order, the Swordbrothers hadn't yet adapted to life in Livonia and we usually undertook no campaigning in the winter months. This would change when we realised that the winter was actually better for us, as the rivers and marshes froze over to allow faster movement for our heavy warhorses. It was also easier to avoid ambushes in the forest due to the lack of leaves able to conceal the local tribesmen and footprints in the snow betrayed the pagan hiding places and movements. But in the early years, we spent the bitter months of winter cooped up in our commandery and castle, training, praying and freezing.

Two days after the Feast of Saint Nicholas, we received news from one of the traders who supplied the commandery with furs and hides that the Gulf of Riga had begun to freeze with a thin film of ice that now made it all but impossible to reach the city by sea. I managed to speak briefly with the man when I stabled his horse and he told me that in a month or so the ice would be thick enough to bear the weight of people. The Düna river would also probably freeze. Unfortunately we sergeants were rarely allowed into the city, so it was impossible for me to see for myself. I tried to imagine what a frozen river would look like, but found it hard to picture.

As the weeks went by, there were no further incidents with Wolfgang or his friends, although I would often see them whispering together and knew from their glances they were sometimes talking about me. There was little I could do about it; Otto had been right when he'd said the chances of getting even would be significantly harder here in the commandery. I tried not to let it bother me, still convinced my time would come if I was patient. And Sighard never paired us together when we were practising in the yard. He knew of our enmity and had no wish to make things worse. However, I did notice a change in some of the older sergeants' behaviour – the ones who had been here before our arrival. They began to shun me. At first, it was very subtle: some of them just ignored me; questions would go unanswered; others avoided speaking to me altogether. Then, a week before the Nativity of Christ, some sergeants moved to another table in the refectory when I sat down. Of course, my friends noticed, but we were forbidden to talk whilst eating and afterwards their joint consensus was not to worry about it. 'They don't talk to me either,' Gerhard said.

Oskar, the kitten I had found in Ascheraden, was still too small to mix with the other cats that lived in and around the commandery, so I kept him hidden in our dormitory and my friends and I brought him milk. With the weather like it was, I had no doubt he would die outside immediately. Sighard knew the kitten was with us but he never said anything further.

Life continued as normal with the Nativity of Christ, Feast of Saint Stephen and Saint John followed by Saint Silvester providing a distraction to the usual routine, and allowing us to eat plenty of the meat that had been denied us during Advent. January saw a week of storms which rattled and banged the shutters of the commandery's buildings and brought yet more heavy snow. Now it was so cold that we were finally allowed a brazier in our dormitory, although it hardly made the room any warmer. My sixteenth birthday came and I spent most of the day clearing the freshly fallen snow and chopping the logs that had been delivered by wagon to feed the fires of the infirmary, kitchen and refectory – the latter acting as a warming room and the only places in the commandery that were heated at all times.

One bright morning a week after my birthday, Sighard ordered Gerhard, Emich and me to help unload a small caravan of supplies that had arrived from the city. We spent most of the morning unloading fleeces of wool, boxes of candles, bags of grain and rye, sides of bacon, barrels of hay and oats into the storerooms adjacent to the main building.

'Sixty fleeces and forty-five sacks of grain,' I checked with the merchant after counting my part of the delivery.

'As agreed,' the man said. He was disinterested, probably keen to get his complimentary cup of wine in the warmth of the refectory.

Because of my master's position in the Order as treasurer, I sometimes had to work as his scribe, recording figures in the ledger. The day after the delivery, I was writing up the accounts in Rudolf's office in the main building. The room was small, with space for the desk where I sat, and a chair behind where Rudolf perched on the armrest while he dictated the figures. Behind him were several wooden crates against the wall. I dipped my quill in the inkpot and prepared to write.

'Forty sacks of rye,' Rudolf said, bored. 'Seventy-eight sides of bacon.'

I scribbled the figures down.

'Sixty-five fleeces of wool.'

I paused and turned around to look at him. 'Sixty-five? But I unloaded them yesterday. There were only sixty.'

'There were sixty-five,' Rudolf insisted.

'But I know there were only sixty,' I said. 'We can go to the storeroom and check. I am sure I'm right…'

Rudolf exploded. 'How dare you contradict me, you little whelp. If I say there are sixty-five, there are sixty-five.'

'But…'

'There are no buts, you little foreign *Arschloch*. Do not forget your place. Get out of my sight before I beat you again for insubordination!'

I came to my feet, stunned by his outburst. I left the room, pausing outside. Rudolf's reaction was totally irrational. I couldn't understand his fury. It just confirmed to me, as if I had any doubt, what a complete bastard my master was. And I knew I was right about the number of sacks. But why would he get so angry over such a minor detail?

It wasn't until much later that I found out the answer.

We endured the worst of the winter despite it being every bit as bad as we had feared. On a bright morning at the beginning of February, with the snow still carpeting the fields and heavy on the wood-shingle roofs of the city, the Lithuanians came. The Lithuanians were the most feared and dangerous of the tribes that lived in the lands to the south. They certainly terrified the more local Livs and Letts, which had probably influenced many of them to give up their pagan ways and convert to Christianity. I was working in the stables when the alarm was called and most of the commandery climbed the wooden staircase to the parapet of the stockade to see for ourselves.

'I've never seen so many men,' Brother Dieter said next to me. 'There must be at least two thousand of them. Let's hope they don't decide to attack the city.'

We watched in silence as more men streamed from the edge of the forest, tramping across the frozen marshland and snowy field to the east of the town. For a long time, our normal routine was interrupted as we kept watching and they kept coming. Some of the Lithuanians were mounted on horses, but the greater number were on foot and most of them ignored us, heading north. However, a crowd of approximately thirty men paused on the other side of the bridge over the Rigebach in the lee of the great snow-covered sand-dune of *Kubsberg*, or Kube Hill.

'What are they doing?' Wenno said, joining us at the parapet. He was accompanied by Berthold, who gave me a smile.

'I do not know,' Dieter said. 'But they don't appear to have any ladders or siege equipment. They will not get over our stockade without them, even with their numbers.'

As we watched, my eyes were drawn to one of the Lithuanians who was simply huge. A giant. He stood far above his compatriots and must have been at least seven feet tall. Further along the Great Sandy Way, a dozen men came from the direction of the city. They crossed the bridge and began talking with the group of Lithuanians, including the giant.

'They look German from their dress,' the Master said. 'Why are they talking with the pagans?'

No one knew the answer to that question. We continued to watch as the group began sharing several jugs with the invaders. The Master frowned but said nothing further. Another group of Lithuanians on horseback peeled away from the main column and joined the group, dismounting and sharing in the jugs being passed around.

By now most of the army had passed, the churned-up snow attesting to their massive numbers, and only the last few stragglers were passing in their wake. Presently, the Lithuanians who had paused moved on too, as the townsmen who had been drinking with them returned back into the city. There was nothing more to see. The danger had passed and when the bell rang for Sext we all descended from the walkway and went to the chapel.

Three days later a chieftain from one of the allied Semigallian tribes to the south-west came to Riga with his entourage. His name was Viesthard, but he liked to be called King Vester, and he wanted a meeting with Bishop Albert. However, finding the bishop was not in Livonia, he decided to talk to Theodoric and the city authorities. Naturally, Wenno, Volkwin, Berthold and my master, Rudolf, all wanted to attend any meeting and they needed their squires, so two other sergeants and me were detailed to provide an escort. The meeting was to take place in the town hall near the market square and we left after Nones. We sergeants led our masters' horses through the slush and mud of the streets. I was excited, as I had seen so little of the city that lay outside the gates of the commandery. It was busy, and there was a palpable buzz of excitement due to the arrival of the strangers, and in the market square even more people gathered. By the town hall, Viesthard's escort waited, a dozen Semigallian warriors who looked ill at ease, nervously fingering their weapons and looking around warily at the growing mass of people.

We drew up at the town hall and the crowd parted at our approach. I held Rudolf's horse as he and the others dismounted. Wenno ordered one of the sergeants to look after the horses and nodded that the other sergeant and I should accompany them inside. I followed the senior knight-brothers through the reinforced wood door into a hall that was already crowded with the city's top merchants, Englelbert – the provost of Saint Mary's and Bishop Albert's brother – and a few of the secular nobles who were vassals of Bishop Albert. I heard Theodoric's booming voice before I saw him, and as the men moved to give us room, I saw he was already talking to the Semigallian chieftain.

Viesthard was an imposing figure, with a broad chest and a bushy black beard. He wore a blue coat with embroidered sleeves and a good deal of fur, with a large bear pelt wrapped around his shoulders fastened by a gold circular clasp in the shape of a snake, making him look even bigger and not unlike a bear himself. On both of his lower arms he wore several bands and his fingers were festooned with rings of silver and gold. A thick, gold chain hung around his neck and he looked every inch the king he was supposed to be. With him were several other Semigallians, and he was talking with Theodoric with the help of a priest who was translating. At our arrival they paused, while Viesthard looked our party over before Theodoric introduced us.

'King Vester is not happy,' Theodoric explained. There was a rumble of discontent from some of the other Germans gathered around us. 'The Lithuanians raided Semigallian land on their way north. He is upset we allowed them to cross our territory unimpeded and some of the townspeople drank beer with them.'

'What could we have done?' Wenno said. 'Their numbers were too great.'

'I already explained that we don't want to engage the pagans until Bishop Albert returns with a new army,' Theodoric said. Some of the Germans murmured agreement.

Viesthard began talking. He had a deep voice and spoke in an animated way, moving his arms and hands, and his words, even though I couldn't understand them, were passionate. We waited for the priest to translate. 'It is bad that they were here. Now that the Lithuanians have seen the city they might decide to attack at another time. The Lithuanians are very bad people – they are like monsters. They have a very strong man… a champion. His name is Ąžuolas – means oak tree in their language. This man is as large as an oak and no one can kill him. But King Vester is not scared. The king says we should band together and attack these monsters – kill this giant man and his army. He says he can bring a mighty throng to help attack them when they return from their raiding. If you could provide him with a few good men who know how to organise and drill an army for battle, we would surely be victorious.'

'That is a good offer,' Theodoric said. 'But I must speak with my compatriots first.' The Germans turned around, moving a few feet away before huddling together. 'This could help our cause,' Theodoric said. 'As a condition we can demand they accept some of our priests, which will lead to conversion. This could be a big success for us.'

'But we can't field even half the number of the Lithuanians,' another man said, a merchant from the rich clothes he wore.

'The Militia of Christ are worth far more than our small numbers,' Wenno said, 'with or without a superhuman giant on their side.' My master nodded in agreement. 'If Viesthard can amass the majority of the forces needed, we can prevail.'

'That depends on how far we are willing to trust the Semigallians,' another man said. He was German, dressed like a noble, with his cloak edged in fox fur that partially covered a fine-looking longsword. I assumed from the deference he received from some of the other men that he was the most senior of Bishop Albert's secular nobles.

'Hostages,' Wenno said. 'We get them to hand over hostages to guarantee their good faith. It has worked in the past with some of the Liv tribes.'

Theodoric nodded. 'If Viesthard agrees we should accept his offer. We gather our forces and send scouts to track the Lithuanian army, that shouldn't be a problem in the snow. We know they are going to Estonia. When they return to Livonia, we will be waiting for them.'

'But we don't have enough men – even with the Semigallians,' the merchant said. 'We should wait until the bishop has returned...'

'Imagine the glory we will achieve if we beat the Lithuanians,' the noble said.

'Glory that will belong to Our Lord,' Theodoric said, 'as will the new souls we convert from paganism. So, we are decided, we accept the Semigallian offer?'

There was a murmur of agreement. Only the merchant looked unhappy.

Theodoric turned back to Viesthard. 'We are prepared to accept your offer on two conditions. The first is to admit priests into your lands to peacefully preach the word of God. They are not to be harassed and are to be allowed to go where they wish.'

The priest translated. Viesthard listened impassively as one of his companions whispered in his ear.

'And secondly, we will require hostages from each of your forts to ensure your goodwill. If this is agreed, we will send some men to help train your forces.' The abbot looked to Wenno who nodded. 'These will be experienced men from the Militia of Christ. Master Wenno will arrange it.'

Viesthard smiled and said something to the man next to him and they both laughed. The priest translated the words that followed. 'King Vester is happy with this outcome. He will return to his tribe and assemble the army. He will bring the army here by the new moon.'

'It is agreed,' Theodoric said, beaming. He called for wine.

I felt a rising excitement at the agreement reached with the Semigallians. It meant the everyday monotony was about to change. We were going into battle again.

CHAPTER TWENTY-FIVE

The Master sent Volkwin and two other knights and their sergeants to help train the Semigallians. This included Brother Arnold, Otto's master, so I found myself without my best friend for the first time since we had met in Lübeck. Our own training was increased and we spent more time in the practice yard preparing for the fight to come. A day later, we received a delivery of twenty-five horses, on loan from the town, and I was told I would be one of the sergeants who would now get the chance to ride into battle. This was very good news. Finally, I would get the chance to fight in the way I had been taught back home in England.

True to his word, two and a half weeks later with the new moon, Viesthard came with his army and the agreed hostages. They arrived from the south and crossed the Düna, which was still frozen, to the east of the city. Our preparations were already completed and we left Riga early the next morning, when we got our first view of the Semigallian army. I was mounted on a grey mare, whose name I never found out, which Emil told me belonged to one of the merchants who had attended the meeting with Viesthard.

Virtually the entire Order was again in the field with nearly fifty knight-brothers supported by almost one hundred mounted sergeants, including me and Hinz. Gerhard, Emich and Uli remained as crossbowmen and I was secretly glad not to have to care for Gerhard when battle was joined. Otto, of course, would be fighting with the Semigallians. There were five hundred or so tribesmen, and they were dressed in fur and armed mostly with spears, javelins and axes. The majority had shields, but few wore any kind of armour. Nevertheless, they looked fierce. I just hoped the Lithuanians thought so too. There was another group of mixed German and Livonian militia from Riga. They numbered around two hundred, armed with an assortment of weapons, sprinkled with Bishop Albert's own knights, about a score strong and led by Conrad von Meiendorf. Conrad would hold joint command of the entire army, along with Viesthard and Wenno.

So, we numbered approximately nine hundred men and the best estimates put the Lithuanians at nearly two thousand. These were not good odds and I found my enthusiasm to take part in a battle again tempered by the feeling that it would probably be my last. But then again, at least I would die on horseback.

The army headed north through ancient paths carved through the forest. Scouts were sent out towards Treiden to the north to locate the Lithuanians. Their job was to discover the route the enemy would use to return to their lands – we knew they had gone north to attack Estonia, but there were several routes they could use to get home and we didn't want them to slip past us. In the meantime, we made camp at the edge of the forest one day north of Riga, erecting our tents, digging latrines and felling trees, before settling down into a game of waiting. I shared a tent with Hinz and two older sergeants who made it clear from the beginning they wanted nothing to do with either of us. It was freezing, but the bitter cold of January was thankfully behind us and there was enough work to keep us warm.

In the late afternoon of our first day, I was walking back through the camp after attending on my master, picking my way past the knight-brothers' tents. When I got to the sergeants' tents, I saw Gabriel coming towards me carrying two urns of water. I put my head down, intending to ignore him, but when I got closer, he stopped, put down the urns and blocked my path.

'What do we have here?' Gabriel said. 'A little runt...'

'Let me pass,' I said. Gabriel was at least a head taller than me and I felt a tremor in my chest.

My heart sank as I recognised Wolfgang's voice behind me. 'He thinks he is our equal now he's got himself a proper horse.'

Gabriel spat on the ground. 'The stumpy horse he had before suited him better.'

I turned around as Wolfgang came closer. No one else sat around their fires paid us any attention. Would they be so brazen to attack me again in the middle of our camp? I was trapped between them, and when they both took a step closer I prepared for what I knew was coming.

A voice suddenly interrupted us. 'What is going on here?' It was Sighard.

'Nothing, Brother Sighard,' Wolfgang said quickly.

'Priest-brother Berthold has an errand for you, Sergeant-brother Wolfgang. Report to him immediately. He is with the Master.' Sighard turned to Gabriel. 'And you better finish taking that water to wherever you're taking it.'

Gabriel bowed his head, picked up the two urns, and pushed past me.

My thanks were waved off by Sighard as he marched off to harangue some other poor sergeants. I returned to my tent to find Hinz sitting by our fire sharpening his sword with a whetstone. I told him about what had happened.

'The bastards,' Hinz said. 'Be careful, Richard. They will try again, especially if there is a battle.'

He was right; a knife in the back during the heat of combat was a real risk and hard to guard against. I had no doubt they would try if given the chance; they hated me enough. I would have to make sure I was careful and avoid them in battle.

We sat and talked a little about Lübeck. I asked him how he knew Detmar.

'He married my sister,' Hinz said. 'Our fathers were friendly. Both are in the business of trading salt.'

'So, you are Brigitta's brother,' I said. 'I met her once, at the Christmas feast.'

'I don't think he treats her very well.' Hinz shook his head. 'I never liked him, but it was a political marriage between our two families.'

'All marriages are political. He's a little bastard anyway but I broke his nose.' I remembered catching him in the warehouse, but there seemed no point in telling Hinz any more. It was all part of my previous life. 'But why did you give up everything and come here?'

Hinz sighed. 'I am beginning to wonder myself. I wanted adventure... My older brother will take over my father's business so I wasn't needed at home. I originally wanted to take the cross and go to the Holy Land, but when that fell through, I decided to come here. I'm not sure now if I made the right decision.'

I shrugged. 'At least you had the choice. If I hadn't come here, I would be a fugitive or an outlaw.'

We relapsed into our own thoughts. A short time later, a welcome face caused me to look up from my task of darning my black surcoat. It was Otto.

'I've been searching the whole camp for you two.' Otto grinned. 'I had some free time so I thought I would come and see how you were faring.'

'You're a sight for tired eyes,' I said. 'How goes it with the heathens?'

'It's very different from the commandery,' Otto said. 'About as different as it can be. We have been training them at one of their forts. The Semigallians are a wild folk. Most are pagan, but there are a few Christians among them and they don't seem to be treated any differently. I don't understand a word they say but they laugh and drink plenty. I like them.' He went on to explain about how they were teaching the tribesmen discipline and the need to obey the orders of their leaders. 'But they are daunted about fighting the Lithuanian champion – the giant we saw when they came to Riga.'

'I think he's called Ąžuolas,' I said. 'Something about an oak tree.'

'Yes. They say he has killed over a hundred men with his axe. Many in single combat. I hope we do not meet in battle.'

I shrugged. I would let the more experienced knight-brothers worry about fighting him.

'But after we've beaten the Lithuanians we are to return to Riga. My master, Brother Arnold, cannot get back quick enough.'

'It will be good to have you back,' I said with a laugh. 'I've missed beating you in the practice yard.'

'And I've missed seeing your ugly face.'

Otto stayed for a while and we exchanged tales about the last few weeks, before he returned to where the Semigallians were encamped, further into the forest.

Our army remained camped for the next two days and we spent the time foraging, chopping wood and making any last preparations before battle. On the morning of the third day we received news from our scouts. The Lithuanians were on their way back home, heading southwards. They had spent a night at the fort of Caupo in Treiden, the same chieftain I had met with Theodoric on the *Saint Maria*. Our scouts had found out they intended to travel back through the village of Rodenpois, which was less than half a day's march away from our encampment.

An unmistakable excitement coursed through the army and I felt the same nervous energy as we struck camp and packed our tents and equipment. Finally I would get to fight a proper battle, something I had dreamed about since being a young child. The skirmish at Lennewarden or the fight with the pirates did not count – I wanted to take part in the greatest contest of combat, a proper fixed battle with thousands of soldiers involved. I wanted to prove myself.

Hinz and I collected our horses from the large corral that had been built next to the knight-brother's tents and, after what seemed an age, we were finally on the move again. We crossed a large expanse of open ground where the snow had been blown into huge drifts by the wind, which continued to lash our faces and sting our eyes. It was bitterly cold, especially as we were all in mail with our heads wrapped in scarves against the gusts that blew clouds of snow up into the air like dancing ghosts. Progress was painfully slow, but it was easier for us on horseback than the poor soldiers on foot who trudged and stumbled, trying to follow in the footprints of their comrades, surrounded by a landscape of whiteness that stretched all around. Above us, the stone-coloured sky seemed to press down oppressively, threatening yet more snow. Nevertheless, despite the hardship, our spirits were high at the thought of the coming battle.

We had to move fast if we wanted to get into position to attack the Lithuanians near Rodenpois, and we were hounded by the Master to keep up the pace, despite the difficult terrain, not even stopping to pray. After passing into another forest, we picked up a track, the snow crunching under our feet while flakes drifted down on the breeze from the grey tree-trunks that surrounded us like a palisade. Sometime later, we reached our position, forming up abreast at the edge of the trees to where a gentle slope of open ground ran down to the road, obscured by snow, where the Lithuanian army was expected to march. The Semigallians sent out more scouts and we dismounted, fed the horses and collected our heavy weapons from the packhorses. There was little conversation. The mounted sergeants were mixed in with the knight-brothers as a combined cavalry force, and those of us acting as squires were expected to support our masters when battle was joined. I held Rudolf's lance and shield as he spoke tactics nearby with Wenno. We watched Conrad von Meiendorf lead the men of Riga and half of Viesthard's Semigallians out of the cover of the forest, streaming across the snow-covered ground, over the road to the line of trees opposite, some two or three hundred paces further from our position. The plan was to ambush the Lithuanians from both sides, charging out of the forest and smashing into them with our heavy cavalry. The rest of the army on foot would follow as quickly as possible, engaging the enemy in support of the knights.

All eyes turned to look as a rider came along the road, galloping as fast as he could in the snow. It was one of the Semigallian scouts. He steered his horse towards the trees where we waited and I saw how exhausted the animal was, its flanks frothy and wet with sweat and nostrils flared. The scout reported to Viesthard, who was some way along the treeline and out of my sight, but word was immediately passed along the line and a few moments later everyone knew. The Lithuanian army had been sighted.

In order not to be seen, we withdrew further back into the trees. Rudolf turned to me. 'When we attack, you are to stay with me. Whatever happens you stay with me. Do you understand?'

I nodded, handing him his lance and shield, followed by his helm that encased the entire head. I mounted my own horse, slipping my shield from my back to my arm and loosening my sword in its scabbard. I placed my flat-topped nasal helmet over my mail *coif*. Now we were ready. Everyone strained their eyes to catch the first glimpse of our foe. I swung my gaze along our line, eyes locking with Wolfgang who was sitting on his horse some fifty paces to the left of me. He made an obscene gesture but I didn't care, turning away, far more concerned about spotting the enemy.

And then suddenly in the distance the Lithuanians appeared and I felt my throat constrict with dryness, sweat dripping down the small of my back under my padded armour and mail despite the cold.

There were hundreds and hundreds and hundreds of them.

For the next few anxious moments we watched as the Lithuanian army came closer. They were packed together in a long column on the road, due to the deep snow, and they stretched back as far as the eye could see. As they slowly approached, I could see the vanguard numbered hundreds, more than our entire army. Behind was a large group of people tied together by ropes, and I realised they must have been the prisoners they had picked up on their raid, probably Estonians. More than a score of wagons and carts loaded with plunder struggled along in the wake of the prisoners. Dozens and dozens of animals accompanied them, sheep, and cattle for the most part, ploughing through the snow at the edge of the army. To our right, I heard the Semigallians murmuring in discontent, only increasing my own uncertainty. They were scared of the enemy's numbers.

And so was I.

The Lithuanians at the very front of their army were now directly between us and Conrad von Meiendorf's men hidden in the trees opposite. There was some commotion between the men at the head of the column and suddenly they stopped.

'They've seen the tracks Conrad's men made in the snow,' Dieter said on his horse in front of me.

And he must have been right because some of the Lithuanians were quite agitated, waving their arms about while others looked towards the trees where we were concealed. I could clearly see the Lithuanian giant, Ąžuolas, looming above everyone else, his huge axe over his shoulder, pointing towards the trees. But the men following, not realising the front of the column had halted, continued walking, bumping into the people before them and massing together in one huge group.

Conrad von Meiendorf chose this moment of confusion to launch his attack. With his Germans on the far side of the enemy, pitifully few in number, they came charging out of the trees screaming a challenge.

'Where are the Semigallians?' Wenno said loudly in front of me. 'Why are they not supporting Conrad?' It was true; only the Germans were attacking. The Semigallians were still in the trees opposite. Had they betrayed us? A flash of movement out of the corner of my eye attracted my attention, distracting me from the Master's words.

From our left flank, I saw Wolfgang, Gabriel, and another dozen sergeants break ranks without orders and charge across the snow to attack the Lithuanians. They ploughed into the mass of men at the head of the column, but they were so few and the enemy so many. They were in trouble immediately.

But no one else seemed to have noticed them. For a moment, Wenno hesitated before bellowing the order to attack in the centre. There was a roar of, 'Saint Mary!' as the knights and sergeants kicked their horses forward and Wenno led them out of the trees towards the main mass of Lithuanians. I drew my sword, looking over to the left where Wolfgang and his comrades, seemingly forgotten, were desperately chopping at the crush of men around them, isolated from the rest of our army.

I knew what I had to do. Steering my horse across our line of attack, I galloped towards the front of the enemy's column, crouching low in my saddle, determined to help the tiny group of sergeants before they were overwhelmed. It was hard for the horse in the snow, the drifts considerably slowing down my speed, but I forced the mare on and looked back, screaming to my comrades about the danger ahead of me, but most were too occupied, continuing their charge towards the middle of the enemy army. Nevertheless, I saw Dieter hear my words and look towards the head of the Lithuanian column. Behind me, above the din of the assault, my master shouted my name. I ignored him, pulling away from the main direction of our attack. Despite the snow, Wenno and our main force hit the Lithuanian centre, some fifty paces to my right, carving a bloody path through the multitude of men.

The first Lithuanian appeared in front of me, stabbing upwards with a spear aimed at my stomach. I pivoted to avoid the thrust and brought my sword down on top of the man's head, cutting into his skull and dropping him in a welter of blood and brain. Almost immediately, I was besieged by more Lithuanians. I turned to confront a large man with an axe as another tugged at my leg, trying to pull me from the saddle.

Everything was in confusion. A rising panic exploded in my chest when I realised I was surrounded by a heaving press of people. I slashed and struck with my sword at everyone around me, feeling it connect with several people and taking at least two blows on my shield. I knew that my only chance was to keep moving, and my fear propelled me on. My horse drove through the crowd and suddenly I was clear, with an open space a few feet wide revealing bloody snow. Five paces in front, I saw Wolfgang being dragged from his horse by two Lithuanians, knocking his helmet off, his blond hair matted with blood. I spurred my horse forward and took the first man in the chest, swinging my sword back and parrying another spear that someone else thrust at me. Behind, I heard more riders slam into the enemy ranks, alerted by the danger facing their comrades. The Lithuanians to my back were now busy fighting the new arrivals and I was able to stab the second man who had unseated Wolfgang, my thrust taking the unarmoured man high in the back. He screamed as he went down.

'Get back on your horse!' I shouted to Wolfgang. 'I'll protect you.' I wheeled my own horse around to shield him and sliced my sword across the face of another Lithuanian, mangling it into a gory, teeth-filled mess of blood and snot. He fell back clawing at his wound.

'I don't need your help!' Wolfgang snarled. He came to his feet and said something I didn't hear.

A bolt of agony seared down my leg from a sword thumping into my mailed thigh. Luckily, the chain links of my *hauberk* held but the pain was still intense. In response, I barged my horse sideways into my aggressor, knocking him forward into the snow. But he recovered quickly, scrambling to his feet again, snarling in defiance. And he was wild, with a long, bushy beard and a mouthful of black stumps for teeth.

Screaming a war cry, he threw himself forward, slashing at my horse who reared upwards to escape the stroke. I hung on desperately and when the horse came down, I hacked again at the Lithuanian, but he blocked my blow with his shield. A second later, he reeled back as another sergeant smacked him around the head with a mace.

Wolfgang was bleeding from another wound on the leg, but he seemed to have no problem putting his foot in the stirrup and hauling himself up onto his horse. A Lithuanian grabbed the reins of my own horse and I kicked him in the face, looking to find where the rest of our army was. Near me, the few sergeants still mounted were like islands in a sea of pagans, desperately raining blows down on the mass of Lithuanians, and I saw Gabriel slice his sword across a bearded Lithuanian's face. Screams and shouts pierced the air around us, and I knew we wouldn't last much longer than a few more seconds. My breath rasped in my ears under my helmet and mail. There was still no sign of the Semigallians. The bastards had probably run away.

And then they came.

A panic rose up in the ranks of the Lithuanians as the Semigallians came screaming out of the forest and across the snow like they were possessed. They slammed into the Lithuanians with a force and ferocity that was too much for our enemy. Despite their overwhelming numbers, they started to break.

As I learnt later in subsequent battles it started like it always does. The first few Lithuanians turned away from the fury that had been unleashed, dropping their weapons in their haste to escape. The panic spread rapidly like a raging town-fire and suddenly everyone was in a mad rush to get away, scrambling to flee the death that had descended on them. An unseen hand grabbed my mail-coat from behind and yanked me hard, making me lose my balance and pulling me from my saddle. My fall was broken by the body of a dead Lithuanian and my own shield, but I managed to keep a grip on my sword. With an instinct learned from years of training I sliced it upwards, cutting into the leg of the man who had pulled me down. He screamed and dropped to his knees, the front of his fur breeches seeping blood. I came to my feet and finished him with a swift lunge that pierced his stomach.

And then I heard a bellow of fury and caught a flash of movement out of the corner of my eye. I just managed to raise my shield in time when I was hammered off my feet from the massive blow of an axe, the force driving me into the snow with only my shield between me and my enemy. It was Ąžuolas.

The giant Lithuanian roared again, smashing his axe down on my shield with another huge thump, splitting the wood as the blade came within a hand's-breadth of my face. I pushed back with all my strength, letting go of the shield's handle, squeezing out of the hollow in the snow the impact had forced me into while the Lithuanian stepped back, the tangle of wood and metal from my ruined shield hanging from his blade. I came to my feet, dazed and battered as more Lithuanians streamed past me. In the moment's respite I struck at the giant, my sword striking the mail of his chest, but there was no power in the blow and the metal links held. He shrugged it off.

Only my agility saved me when the axe whirled past my ear again at an incredible speed. Ąžuolas might have been large, but he was also fast – far faster than someone of his size should have been. There was no doubt in my mind: the man was superhuman and he was going to kill me.

I lunged at him with my sword and he easily stepped aside, bringing his axe back to strike me again. His bearded face snarled in a rictus of hate and spittle. Another man, a Semigallian, I think, shouted something and swung his own axe at the giant. Ąžuolas parried it with ease, smashing his great axe down on the tribesman's head, splitting it like an overripe apple. The Semigallian collapsed in a gush of blood, showering me with his gore.

The giant came for me again in two great strides and in panic I grabbed a fleeing Lithuanian, thrusting him between us as I stumbled backwards. Ąžuolas flung his countryman out of the way like a child's rag doll in his haste to get to me, swinging his axe again, but I stumbled backwards and slipped in the snow, falling onto my back. His axe missed, hacking into the ground next to my head, showering me in snow. The giant Lithuanian leaped forward and I thrust my sword upwards, into his stomach, his own momentum driving him onto my blade. The chain links of his mail splintered apart and he dropped the axe, but he still came on, driving himself further onto my sword, reaching for my neck. I could feel his fetid breath on my face as his huge hands found my throat. Ąžuolas's fingers began squeezing and in rising panic I bit at his thumb, clamping my teeth shut with all my power. The metallic taste of blood filled my mouth and the giant bellowed in pain, his fingers choking the life from me. Stars exploded in my head and I knew that any moment my windpipe would be crushed. I was about to black out when the giant's fingers suddenly released their grip and the huge weight on my chest relented.

Standing above me was Dieter, a bloody sword in his hand. I rolled to the side and retched, spitting out the remains of the giant's thumb. The bitter taste of flesh lingered long in my mouth.

I was battered and bruised and my throat was on fire. Ąžuolas's body lay to the side, drenched in blood with my sword still in his guts. Dieter helped me back to my feet but, after checking I was all right, he remounted his horse. 'I have to help stop the Semigallians killing the prisoners,' he explained. He wheeled his destrier around before cantering off.

I recovered my sword, looking to retrieve my own horse with the remaining Lithuanians still stampeding around me. All of them were eager to escape the battle and they ignored me, most of them no longer interested in fighting. I saw my horse not so far away and looked up as Volkwin and three other knights trotted past, cutting down the fleeing Lithuanians from behind. What followed was a massacre.

As Dieter had said, the Semigallians were in among the terrified Lithuanians, slaughtering as many as possible. They were merciless, killing the ones who yielded as well as those ones fighting to the death. And they did not stop with the Lithuanians. When I got back on my horse, I looked over the battlefield and saw them killing the Estonian captives too. Many of the enemy had already fled further down the road or dispersed into the forest, leaving hundreds of heaped bodies in the snow to mark their progress. I saw one Semigallian hacking off a dead man's head, proudly holding it aloft afterwards to great jubilation from his comrades. Close by, Wolfgang was chasing down Lithuanian stragglers, bare-headed, his face animated in the cold air, laughing. I turned away in disgust. Where was the honour in killing defenceless men who were running away?

Now the battle was all but over. Dead and dying, mostly Lithuanians, littered the snow-covered ground and the last few pockets of resistance were being overcome. A cow, eyes wide with terror, loped past me, mooing in distress. The brutality of our tribesmen allies sickened me. I sat slumped on my horse, completely drained. My leg was hurting badly and my arms ached from fighting, but it was my throat that pained me the most. And knowing how close I had come to dying. I looked up at the sound of hooves nearby and smiled in relief to see Otto mounted on a brown courser, his sword still unsheathed. Thankfully, he was uninjured.

'*Mein Gott*, Richard, you look terrible,' he said. 'You are covered in blood. Are you wounded?'

'With God's grace I will live. Most of the blood is not mine. And I'm glad to see your ugly face is in one piece. But what happened with the Semigallians? I thought they had abandoned us.'

Otto shook his head. '*Ach*, when they saw the huge number of Lithuanians they wanted to go home. Their king, Viesthard, argued with them, but it was only after our people charged and they saw the enemy's fear did they decide to attack. Now they are filling a captured cart with as many Lithuanian heads as possible. Once battle began, they didn't listen to us…'

'It is barbaric. What about the others?'

'All our friends survived,' Otto said. 'Although Emich is slightly wounded, but only a cut on his arm, nothing serious. You are the last I have seen. How was it?'

I told him about fighting the giant, walking our horses over to show him the body, partially decapitated from Dieter's sword.

'That's incredible, Richard. How did you manage…?'

I explained what happened in the battle. More knights and sergeants galloped past us.

'Why did you help Wolfgang after everything that's happened?' Otto was incredulous. 'He would have left you to die. Why get yourself killed for that little turd? I bet he wasn't even grateful.'

I was saved from answering by the arrival of a group of mounted Swordbrothers, picking their way through the dead bodies and celebrating Semigallians. I saw they were led by

Master Wenno and behind him rode Dieter, Berthold and several other knights. The Master smiled when he saw me.

'By the Holy Mary, I am glad to see you alive,' Wenno said. 'It seems you are a hero! Brother Dieter informs me you fought and fatally wounded the giant Lithuanian champion. That is truly incredible!'

'Without Brother Dieter's help, he would have killed me.'

Wenno smiled. 'And he also tells me you rode to help the sergeants who charged without orders. They will be punished for their lack of discipline, if they are still alive. It was very foolish of them.'

'I tried to support you,' Brother Dieter said. 'But there were too many Lithuanians and we couldn't break through until after the bulk of their army had broken. But I caught a glimpse of you. You fought well – even before the combat with their champion.'

I remembered hearing my comrades attacking the enemy behind me; that must have been Dieter. 'You helped to tie up many of the enemy...'

'Their numbers were countless,' Dieter said. 'I thought we were all going to die. Especially before the Semigallians arrived.'

Wenno turned his attention to Otto, asking him about what had happened with our allies, whilst I looked across the battlefield, exhausted and strangely detached from everything around me. Approximately two hundred paces away, a rider galloped across the snow towards us. Even from that distance the mounted man cut a fine figure, his black horse and raven-coloured hair a stark contrast against the white tabard he wore and the blood-splattered snow.

It was Rudolf.

The last I had seen of him was when he had ordered me to stay close in the battle, and I remembered hearing him shout my name as I'd ridden to help Wolfgang and the others. Now there would be a reckoning for my disobedience.

He pulled his horse up in a flurry of snow where we waited, his face a mask of fury, but Wenno turned to him before he could speak. 'Your squire is a hero, Brother Rudolf. He killed the Lithuanian champion and fought outstandingly with valour. We are very lucky to have him in our Order. You must be proud.'

'He deliberately disobeyed a direct order. The boy should be chastised, not celebrated!'

'You would chastise a man for trying to aid his comrades?' Berthold said. 'Not to mention slaying the most fearsome of the enemy's warriors?'

'That is what you say,' Rudolf sneered. 'I saw nothing. But you miss the point, Priest-brother Berthold. It is about discipline. Where are we without discipline?'

The Master rubbed his beard and nodded. 'That is true, discipline is very important – it is fundamental to our Order.' Wenno looked at me. 'Did you disobey a direct order from Brother Rudolf?'

'I heard no order,' I lied. 'Before the battle, Brother Rudolf instructed me to support him, but when I saw the other sergeants in trouble, I knew I had to help them…'

Rudolf snorted. 'He is an impertinent young pup and needs to be punished!'

'Punishment!' Berthold said. 'That is all that ever interests you, Brother Rudolf. Sergeant-brother Richard has fought and behaved admirably, especially considering his age.'

'I agree,' Wenno said, turning to my master. 'If you are still unhappy, Brother Rudolf, we can review the matter later at the chapter meeting.'

'But—'

Wenno raised his hand. 'That is enough. The matter is closed – at least for now.'

'I would like to say a prayer with the whole army when we are finished here,' Berthold said to the Master. 'But let us say a short thanks for our victory. Without God's favour, we would all be dead now.'

We dismounted and knelt together on the ground, the corpses of Lithuanians heaped around us and the cheers of the Semigallians drifting across the battlefield. Berthold began to recite a prayer but I was not listening. A flood of relief flowed through me, followed by a surging feeling of pride. I had survived my first proper battle and won glory by defeating the enemy champion. It was a story worthy of the bards and jongleurs, fit for any lord's great hall. It was hard to believe it was true. On my journey to this point I may have lost everything that had been dear to me, but my life had also taken on a new meaning.

Berthold continued. *'Many enemies were around me; but I destroyed them by the power of the Lord! They were around me on every side; but I destroyed them by the power of the Lord! They swarmed around me like bees, but they burned out as quickly as a brush-fire; by the power of the Lord I destroyed them.'*

And maybe now, after distinguishing myself, I would finally find acceptance in my new life on the frontiers of the Christian world.

Berthold came to the end of the prayer. *'The Lord makes me powerful and strong; he has saved me.'*

We all recited the paternoster before coming to our feet.

Rudolf was glaring at me again but I ignored him, turning to Wenno. 'I would ask permission to go and check on the health of my comrades, sir.'

The Master nodded. 'Agreed. And make sure you seek out Brother Burkhardt to attend to your wounds.'

I nodded, walking back to my horse. Otto followed me and we both remounted, leading our horses away from the group of knight-brothers. I turned my horse away, as flurries of new flakes began to fall, gently covering the heaped bodies and the bright blood on the trampled snow of the battlefield.

'Your master looked furious.' Otto grinned. 'He hates that you killed the champion and outshone him.'

Otto was right. I could hear his angry words with Wenno but I didn't care. There would be a reckoning, but it would have to wait.

Rudolf could go to hell. I was going to find the rest of my friends.

Gorodische,
Novgorod Republic,
June 1242

'So why did you help your enemies?' Fergus asked. We were alone in the scriptorium. A light rain pattered down on the roof. 'If they had been killed in the battle your problems would have been solved.'

And that was true. If I'd expected any thanks from Wolfgang, I was to be well and truly disappointed. But that comes later in my story. It was a good question and the same one that Otto had asked just after the battle. Why had I risked the wrath of Rudolf and disobeyed my orders to save a group of ungrateful bastards?

'Honour,' I said. 'You wouldn't understand it. Honour is everything. Honour is more important than life. If you live without honour you might as well be dead.'

'I prefer living my life following the teachings of Our Lord and the Bible.'

'Well, I wouldn't expect you to understand,' I said. 'You are only a scholar.'

Fergus closed his eyes and gritted his teeth, doing his best to control his temper. I enjoyed baiting him.

'And although they were my enemies, they were also my comrades, despite our hostility to one another. We fought under the same banner for the same God. In those days, Livonia was far more of a wilderness than it is now. I could no more leave them to die than I could Otto or my other friends.'

Fergus shook his head. He clearly did not understand.

Of course, I still intended to get my own back on them, and I did, as my tale will later show. But in battle, against our enemies, we were united.

'Why are we even doing this?' Fergus said suddenly. 'I have more important work rather than waste time here.'

'You know why,' I said. 'I want to record an account for my son, so he knows about my life and the inheritance that was stolen from my family. And your master wants another chronicle for his library.'

'But you will never recover your barony in England. And it's arrogant of yourself to think otherwise. It's been nearly forty years now. You are too old to do anything about it, so you are. What makes yourself think your son even cares about your story or your damned inheritance? You hardly know him.'

'He will care.' I felt my familiar anger rising. 'Because he has honour and because he has pride. These are things you know nothing about—'

We were interrupted by the arrival of Miroslav. Fergus took this opportunity to storm from the room. I was tired and needed to rest, so Miroslav helped me back to my own small cell where I lay down on my pallet, my mind brimming over the argument with the Irishman.

Despite what I had said, it was true I hardly knew my son and it was true I didn't know if he would even read my story or whether it would inspire him to seek the revenge I wanted – the revenge I craved. Maybe Fergus was right, maybe I was wasting my time. A wave of despair hit me like a hammer.

For forty years I had dreamed and nourished the thought of regaining Cranham and finally gutting my uncle, Gilbert, if he was still alive, or more likely his son, Walter. Although I had never returned to the land of my birth since I had fled, the thought of righting the wrongs of my youth had sustained me through many a bitter winter's night in Livonia. Even though Cranham was just a very distant memory, the vengeance bubbling within me had been the overriding theme of my life and I had never really considered it might never happen. Of course, my age made it highly unlikely I could fulfil this wish myself and my vows and position in the Teutonic Order made it impossible, but I had known this for a long time. This was why I had focussed my hopes on my son achieving it for me. Fergus's words had planted doubt in my mind, a doubt that had not existed previously. But he was right; what if my son refused the burden and obligation I was forcing, unasked, upon him?

No, I told myself; my son would not do this to me. This was why it was imperative that I finished my story so that he understood everything that was at stake. Only then would he understand his destiny. The goal that had tormented me for forty years was a matter of family honour. So even though I disliked Fergus intensely, I needed the Irishman to help finish my story. I needed the Irishman to help recover everything that had been stolen from me.

The next day was the *veche* in Novgorod. We left in the early afternoon, Prince Alexander accompanied by a score of his *druzhina*, half-a-dozen priests and monks, including Miroslav and Fergus. There was concern about me riding, due to my injury, even though the distance was less than two miles. I waved off Brother Miroslav's fears and Prince Alexander accepted my word that I was able to make the journey. 'I am not an invalid yet,' I said. 'I've been riding since I was five years old. A short ride will not kill me.'

Nevertheless, it was harder than I imagined. My wound felt like an inferno, but I was damned if I would complain or show any sign of the corruption surging through my body. We travelled slowly, no faster than walking pace, which enabled me to examine Novgorod as we approached along the Volkhov river. Across the water I could see the walls of the *detinets*, the citadel, and the onion cupolas of the Saint Sophia Cathedral behind. But Miroslav told me that we were heading for Yaroslav's Court, located in the jumble of wooden buildings in the commercial quarter of the city on the east bank. 'This is where the *veche* will take place,' the monk explained. 'There will be many people in attendance and it could get unruly... Prince Alexander has had problems in the past.'

Prince Alexander and Fergus dropped back from the head of the column to speak with me in a serious voice, although it was Miroslav who translated. 'As discussed, Prince Alexander asks that you explain to the *veche* that your Order will no longer threaten the lands of Veliky Novgorod.'

'But I have had no contact with my Order since the battle. How can I possibly speak for them? I have no idea what my comrades are planning.'

'Prince Alexander knows this,' Miroslav said. 'But you are a senior knight in the Livonian Order and you must know about any long-term plans or designs on our land. If you speak on his behalf then it will go better for you when we negotiate your ransom.'

Of course, preventing the victorious Russians from attacking our holdings in Estonia and Livonia was certainly desirable, so there was no reason for me not to help Alexander convince his people. I agreed to his request and he gave a tired smile. Fergus said nothing.

We rode through the outskirts of the city, a maze of wooden buildings outside the walled town. A bell began ringing as our horses clopped over the timber boards that paved the street and I noticed that there were relatively few people considering the time of day. 'That is the bell ringing for the *veche*,' Miroslav said. 'That is where most of the people will be.'

Shortly before reaching our destination in the broad area ahead, we drew up by a large stables. I dismounted with the others, wincing at the pain, feeling a wave of dizziness wash over me that caused me to pause for a moment until it passed. Miroslav looked over in alarm but I waved away his concern.

The market square which hosted the *veche* was next to the river and was huge. It was dominated by several Orthodox churches, mostly wooden, but there was one large cathedral built from stone with a domed roof, connected to various other buildings that Miroslav explained were part of the palace complex that used to belong to the princes of the city. Nearby rang a big bell, mounted on a wood structure under a canopy. As expected, there was a large crowd and I was surprised to learn that the assembly was not just confined to the *boyars*, the nobles, but also included the lower class, who were loud and boisterous.

After a moment, we approached a raised stage in front of the palace, covered by a stone arcade where a dozen or so men were talking. At Alexander's arrival, some of the crowd cheered, but I noticed that a sizeable number did not, making me wonder about the complicated relationship the prince seemed to have with his city. Alexander sought out a portly man in a long burgundy-coloured coat of high quality who was in a heated discussion with three other nobles.

Around us it was very loud, with people talking and the sound of music coming from minstrels in the crowd. I was ignored by everyone except Miroslav, who had obviously been given the task of looking after me. Rather him than Fergus anyway.

'That is the *posadnik*, the mayor.' Miroslav pointed to the portly man now in conversation with Alexander. 'He is Stepan Tverdislavich and is an ally of the prince. But be careful... his brother Domash was killed shortly before the battle on the ice and he hates Germans.'

'I am not German,' I said.

Miroslav smiled. 'I'm afraid this little detail will not be recognised by anyone here.'

I shrugged. What did it matter? I was used to being hated.

Finally, to my relief, the bell stopped ringing. At Miroslav's prompting we joined Alexander on the stage as the prince's *druzhina* took up station facing the crowd. Miroslav bowed his head at a cleric dressed in a long cassock whom I recognised as the archbishop I had seen at Yuriev Monastery. He looked at me briefly before joining the conversation with Alexander. Fergus stood nearby, looking as out of place as I felt.

After a few moments, the small talk was over and the *veche* could begin. The crowd slowly fell silent as the *posadnik* addressed them. He spoke but no one translated for me. Then it was Alexander's turn. The prince spoke for a long time and, despite not understanding a word, I heard the passion in his voice as he cajoled, pleaded and lectured the mass of people. A group of men that looked like noblemen were talking among themselves and from the looks on their faces they were not in agreement. At least I knew now who the enemy were.

Alexander stopped talking and there was a smattering of applause before several people started shouting. One of the nobles began speaking, a tall man with a black beard and booming voice, pointing to the prince as he addressed the crowd, whipping up a large segment who roared and cheered in support. I wanted to sit down but I wasn't going to ask for a chair.

'He wants to attack Estonia and destroy your Order,' Miroslav whispered to me.

It was as I thought. The archbishop came forward to the edge of the stage and held up his hands to quieten the people. He waited for a few moments until the crowd fell silent and then spoke in a voice, surprisingly strong in a man who was at least twenty years older than me, preaching to the townspeople rather than the nobles. The crowd listened intently to what the man said, some of them making the sign of the cross. After he had finished, the archbishop said a prayer and turned back to the others on the stage.

Alexander said something and pointed to me. Fergus translated into French. 'The prince would like you to explain that your Order would welcome peace.'

Everyone looked at me and I felt the hostility in those stares. A mumbling of discontent rumbled from the crowd. I hesitated for a moment, swallowing my nerves. 'It is true that my people would welcome peace, if your terms are generous,' I said. 'We were heavily defeated in the battle and would pose no further threat to Novgorod.' It was a fair assumption and probably even true. 'But remember,' I cautioned. 'Our army was led by Bishop Hermann, not the Livonian Order... You will have to treat with him.' I waited while Fergus translated.

A noble shouted something at me. 'How can we believe your words, German. You people only understand strength. Now is the time to crush you decisively!'

'That didn't fare well for you last time,' I retorted. 'If you invade Livonia or Estonia again then the Danes and Germans will bring all their forces to resist you. My Order remains strong and our castles many. What makes you think the result will be any different from before?'

My words were translated but I didn't understand his answer. The crowd was becoming angry and a group of drunken peasants near where I stood were being particularly abusive, beating their chests and shouting at me. Alexander said something, provoking an argument between the nobles on the stage.

The *veche* was getting out of hand.

Miroslav tried to pull me gently away, but I brushed off his arm. I wasn't going to be intimidated by a bunch of peasants, even if I was a prisoner and unarmed. Behind me, Alexander was now shouting but no one was listening. All around there was uproar, and the first men barged past the terribly outnumbered *druzhina* who were attempting to keep the crowd back, and rushed the stage.

One of the peasants ran at me and I kicked him in the knee, causing him to fall flat on his face and I kicked him again, this time in the head. More of the townspeople were on the raised stage, trying to get past the *druzhina* to attack me. Miroslav was still trying to pull me away but I was hemmed in on all sides. Excruciating pain exploded in my shoulder as someone grabbed me, tearing my wound. More guards, city militia this time, pushed forward to beat back the crowd but I felt a blackness rise and engulf me.

I passed out.

I awoke a few moments later, covered in blood, staring up at an array of concerned faces. Among them was Fergus, who to my surprise sighed in relief and actually looked upset. It was as though his mask of sneering indifference had dropped for a moment, but when I looked again, he turned away.

Had I imagined the expression of grief on his face? Did my antagonistic Irish scribe care about my well-being? It seemed absurd, considering the number of arguments and bad words we'd exchanged since working together.

Nearby, I could hear the guards and *druzhina* beating back the crowd. Miroslav and two other men helped me to my feet. I clenched my teeth together to stop from screaming. Fresh blood flowed down my left arm, dripping from my hand to pool on the ground. The men helped support me as we retreated from the crowd, leaving the stage and back in the direction we had come. We were joined by Alexander and the rest of his *druzhina*, the prince with a face of fury and his sword drawn, although it was unbloodied. The hostility against the prince was so overwhelming it was unclear if any of us would make it back to Gorodische alive.

I was delirious and my shoulder burned like a blacksmith's forge. In my state, I wasn't sure I would survive the return trip even if we did manage to get back. My legs suddenly failed and I lurched forward, but strong arms grabbed me, pulling me up and dragging me further away. Blackness surged up and I heard a dog barking very close. Was this what death felt like?

Flashes of my life exploded in my head. Images of the battle on the ice of Lake Peipus. The carnage and slaughter of our army, the arrows, the pitiful rout of the Estonians. Horrible images. And I had been largely to blame – for heavily pushing the campaign in the first place against much opposition from my brethren. That was something I had not told Fergus.

But what had I actually achieved in my life? Fergus had said my son would not care about my life account, and now the bone-numbing truth of that statement settled in my gut like an anchor stone. Why would he care? My entire life had been dreaming of my vengeance – a vengeance that probably only ever existed in my mind. And where had it brought me? Nowhere.

If I died who would remember me?

Now was probably a good time to make my peace with God. We'd had a mixed acquaintanceship. It was strange that, after a life of scepticism and disinterest, the prospect of death thrust the thought of God into my mind. A God I had spent most of my life trying to avoid. But I had fought to bring His word to many new converts over the last nearly forty years and

I hoped he would look kindly upon me. Maybe there would even be a place for me in Heaven?

I was vaguely aware of Fergus beside me. 'What were you thinking of? We're leaving now, so we are. But you can't fight everyone!'

That was something I was more than aware of. Not anymore.

'But don't you be dying on me now. You have a chronicle to finish. Forget your bloody son, forget your bloody vengeance! You have to live and finish your story – for its own sake if nothing else!'

I heard shouting behind me but the world was spinning and I stumbled again. They dragged me further down the street, through the buildings, away from the noise. Shadows hovered at the edge of my vision like distant wraiths. Perhaps I would be going to Hell after all. I was about to pass out again.

But with Miroslav's help, I managed to remain conscious. We reached the stables and several men helped me onto my horse, the exertion exhausting me and causing more blood to flow from my freshly opened wound. The others quickly mounted and with as much dignity as we could muster, we kicked our horses forward, back the way we had come. Behind, I could still hear shouting. Alexander led the way, in no mood to stop, ready to trample under the hooves of his horse anyone foolish enough to stand in our way.

Our trip had been a disaster for all of us, not just me. Prince Alexander had seen his authority questioned and ultimately thwarted, forcing him to flee his own city in ignominy.

And so we withdrew to Gorodische, leaving the mayhem of Novgorod in our wake.

TO BE CONTINUED

HISTORICAL NOTE

The Baltic Crusades are a fascinating period of history, traditionally overshadowed by the crusades in the Middle East (or Outremer as the Franks called the Latin Kingdoms in the Levant), over which many hundreds of non-fiction books and novels have already been written. The crusades in the eastern Baltic differed significantly from those in Outremer because the local tribes were not in control of any holy sites, nor were they a threat to Christian pilgrims. It was therefore harder for the Latin Church to justify. In order to attract people willing to undertake the hardships of life on the eastern frontier of Christendom, Pope Celestine III authorised full crusading privileges to anyone willing to make an armed pilgrimage to Livonia and this was confirmed by his successor Pope Innocent III in 1198. Thousands of volunteers travelled every year to this far-flung region to campaign and fight, predominantly Germans, but also Danes, Swedes, Slavs and Frisians. Eric Christiansen's excellent *The Northern Crusades* details their history and was the first book that got me initially interested in this little-known period.

However, the principal first-hand source is *The Chronicle of Henry of Livonia*, which was written by a priest, Henricus des Lettis, probably around 1229. The chronicle deals with events in the eastern Baltic between 1180 to 1226. Hardly surprisingly, it is written from the German point of view and describes the role of the Latin Church in colonising and spreading Christianity to the local pagan tribes. His chronicle is a highly detailed account, rich in human history, and he provides eyewitness testimony of the events at this time, depicting not only the military campaigns but interesting facts about the local people themselves. This is particularly valuable as there is practically no other first-hand evidence of the events of the early Christian settlement in what is now Latvia and Estonia.

But it is Bishop Albert von Buxhövden who holds the central place in Henry's account. As a canon from Bremen Cathedral, Albert was ordained as the third Bishop of Uexküll (Ikšķile in Latvian) in 1199. He was one of the most energetic, charismatic and relentless empire builders of his time. Albert came to Livonia to conquer land in the name of the Church and to convert the inhabitants, by force if necessary. One of his first acts was to move the seat of the bishopric from Uexküll, which was considered too far up the Düna river, and found the new town of Riga on the site of an old Liv fishing and trading port in a sheltered natural harbour where cogs could anchor. From the chronicle, Henry's admiration of Bishop Albert is clear, and he probably came to Livonia as a young man in 1205, working as a scholar in the bishop's household. In 1208, the bishop ordained him as a priest and gave him a parish to administer, where he lived among the Letts, remaining in the country until reaching old age. Bishop Albert returned to Germany every year to preach the crusade until 1224, travelling around Northern Germany drumming up support for his mission. In this story, Albert has only a very peripheral role, but he will feature prominently later.

A further achievement of Bishop Albert was sanctioning the formation of the Livonian Brothers of the Sword (Latin: *Fratres militiæ Christi Livoniae*, German: *Schwertbrüderorden*), although this was probably accomplished by Abbot Theodoric, who as in our story did arrive with the Livonian chief Caupo on the three ships in September 1204 after visiting and getting sanction from Pope Innocent III in Rome. This new monastic Order of warrior monks was given the same Rule as the Knight Templars and the first Master was Wenno von Rohrbach. But more about that in the next book! The Order was under the command of Bishop Albert, but unlike the more prestigious and larger organisations like the Teutonic Knights, the Swordbrothers were always considered second class – smaller, poorer and with less prestige. Nevertheless, whereas prior to their formation crusader armies would arrive in the spring and campaign over the summer, now the mission could be protected all year round. The Swordbrothers built castles, protected missionaries and acted as a military force to compel the local tribes to convert. But they were always impoverished, depending on the land they conquered and the tithes they needed in order to survive. This led them into dispute with Bishop Albert, with whom they would later fall out over the division of new lands and spoils. The Swordbrothers themselves appear to be of very mixed origins, many of them from the *ministeriales* class, earning their living from service rather than by the resources of their own lands, and who made up the bulk of German knighthood at this time. Others were the sons of merchants and hardly noble at all, and some were criminals, although Volkwin von Naumburg zu Winterstätten was probably the son of the count of Naumburg. The Order had a reputation for being unrefined and hard to control, and by the end of their short history there were few crimes of which they had not been accused. Nonetheless, they successfully endured the severe hardships of the frontier and were triumphant in most of the battles they fought, mainly due to their superior weapons and the use of heavy knights, which despite being unsuitable in the marshy, forested terrain, proved devastating against the more lightly armed pagan tribes.

However, the problems for the Swordbrothers were mounting, as were their enemies. Pope Honorius III rebuked them for squeezing too much money from their peasants to help fund their wars, causing an uprising, and when they seized the king of Denmark's land in Estonia, defying a papal legate, their legal disputes only increased. The Swordbrothers were getting a bad reputation and Volkwin tried to solve the issue by enlisting the help of the Teutonic Knights to admit his men into their Order as knights-brethren. After a tour of inspection, the latter were unimpressed by the lack of discipline, and when they reported back to their chapter meeting the Teutonic Knights decided to reject the request. Hartmann von Heldrungen wrote that the Swordbrothers, 'were people who followed their own inclination, and did not keep their Rule properly, and merely wanted to be given *carte blanche*, and not have their conduct looked into unless they agreed to it'. It was this rough-and-ready attitude that interested me most about the Swordbrothers in the first place and ignited my study of this little-known period.

Another historian who has proven invaluable in my research is William Urban, especially his book *The Baltic Crusades* and his translation with Jerry C Smith of *The Livonian Rhymed Chronicle*. A professor of History and International studies at Monmouth College, Illinois, he is probably the foremost English-speaking historian who has devoted his career to studying this period and whose knowledge on the subject is considerable. Mr Urban was kind enough to read over and give his opinion on the first draft of this book.

The *Livonian Rhymed Chronicle* itself is written by an unknown member of the Teutonic Order in the late 13th century. It covers the years from 1180 to 1290 and is the only primary source from the years 1267–1290, differing from *The Chronicle of Henry of Livonia* in that it deals almost exclusively on the military affairs of the Teutonic Knights. Urban and Smith speculate that perhaps it was used as a *Tischbuch*, a book that would have been read aloud to members of the brethren during mealtimes, although this is hard to know for certain.

Much of the book takes place in Lübeck, one of the most famous medieval cities in Germany. The city was the main point of departure for the Baltic Crusades, although in 1204 it was far from being the 'Queen of the Hanseatic League' that it would later become. The Hanseatic League (*Hanse* in German) was a trading organisation that encompassed much of northern Europe, from the North Sea to the Baltic, acting as a commercial and a defensive confederation of cities. The actual word *Hanse* itself was not used until the middle of the 13th century. Most of the latter medieval buildings that now define Lübeck for tourists like the Holsten Gate (*Holstentor*), Saint Mary's Church (*Marienkirche*), Saint Peter's Church (*Petrikirche*), the *Salzspeicher*, or even the brick-built gabled houses, were not built at the time of this book. Only the cathedral that still stands (*Dom zu Lübeck*) existed and was under construction although it was modified many times since and was almost completely destroyed in the Second World War. The *Holstenbrücke* (Holsten Bridge) was first mentioned in 1216 but it was conceivable that a bridge existed beforehand, although I have chosen otherwise. This would have been constructed from wood.

Throughout the book, I have generally (although not exclusively) kept to the German spellings of people and places. This is partly because Richard is fighting for a German Order and obviously speaking Low German which was the language of most of the crusaders. It is also intended to add to the atmosphere and help in the reader's immersion, and hopefully it achieves that.

Very little is known about the battle that took place near Rodenpois (Ropaži in Latvian) around Lent 1205. Almost all of the available information is contained in *The Chronicle of Henry of Livonia* and it was a crushing defeat for the Lithuanians and the first real victory for the Swordbrothers. The chronicle states, *Thus the army was assembled and the Lithuanians were dispersed on all sides of the road like sheep. About twelve hundred of them were cut down by the sword.* Most of the thousand or so Estonian prisoners that the Lithuanians were taking home were butchered by the victorious Semigallians. The battle is a clear example of the crusaders' strategy of divide and conquer, using the rivalry and hatred the pagan tribes had for each other in order to dominate them all. And in this they were very successful.

Prince Alexander Yaroslavich, better known as Alexander Nevsky, is one of the greatest heroes of Russian history. He was born around 1220 and spent most of his childhood and youth in the Principality of Pereyaslavl-Zalessky, ruled over by his father, with eight brothers and an unknown number of sisters. When his elder brother Fedor died, he became the most senior and was summoned by the people of Novgorod to be *knyaz* (prince) in 1236. After beating the Swedes at the battle of Neva in 1240 at the young age of nineteen, he received the name 'Nevsky' (of Neva), which helped cement his power but made him unpopular with some of the *boyars* or nobles. This culminated with him being banished by the city during the winter of 1240/41, for reasons unknown. However, two years later, he was recalled again and went on to beat the combined Danish, German and Estonian army in the famous battle on the ice at Lake Peipus. This is commemorated in the famous 1938 film by Sergei Eisenstein, *Alexander Nevsky*, a film beloved by Stalin. As mentioned in the book, his primary concern was the threat of the Mongols, who had already swept across Asia and Russia, sacking Kiev in 1240. Alexander realised their overwhelming power and submitted to them, using them as allies against any further possible western aggression. He has received criticism for this, but there is little doubt that this far-sighted and astute move saved Novgorod from the same fate of many other Russian cities. His loyalty was rewarded, and the Mongols allowed him to become Grand Prince of Vladimir (*Veliki Knyaz*), the supreme ruler of Russia in 1252, which he remained until his death in November 1263.

Alexander Nevsky was canonised by the Orthodox Church in 1547, and in 1725 Empress Catherine I introduced the Imperial Order of Saint Alexander Nevsky, one of the highest decorations in Russia. He is probably best remembered for the line, 'Whoever comes to us with a sword, from a sword will perish...'